Charles Garv

Leslie's Loyalty

Charles Garvice

Leslie's Loyalty

1st Edition | ISBN: 978-3-75234-663-3

Place of Publication: Frankfurt am Main, Germany

Year of Publication: 2020

Outlook Verlag GmbH, Germany.

LESLIE'S LOYALTY

I-Y
CHARLES GARVICE

NEW YORK
STREET &: SMITH, Pvau se1u

CHAPTER I.

LESLIE LISLE.

Nobody ever goes to Portmaris; that is to say, nobody who is anybody. It lies —but no matter, ours shall not be the hand to ruin its simplicity by advertising its beauties and advantages, and directing the madding crowd to its sylvan retreat. At present the golden sands which line the bay are innocent of the negro troupe, the peripatetic conjurer, and the monster in human form who pesters you to purchase hideous objects manufactured from shells and cardboard.

A time may come when Portmaris will develop into an Eastbourne or a Brighton, a Scarborough or a Hastings; but, Heaven be praised, that time is not yet, and Portmaris, like an unconscious village beauty, goes on its way as yet ignorant of its loveliness.

At present there are about a dozen houses, most of them fishermen's cottages; a church, hidden in a hollow a mile away from the restless sea; and an inn which is satisfied with being an inn, and has not yet learned to call itself a hotel.

Two or three of the fisherfolk let lodgings, to which come those fortunate individuals who have quite by chance stumbled upon this out-of-the-way spot; and in the sitting-room of the prettiest of these unpretentious cottages was a young girl.

Her name was Leslie Lisle. She was nineteen, slim, graceful, and more than pretty. There is a type of beauty which, with more or less truth, is generally described as Irish. It has dark hair, blue eyes with long black lashes, a clear and colorless complexion of creamy ivory, and a chin that would seem pointed but for the exquisite fullness of the lips. It is a type which is more fascinating than the severe Greek, more "holding" than the voluptuous Spanish, more spirituel than the vivacious French; in short, it is a kind of beauty before which most men go down completely and forever vanquished, and this because the wonderful gray-blue eyes are capable of an infinity of expressions, can be grave one moment and brimming over with fun the next; because there lurks, even when they are most quiescent, a world of possibilities in the way of wit in the corners of the red lips; because the face, as you watch it, can in the course of a few minutes flash with spirit, melt with tenderness, and all the while remain the face of a pure, innocent, healthy, light-hearted girl.

The young men who crossed Leslie Lisle's path underwent a sad experience.

At first they were attracted by her beauty; in a few hours or days, as the case might be, they began to find the attraction lying somewhat deeper than the face; then they grew restless, unhappy, lost their appetites, got to lying awake of nights, and lastly went to pieces completely, and if they possessed

sufficient courage, flung themselves perfectly wretched and overcome at the small feet of the slim, girlish figure which had become to them even that of the one woman in the world. And to do Leslie justice, she was not only always surprised, but distressed. She had said nothing, and what is more, looked nothing, to encourage them. She had been just herself, a frank yet modest English girl, with an Irish face, and that indescribable sweetness which draws men's hearts from their bosoms before they know what has happened to them.

She was seated at the piano in the sitting-room of the cottage which the fisherman who owned it had christened Sea View, and she was amusing herself and a particularly silent and morose parrot by singing some of the old songs and ballads which she had found in a rickety music-stand in the corner; and for all the parrot glanced at her disapprovingly with his glassy eye, she had a sufficiently sweet voice, and sang with more than the usual amount of feeling.

While she was in the middle of that famous but slightly monotonous composition, "Robin Grey," the door opened, and a tall, thin man entered.

This was Francis Lisle, her father. He was a man this side of fifty, but looked older in consequence, perhaps, of his hair, which was gray and scanty, a faded face, with a dreamy far away look in the faint blue eyes, and a somewhat bent form and dragging gait. He carried a portable easel in one hand, and held a canvas under his arm.

As he entered he looked round the room as if he had never seen it before, then set the easel up in a corner, placed the canvas on it upside down, and crossing his hands behind his back, stood with bent head gazing at it for some moments in silence. Then he said, in a voice which matched the dreamy face:

"Leslie, come here."

Leslie stopped short in the middle of the most heart-rending line of the cheerful ballad, and walked—no; glided? scarcely; it is difficult to describe how the girl got across the small room, so full of grace, so characteristic was her mode of progression, and putting both hands on his shoulders, leaned her cheek against his head.

"Back already, dear?" she said, and the tone fully indicated the position in which she stood toward her parent. "I thought you were going to make a long day of it."

"Yes, yes," he said, without taking his eyes from the sketch. "I did intend doing so. I started full of my subject and—er—inspired with hope, and I don't think I have altogether failed. It is difficult—very. The tone of that sky would fill a careless amateur with despair, but—but I am not careless. Whatever I may be I am not that. The secrets of art which she hides from the unthinking and—er—irreverent she confides to her true worshipers. Now, Leslie, look at that sky. Look at it carefully, critically, and tell me—do you not think I have caught that half tone, that delicious mingling of the chrome and the ultramarine? There is a wealth of form and color in that right hand corner, and I—yes, I think it is the best, by far the best and truest thing I have as yet done."

Leslie leaned forward, and softly, swiftly, placed the picture right side up.

It had not very much improved by the transposition. It was—well, to put it bluntly, a daub of the most awful description. Never since the world began had there ever, in nature, been anything like it. The average schoolboy libeling nature with a shilling box of colors could not have sinned more deeply. The sea was a brilliant washerwoman's blue, the hills were heaps of muddy ochre, the fishing vessels looked like blackbeetles struggling on their backs, there was a cow in the meadow in the foreground which would have wrung tears from any one who had ever set eyes on that harmless but necessary animal, and the bit of sky in the corner was utterly and completely indescribable.

Leslie looked at it with a sad little expression in her eyes, the pitying look one sees in the face of a woman whose life is spent in humoring the weakness of a beloved one; then she said, gently:

"It is very striking, papa."

"Striking!" repeated Francis Lisle. "Striking! I like that word. You, too, are an artist, my dear Leslie, though you never touch a brush. How well you know how to use the exact expression. I flatter myself that it is striking. I think I may say, without egotism, that no one, no real critic could look at that sketch—for it is a mere sketch—without being struck!"

"Yes, papa," she murmured, soothingly.

He shaded his eyes with his thin white hands in the orthodox fashion, and peered at the monstrosity.

"There is, if I may say so, an—er—originality in the treatment which would alone make the sketch interesting and valuable. Tell me, now, Leslie, what it is in it that catches your fancy most."

Leslie looked at it carefully.

"I—I think that heap of sea-weed nicely painted, papa," she said, putting her arm round his neck.

"Heap of sea-weed?" his brows knitted. "Heap of sea-weed? I don't see anything of the kind."

"There, papa," she said, pointing.

"My dear Leslie, I have always suspected that your sight was not perfect, that there was some defect in its range power; that is not a heap of sea-weed, but a fisherwoman mending her nets!"

"Of course! How stupid of me!" she said, quickly. "I'm afraid I am near-sighted, dear. But don't you think you have done enough for to-day? Why not put it away until to-morrow?"

"There is no to-morrow, Leslie," he said, gravely, as he got out his palette. "'Art is long and life is fleeting.' Never forget that, my dear. No, I can stipple on a little. I intend finishing this sketch, and making a miniature—a cabinet picture. It shall be worthy of a place among those exquisite studies of Foster's. And yet——," he sighed and pushed the hair from his forehead, "and yet I'll be bound that if I tried to sell it, I should not find a dealer to give me a few paltry pounds for it. So blind and prejudiced! No, they would not buy it, and possibly the Academy would refuse to exhibit it. Prejudice, prejudice! But art has its own rewards, thank Heaven! I paint because I must. Fame has no attraction. I am content to wait. Yes, though the recognition which is my due may come too late! It is often thus!"

The girl bent her beautiful head—she stood taller than the drooping figure of her father—and kissed, ah! how tenderly, pityingly, the gray hair.

Francis Lisle, Esquire, the younger son of an old Irish family, had been a dreamer from his youth up. He had started with a good education and a handsome little fortune; he had dreamed away the education, dreamed away the small fortune, dreamed away nearly all his life, and his great dream was that he was an artist. He couldn't draw a haystack, and certainly could not have colored it correctly even if by chance he had drawn it; but he was persuaded that he was a great artist, and he fancied that his hand transferred to the canvas the scenes which he attempted to paint.

And he was not unhappy. His wife had died when Leslie was a mite of a thing, and how he had managed to get on until Leslie was old enough to take care of him can never even be surmised; but she began to play the mother, the guardian, and protector to this visionary father of hers, at an extremely early age. She managed everything, almost fed and clothed him, and kept from him all those petty ills and worries which make life such a burden for most people.

They had no settled home, but wandered about, sometimes on the Continent, but mostly in England, and Francis Lisle had hundreds of sketches which were like nothing under heaven, but were supposed to be "ideas" for larger pictures, of places they had visited.

They had been at Portmaris a couple of months when we find them, and though Francis Lisle was just beginning to get tired of it, and restlessly anxious to be on the move again, Leslie was loth to leave. She had grown fond of the golden sands, the strip of pebbly beach, the narrow street broken by its wind-twisted trees, the green lanes leading to the country beyond, and still more fond of the simple-hearted fisher folk, who always welcomed her with a smile, and had already learned to call her Miss Leslie.

Indeed, Miss Lisle was a dangerous young woman, and the hearts of young and old, gentle and simple, went down before a glance of her gray-blue eyes, a smile from the mobile lips, a word from her voice which thrilled with a melody few could resist.

Francis Lisle went on daubing, his head on one side, a rapt, contented look on his pale, aristocratic face.

"Yes, this is going to be one of my best efforts," he said, with placid complacency. "Go and sing something, Leslie. I can always work better while you are singing. Music and painting are twin sisters. I adore them both."

Leslie went back to the piano with that peculiarly graceful motion of hers, and touched a note or two.

"Were there no letters this morning, dear?" she asked.

"Letters?" Lisle put his hand to his forehead as if rudely called back to earth from the empyrean. "Letters? No. Yes, I forgot. There was one. It was from Ralph Duncombe."

Leslie turned her head slightly, and the rather thick brows which helped the eyes in all their unconscious mischief straightened.

"From Ralph? What does he say?"

"I don't know," replied Lisle, placidly. "I can never read his letters; he writes so terribly plain a hand; its hardness jars upon me. I have it—somewhere?"

He searched his pockets reluctantly.

"No, I must have lost it. Does it matter very much?"

Leslie laughed softly.

"I don't know; but one generally likes to know what is in a letter."

"Well, then, I wish I could find it. I told the postman when he gave it to me that I should probably lose it, and that he had better bring it on to the house;

but—well, I don't think he understood me. I often think that we speak an unknown language to these country people."

"Perhaps he did not hear you," said Leslie. "Sometimes, you know, dear, you think you have spoken when you have not uttered a word, but only thought."

"I dare say," he assented, dreamily. "Now I come to think of it, I fancy Duncombe said he was coming down here——."

The slender white hands which had been touching the keys caressingly stopped.

"Coming here, papa!"

"Yes. I think so. I'm not sure. Now, what could I have done with that letter?"

He made another search, failed to find it, shook his head as if dismissing the subject, and resumed his "work."

Leslie struck a chord, and opened her lips to sing, when the sound of the wheels belonging to the one fly in the place came down the uneven street. She paused to listen, then leaned sideways and looked through the window.

"The station fly!" she said. "And it has stopped at Marine Villa, papa. It must be another visitor. Fancy two visitors at the same time in Portmaris! It will go wild with excitement."

The cranky vehicle had pulled up at the opposite cottage, and Leslie, with mild, very mild, curiosity, got up from the piano and went to the window.

As she did so a man dressed in soft tweed got down from beside the driver, opened the fly-door, and gave his arm to a young man whose appearance filled Leslie's heart with pity; for he was a cripple. His back was bent, his face pale and gentle as a woman's, marked with lines which were eloquent of weary days, and still more weary nights; and in the dark eyes was that peculiar expression of sadness which a life of pain and suffering patiently borne sets as a seal.

The young fellow leaned on his stick and the man's arm, and looked round him, and his eye, dark and full of a soft penetration, fell upon the lovely face at the opposite window.

Leslie drew back, when it was too late, and breathed an exclamation of regret.

"Oh, papa!"

"What is the matter?" asked Lisle, vacantly.

"I am sorry!" she said. "He will think I was staring at him—and so I was. And that will seem so cruel to him, poor fellow."

"What is cruel? which poor fellow?" demanded Lisle with feeble impatience.

"Some one who has just got out of the fly, dear; a cripple, poor fellow; and he saw me watching him." And she sighed again.

"Eh?" said Lisle, as if he were trying to recollect something. "Ah, yes, I remember. Mrs. Whiting told me that he was expected some time to-day; they had a telegram saying he was coming."

"He? Who?" said Leslie, going back to the piano.

"Who?" repeated Lisle, as if he were heartily sorry he had continued the subject. "Why, this young man. Dear me, I forget his name and title——."

"Title? Poor fellow! Is he a nobleman, papa? That makes it seem so much worse, doesn't it?"

Lisle looked round at her helplessly.

"Upon my word, my dear," he said, "I do not wish to appear dense, but I haven't the least idea of what you are talking about, and——," he went on more quietly, as if he feared she were going to explain, "it doesn't matter. Pray sing something, and—and do not let us worry about things which do not concern us."

Leslie began to sing without another word.

CHAPTER II.

FATE.

The crippled young man, with the assistance of his companion, made his way into the sitting-room of Marine Villa; an invalid's chair was hauled from the top of the fly and carried in, and the young man sank into it with a faint sigh.

"Leave me, Grey," he said. "When Lord Auchester arrives let him come to me at once; and, Grey, be good enough to remember what I told you——."

"Yes, your grace," said the man; then, as his master lifted the soft brown eyes with gentle reproach, he added, correcting himself, "yes, sir."

The young man smiled faintly.

"That is better. Thanks."

The valet unlocked a morocco traveling case, and took out a vial and medicine chest.

"The medicine, your gra——, sir, I mean."

"Ah, yes, I forgot. Thank you," said the young man, and he took the draught with a weary patience. "Thanks. Let me know when his lordship arrives. No, I want nothing more."

The valet went out, shutting the door softly after him, and his master leaned his head upon his hand, and closed his eyes.

Fate had dealt very strangely with this young man. With one hand it had showered upon him most of the gifts which the sons of men set high store by; it had made him a duke, had given him palaces, vast lands, money in such abundance as to be almost a burden; and with the other hand, as if in scorn and derision of the thing called Man, Fate had struck him one of those blows under which humanity is crushed and broken.

A nurse had let him, when a child, slip from her arms, and the great Duke of Rothbury was doomed to go through life a stunted and crooked-back object, with the grim figure of pain always marching by his side, with the bitter knowledge that not all his wealth could prevent the people he met in the streets regarding him with curious and pitying glances, with the bitter sense that the poorest of the laborers on his estates enjoyed a better lot than his, and was more to be envied than himself.

He sat perfectly motionless for some minutes; then he opened his eyes and started slightly; Leslie had just begun to sing.

He wheeled his chair to the window, and set it open quietly, and, keeping behind the curtains, listened with evident pleasure.

The song was still floating across to him when a young man came marching up the street.

Youth is a glorious thing under any circumstances, but when it is combined with perfect health, good temper, a handsome face, and a stalwart form it is god-like in its force and influence.

The little narrow street of Portmaris seemed somehow to grow brighter and wider as the young man strode up it; his well-knit form swaying a little to right and left, his well-shaped head perfectly poised, his bright eyes glancing here and there with intelligent interest, the pleasure-loving lips whistling softly from sheer light-heartedness. He stopped as he came opposite Sea View, and listened to Leslie's song, nodding his head approvingly; then he caught sight of the "Marine Villa" on the opposite house, and walked straight into the little hall.

"Hallo, Grey," he said, and his voice rang, not hardly and unpleasantly, but with that clear golden timbre which only belongs to the voice of a man in perfect health. "Here you are, then! And how is——."

Grey smiled as he bent his head respectfully; everybody was glad to see the young man.

"Yes, my lord. Just got down. His gra——. We are pretty well considering the journey, my lord. He will see your lordship at once."

"All right," said the young fellow. "I rode as far as Northcliffe, but left the horse there, as I didn't know what sort of stables they'd have here."

"You were right, my lord," said Grey, in the approving tone of a confidential servant. "This seems a rare out-of-the-way place. And I should doubt there being a decent stable here."

"Ah, well, the duke will like it all the better for being quiet," the young fellow said.

Grey put his hand to his lips, and coughed apologetically.

"Beg pardon, my lord, but his gra——, that is—well, you'll excuse me, my lord, but we're down here quite incog., as you may say."

As Lord Auchester, staring at the man, was about to laugh, the clear, rather shrill voice of the invalid was heard from the room.

"Is that you, Yorke? Why do you not come in?"

The young fellow entered, and took the long thin hand the duke extended to him.

"Hallo, Dolph!" he said, lowering his voice. "How are you? What made you think of coming to this outlandish spot?"

The duke, still holding his cousin's hand, smiled up at him with a mixture of sadness and self raillery.

"I can't tell you, Yorke; I got tired of town, and told Grey to hunt up some place in Bradshaw that he had never heard of, some place right out of the beaten track, and he chose this."

"Poor unfortunate man!" said Lord Auchester, with a laugh.

"Yes, Grey suffers a great deal from my moods and humors; and so do other persons, yourself to wit, Yorke. It was very kind of you to come to me so soon."

"Of course I came," said Lord Auchester. "I wasn't very far off, you see."

"Fishing?" said the duke, with evident interest.

"Y-es; oh, yes," replied the other young man, quickly. "I rode over as far as Northcliffe——."

The duke sighed as his eyes wandered musingly over the stalwart, well-proportioned frame.

"You ought to have been in the army, Yorke," he said.

Lord Auchester laughed.

"So I should have been if they hadn't made the possession of brains a *sine qua non*; it seems you want brains for pretty nearly everything nowadays; and it's just brains I'm short of, you see, Dolph."

"You have everything else," said the duke, in a low voice.

He sighed and turned his head away; not that he envied his cousin his handsome face and straight limbs.

"You haven't told me what you wanted me for, Dolph," said Lord Auchester, after a pause, during which both men had been listening half unconsciously to the sweet voice in the cottage opposite.

"I wanted—nothing," said the duke.

"There is nothing I can do for you?"

"Nothing; unless," with a sigh and a wistful smile, "unless you can by the wave of a magician's wand change this crooked body of mine for something like your own."

"I would if I could, Dolph," said the other, bending over him, and laying a pair of strong hands soothingly on the invalid's bent shoulders.

"I know that, Yorke. But you cannot, can you? I dare say you think I am a peevish, discontented wretch, and that I ought, as the poor Emperor of Germany said, to bear my pain without complaining——."

"No, Dolph; I think you complain very little, and face the music first rate," put in the other.

"Thanks. I try to most times, and I could succeed better than I do if I were always alone, but sometimes——," he sighed bitterly. "Why is it that the world is so false, Yorke? Are there no honest men besides you and Grey, and half a dozen others I could mention? And are there no honest women at all?"

Yorke Auchester raised his eyebrows and laughed.

"What's wrong with the women?" he said.

The duke leaned his head upon his hand, and partially hid his face, which had suddenly become red.

"Everything is wrong with them, Yorke," he said, gravely and in a low voice. "You know, or perhaps you do not know, how I esteem, reverence, respect a woman; perhaps because I dare not love them."

Yorke Auchester nodded.

"If all the men felt as you do about women there would be no bad ones in the world, Dolph," he said.

"To me there is something sacred in the very word. My heart expands, grows warm in the presence of a good woman. I cannot look at a beautiful girl without thinking—don't misunderstand me, Yorke."

"No, no, old chap!"

"I love, I reverence them; and yet they have made me fly from London, have caused me almost to vow that I will never go back; that I will hide my misshapen self for the rest of my weary days——."

"Why Dolph——."

"Listen," said the duke. "Look at me, Yorke. Ah, it is unnecessary. You know what I am. A thing for women to pity, to shudder at—not to love! And yet"—he hid his face—"some of them have tried to persuade me that I—*I*—could inspire a young girl with love; that I—*I*—oh, think of it, Yorke!—that I had only to offer myself as a husband to the most beautiful, the fairest, straightest, queenliest of them, to be accepted!"

Yorke Auchester leaned over him.

"You take these things too seriously, Dolph," he said, soothingly. "It's—it's the way of the world, and you can't better it; you must take it as it comes."

"The way of the world! That a girl—young, beautiful, graceful—should be sold by her mother and father, should be willing to sell herself—ah, Yorke!—to a thing like me. Is that the way of the world? What a wicked, heartless, vicious world, then; and what an unhappy wretch am I! What fools they are, too, Yorke! They think it is so fine a thing to wear a ducal coronet! Ha, ha!" He laughed with sad bitterness. "So fine, that they would barter their souls to the evil one to feel the pressure of that same coronet on their brows, to hear other women call them 'Your Grace.' Oh, Yorke, what fools! How I could open their eyes if they would let me! Look at me. I am the Duke of Rothbury, Knight of the Garter—poor garter!" and he looked at his thin leg—"and what else? I almost forget some of my titles; and I would swap them all for a straight back and stalwart limbs like yours. But, Yorke, to share those titles, how many women would let me limp to the altar on their arms!"

He laughed again, still more bitterly.

"Sometimes, when some sweet-faced girl, with the look of an angel in her eyes, with a voice like a heavenly harmony, is making what they call 'a dead set' at me, I have hard work to restrain myself from telling her what I think of her and those who set her at me. Yorke, it is this part of the business which makes my life almost unendurable, and it is only by running away from every one who knows, or has heard of, the 'poor' Duke of Rothbury that I can put up with existence."

"Poor old chap," murmured Lord Auchester.

"Just now," continued the duke, "as we drove up to the door, I caught sight of a beautiful girl at the window opposite. I saw her face grow soft with pity, with the angelic pity of a woman, which, though it stings and cuts into one like a cut from a whip, I try to be grateful for. She pitied me, not knowing who and what I am. Tell her that I am the Duke of Rothbury, and in five minutes or less that angelic look of compassion will be exchanged for the one which you see on the face of the hunter as his prey comes within sight. She will think, 'He is ugly, crooked, maimed for life; but he is a man, and I can therefore marry him; he is a duke and I should be a duchess.' And so, like a moral poison, like some plague, I blight the souls of the best and purest. Listen to her now; that is the girl singing. What is it? I can hear the words."

He held up his hand. Leslie was singing, quite unconscious of the two listeners.

> "My sweet girl love with frank blue eyes,
> Though years have passed I see you still;
> There, where you stood beside the mill,
> Beneath the bright autumnal skies.
> Though years have passed I love you yet;
> Do you still remember, or do you forget?"

"A nice voice," said Yorke Auchester, approvingly.

"Yes; the voice of a girl-angel. No doubt she is one. She needs only to be informed that an unmarried duke is within reach, and she'll be in a hurry to drop to the earth, and in her hurry to reach and secure him will not mind dragging her white wings in the mud."

"Women are built that way," said Yorke Auchester, concisely.

The duke sighed.

"Oh, yes, they are all alike. Yorke, what a fine duke you would have made! What a mischievous, spiteful old cat Fate is, to make me a duke and you only a younger son! How is it you don't hate and envy me, Yorke?"

"Because I'm not a cad and a beast, I suppose," replied the young fellow, pleasantly. "Why, Dolph, you have been the best friend a man ever had——."

"Most men hate their best friends," put in the duke, with a sad smile.

"Where should I have been but for you?" continued Yorke Auchester, ignoring the parenthesis. "You have lugged me out of Queer Street by the scruff of my neck half a dozen times. Every penny I ever had came from you, and I've had a mint, a complete mint—and, by the way, Dolph, I want some more."

The duke laughed wearily.

"Take as much as you want, Yorke," he said. "But for you, the money would grow and grow till it buried and smothered me. I cannot spend it; you must help me."

"I will; I always have," said Yorke Auchester, laughing. "It's a pity you haven't got some expensive fad, Dolph—pictures, or coins, or first editions, or racing."

The duke shrugged his shoulders.

"I have only one fad," he said; "to be strong and straight, and that not even the Rothbury money can gratify. But I do get some pleasure out of your expenditure. I fancy you enjoy yourself."

"I do."

"Yes? That is well. Some day you will marry——."

Yorke Auchester's hand dropped from the duke's shoulder.

"Marry some young girl who loves you for yourself alone."

"She's not likely to love me for anything else."

"All the better. Oh, Heaven! What would I not give for such a love as that?" broke out the duke.

As the passionate exclamation left his lips the door opened, and Mrs. Whiting, the landlady, came in. Her face was flushed; she was in a state of nervous excitement, caused by a mixture of curiosity and fear.

"I beg your pardon, your grace," she faltered, puffing timorously; "but did you ring?"

The duke looked straight at the woman, and then up at Yorke Auchester.

"No," said Yorke.

"I beg your grace's pardon," the curious woman began, stammeringly; but Grey coming behind her seized her by the arm, and, none too gently, swung her into the passage and closed the door.

The duke looked down frowningly.

"They've found you out, Dolph," said Yorke.

The duke was silent for a moment, then he sighed.

"Yes, I suppose so; I do not know how. I am sorry. I had hoped to stay here in peace for a few weeks, at any rate. But I must go now. Better to be in London where everybody knows me, and has, to an extent, grown accustomed to me."

He stopped short, and his face reddened.

"Yorke," he said, "do you think she knew which of us was the duke?"

"I don't know," replied Yorke; "I don't think she did."

"She would naturally think it was you if she didn't know," said the duke, thoughtfully, his eyes resting on the tall form of his cousin, who had gone to the window and was looking at the cottage opposite. "She would never imagine me, the cripple. Don't some of these simple folk think that a king is always at least six feet and a half, and that he lives and sleeps in a crown? Yes, you look more like a duke than I do, Yorke; and I wish to Heaven you were!"

"Thanks," said Yorke Auchester, not too attentively. "What a pretty little scrap of a place this is, Dolph, and—ah——." He stopped short. "By Jove! Dolph, what a lovely girl! Is that the one of whom you were speaking just now?"

The duke put the plain muslin curtain aside and looked.

Leslie had come to the window, and stood, all unconscious of being watched, with her arms raised above her head, in the act of putting a lump of sugar between the bars of the parrot's cage.

The duke gazed at her, at first with an expression of reverentadmiration.

"Ah, yes, beautiful!" he murmured; then his face hardened and darkened. "How good, how sweet, how innocent she looks! And yet I'll wager all I own that she is no better than the rest. That with all her angelic eyes and sweet childlike lips, she will be ready to barter her beauty, her youth, her soul, for rank and wealth." He groaned, and clutched his chair with his long, thin, and, alas! claw-like hands. "I cannot bear it. Yorke, I meant to conceal my title, and while I staid down here pretend to be just a poor man, an ordinary commoner, one who would not tempt any girl to play fast and loose with her soul. I should have liked to have made a friend of that girl; to have seen her, talked with her every day, without the perpetual, ever-present dread that she would try and make me marry her. But it is too late, it seems. This woman here knows, everybody in the place knows, or will know. It is too late, unless ——."

He stopped and looked up.

"Yorke!"

"Hallo!" said that young fellow, scarcely turning his head.

"Will you—do you mind—you say you owe me something?" faltered the duke, eagerly.

"Why, of course," assented Yorke Auchester, and he came and bent over him. "What's the matter, Dolph? What is it you want me to do?"

"Just this," said the duke, laying his hand—it trembled—on the strong arm; "be the Duke of Rothbury for a time, and let this miserable cripple sink into the background. You will not refuse? Say it is a whim; a mere fad. Sick people," he smiled, bitterly, "are entitled to these whims and fads, you know, and I've not had many. Humor this one; be the duke, and save me for once from the humiliation which every young girl inflicts upon me."

Yorke Auchester's brow darkened, and he bit his lip.

"Rather a rum idea, old chap, isn't it?" he said, with an uneasylaugh.

"Call it so if you like," responded the duke, with, if possible, increased eagerness. "Are you going to refuse me, Yorke? By Heaven!"—his thin face flushed—"it is the first, the only thing I have ever asked of you——."

"Hold on!" interrupted Yorke Auchester, almost sternly. "I did not say I would refuse; you know that I cannot. You have been the best friend——."

The duke raised his hand.

"I knew you would not. Ring the bell, will you?" His voice, his hand, as he pointed to the bell, trembled.

Yorke Auchester strode across the room and rang the bell.

Grey entered.

"Grey," said the duke, in a low voice, "how came this woman to know my name?"

"It was a mistake, your grace," said Grey, troubled and remorseful. "I let it slip when I was wiring, and the idiot at the telegraph station in London must have wired it down to the people on his own account. But—but, your grace, she doesn't know much after all, for she didn't know which is the dook, as she calls it, beggin' your pardon, your grace."

The duke nodded, clasping his hands impatiently and eagerly.

"Ring the bell. Stand aside, and say nothing," he said, in a tone of stern command which he seldom used.

The landlady, who, like Hamlet, was fat and scant of breath, was heard panting up the stairs, knocked timidly, and, in response to the duke's "Come in," entered, and looked from one to the other, in a fearsome, curious fashion.

"Did you ring?"

She would not venture to say "Your grace" this time.

The duke smiled at her.

"Yes," he said, gravely but pleasantly. "His Grace the Duke of Rothbury will stay with me for a few days if you can give him a room, Mrs.—Mrs.——."

"Whiting, sir, if you please. Oh, certainly, sir," and she dropped a courtesy to Yorke Auchester. "Certainly your grace. It's humble and homely like, but ——."

Grey edged her gently and persuasively out of the room, and when he had followed her the duke leaned back his chair, and looking up at the handsome face of his cousin, laughed.

"It's like a scene in one of the new farces, isn't it, Yorke—I beg your pardon, Godolphin, Duke of Rothbury?"

Farce? Yes. But at that moment began the tragedy of Leslie Lisle's life.

CHAPTER III.

RALPH DUNCOMBE.

The "great artist" went on painting, making the sketch more hideously and idiotically unnatural every minute, and was so absorbed in it that Leslie could not persuade him to leave it even for his lunch, and he maundered from the table to the easel with a slice of bread and butter in his hand, or held between his teeth as if he were a performing dog.

Leslie had played and sung to him until she was tired, and she cast a wistful glance from the window toward the blue sky and sunlit sea.

"Won't you leave it for a little while and come out on the beach, dear?" she said, coaxingly.

But Francis Lisle shook his head.

"No, no. I am just in the vein, Leslie; nothing would induce me to lose this light. But I wish you would go. It—it fidgets and unsettles me to have any one in the room who wants to be elsewhere. Go out for your walk; when you come back you will see what I have made of it; I flatter myself you will be surprised."

If she were not it would only be because she had seen so many similar pictures of his.

She put on her hat and dainty little Norfolk jacket of Scotch homespun, and went out with a handkerchief of his she was hemming in her pocket.

The narrow street was bathed in sunshine; at the open doors some of the fisher wives were sitting or standing at their eternal knitting, children were playing noisily in the road-way. The women, one and all, looked up and smiled as she appeared in the open doorway, and one or two little mites ran to her with the fearless joyousness which is the child's indication of love.

Leslie lifted one tiny girl with blue eyes and clustering curls and kissed her, patted the bare heads of the rest, and nodded pleasantly to the mothers.

"Mayn't we come with 'oo?" asked the mite; but Leslie shook her head.

"Not this afternoon, Trotty," she said, and ran away from them down the street which led sheer on to the beach.

As a rule she allowed the children to accompany her, and play round her as she sat at work, but this afternoon she wanted to be alone.

The arrival of the letter which her father had lost had disturbed and troubled her.

The man from whom it had come was a certain Ralph Duncombe, and he was one of the many unfortunates who had fallen in love with her; but, unlike the rest, he had not been content to take "No" for an answer, and gone away and got over it, or drowned himself, but had persisted in hoping and striving.

She had met him at a sea-side boarding house two years before this, had been pleasant and kind to him, as she was to everybody, but had meant nothing more than kindliness, and was surprised and pained when he had asked her to be his wife, and declined to take a refusal.

Since that time he had cropped up at intervals, like a tax collector, and it seemed as if Leslie would never convince him that there was no hope for him. His persistence distressed her very much, but she did not know what she could do. He was the sort of man who, having set his heart upon a thing, would work with a dogged earnestness until he had got it; and could not be made to understand that women's hearts are not to be won, like a town, by a siege, however long and stringent it may be.

She went down to the breakwater, and sat down in her favorite spot and got out her handkerchief; and two minutes afterward there was a patter-patter on the stones behind her, and a small black-and-tan terrier leaped on her lap with a joyous yap.

She laughed and hugged him for a moment, then forced him down beside her.

"Oh, Dick, what a wicked Dick you are! You've run the needle into my finger, sir!" she said. "Look there." And she held out a tapering forefinger with one little red drop on it.

Dick smiled in dog fashion, and attempted to bite the finger, but to his surprise and disgust Leslie refused to play.

"I'm too busy, Dick," she said, gravely. "I want to finish this handkerchief; besides, it's too hot. Suppose you coil yourself up like a good little doggie, and go to sleep——. Well, if you must you must, I suppose!" And she let him snuggle into her lap, where, seeing that she really meant it, he immediately went to sleep.

It was a lovely afternoon. There was no one on the beach excepting herself, and all was silent save for the drowsy yawing of the gulls and the heavy boom of the tide as it went out, for the sea was very seldom calm at Portmaris, and in the least windy of days there was generally a ground-swell on.

Leslie sat and worked, and thought, thought mostly of Mr. Ralph Duncombe, her persistent suitor; but once or twice the remembrance of the deformed cripple who had come to lodge at Marine Villa crossed her mind, and she was thinking of him pityingly when the sound of footsteps crunching firmly and uncompromisingly over the pebbles made her start, and caused the terrier to leap up with the fury of its kind.

Leslie's brows came together as she looked up.

A middle-sized young man, with broad shoulders and a rather clumsy but steady gait, was coming down the beach. He was not a good-looking man. He had a big head and red hair, a large mouth and a square jaw; his feet and hands were also large, and there was in his air and manner something which indicated aggressiveness and obstinacy.

Sharp men who had seen him as a boy had said, "That chap will get on," and, unlike most prophets, they had been correct; Ralph Duncombe had "got on." He had started as an errand boy in a city office, and had risen step by step until he had become a partner. Rawlings & Co. had always been well thought of in the city, but Rawlings and Duncombe had now become respected and eminent.

His square, resolute face flushed as he saw her, but the hand with which he took off his hat was as steady as a rock.

"Good-morning, Miss Lisle," he said, making his voice heard above the dull roar of the sea and the shrill barking of the terrier.

Leslie held out one hand while she held the furiously struggling Dick with the other.

He took her hand in his huge fist, and dropped heavily on the shingle beside her.

"I didn't know you had a dog," he said, glancing at her and then at the dog, and then at the sea, as a man does who is so much head-over-heels in love that he cannot bear the glory of his mistress' face all atonce.

"I haven't," said Leslie, laughing in the slow, soft way which her adorers found so bewitching—and agonizing. "He doesn't really belong to me, though he pretends that he does. He is the abandoned little animal of Mrs. Merrick, our landlady; but he will follow me about and make a nuisance of himself. Be quiet, Dick, or I shall send you home."

"I'm not surprised," said Ralph Duncombe, with a slight flush, and still avoiding her eyes. "I can sympathize with Dick."

Leslie colored, and took up her work, leaving Dick to wander gingerly round the visitor and smell him inquisitively.

"You got my letter, Miss Leslie?"

"No," she said. "I am very sorry; but papa lost it."

He smiled as if he were not astonished.

"It doesn't matter," he said. "It only said that I was coming and—here I am."

"I—I will go and tell papa; you will come and have some lunch?"

"No don't get up," he said, quickly putting out his hand to stay her. "I've had my lunch, and I can go and see Mr. Lisle presently if——," he paused. "Miss Leslie, I suppose you know why I have come down here?"

Leslie bent her head over her work. She could guess. Such a man as Mr. Ralph Duncombe was not likely to come down to such a place as Portmaris in obedience to a mere whim.

"I've come down because I said that I would come about this time," he went on, slowly and firmly, as if he had well rehearsed his speech—as, indeed, he had. "I'm a man who, when he has set his heart upon anything, doesn't change or give it up because he doesn't happen to get it all at once. I've set my heart upon making you my wife, Miss Leslie——."

Leslie's face flushed, and she made a motion as if to get up, but sank back again with a faint sigh of resignation.

"That's been my keenest wish and desire since I saw you two years ago; and it's just as keen, no less and no more, as it was the first half hour I spent in your society."

"You—you told me this before, Mr. Duncombe," said Leslie, not angrily nor impatiently, but very softly.

"I know," he assented. "And you told me that it couldn't be. And I suppose most men would have been satisfied—or dissatisfied, and given it up. But I'm not made like that. I shouldn't be where I am and what I am if I were. I dare say you think I'm obstinate."

The faintest shadow of a smile played on Leslie's lips.

"Yes!" she said. "But—but may I not be obstinate, too?" pleadingly.

"No," he said, gravely. "You are a woman, a girl, little more than a child, and I'm a man, a man who has fought his way in the world, and knows what it is; and that makes it different."

"But——."

"Wait a minute," he said. "You said 'no' because—well, because I'm not good-looking, because I haven't the taking way with me which some men have; in short, because there's nothing about me that would be likely to take a romantic girl's fancy——."

Leslie laughed softly.

"Who told you that I am romantic, Mr. Duncombe?" she said.

"All girls—young girls who don't know the world—are romantic," he said, as if he were remarking that the world is round, and that two and two make four. "You look at the outside of things, and because I'm not handsome and a—swell—you think you couldn't bring yourself to love me, and that I'm not worth loving."

Leslie shook her head.

"I respect you very much. I like you, Mr. Duncombe," she said, in a low voice.

"Very well. That's all I ask," he retorted, promptly. "Be my wife and I'll change your respect into liking, your liking into love. I'm satisfied with that. When a man's starving he is thankful for half a loaf."

He didn't plead his cause at all badly, and Leslie's gray eyes melted and grew moist.

"Don't shake your head," he said. "Just listen to me first. You know I love you. You can't doubt that. If you did, and you knew what I've given up to come down here, you wouldn't doubt any longer. And you wouldn't if you knew what this love of mine costs me. A business man wants all his wits about him if he means to succeed; he wants all his thoughts and energies for his business; and for the last two years my wits and my thoughts have been wandering after you. It's a wonder that I have succeeded; but I have. Miss Leslie, though I'm plain to look at, I believe I've got brains. If I can't offer you a title——."

Leslie smiled; it was so likely that anyone would offer her a title!

"I can at least make you a rich woman."

Her face flushed.

"Mr. Duncombe——."

"I know what you are going to say. All girls declare that they don't care for money, and they mean it. But that's nonsense. A beautiful woman's beautiful whether she's poor or rich, but she's more likely to be happy with plenty of money. And you shall have plenty. I am a rich man now, as times go, and I mean to be richer. I've been working these two years with one object before me. I've made the money solely that I might become less unworthy to offer myself. Miss Leslie, my heart is yours already, such as it is. Be my wife, and share my home and fortune with me!"

Leslie's lips trembled.

"Oh, if I could!" she murmured, almost inaudibly. "I am so sorry, so sorry!"

He took up a pebble, looked hard at it, and cast it from him.

"You mean that you can't love me?" he said, rather hoarsely.

Her silence gave assent.

He drew a long breath.

"I expected you to say that, but I thought I should persuade you to—try and trust yourself to me, and wait for the love to come." He paused a moment. "Miss Leslie, do you ever think of the future?"

"Of the future?" She turned her startled eyes on his face, grave almost to sternness.

"Yes. Forgive me if I speak plainly. You and your father are alone in the world."

"Yes, ah, yes!" dropped from her parted lips.

"And he—well, even now it is you who are the protector; some day—Leslie, it makes my heart ache to think of you alone in the world, alone and poor. I know that the little he has goes with him. Don't be angry! I am thinking only of you. I cannot help thinking of you and your future. If you would say 'yes,' if you would promise to be my wife, not only would your future be secure, but your present, his present, would be easier, happier; for your father's sake if not for your own——."

He stopped, for Leslie had risen, and stood looking down at him, her lips quivering, her hands clasped tightly.

"No, no!" she panted; "not even for—for his sake! Oh, I could not! I could not!"

He arose. His face was pale, making his red hair more scarlet by contrast.

"I understand," he said. "It isn't that you do not love me, but that you—well, yes, dislike me!"

"No!"

"Yes, that's it," he said, his eyes resting for a moment on the lovely face with the wistful, hungry, half fierce look of a famishing man denied the crust which might save his life. Then his eyes sank to the stones. "I see now that I have been a fool to go on hoping, that my case is hopeless. Don't"—for she had shrunk from his almost savage tone—"don't be afraid. I am not going to bother you any more. I wish I could say that I am going to give up loving you; but I can't do that. Something tells me," he struck his breast, as if he were glad of something to strike, "that I shall go on loving you till I die! See here, Les—Miss Lisle. It's evident that I can't be your husband; but I can be your friend. No,"—for she turned her head away—"no, I don't mean that I am going to hang about you and pester you. I couldn't. The sight of you would be torture to me. I hope—yes, I hope I sha'n't see you for years. But what I want to say is this; that if ever you need a friend remember that there is one man in the world who would give his right hand to serve you. Remember that at any time—any time, in one year, two, or when you are old and gray—that you have only to say 'Come!' to bring me like a faithful dog to your feet. That time will never come, you think. Very good. But still you may need me. If you do send to me. I devote my life to you—oh, there's no merit in it. I can't help it. I'm romantic in a way, you see." He smiled with bitter self-scorn for his weakness. "You are the one woman in the world to me. Your case is mine, your friends shall be mine, your foes mine. If you need a protector send for me; if one wrongs you, and you want revenge, send to me, and as there is a heaven above us, I will come at your call to help to avenge you."

His face was white, his eyes gleaming under their red brows. So transformed was he by the master passion that if any one of his city friends had seen him at that moment they would scarcely have recognized him.

Ralph Duncombe talking the "rant" of melodrama! Impossible!

Leslie drew back, her eyes fixed on him in a fascinated kind of gaze, her bosom heaving.

He made an evident effort to regain his self-command, and succeeded. With a long breath he allowed his face to regain its usual hard, self-possessed expression.

"I have frightened you," he said, still rather hoarsely, but calmly. "Forgive me. I told you how I loved you, and you see a man doesn't tear from his heart the hope that has grown there for two years without feeling it. I am going now. You can make any excuse to your father, or you need not tell him you have seen me. Good-by—Leslie! It's the last time I shall call you so."

He held out his hand. It was firm as a rock, and gripped hers so tightly that she winced.

"I've hurt you," he said; "I, who would lay down my life to save you a moment's pain." He looked at his hand. "It was my ring. Ah!" he exclaimed, as if an idea had occurred to him, and he drew the ring from his finger. "Take this," he said, and he took her hand, opened it, and placing the ring on her palm, closed her fingers over it gently and yet firmly, as if he would accept no refusal. "If ever you need a friend, either for yourself or another, if ever you need to be avenged on a foe, send this ring to me—it will not be necessary to send a word with it—and I will come to you. Good-by!"

He raised her hand toward his lips, then with a sound that was half sigh, half groan, he let it fall, and without looking round climbed the beach and was lost to sight.

CHAPTER IV.

THE NEW DUKE.

The expression on Yorke Auchester's face as his cousin introduced him as his grace, the Duke of Rothbury beggars description.

He stared at the duke and colored, with a mixture of amazement and annoyance, which caused the duke to lean back in his chair and laugh; he did not often laugh.

"That was neatly done, Yorke," he said. "It isn't often a man is made a duke so easily."

"N-o," said Yorke; "but—but it's rather a large order, Dolph," and he turned to the window with something like a frown on his handsome face.

"Not at all," said the duke, cheerfully and airily. "You will find it easy and natural enough after the first half hour. There is very little difference between the duke and the dustman nowadays; indeed, if the dustman can only talk and manage to get into Parliament he is often a greater man than the duke, and he is quite certain to put on more 'side.' Come, Yorke, you are not angry?"

"No, no!" responded Yorke Auchester; "rather surprised, that's all. My elevation is somewhat sudden, you see," and he laughed. "The whim seems to give you pleasure, and it won't hurt me, and it won't last long. You only want me to take your place while you are down here?"

"Just so," said the duke. "I'm afraid you couldn't manage it in London. 'That poor cripple, Rothbury,' is too well known there. Seriously, my dear Yorke, I am very much obliged to you. You have made it possible for me to enjoy a few weeks of quiet and repose. These simple folk won't take any notice, after the first day or two, of a hunchback who is only a common Mr.—let me see; what shall I call myself—Brown, Jones, Robinson? No; there are quite enough of those honored names in the directory already. I'll call myself Temple; there is a Temple in the family nomenclature. Yes; Mr. Temple. There is no fear of our little arrangement becoming known. I'm not one of those men who delight in seeing their coat of arms emblazoned on everything they wear and use. I don't think there is a coronet to be found anywhere about me, and Grey is the pink and pattern of discretion. You can wear the lion's skin—poor lion!—down here at Portmaris in perfect security. Be a good duke, Yorke. Keep up the honor of the old title." He laughed again. "At any rate, you will look every inch of one. And now about that money—a duke must have the means of keeping up his state, you know. Will you hand me up that dispatch box, or shall I ring for Grey?"

Yorke Auchester placed the writing case on the table, and the duke took out his check book.

"How much shall it be, Yorke?" he asked, without looking up, and with a certain shyness, as if it were he who was about to receive the money instead of giving it.

Yorke Auchester looked down at him with an expression on his face which made it nice to look at.

"You are very good to me, Dolph," he said. "It is only the other day you sent me——."

"Sufficient for the day only is the check thereof," cut in the duke, as if to stop any thanks. "I dare say that is all spent."

"It is, indeed," assented the young man, candidly.

The duke laughed easily.

"Who cares? Not you, who, I dare say, have had your enjoyment out of it; not I, who have more money than I know what to do with. How much? Shall we say a thousand, Yorke?"

Yorke Auchester's face flushed.

"I should like to say it is too much," he said. "But you wouldn't believe me if I did, Dolph."

The duke smiled.

"I certainly should not. I can guess how quickly money flies when one is young and strong, blessed with youth's appetite for pleasure."

He filled in the check in a sharp, pointed hand and gave it to his cousin.

"There you are. You must spend some of it down here for the honor of the name."

Yorke laughed.

"All right," he said, "though I don't quite know what I can buy. Sixpence in periwinkles would go a long way."

"Yes," said the duke; "that is what I find. Money is a burden and a nuisance if you don't know how to get rid of it. Suppose you buy half a crown's worth of winkles and a lobster or two."

When Grey came in with the lunch he was surprised to find his master in so bright a humor.

"You quite understand the arrangement between Lord Auchester and me, Grey?" said the duke.

"Yes, your gra—sir."

The duke smiled.

"My name is Temple, Grey," he said; "this gentleman is the Duke of Rothbury. Don't forget that, and don't, by a slip, let the cat out of the bag. I want to be quiet, and to avoid the worry of being called upon and stared at while I am down here. You're sure you understand, Grey?"

"Quite, sir; oh, quite," said Grey, who was an admirable servant; and in addition to being, as the duke had said, the pink and pattern of discretion, had lived long enough with his grace to know him thoroughly, and to appreciate a good master, who, with all his whims and fads, was tenderness and liberality personified.

"Of course you do," said the duke. "You must be as glad of a little quiet as I can be, and we shall get it down here under this arrangement. Now, mind, be careful and keep the secret. Have you brought up my beef tea? Very well, you need not wait."

Grey wheeled his master to the table, cast a glance of respectful astonishment at Lord Auchester, which meant, "You and I must humor him, of course, my lord," and left the room.

"A nice lunch, isn't it, Yorke?" said the duke, looking round the table. "Ihope you will enjoy it. You are nearly always hungry, aren't you?" and he sighed as he smiled.

"Quite always," assented Yorke Auchester. "Chops, soles, and a custard pudding. Right. Sure you won't have any, Dolph?"

The duke shook his head.

"This is as much as I can digest," he said, tapping the basin before him indifferently. "Now tell me the news, Yorke—your grace."

Yorke laughed.

"News? I don't think there's any you don't know."

"Not London news, I dare say," said the duke; "though I don't know much of that. I don't go out more often than I am obliged to. I don't dance, you see," he smiled, "and if I go to the theater I find that I distract the attention of the audience from what is going on upon the stage. I suppose they consider me as interesting, as good, if not better than any play. And as to plays, there aren't many good ones now. The last time I went was to that burlesque at the Diadem Theater, and everybody seemed 'gone,' as you call it, on that dancer. What's her name, eh?"

Yorke Auchester was in the act of disboning his second sole. He stopped and looked up, paused for a moment with a rather singular expression on his frank, handsome face.

"Finetta, do you mean?" he said, slowly.

"Yes, that's the name, I think," said the duke, stirring his beef tea as if he hated it; "so called, I suppose, because she has finished so many good men and true. They tell me that she has completely ruined poor Charlie Farquhar. Is that so, Yorke?"

Yorke seemed very much ingrossed in his sole.

"Oh, Farquhar!" he said. "Yes, he is stone-broke; but I don't know that Fin—I mean Finetta—has had so much to do with it. Charlie was under the delusion that he understood horses, and——."

"I see," said the duke. "Poor lad! I suppose if I offered to help him he would be quite offended?"

"I don't know. You might try," said Yorke, dryly.

"I'll see. But about this same Finetta. She was pretty——."

Yorke Auchester looked up with a laugh. It was not a particularly merry one.

"Only pretty?"

"Well, yes, to my eyes; but I'm rather particular and hard to please, I'll admit. Oh, yes, she was pretty, and she danced," he smiled, "yes, she danced without doubt. The young men in the stalls seemed infatuated; but I didn't fall down and worship with the rest. Perhaps I'm old-fashioned, though I'm not much more than your age. Anyhow, a very little of Mlle. Finetta goes a long way with me. Do you know her, Yorke?"

"Oh, everybody knows Finetta," replied Yorke Auchester, carelessly—a little too carelessly.

"And some, it seems, like poor Charlie Farquhar, know her not wisely but too well. Well, I've not been to the theater since, and that's six weeks ago. Is that chop tender?"

"First rate; try it."

"I dare not; but I enjoy seeing you eat it. I've often had thoughts of having a man with a good appetite that I might have the pleasure of seeing him eat a square meal while I sit cursing my beef tea and gruel. The night I went to the Diadem I took Eleanor——."

Yorke Auchester suspended his fork half way to his mouth, and looked at his cousin.

"Oh," he said, and whatever the "Oh" might have been intended to mean it was singularly dull and inexpressive.

"Yes, it was her birthday, and she asked me to take her. That was kind of her, wasn't it?"

"Was it?" said Yorke, dryly.

"Well, I think so. You mean that most young girls would like to go to the theater with the Duke of Rothbury, or for the matter of that any other duke—unmarried; but that's because they would go with the hope of repeating the visit some day as his duchess. But Eleanor knows that I should not marry her; we have come to a plain understanding on the subject."

"I see," said Yorke Auchester. "I suppose this is Dartmoor mutton? It's very good."

"I dare say," assented the duke, with a smile. "But to return to *my* mutton, which is Eleanor. It was her birthday, and I took her to the theater and gave her a small present; the Rothbury pearls."

"Some persons would call an elephant small," remarked Yorke, laconically.

"Did—did you give her anything, Yorke?" asked the duke, almost shyly, ignoring the comments.

Yorke Auchester took a draught of the admirable claret which Grey had brought down with him, before replying.

"I?" he said, carelessly. "No. Why should I? What would be the use. She doesn't expect anything better than a penwiper or a shilling prayer book from a pauper like me, and she has tin enough to buy a million of 'em if she wants them," and he attacked the custard.

The duke leaned back in his chair, and looked at the handsome face of his cousin, with its frank and free, and happily devil-may-care expression.

"I've a notion that Eleanor would value anything in the way of a penwiper or a prayer book you might give her, Yorke," he said.

"Not she. It's only your fancy."

"I think not," said the duke.

He was silent for a moment, then he said, thoughtfully and gravely:

"At the risk of repeating myself, I will say once more that it is a pity you are not the Duke of Rothbury, Yorke."

"Thanks, but a better man's got the berth, you see."

"And a still greater pity that you can't be the future one. But you can't, can you, Yorke?"

"Not while Uncle Eustace and his two boys come before me, and as they are all as healthy as plowboys, and likely to live to the eighties, every one of 'em, there doesn't seem much chance, Dolph!"

"No," said the duke, in a low voice. "It's rather hard on the British Peerage that the present Duke of Rothbury should be a hunchback and a cripple, and that the next should be a miser, while the young man who would adorn the title——."

"Should be a penniless young scamp," put in Yorke, lightly.

The duke colored.

"Well, barring the scamp, that was in my thoughts. Do you ever think of the future, Yorke?"

"Never, if I can help it," responded the young fellow, cutting himself a piece of stilton.

The duke smiled, but rather gravely.

"I do, and when I think of it, I wish that I could secure it for you. But you know that I can't, Yorke. Every penny, or nearly every penny, goes to Lord Eustace."

"Don't let it trouble you, Dolph," said Yorke Auchester. "Of course the money must go to keep up the title. Every fellow understands that. Heaven knows I've had enough as it is."

"And so you didn't give Eleanor a birthday present," said the duke, slowly. "That was—to put it delicately, Yorke—thoughtless of you. Will you give me that box, the leather one? Thanks."

He opened the box and took out a small morocco case, and tossed it across the table.

"I had an idea you would forget it, and so——."

"By Jove, that's pretty!" broke in Yorke.

He had opened the case and revealed a gold bracelet, not set with diamonds, but of plain though first-rate workmanship. Just the sort of gift which a rather poor young man could manage.

"I'm glad you like it. I am sure Eleanor will, especially as it comes from you."

Yorke Auchester colored, and he looked for a moment as if he were about to decline the piece of jewelry; but, checking the words that rose to his lips, he put the case in his pocket.

"It's a shame to let her think it came from me, but I'll give it to her, because ——." He paused.

"Because you are too good-natured to disoblige me," said the duke.

"She'll think I've been committing burglary."

"In that case she will value the thing all the more highly," retorted the duke. He leaned back and rested his head on his hand.

"Go out and smoke, Yorke," he said presently.

Yorke Auchester was accustomed to his cousin's peremptory words. They were just those of a sick man, and had nothing of discourtesy in them.

"All right," he said. "I'll stroll down to the parade."

The duke smiled.

"I expect you will find nothing but a strip of beach," he said. "There are some cigars in that traveling case."

But Yorke said he had some cigars, and tossing on his hat made his way out into the sunshine.

For the first few minutes, as he went down the village street and along the narrow quay which stood for parade, his face was unusually grave and thoughtful.

We suppose by this time the intelligent reader will have formed some opinion respecting Yorke Auchester. At any rate we are not going to try and persuade the reader that the young fellow was an angel. He was no worse, perhaps a shade better, than most young men of his class. He was idle, but then he had never been taught to work, though in the way of sport he would cheerfully undergo any amount of toil, and endure any amount of hardship. He was thoughtless because he had nothing to think about, except the ever recurring problem—how best to kill time; he was extravagant because, never having earned money, he had no idea of its value. But he would share his last five-pound note with a friend, would sit up beside that friend all night and many nights, if he happened to fall sick, and behind his happy-go-lucky manner hid a heart as tender as a woman's, more tender than most women's, perhaps; and, like the antique hero, feared neither man nor beast. Children and dogs loved him at first sight; but, alas! that was perchance because of his handsome face, his bright smile, and his short, light-hearted laugh, for dogs and children have an unfair partiality for cheerful and good-looking people, and too often unwisely judge by appearances. Anyhow, there he was with all his faults, and so we have got to take him.

He created quite a little sensation as he sauntered along with his hands in his Norfolk jacket, his hat a little on one side, his big L'Arranaga in his mouth; the simple folk of Portmaris had never before seen anything so splendid. But Yorke did not notice them. He was thinking; wondering what his cousin, the duke, would say if he knew how far too well he, Yorke, knew Finetta; wondering whether he hadn't better cut town and marry Eleanor Dallas and her fifty thousand pounds; wondering——.

"Oh, dash it!" he exclaimed at last, as he felt the crisp check in his pocket. "What's the use of bothering, on such a morning, too!" and he threw off the "pale cast of thought," and began to sing under his breath.

Then he stopped suddenly, for he saw a young girl sitting on the shingle with her back to the breakwater.

It was Leslie, sitting as Ralph Duncombe had left her. She held the ring in her hand, her bosom still heaving, her heart troubled, her eyes fixed on vacancy. There was a tear trembling on the long black lashes, and a faint quiver on the parted lips, and Yorke Auchester, as, unseen by her, he stood and looked at her, saw this.

Now, one of this young man's foibles was the desire, when he saw people in distress or trouble, to help them out of it, or, failing to do that, to at any rate try and cheer them up and console them.

"That's the pretty girl from over the way," he mused. "Pretty! It's a lovely face, perfectly lovely. Now, what's the matter with her, I wonder? She can't be up to her neck in debt, and—and the rest of it. Got into a scrape, I expect, and somebody—papa or mamma, I suppose—has been bullying her. I should think whoever they are they must find it difficult to worry such an angel as that. She's been crying, or going to cry. Now what an ass of a world this is! If I were to go down to her, and ask her what was the matter, and try and cheer her up, and tell her there wasn't anything in the universe worth crying for, she'd jump up like a young wild-cat, feel herself insulted, scream for her brother or her father, and there'd be a row. And yet where would be the harm? I know this, that if I were sitting there down on my luck, I should like her to come and console me; but that's different, I suppose. Well, as the man said when his mother-in-law tumbled out of the second floor window, it's no business of mine."

But though he made this philosophical reflection, he still stood and looked at her wistfully, until, afraid that she might turn her head and see him, he went down the beach and sat down on the other side of the breakwater.

Leslie did not hear him, was quite unconscious of his proximity, did not even notice the perfume of the choice Havana. What was troubling her was the memory of Ralph Duncombe's passionate words and melodramatic promise; and the question, what should she do with the ring? She would have died rather than have put it on her finger; she didn't like—though she wanted—to pitch it in the sea. So she still held it in her soft, hot little palm. Happy ring!

So these two sat. Presently that peculiar desire which assails everybody who sits on the beach at the sea-side began to assail Yorke. Why it should be so difficult to refrain from flinging stones into the sea it is impossible to say; the clever people have found out most things, or say they have, but this still beats them.

Yorke, like everybody else, found the desire irresistible. Half unconsciously he took up a stone and shied it at the end pile of the breakwater. He missed it, mechanically took another aim, and hit it, then he absently found a piece of wood—the fragment of some wreck which had gone down outside in the bay, perhaps—and threw that as far as he could into the sullen, angry waves, which rolled and showed their teeth along the sand.

A minute, perhaps two, afterward, he heard a cry of distress behind him, and looking round saw Leslie standing and gazing seaward, with a troubled, anxious look in her gray eyes.

Yorke was astounded. What on earth had happened? Had she caught sight of a vessel going down, a boat upset—what?

She began to run down the beach, her small feet touching the big bowlders with the lightness and confidence of familiarity, and once more she cried out in distress.

Yorke strode after her, and gained her side.

"What's the matter?" he shouted above the dull sea roar.

She turned her face to him with a piteous look of entreaty and alarm.

"Dick! It's Dick!" she said.

"Dick! Who—which—where?" he demanded, looking in the direction of her eyes.

"It's a little dog—there!" she answered, quickly, and pointing. "A little black and tan, don't you see him? Ah, he is so small!"

"I see him!" said Yorke. "What's he doing out there? And can't he swim?"

"Yes, oh, yes, but the tide is going out, and he has got too far, and the current is dreadfully strong. Oh, poor, poor Dick! He went out after a piece of wood or something that some one threw."

Yorke flushed. He felt as guilty and uncomfortable as if he had been detected in an act of killing a human being.

"See, he cannot make any way! Oh, poor little Dick! I am—so—sorry. I am so fond of him, and he is such a nice——." She stopped and turned her head away as if she could not go on, and could look no longer.

"I threw the piece of wood," said Yorke. "I didn't see the dog; he's so small—oh, for goodness sake, don't cry! It's all right."

He got out of his coat with the cool quickness of a man who is used to emergencies in the sporting way, and running across the sand, sprang into the sea, and struck out.

Leslie was too astonished for a moment to realize what he had done, then she raised her voice with a warning cry.

"The current!" she called to him. "The current. Oh, come back, please come back!"

CHAPTER V.

APPRECIATED GENIUS.

Yorke soon found himself out of his depth, and almost as quickly discovered what the young lady meant by shouting, "The current!" But he was a good swimmer—there was scarcely anything Yorke Auchester could not do, except earn his living—and, though he found his boots and clothes very much in the way, he got through the waves at a fair pace, and reached the black and tan.

Saving a fellow creature is hard work enough, but it is almost as bad to rescue a dog, even so small a one as Dick, from a watery grave.

When Yorke had succeeded in getting hold of him with one hand Dick commenced to scratch and claw, no doubt under the impression that the great big man had come to hasten his death rather than prevent it, and Yorke was compelled to swim on his back, and hold the clawing, struggling little terrier pressed hard against his chest.

It was hard work getting back, but he found himself touching the sand at last, and scrambling to his feet waded through what remained of the water, and set Dick upon his four legs at Leslie's feet.

Of course the little imp, after shaking the water off his diminutive carcase, barked furiously at his preserver.

Now the handsomest man—and, for that matter, the prettiest woman also—is not improved in appearance by a bath; that is, before he has dried himself and brushed his hair.

The salt water was running off Yorke's tall figure at all points; his short hair was stuck to his forehead; his mustache drooped, his eyes were blinking, and his clothes adhered to him as if they loved him better than a brother. He didn't look in the least heroic, but extremely comical, and Leslie's first impulse was to laugh.

But the laugh did not—indeed, would not—come, and she picked up the damp Dick and hugged him, and looked over his still snarling countenance at his preserver with a sudden shyness in her eyes and a heightened color in her face.

She looked so supremely lovely as she stood thus that Yorke forgot his sensation of stickiness, and gazed at her with a sudden thrill agitating his heart.

Leslie found her voice at last, but there only came softly, slowly, the commonplace—

"Thank you."

It sounded so terribly commonplace and insufficient that she made an effort and added:

"It was very kind of you to take so much trouble. How wet you must be! You must not stand about."

Yorke smiled, and knocked the hair from his forehead and wrung his shirt sleeves.

"It's all right," he said. "It was my fault. If I hadn't chucked the piece of wood he wouldn't have gone in. He hasn't come to any harm apparently."

"Oh, no, no. He's all right," said Leslie. "He can swim very well when the tide is coming in, but when it is going out it is too strong for him, and—he would have been drowned if you had not gone after him," and her eyes dropped.

"Poor little chap," said Yorke, putting on his coat. "That would never have done, would it, doggie?"

"It is a very dangerous place for bathing," said Leslie. "The current is very strong, and that is why I called out."

"Yes thanks," he said, to spare her the embarrassment of explaining that sudden frightened cry of hers. "I could feel that. But I have to thank Dick for an enjoyable bath, all the same. I suppose he will never forgive me; the person whose life you save never does."

He sat down on the breakwater and began to empty his pockets. There were several papers—bills—reduced to semi-pulp; Yorke did not sorrow over them. His watch had stopped; his cigars and cigar case were irretrievably ruined. He held them up with a laugh, and laid them on top of the breakwater in the sun; then suddenly his happy-go-lucky expression grew rather grave as he took up an envelope and looked at it.

"By George!" he said. "All the rest doesn't matter, but this doesn't belong to me."

Leslie stood and looked down at him anxiously. She was thinking of colds and rheumatism, while the young fellow sat so perfectly contented in his wet clothes.

"Don't you think—had you not better go home and change your things as quickly as possible?" she said, forgetting her shyness in her anxiety.

He looked up from the envelope.

"Why, I shall be dry in ten minutes," he said, carelessly, "and I sha'n't take any harm if I'm not. I never caught cold in my life; besides, salt water never hurts."

Leslie shook her head gravely.

"I don't believe that; it's a fallacy," she said. "Some of the old fishermen here suffer terribly from rheumatism."

"That's because they're old, you see," he said, smiling up at her. "And if you think it's so dangerous hadn't you better put Master Dick down? He is making you awfully wet."

She shook her head, and held Dick all the more tightly.

"I am so glad to get him back," she said, half to herself, "that I don't mind his making me a little damp; but I do wish you would go."

He did not seem to hear her, but after another glance at the letter, said:

"I picked this up just over there," and he nodded in the direction of the cliffs, "and I should like to find its owner; though I expect she won't thank me much when she sees its condition. Have you been here long? Do you know the people here pretty well?"

"We have been here some months," said Leslie, "and—yes, I think I know them all."

"Now, who does she mean by 'we?' Her husband?" Yorke asked himself, and an uncomfortable little pain shot through him. "No!" he assured himself; "she can't be married; too young and—too happy looking! Well, then, perhaps you know a young lady by the name of Lisle—Leslie Lisle," he said.

Leslie smiled.

"That is my name; it is I," she replied.

"By George!" he exclaimed. "Then this is your property!" and he held out the letter.

Leslie took it, and as she looked at the address flushed hotly. It was Ralph Duncombe's missing letter.

Yorke noticed the flush, and he looked aside.

"My father dropped it," she said, with an embarrassment which, slight as it was, did not escape him. "Thank you."

"I'm sorry that I didn't put it in my coat pocket instead of my waistcoat," he said. “But I knew if I did that I should forget it perhaps for weeks. I always forget letters that fellows ask me to post. So I put it in with my watch, that I might come across it when I looked at the time, and so it’s got wet; but as it was opened you have read it, so that I hope it doesn’t matter so much.”

“No, I haven’t read it. Papa always opens my letters—he doesn’t notice the difference. It does not matter in the least; I know what was in it, thank you,” she said, hurriedly.

“I wish some one would always open and read my letters, and answer them, too,” said Yorke, devoutly, as he thought of the great pile of bills which awaited him every morning at breakfast. “Are you staying—I mean lodging, visiting here, Miss Lisle?” he asked, for the sake of saying something that would keep her by his side for at least a few minutes longer.

“Yes,” said Leslie. “We are staying in ‘The Street,’ as it is called at Sea View.”

Yorke was just about to remark, “I know,” but checked himself, and said instead:

“It is a very pretty place, isn’t it?”

“Very,” assented Leslie; “and quiet. There is no prettier place on the coast than Portmaris.”

“So I should think,” he said, looking round, then returning to the beautiful face. “I am a stranger, and only arrived an hour or two ago.” He looked down, trying to think of something else to say, anything that would keep her; but could think of nothing.

Leslie stood for a moment, silent, too, then she said:

“Will you not go and change your things now? Dick would be very sorry if you were to catch cold on his account.”

It was on the tip of Yorke’s tongue to ask, “Only Dick?” but once more he checked himself. The retort would have come naturally enough if he had been addressing a London belle; but there was something in the beautiful gray eyes, an indescribable expression of maidenly dignity and reserve, which, sweet as it was, warned him that such conversational small change would not be acceptable to Miss Lisle, so instead he said, with a smile:

“Oh, Dick won’t mind. Besides, he knows I am almost as dry as he is by this time.”

Leslie shook her head as if in contradiction of his assertion, and with Dick still pressed to her bosom, said:

“Good-morning, and—and thank you very much,” she added, with a faint color coming into her face.

Yorke arose, raised his hat, and watched her graceful figure as it lightly stepped up the beach to the quay; then he collected his various soaked articles from the breakwater, and followed at a respectful distance.

"Leslie Lisle," he murmured to himself. "The name's music, and she——."

Apparently he could not hit upon any set of terms which would describe her even to his own mind, and, pressing the water from his trousers, he climbed the beach, still looking at her.

As he did so he saw a tall, thin gentleman coming toward her. He held a canvas in his hands, gingerly, as if it were wet, and was followed by a small boy carrying a portable easel and other artistic impedimenta, and, as Leslie spoke to the artist and took the easel from the boy, Yorke muttered:

"Her father! Now, if I go up to them she'll feel it incumbent upon her to tell him of my 'heroic act,' and he'll be bored to death trying to find something suitable to say; and she'll be embarrassed and upset, and hate the sight of me. She looks like a girl who can't endure a fuss. No, I'll go round the other way —if there is another way, as the cookery books say."

He looked round, and was on the point of diving into a narrow street opposite him when an invalid chair came round the corner, driven by Grey, and the occupant, whose eyes were as sharp as his body was frail and crooked, caught sight of the stalwart figure, and held up a hand beckoningly.

Yorke looked very much as if he meant making a run for it; then, with a muttered, "Oh, confound it!" he stuck his hands in his pockets, tried to look as if nothing had happened, and sauntered with a careless, leisurely air up the quay.

By this time Francis Lisle had stuck up his easel right in the center of the narrow pavement, and arranged his canvas, and Grey was in the act of dragging the invalid chair round it, when Leslie, bending down, said, in a whisper:

"Papa, I must move the easel; they cannot pass."

"Eh?" said Francis Lisle, looking round nervously. "I beg your pardon, I will move; yes, I will move."

"Do not, please," said the duke, his thin voice softening as it always did in the presence of a lady. "There is plenty of room. You can go round, Grey?"

"Yes, your—yes, sir," said Grey.

His master shot a warning glance at him.

"There is not room," said Leslie, in a low voice, but the duke held up his hand.

"Please do not trouble," he said; "I am not going any further. I only want to speak to this gentleman coming along. I beg you will not trouble to move the easel. Artists must not be disturbed, or the inspiration may desert them," he added to Francis Lisle, with a pleasant smile.

"Thank you, thank you," said Lisle, still clutching the easel; but Grey had turned the chair with its front to the sea, and the duke called to Yorke, who had come upon them at this juncture.

"What a pretty place, Yorke!" he said. "Have you had your stroll? Shall we go back?"

Yorke had discreetly kept behind the chair, and out of sight of his cousin's sharp eyes.

"All right," he assented.

"Will you give me a cigar?" said the duke.

Yorke came up to the chair and put his hand in his pocket, and thoughtlessly extended the cigar case.

"Thanks. Good gracious! Why, it is soaking wet! Hallo, Yorke," and the duke screwed his head round. "Why, where have you been? What have you been doing?"

Yorke flushed, and cast an appealing glance at Leslie's downcast face. To be made the center of an astonished and absurdly admiring group, to be made a cheap twopenny-halfpenny hero of, was more than he could stand.

"Oh it's nothing," he growled. "Had an accident—tumbled into the sea."

"An accident!" exclaimed the duke, staring at him. "Tumbled in the sea! How did you manage that, in the name of goodness?"

Yorke got red, and looked very much like an impatient schoolboy caught playing truant or breaking windows.

"What's it matter!" he said. "Fell off breakwater. Go and get the cigars, Grey; I'll look after his——."

The duke cut in quickly before the word "grace."

"Nothing of the sort," he said. "You get home and change your things. Fell off the breakwater!" He stared at him incredulously.

Mr. Lisle, too, gazed at him with blank astonishment, as if he were surprised to find that it was a man and not a little boy in knickerbockers, who might not unnaturally be expected to tumble off the breakwater.

Leslie meanwhile stood with downcast eyes, then suddenly she said, addressing her father and carefully avoiding the other two:

"This gentleman swam in to save Dick, papa; that is why he is wet."

The duke scanned her face keenly, and smiled curiously.

"That sounds more probable than your account, Yorke. It is a strange thing," he turned his head to Lisle, "that a man is more often ashamed of committing a good or generous action than a bad one. How do you account for it?"

Mr. Lisle looked at him helplessly, as if he had been asked a conundrum which no one could be expected to answer.

"Because there is always such a thundering fuss about it," said Yorke, stalking off.

The duke looked after him for a minute or two, apparently lost in thought, then he turned to Lisle again.

"You are an artist, sir?" he said.

Mr. Lisle flushed.

"I am, at least, an humble worshiper at the throne," he replied, in the low, nervous voice with which he always addressed strangers, and he resumed his painting.

The duke signed to Grey to help him to get out of the chair, which was so placed that he could not see the canvas.

Grey came round, and in opening the apron let the duke's stick fall. Leslie hesitated a moment, then stepped forward and picked it up. The duke took it from her with a faint flush on his pale, hollow cheeks.

"Thank you," he said. "I am afraid I could not get on without it. At one time I could not walk even with its aid. Please don't say you are sorry or pity me," he added, with an air of levity that barely concealed his sensitive dread of any expression of sympathy. "Everybody says that, you know."

"I was not going to say so," said Leslie, looking him full in the face, and with a sweet, gentle smile.

He looked at her with his unnaturally keen eyes.

"No," he said, quietly. "I don't think you were. And this is the picture——." He stopped as he looked at the awful monstrosity, then caught Leslie's eyes gazing at him with anxious, pleading deprecation, and went on, "Singular effect. You have taken great pains with your subject, Mr. ——."

"Lisle—my name is Lisle," he said, hurriedly. "Yes, yes, I have not spared pains! I have put my heart into my work."

"That is quite evident," said the duke, with perfect gravity, and still regarding the picture. "And that which a man puts his heart in will reward him some day; does, indeed, reward him even while he works."

"True, true!" assented the dreamer, with a gratified glance at the speaker and at Leslie, who stood with downcast eyes, to which the brows were dangerously near. "It is with that hope, that heart, that we artists continue to labor in face of difficulties which to the careless and irreverent seem insurmountable. You think the picture a—a good one, sir; that it is promising?"

The duke was floored for a moment, then he said:

"I think it evidences the painter's love for his art, and his complete devotion to it, Mr. Lisle."

The poor dreamer's face had fallen during the pause, but it brightened at the diplomatic response when it did come, and Leslie, casting a grateful glance at the pale face of the cripple, murmured in his ear:

"Thank you!"

The duke looked at her with a glow of sympathy in his eyes.

"This is your daughter, I presume, Mr. Lisle?" he said.

Lisle nodded.

"Yes," he said. "My only child. All that is left me in the world—excepting my art. You are not an artist also, sir? Pardon me, but your criticism showed such discrimination and appreciation that I was led to conclude you might be a fellow-student."

The duke hesitated a moment.

"No," he said, quietly. "I am not an artist, though I am fond of a good picture ——," poor Lisle gazed at the daub, and nodded with a gratified smile. "I am what is called—I was going to say a gentleman at ease, but I am very seldom at ease. My name is Temple, and I am traveling for the benefit of my health."

Lisle nodded again.

"You will find this an extremely salubrious spot," he said. "My daughter and I are very well here."

The duke glanced at Leslie's tall, graceful figure, and smiled grimly.

"But then she is not a cripple," he said.

"A cripple!" Mr. Lisle looked startled and bewildered. "Oh, no; oh, no."

The duke smiled, and leaning upon his stick, seemed to be watching the painter at his work, but his eyes wandered now and again covertly to the beautiful girl beside him. He noticed that her dress, though admirably fitting, was by no means new or of costly material, that her gloves were well worn and carefully mended in places, that her father, if not shabby, had that peculiar look about his clothes which tells so plainly of narrow means; and when Leslie, becoming conscious of his wandering glance, moved away and stood at a little distance on the edge of the quay, the duke said:

"Have you disposed of your picture, Mr. Lisle?"

Francis Lisle started and flushed.

"N-o," he replied. "That is, not yet."

"I am glad of that," said the duke. "I should like to become its purchaser, if you are disposed to sell it."

Lisle's breath came fast. He had never sold a "picture" in his life, had long and ardently looked forward to doing so, and—and, oh! had the time arrived?

"Certainly, certainly," he said, nervously, and his brush shook. "You like it so much? But perhaps you would like some others of mine better. I—I have several at the cottage. Will you come and look at them?"

"With pleasure," said the duke. "Meanwhile, what shall I give you for this?"

Lisle gazed at the picture with pitiable agitation; he was in mortal terror lest he should scare his customer away by asking too much.

"Really," he faltered, "I—I don't know its value, I have never——," he laughed. "What should you think it was worth?"

The duke ought, if he had answered truthfully, to have replied, "Rather less than nothing," but he feigned to meditate severely, then said:

"If fifty pounds——."

Poor Lisle gasped.

"You—you think—I was going to say twenty."

"We will say fifty," said the duke, as if he were making an excellent bargain. "You have not finished it yet."

"No, no," assented Lisle, eagerly. "I will do so carefully, most carefully. It—it shall be the most finished picture I have ever painted."

"I am sure you will do your best," said the duke. "I will accept your kind invitation to see your other pictures, and now I must be getting back. Good-morning."

"Yes, yes! Good-morning! What did you say your name was?"

"Temple," said the duke.

He glanced at Leslie, raised his hat, was helped into his chair by Grey, who had stood immovable and impassive just out of hearing, and was wheeled away.

Lisle stood all of a quiver for a moment, then beckoned to Leslie.

"What is it, dear," she said, soothingly, as she saw his agitation. Had the crippled stranger told him what the sketch was really like?

"That—that gentleman has bought the picture, Leslie!" he exclaimed, in a tone of nervous excitement and triumph. "You see! I told you the day would come, and it has come. At last! Luck has taken a turn, Leslie! I see a great future before me. I only wanted some one with an appreciative, artistic eye, and this Mr.—Mr. Temple is evidently possessed of one. He saw the value of this at once. I noticed his face change directly he looked at it."

Leslie's face gradually grew red.

"What—what has he given you for it, dear?" she asked.

"Fifty pounds!" exclaimed Lisle, exultingly. "Fifty pounds! It may not be as much as it is worth; but it is a large sum to us, and I am satisfied, more than satisfied! I wonder what he will do with it? Do you think he will let me exhibit it? I will ask him—not just now, but when it is finished. I must finish it at once! Where is my olive green? I have left it at home. Bring it for me, Leslie; it is on the side table."

She went without a word. At the corner of the street she overtook the invalid chair, hesitated a moment, walked on, and then came back.

The duke peered up at her from under his brows.

"I want to speak to you," she said, her breath coming and goingquickly.

He motioned to Grey to withdraw out of hearing, and struggling to keep her voice steady, Leslie went on:

"I want to thank you—but, oh, why did you do it? I know—you know that it —it is not worth it—why?"

The duke smiled.

"Do not distress yourself, Miss Lisle," he said, gently. "You refer to my purchase of your father's picture?"

"Yes!" she said, in a troubled voice. "It was kind of you, and it has given him, oh! you cannot tell what pleasure."

"Yes, I think I can. It is not the money."

"No."

"Just so. I understand. And don't you understand that I have bought something more than the sketch? Miss Lisle, I'm not the richest man in England,"—he was just within the truth—"but I can afford the luxury of bestowing pleasure on my fellow creatures now and again. Please don't begrudge or deny me that! I have not too many pleasures," and he glanced downward at his stunted figure. "Of the two, I fancy I am more pleased than your father. Don't say any more, and please don't look so heartbroken, or you will rob me of more than half my satisfaction. Miss Lisle, forgive me, but I think you love your father?"

"Yes; oh, yes!" she breathed.

"Very well, then," he said. "Be careful you do not let him see that you think he has got too good a price for his picture. Let him be happy; happiness comes too seldom for us to turn it aside with a cold welcome."

Leslie looked down at the worn and lined face with eyes that glowed with gratitude.

"I—I can't thank you, Mr. Temple!" she said, in a low voice, that thrilled like some exquisite music. "You have made me happy, and—ah, I can't tell you what I feel!" and she trembled and turned up the street.

The duke looked after her with a wistful expression on his pale face.

"She is an angel!" he murmured.

Then his face changed, grew harder and cynical.

"Yes, an angel at present," he said. "But tell her that I am the Duke of Rothbury, and she will become transformed into a harpy, and want to marry me, like the rest. Grey, where are you! Have you gone to sleep? Are you going to keep me here all day?"

CHAPTER VI.

TAKING A SAIL.

The moon rose early that evening and flooded Portmaris with a light that transformed it, already picturesque enough, into a fairy village beside an enchanted ocean. Leslie sat at the open window of her room, her head resting on her hand, her eyes fixed on the sea, now calmly rippling as if it were rocking itself to sleep in the moonbeams.

Her father had gone to bed, early as it was, worn out with his long day's work and the excitement produced by the sale of his picture, and Leslie was free to recall the events of the day.

Her life hitherto had been so gray and sober, so uneventful, that the incidents which had been crowded into this day had almost bewildered her.

She ought, in common fairness to that individual, have thought first and most of Ralph Duncombe; but it was upon that other young man who had plunged into the waves to reach Dick that her mind was fixed.

Beauty, man's beauty, doesn't count much with women; indeed, it has been remarked by the observant that some of the ugliest men have married the prettiest girls, and it was not Yorke's handsome face which had impressed Leslie. It would be hard to say exactly what it was in him that had done so; perhaps it was the frank smile, the free and musical laugh, that devil-may-care air of his, or the pleasant voice which seemed to float in through the window upon the moonbeams, and find an echo in Leslie's heart. Once or twice she tried to cast him out of her mind. There seemed to her something almost approaching unmaidenliness in dwelling so much upon this stranger; the young man whom she had seen for only a few minutes, and whom she might never see again. Why, she did not even know his name, or at any rate only a part of it. "Yorke," Mr. Temple had called him, and she murmured it absently. "Yorke." It seemed to her to fit him exactly. It had a brave, alert sound in it. She could fancy him ready for any danger, any emergency. He had plunged into the waves after Dick, as if it were quite a matter of course that he should do so, had done it as naturally as if there were no other course open to him. She could see him now, as he came out, with Dick in his arms, his hair plastered on his face, his eyes bright and laughing.

And how anxious he had been to avoid any thanks or fuss! It was wicked of him, of course, to tell a story and account for his besoaked condition by stating that he had fallen off the breakwater—Leslie smiled as she thought of the thinness of the excuse—but she understood why he had fibbed, and—forgave him.

"Don't you like this Mr. Yorke, Dick?" she said to Dick, who lay in a contented coil on her lap. "You ought to do so, for if it had not been for him you would be at the bottom of the sea, little doggie, by this time."

Probably Dick would have liked to have retorted, "And if it hadn't been for him I shouldn't have gone in at all."

Then her thoughts wandered to the crippled hunchback, and her heart thrilled with gratitude as she thought of his kindness; Mrs. Whiting had said that he was a nobleman, but there had evidently been a mistake; very likely the simple-minded landlady had concluded that no one traveling with a man-servant could be less than a man of title.

Leslie thought of the two men—but most of "Yorke"—and all they had said and done for some time before Ralph Duncombe insisted upon his share in her reflections, and as she thought of him she sighed. She pitied him, and was sorry for him, but she did not want to see him again. He had frightened as well as touched her by the passionate avowal which had accompanied the ring.

The ring! She had utterly forgotten it! She put her hand to her pocket, turned it out, but the ring was not there. What had she done with it? It was fast closed in her hand, she remembered, when she heard Dick's piteous yap; and then she had sprung up, and run down the beach. She must have dropped it among the pebbles.

Her heart smote her reproachfully. The least she could do in return for the passionate love Ralph Duncombe had lavished so uselessly upon her was to keep his ring! She rose, troubled and remorseful. The tide had been going out when she dropped it; it was not likely that it would be seen by any one, and it was probably lying where it had fallen. She seemed to see the plain gold circlet lying there in the silent night, neglected and despised.

Her hat and jacket lay on the bed; she snatched them up, put them on hastily, and left the house.

A light burned behind the windows of Marine Villa opposite, and she glanced up at it, trying to picture to herself the two men in the sitting-room; the one so strong and stalwart, the other so weak and crippled.

As she went quickly down the street she was conscious of a new and strange feeling; it was half pleasant, half painful. It seemed to her as if some spirit of change had entered her quiet, peaceful, uneventful life, as if she were on the verge of some novel experience. The feeling disquieted her. She looked up at the stars almost hidden by the haze of the glorious light thrown broadcast by the moon, and there came into her mind some verses—they were from the Persian, though she did not know it—which she had seen under a picture in one of the Academy exhibitions—

"Love is abroad to-night; his wings
Beat softly at Heaven's gate!"

Murmuring the musical lines, she passed to the quay, and leaping lightly onto the beach, made her way to the breakwater.

At nine o'clock Portmaris, as a rule, goes to bed.

No one was stirring; the street, the quay, were empty. The tide was far out now, and the sands lay a golden beat between sea and beach, unbroken save where at the very margin of the lapping wavelets a boat lay at anchor.

Not even a greater enthusiast than Francis Lisle could have desired a more delicious picture than she made flitting slowly yet lightly over the beach, her graceful figure casting a long shadow behind her. "Night is youth's season," says the poet, and Leslie's heart was beating to-night with a strange pulsation.

She reached the spot where she had sat with Ralph Duncombe's ring in her hand, and going down on one knee searched carefully. The bright light revealed every pebble, and, convinced at last that it was not there, but that she must have held it until she had run some way down the sands, before she dropped it, she rose from her knees with a sigh, and was going back when she saw a man's form lying full length on the top of the breakwater.

It was a young fisherman apparently, for he was clad in the tight-fitting blue jersey and long sea boots, and wore the red woolen cap common to men and boys in Portmaris. He was stretched out full length with his head resting on his arms, his face upturned, perfectly still and motionless.

It occurred to Leslie that he might have picked up the ring, and, well aware that his class was as honest as the day she went up to him, saying:

"Have you found a ring on the beach, just here?"

The man did not answer nor move, and when she got quite up to him she saw that he was asleep.

She saw, too, something else; that it was not a Portmaris fisherman, but the young man whom Mr. Temple had called "Yorke."

With a sudden rush of crimson to her face she was about to beat a retreat when Yorke started slightly, opened his eyes, and stared up at her.

The next instant he was off the breakwater and on his feet.

"By George!" he exclaimed, with a bated breath. "It is you, Miss Lisle!"

"Yes, it is I," said Leslie as calmly and composedly as she could, and from the effort for composure her voice sounded rather cold.

"I beg your pardon. Of course it is. But——," he hesitated a moment. "Well, the fact is, I was dreaming about you——." He stopped, as if he were afraid he had given offense.

But Leslie smiled.

"It must have been an uncomfortable dream," she said, glancing at the breakwater.

"No," he said. "I was never more comfortable in my life. I'm more used to roughing it than you'd think. I suppose it was the beauty of the night that tempted you as it tempted me?" he went on, with his frank eyes on her face.

Leslie looked down. She could not ask him the question she had put to the supposed fisherman—if he had found her ring, of course, he would give it to her.

"Yes," she said.

"I told Dolph it was too good to sit indoors," he went on. "That's my cousin, the man you saw to-day, you know."

"Mr. Temple?" said Leslie.

"Mr.—yes, Mr. Temple," he assented, after a moment's hesitation. "And I tried to lure him out; but he doesn't care about stirring after dinner, poor old chap——," he broke off with a laugh. "You are looking at my get-up?" he said.

Leslie smiled.

"I suppose you took me for one of the marine monsters who abound here. Fact is, I found my things wetter than I supposed——."

"I knew you would!" said Leslie, with an air of gentle triumph.

"Yes, and as I hadn't a change with me I borrowed a suit from the landlady's boy; a 'boy' about six feet high. I fancy I rather upset my cousin's man sitting down to dinner in 'em; but they're astonishingly comfortable. I'm half inclined to take to them as a regular thing. After all, one might be worse than a fisherman, Miss Lisle."

"Very much," said Leslie, with a smile.

"Oh, you're surely not going!" he said, as she half turned toward the quay. "It's far better out here than indoors; and it's early, too. Won't you walk across the sand to the edge of the sea? It's quite dry."

He moved in that direction as he spoke, and Leslie, with a twinge of conscience, moved also.

“It’s a pity all life can’t be a moonlight night,” he said, after a pause, and with a faint sigh. “By George, it would be grand on the water to-night. There’s just enough wind to keep a boat going—and there’s a boat!” he exclaimed, pointing to the boat lying at anchor at the edge of the water as if he had made a discovery which was to render this weary world happy for evermore. “What do you say to going for a little sail, Miss Lisle?”

He put the question very much as one truant from school might put it to another, only a little more timorously.

“It would be splendid, a thing to be remembered. Oh, don’t say no! I’ve set my heart upon it——.”

“Why should you not go?” said Leslie, trying to smile, and to keep from her eyes the wistful longing which his audacious suggestion had aroused.

“By myself!” he said, reproachfully, and with a kind of high-minded wonder. “I wouldn’t be so selfish. Come, Miss Lisle—I—I mean we—may never have another chance like this. You don’t get such nights as this in England often. And you need not be nervous. I can manage a boat in half a gale. But never mind if you think you wouldn’t be safe.”

This may have been a stroke of artfulness or pure ingenuousness; it settled the matter.

“I have never been afraid in my life—that I remember,” said Leslie, conscientiously.

“Then that settles it!” he said, in that tone of free joyousness which appeals to a woman more than any tone a man can use. “Here we are—and by Jove, here’s a real sea-monster asleep in the boat. Hallo, there!” he called out to an old man who lay curled up in the bottom of the boat.

Leslie laughed softly.

“It is of no use calling to him,” she said. “He is stone deaf. It is old Will, and he is waiting for the turn of the tide.”

“Like a good many more of us,” said Yorke, cheerfully, and he was about to shake the man, but Leslie put her hand on his arm and stayed him.

“I—I think I had better wake him,” she said. “He is old, and not very good-tempered, and——.”

“I see. All right,” said Yorke. “I’ll keep here in the background. If he refuses to go tell him we’ll take his boat and do without him.”

Leslie bent over the gunwale, and touched the old man gently. He stirred after a moment or two, and got up on his elbow, frowning at her.

Leslie indicated by expressive pantomime that they wanted to go for a sail, and, after glancing at the sky and at Yorke, the old fellow nodded surlily, and got out of the boat.

Yorke helped him to push the boat into the water.

"And now how are you going to get in?" he said to Leslie, but before she could answer the question old Will took her in his arms and carried her bodily into the boat.

Leslie smiled.

"He is a very self-willed old man, and no one in Portmaris interferes with or contradicts him, perhaps because he is deaf."

"I see," said Yorke. "I never realized until to-night the great advantages of that affliction."

He went forward as he spoke to assist with the sail, but the old man surlily waved him back into the stern.

"All right, William, I'll steer then," he said; but he had no sooner got hold of the tiller than Will angrily signed to him to release it, and pointed to Leslie.

"I think he wants me to steer," she said, with a faint blush. "I am often out sailing with him."

"He evidently regards me as a land lubber, whatever that is," said Yorke. "But, right! the password for to-night is, 'Don't cross old William!'"

He dropped down at her feet and leaned his head upon his hand, and sighed with supreme, unbounded content, and there was silence for a few minutes as the boat glided out to sea; then he said:

"Do you think old William would fly into a paroxysm of rage if I offered him a pipe of tobacco, Miss Lisle?"

"You might try," said Leslie, and the tone of her voice was like an echo of his. The two truants were enjoying themselves, and had no thought of the schoolmaster—just then.

Yorke took out his pouch, and flung it with dextrous aim into the old man's lap. He took it up, glowered at the donor for a moment, then nodded surlily, and, filling his pipe, pitched the pouch back.

"We still live!" said Yorke, and he was about to fill his own pipe, but remembered himself and stopped.

"Please smoke if you wish to," said Leslie, "I do not mind. We must not go far," she added.

"Not farther than Quebec or, say, Boulogne," said Yorke. "All right, Miss Lisle, we'll turn directly you say so. How delightful this is! I may have been happier in the course of an ill-spent life, but I don't remember it. Are you sorry you came? Please answer truthfully, and don't mind my feelings."

But Leslie did not answer. The strange feeling which had haunted her as she left the house was growing more distinct and defiant, stronger and more aggressive. Was it really she, Leslie Lisle, who was sailing over the moonlit sea with this careless and light-hearted young man, or should she wake presently in her tiny room in Sea View and find it all a dream?

Happy? Was this novel sensation, as of some vague undefined joy, happiness or what?

She was wise to leave the question unanswered!

Yorke smoked in silence for a minute or two, then he turned on his elbow so that he could look up at her.

"Miss Lisle," he said, "were you looking for something when you came down the beach just now? I ask because I thought you looked rather troubled——."

"But you were asleep!" said Leslie.

He colored, and his eyes dropped.

"I've given myself away," he said, penitently. "No, Miss Lisle, I wasn't asleep. But I thought it better to pretend, as the children say, lest you should take fright and run away."

Leslie looked away from him.

"You are angry? Well, it serves me right. But don't think of it. Try and forgive me if you can, for I was half asleep, and I was dreaming of you—there, I've offended you again! But don't you know how you can dream though you are wide awake? I was wondering whether I should see you again—there was no harm in that, was there?—wondering whether I should have seen you or spoken to you at all if it hadn't been for Dick——. By the way, how is Dick?"

"He is all right," she said, the tension caused by his former words suddenly relieved, "but I do not think he will ever forgive you for saving his life."

"I'm afraid not," he said. "But you have not answered my question yet."

"Which one?" asked Leslie, with a smile.

"Whether you had lost anything," he said.

"Yes, I had," she replied, in a low voice.

He put his hand in his waistcoat-pocket, and took out the ring and held it up.

"Is this it?" he said, and his voice was suddenly grave and serious.

Leslie took it from his fingers.

"Thank you. Yes," she said. "Where did you find it?"

He was silent a moment as if lost in thought, then he said, as if with an effort:

"On the beach; just where you had been sitting this afternoon. You dropped it, I suppose?"

"Yes," said Leslie.

There was a pause.

"You are glad to get it back?"

"Yes," she said, looking straight in front of her.

"An old favorite, Miss Lisle?" his eyes fixed on the beautiful face over which the moonbeams fell lovingly.

"N-o," she said, the faint color creeping into her cheeks.

"No! But you were glad to get it back. You didn't seem so very glad, you know."

"No, I was not so very glad," she said, almost inaudibly.

He seemed relieved, and yet rather doubtful still.

"It's singular," he said. "But this is the second thing of yours I have found to-day."

"Yes."

"And they say that if you find two things in one day you are sure to lose something yourself," he murmured, a serious, intent look coming into his dark eyes.

"But the day has gone, and you have not lost anything!" said Leslie, with a smile.

His eyes dropped from his intense regard of her face.

"I am not so sure!" he said.

Did she hear him?

CHAPTER VII.

THE DUKE'S SNEERS.

The boat sails on. Leslie has no mother to watch over her and warn her of sinning against the great goddess Propriety; and as there is no harm to him who thinks none, Leslie is not troubled by conscience because she is out sailing on this Heaven sent evening with a young man and only deaf William for chaperon.

Perhaps this is because of the peculiar nature of the young man. There is no shyness about Yorke, and his manner is just of that kind to inspire confidence; he treats Leslie with a mixture of frankness and respect which could not be greater if he had known her for years instead of a few hours only; and it is but fair to add that his manner toward a duchess would be just the same.

He is happy, is enjoying himself to the utmost, and he assuredly does not trouble his head about the proprieties. But all the same, he is silent after that last remark of his, which Leslie may or may not have heard.

He is lying across the boat, so that without much effort he can see her face. What a lovely face it is, he thinks, and how thoughtful. Is she thinking of that letter he gave her, or of the ring? And who gave her that? It ought not to matter to him, and yet the question worries him not a little. He dismisses it with a half audible "Heigh-ho!"

"I suppose these are what are called dancing waves?" he says at last. "Are you fond of dancing, Miss Leslie? But of course you are."

Leslie lets her dark gray eyes fall on his handsome upturned face as if she had been recalled to earth.

"Oh, yes," she says. "All women are, are they not? But I do not get much dancing. It is years since I was at a party. My father is not strong, and dislikes going out, and—well, there is no one else to go with me; besides, I should not leave him."

He nods thoughtfully, and some idea of what her life must be dawns upon him.

"You must lead a very quiet life," he says.

Leslie smiles.

"Yes, very, very quiet," she assents.

"What do you do to amuse yourself?" he asks.

Leslie thinks a moment.

"Oh," she says, cheerfully, and without a shadow of discontent in her voice or in her face, "I take walks, when my father does not want me, but he usually likes me to stay with him while he is painting; and sometimes William takes me for a sail, and there is the piano. My father likes me to play while he is at work; but when he does not I read."

"And is that all?" he says, raising himself on his elbow that he may better see her face.

"All?" she repeats. "What else is there? It seems a great deal."

He does not answer, but he thinks of the women he knows, the idle women who are always restless and discontented unless they are deep in some excitement, riding, driving, ball and theater going; and as he thinks of the difference between their lives and this girl's, there rises in his breast a longing to brighten her life if only for a few hours a day.

"Well," he says, "it sounds rather slow. And—and have you led this kind of life long?"

"As long as I can remember," replies Leslie. "Papa and I have been alone together ever since I was a little mite, and—yes, it has always been the same."

"And you never go to a theater, a dance, aconcert?"

Leslie laughs softly.

"Never is a big word," she says. "Oh, yes, when we are in London my father sometimes but very seldom takes me to a theater, and now and again there are dances at the boarding houses we stay at."

Yorke almost groans. How delightful it would be to take this beautiful young creature for a whole round of theaters, to see her dressed in full war paint, to watch those dark gray eyes light up with pleasant and girlish joy.

"And which are you most fond of?" he asks. "Walking, sailing, playing, reading?"

She thinks again.

"I don't know. I'm very fond of the country, and enjoy my walks, but then I am also fond of sailing, and music, and reading. Do you know the country round here?"

He shakes his head.

"No, I only came to-day, you know."

“Ah, yes,” she says, and she says it with a faint feeling of surprise; it seems to her as if he had been here at Portmaris for a week at least. “There is a very lovely place called St. Martin; it is about twelve miles out. There is an old castle, or the remains of one, and from the top of it you can see—well, nearly all the world, it seems.”

“That must be worth going to,” he says, and an idea strikes him. “My cousin —I mean Mr. Temple, you know—would like to see that.”

“Yes,” says Leslie. “But he could not walk so far.”

“No. Do you mean to say you can?”

Leslie laughs softly.

“Oh, yes; I have walked there and back several times.”

“You must be very strong!”

“Yes, I think I am. I am always well; yes, I suppose I am strong.”

He still sighs at her; the graceful figure is so slight that he finds it difficult to realize her doing twenty-four miles. The women he knows would have a fit at the mere thought of such an undertaking.

“I think to-morrow is going to be a fine day,” he says, looking up at the cloudless sky with a business-like air.

“Yes,” says Leslie, as if she were first cousin to the clerk of the weather. “It’s going to be fine to-morrow.”

“Well, then,” he says, “I’ll try and get something and drive my cousin over to —what’s the name of the place with the castle?”

“St. Martin.”

“Yes. The worst of it is that he—I mean my cousin, and not St. Martin—so soon gets bored if he hasn’t some one more amusing than I am to keep him company; you see, he’s an invalid, and crotchety.”

“Poor fellow!” murmurs Leslie. “And yet he is so kind and generous,” she adds as she thinks of the fifty pounds he has given for the “picture.”

“Yes, indeed!” he assents. “The best fellow that ever drew breath, for all his whims and fancies; and he can’t help having those, you know. He would like to go to St. Martin to-morrow, especially if you—do you think we could persuade you and Mr. Lisle to accompany us?”

Leslie looks at him almost startled, then the color comes into her face, and her eyes brighten.

"It would be awfully good-natured of you if you would," he goes on, quickly, and as if he knew he was demanding a great sacrifice of her "awfully good nature."

"My father——." Leslie shakes her head. "I am afraid he would not go; he will want to paint if the day is fine."

"He can paint at St. Martin," he breaks in, eagerly. "There must be no end of sketches, studies, whatever you call it, there, you know. I wish you'd ask him! It would do my cousin so much good, and—and," the arch hypocrite falters as he meets the innocent, eagerly wistful eyes, "though I dare say you won't care for the dusty drive, and have seen quite enough of the place, still, you'd be doing a good action, don't you know, and—all that. It will cheer my cousin up sooner than anything."

"Very well," says Leslie. "I will ask my father. But it will not matter if we do not go. You must persuade Mr. Temple."

"Mr. ——. Oh, my cousin, yes," he says, with sudden embarrassment. "Yes, of course. Thank you! It is awfully good of you."

Leslie looks at him, her color deepening; then she laughs softly.

"Why, I want to go, too!" she says. "There is no goodness in it."

Yorke Auchester's glance falls before her guileless eyes.

"Then that settles it," he says, confidently. "What point is that out there, Miss Lisle?"

Leslie starts.

"That is Ragged Points!" she replies. "I had no idea we had come so far; please tell him I am going to put the boat round; it must be very late!"

"No, it isn't," he says. "I can tell by the moon. Can't we go a little farther?"

But she ports the helm, and old William, without a word, swings the sail over, and the boat's nose is pointing to land.

Yorke looks at Portmaris, asleep in the moonlight, regretfully.

"That's the worst of being thoroughly happy and comfortable," he says. "It always comes to an end and you have to come back. What a pace we are going, too!" he adds, almost in a tone of complaint.

"The wind is with us," says Leslie.

"I should like to stay at Portmaris and buy a boat," he says, after a moment or two. "It would be very jolly."

Leslie smiles.

"It is not always fine even at Portmaris," she says. "Sometimes the waves are mountain high, and the sea runs up over the quay as if it meant to wash the village away."

"Well, I shouldn't mind that," he remarks. "I wonder why one lives in London? One is always grunting at and slanging it, and yet one hangs on there." He sighs inaudibly as he thinks of what it must be to-night, with its feverish crowd, its glaring lights, its yelling cabmen and struggling horses; thinks of the folly, and, alas! the wickedness, and glances at the lovely, peaceful face above him with a great yearning—and regret.

"I like London," says Leslie. "But then I go there so seldom, that it is a holiday place to me."

"I know," he responds. "Yes, I can understand that. And I like Portmaris because it is a holiday place to me, I suppose."

Leslie smiles.

"I hope you will not catch cold and be all the worse for this holiday," she says.

He laughs.

"There is no fear of that. I never felt better in my life."

"You must sit firm now," she warns him. "I am going to drive the boat on to the sand."

"Here already!" he remarks, as the keel of the boat touches bottom, and the sails run down with a musical thud; and he steps over the side, and so suddenly that the boat lurches over after him.

He puts out his strong arm to stay her from falling, while old William curses the "land lubber" in accents low but deep.

"I'm about as awkward in a small boat as a hippopotamus," he says, remorsefully. "Will you let me help you ashore?"

He means "carry you," and he holds out his arms, but Leslie shrinks back ever so slightly, and old William comes to the side of the boat and picks her up as a matter of course.

Yorke slips a sovereign into the old man's horny palm, and William, who is not dumb as well as deaf, would probably open his lips now, but for astonishment and amazed delight. He does, however, grin.

As the two walk up the beach Yorke looks behind him at the moonlit sea and the boats, and shakes his head.

"It was a shame to come in," he says, "but never mind, perhaps——." He stops, not daring to finish the sentence, but he feels as if he would cheerfully give half the amount of the check in his pocket for such another sail in the same company.

The quay is empty, the street silent, but as they go up it they see the crippled "Mr. Temple" leaning against the door of Marine Villa.

His keen eyes rest upon them both good-naturedly.

"Where have you been?" he asks.

"Where you ought to have been, Dolph," replies Yorke. "On the water. You can't imagine what it is like."

"Oh, yes, I can," says the duke. "But I am—too old for moonlight sails. I am a day-bird. Have you enjoyed it, Miss Lisle?"

Leslie smiles for answer.

"Look here, Dolph," says Yorke, with affected carelessness. "What do you say to driving out to a place called St. Martin to-morrow? I'm going to try and persuade Miss Lisle and her father to show us the way."

The duke looks at her.

"I shall be very glad," he says. "Will you come, Miss Lisle?"

"If my father——," begins Leslie, and the duke interrupts her.

"We ought to send a formal invitation," he says, with a smile. "Will you give Mr. Lisle our compliments, Miss Lisle, and tell him how much the Duke of Rothbury and Mr. Temple will be indebted to him if you and he will accompany them on a drive to-morrow."

Leslie looks from one to the other for a moment as if she did not understand. The Duke of Rothbury! Can he be jesting?

The duke struggles with a smile as he sees her astonishment, then he says, casually:

"I hope you found the duke a good sailor, Miss Lisle."

Leslie glances at Yorke, who stands staring at his fishermen's boots, with a moody and not well pleased expression on his face.

"I nearly upset the boat," he says, as if to account for his change of countenance.

"It did not matter," she says. "We were on the sands. Yes, I will tell my father, and—thank you very much."

If the duke expected her to be overwhelmed by the announcement of the title he is doomed to disappointment. The first sensation of surprise over, Leslie is as calm and self-possessed as before.

"Good-night," she says, in her sweet, low voice, and a moment afterward the door of Sea View is closed upon her.

The duke looked at his cousin's downcast face with a whimsical smile.

"How well she took it!" he said. "A London girl of the most accomplished type could not have concealed her flutters with greater ease."

"She had nothing to conceal," said Yorke, with averted eyes. "It didn't matter to her that—that you called me a duke. Why should it?"

"Why should it! My dear Yorke, you have grown simple during your moonlight sail. Oh, she was confused and flustered, believe me; but all her sex are actresses from the cradle. Give me your hand, and let us go in."

Yorke helped him up the stairs and into his chair, then stood gazing moodily out of the window.

"Your outing seems to have made you melancholy, Yorke," said the duke. "And yet you looked as if you enjoyed it just now."

"So I did, but——Dolph, I wish to Heaven you hadn't told her that infer—that nonsense!"

The duke leaned back, and looked at him with real or simulated surprise.

"Why not?" he asked. "Have you forgotten our bargain, agreement?"

"Yes, I had forgotten it," replied Yorke, grimly.

"So soon! Why are you so put out? What does it matter? You are going to-morrow——."

"You forget the drive—the appointment; but the best thing I can do is to go, as you say," said Yorke. "You can make some excuse——."

"Nonsense! If you care for this outing, stay and go. It will only mean one more day, and London will not fall to pieces because of your absence for twenty-four hours."

"It is not that——."

"Well, what is it, then? Are you thinking of this girl?"

Yorke flushed, and turned to the window again.

"What does it matter?" went on the duke. "She is a nice girl, but, my dear Yorke," and his voice grew grave, "even if we had not made this little arrangement about the title, she would be nothing more to you than just a pleasant young lady whom you chanced to meet at an outlandish place on the West Coast."

Yorke thrust his hands deep into his pockets—or rather young Whiting's—and the flush on his face grew deeper!

"I know that!" he said, as grimly as before.

"Very well, then! I repeat—what does it matter? If you are annoyed because, in accordance with an arrangement, I introduced you as the duke, why on earth did you consent? It is too late now! Even if I hadn't told her, Grey, or the woman of the house here, or some one else would have done so to-morrow morning——."

"It is too late, I suppose!" broke in Yorke, moodily.

"Quite too late," retorts the duke, decisively. "To tell the truth now would create a sensation and fuss which would be unendurable." He put his hand to his head as he spoke, and moaned faintly as if in pain. "Give me that small vial off the table, will you, please?" he said.

One of his periodical attacks of nervous neuralgia was coming on; and at such times he was wont to grow irritable.

Yorke poured out some of the medicine, and gave it to him.

"Thanks. Yes, it would make a hideous fuss. We should have it in the papers headed, 'A Ducal Hoax,' or something of that kind. But I don't want to force you into anything against your will. I can leave here the first thing to-morrow; I certainly should go if you departed from our arrangement. I came down here for rest and quiet, and I should get none if it were known who I am. Yes, we'd better go to-morrow."

"No, no," said Yorke. "After all, as you say, it does not matter. Besides—besides, I shouldn't care to deprive her of the little bit of pleasure I'd planned for her; I fancy she doesn't get too much of it."

"I dare say not. Very well, then, you'll stay till after to-morrow? For goodness sake try and look a little less funereal. You had no objection to assuming the role till you met this girl. What difference does she make? You think she will make love to you, eh? I should have thought from what I know of you, Yorke, that you would have no very great objection to that."

Yorke swung round almost angrily.

"Look here, Dolph," he said, grimly. "You are altogether mistaken about her. I tell you that she does not care, and will not care, whether I or you are the duke; she is not that sort of girl at all."

The duke was in a paroxysm of pain, intense enough to turn a saint cynical; he sneered:

"I know them all, root and branch," he said, his thin voice rendered shrill and cutting by his agony. "I tell you that she will make love to you; that, thinking you are the duke, she will try and marry you as she would try and marry me if she knew the truth."

"No!" said Yorke, shortly, almost fiercely. "I say that she would not care."

"You seem to have learned her nature very quickly," retorted the duke, with another sneer.

Yorke colored and turned away.

"I tell you that she will turn out like the rest. You deny it, doubt it; very well. Play the part you have assumed, and if I am wrong I will admit I have done her an injustice."

"You do her a cruel injustice!" said Yorke, in a low voice.

"Very well, then!" shouted the duke. "Try her, try her. And then own that I was right. Ah, you're afraid. You know, in your heart, that she would not stand the test! Your innocent, high-minded girl would prove like the rest! Come, you are beaten! Better spare her the disappointment of setting her cap at a false duke; better go to-morrow, my dear Yorke!"

Yorke swung round, his face pale, an angry light in his eyes.

"No, I'll stay!" he said.

CHAPTER VIII.

YORKE AUCHESTER AS A STRATEGIST.

When Leslie wakes next morning she wonders what it is that sends a thrill of happiness through her; then, as with dazed eyes she looks through the sunny window, she remembers the proposed expedition to St. Martin; but she remembers also that the companion of last evening is a duke, and her spirits droop suddenly.

It is difficult to persuade her father to join in the mildest of excursions; it will be very difficult, indeed, to induce him to accept an invitation to drive with a duke. Some women would have experienced an added joy at the thought that they had been honored with civility from a person of such high rank; but the fact rather lessens Leslie's pleasure.

Yorke did her justice; she is not elated nor awed by the ducal title.

When she comes down to breakfast she finds her father posing in front of his picture, his thin hands clasped behind his back, his head bent; and as she kisses him he sighs rather querulously.

"Is anything the matter, dear?" she asks.

"I've got a headache," he replies. "I—I do not feel up to work, and I am so anxious to get on. How do you think it looks?"

Leslie draws him away from the easel to the table, and forces him gently into his chair.

"We will not look at it this morning, at any rate until we have had breakfast, dear," she says. "It is wonderful how much better and brighter this world and everything in it looks after a cup of coffee. But, papa, you must not work to-day, you must take a rest——."

"A rest!" he begins, impatiently.

"Yes; you know how often you say that working against the grain is time and energy wasted. And there is another reason, dear," she goes on, brightly. "We have an invitation for to-day!"

"A what?" he asks, querulously.

"An invitation, dear. We have been asked to drive to St. Martin. Last night," a faint blush rises to her face, "I ran down to the beach to—to find something I had lost, and I saw Mr. Temple's friend, and we went for a sail with old

William; and afterward I saw Mr. Temple outside Marine Villa, and they have been kind enough to ask us to go with them to St. Martin. It was the duke who asked us," she adds, candidly; "but Mr. Temple was just as kind and pressing. I hope you will go, dear."

He puts the thin, straggling hair from his forehead with a nervous gesture.

"What are you talking about, Leslie? what duke?"

Leslie laughs softly.

"It appears that the young man who went in for Dick yesterday, Mr. Temple's friend, is a duke, the Duke of Rothbury," she replies.

Like herself, he is neither elated nor awed, but he lisps a distinct refusal of the invitation.

"The Duke of Rothbury?" he says. "I—I think I've heard the title somewhere. Why do they ask us to go with them? I don't want to go; and I suppose you don't care for it. They are strangers, perfect strangers to us."

"He has already proved himself a very kind friend," says Leslie, gently.

He flushes.

"You mean in buying the picture? Yes, yes. But you know how I dislike strangers, and—and—excursions of this kind. And if you don't want to go very much I'd rather not. Besides, I don't particularly care about making the acquaintance of a duke; I am an artist, a professional man, and I do not believe in associating with persons so far above me in rank. No, we had better decline. I dare say my head will be all right presently, and I shall be able to work, and you can come with me and mix the colors, and so on."

"Very well, dear," she says, struggling to suppress a sigh. "You shall do just as you like. I should have liked to have gone, and the drive would have done you good."

"I am quite well, and I hate long drives," he responds, emphatically, "especially in the company of dukes. What is he doing down here?" he asks, testily. "Did you say you went for a sail with him last evening?"

"Yes," says Leslie, with a sigh that will not be suppressed as she thinks of the moonlit sea, and the pleasant companion who unfortunately has turned out to be a duke. "Yes, and he was very kind and nice, and not a bit like so grand a personage," she adds, with a smile. "He looked exactly like a—fisherman last night, and talked like a young man fresh from school or college. He is not my idea of a duke at all; I fancy I must have thought that dukes talked in blank verse, and habitually wore their coronets and robes."

He waves the subject aside with nervous impatience.

"I don't know anything about them, and I don't want to," he says, getting up and fidgeting round the picture. "I've got this sky too deep, I think, and——." He continues in an inaudible mutter.

Leslie knows that it is useless to say any more, and is silent, and when her breakfast things are cleared away she gets out her plain little desk to write a refusal.

But at the outset she finds herself in a difficulty. "Mr. and Miss Lisle regret," etc., sounds too formal after that eminently informal sail last night, and yet she does not know how to begin her note in the first person. Should she address him as "Dear duke," or "Your grace," or "My lord," or how?

"Did you ever write to a duke, papa?" she asks at last, playing a tattoo with the pen-holder upon her white, even teeth.

"Never, thank Heaven," he says, absently.

"Then you cannot help me?" she says, with a sigh, and ultimately she puts the note in the formal method.

"Miss Lisle presents her compliments to the Duke of Rothbury, and regrets that she and Mr. Lisle are unable to accept his kind invitation for to-day."

"It looks dreadfully stilted and ungrateful," she says to herself; "but it will certainly remove any risk of further acquaintance, and papa will not be worried into knowing such a great personage."

She sends the note over by Mrs. Merrick's small servant, and in five minutes that diminutive maid comes back open-eyed and mouthed with awe and importance.

"If you please, miss, I gave the note to the gentleman what wheels the other gentleman's chair, and he says the duke has gone to Northcliffe, but he'll give him the note when he comes back."

Leslie laughs rather ruefully.

"We need not have worried about the drive to St. Martin, papa," she says. "The duke has forgotten all about it."

But the artist is painting away vigorously, and apparently does not hear her, and with a feeling of disappointment which it is useless to struggle against, she gets out some work and seats herself at the open window.

She has proved more reliable than the usual run of weather prophets, and the day is all she prognosticated. The street is bathed in sunlight, the sea is sparkling as if it had been sprinkled with amethysts; there is a soft breeze laden with the perfume of the early summer flowers in the cottage gardens; a thrush perched on a tree close by is singing with all its might and main. It would have been very pleasant, that proposed drive to St. Martin.

The morning passes slowly onward; the artist, too absorbed by his work to notice the sunlight, or the sea, or the birds, is still painting when, with the striking of the midday hour there mingles the click clack of horses' hoofs on the stony street, and Leslie looking up with a start—for she has been thinking of all she has lost—sees a wagonette and a pair of stylish bays draw up to the door.

On the box is Yorke, no longer in the fisherman's jersey, but clad in Harris tweed, his handsome face bright and cheerful, his whole "get up" and manner suggesting pleasure and a holiday.

After quieting the spirited horses with words and a touch of the whip, he looks down from his high perch, and seeing the startled eyes looking up at him, raises his hat and smiles.

"Are you ready?" he inquires, just as he inquired last night.

Leslie shakes her head, and tries to smile, but the effort is a failure, and putting down her work, she comes to the open door.

"Oh, I am so sorry," she says. "Did you not get my note?"

"What note?" he asks. "Stand still, will you! No, I haven't seen any note. What was it about?"

"We cannot come," she says, with a look at the horses which is more wistful even than she knows.

His face clouds instantly.

"Not come! Oh, I say! Has anything happened? Why not? It's the loveliest day——."

"Yes, isn't it?" she assents, shading her eyes and looking round. "But my father is not well. He has a headache, and——."

"Why, that's all the more reason he should go!" he responds, promptly. "The drive would set him straight!" he urges, remonstratively. "Look here, I'll go and speak to him."

"And while you do the horses will run away straight into the sea," she says, with a smile.

"No, they won't. If you don't mind just standing by this one, the near one. If he moves growl at him like this, 'Stand still!' He'll stop directly."

"Well, I'll try," she says, laughing in spite of herself; and he goes straight into the room.

Lisle looks up at him with impatient surprise and half-dazed; it is as if the young fellow had brought the brilliant sunlight in with him.

"Mr. Lisle, you don't mean to say you aren't coming?" says Yorke.

"Coming? Where?" He has forgotten all about the invitation.

"Why, to St. somewhere or other," says Yorke. "It never entered my head that you'd refuse. Why should you? If you don't care about it yourself, you ought to go for Miss Leslie's sake. She wants a change, an outing; any one can see that. Perhaps you haven't noticed how pale she looks this morning."

Oh, Yorke!

"Leslie is all right," says Lisle, irritably; "she is always strong and well. I'm sorry we cannot accompany you, but I beg your pardon, you are standing in my light. Thank you."

Yorke looks from the pale, livid face of the dreamer to the impossible picture on the easel, and bites his lips. He is sorely tempted to catch up the artist, easel and all, and bundle them into the carriage. Then a far better and more feasible idea strikes him.

"I'm sorry you can't go, Mr. Lisle," he says as indifferently as he can, "because I thought of asking you to make a rough sketch of the castle for me. Want it for my own room, you know. I'm awfully mad on water colors."

Mr. Lisle looks up with awakened interest.

"There is a good sketch to be got out of the west end, the turret," he murmurs, absently.

"That's just what I wanted," Yorke strikes in promptly. "That's the bit I was going to ask you to paint. Come along, sir; allow me," and he catches up the portable easel and paint box and carries them out before Lisle can realize what is being done.

"All right!" Yorke cries to the astonished Leslie: "he is coming. Run in and put your things on, and don't give him time to think."

"But," falters Leslie, a smile beginning to break on the lovely face.

"But nothing!" he cuts in. "Please be quick, or he'll have time to change his mind."

Leslie runs in, laughing, and Yorke, stowing the easel under the seat, shouts out for Grey.

"Tell the—Mr. Temple we're ready," he says quickly. "Got that hamper?"

"Yes, your grace," says Grey.

"Confound——all right then. Get your master down as soon as possible; and Grey, bring me out a glass of ale. Heigh-ho, that was a narrow squeak," and he draws a long breath. "What, let him deprive her of her outing? Not if I had to take the house as well!"

Presently the duke and Grey come out, and Grey helps him into his seat. They have not long to wait for the other two, and Yorke looks approvingly at the slim, graceful figure, which plainly dressed though it may be, is unmistakably that of a lady.

Mr. Lisle, scarcely knowing what they are doing with him, is bundled in; and Yorke, as a matter of course, stands by to assist Leslie to the seat on the box beside him.

"But would not some one else like to sit there?" she says, hesitatingly.

"I am sure Mr. Lisle would be more comfortable inside," he says. "And we mustn't keep the horses waiting longer than we can help, please," he says, and he puts his hand under her elbow and hoists her up carefully.

Then he springs into his place, touches the horses with the whip, and away they go.

Leslie draws a long breath. It is not until they have got to the open country that she can believe that they have actually started.

"It was a near thing," he says, as if he were reading her thoughts.

"Yes," and she smiles; "I don't know how you managed it."

He laughs light-heartedly.

"It was done by force of arms. I meant you—I mean Mr. Lisle—to go, and when I mean a thing I'm hard to obstruct."

"This is rather a grand turn-out, Yorke," remarks the duke. "May one ask where and how you got it? It doesn't look like a hired affair."

"It isn't," he replies. "When I got to Northcliffe I ran against little Vinson, who appears to be staying there. The wagon was standing outside and he asked me if I would like to go for a drive. I said I should if he'd let me have the horses and not ask to go with me. He stared for a minute, then he took off his gloves, and—here you are, you know."

"Wasn't that rather cool?" asks the duke.

Yorke laughs.

"Oh, he's a good-natured little chap, and didn't seem to mind. Said he'd go for a sail instead."

"He must be very good-natured," said Leslie, smiling in spite of herself.

"So he ought to be. He's as rich as Crœsus, and hasn't a care in the world. His father, Lord Eastford, you know, bought up a lot of nursery gardens just outside what was then London, and they've turned out a gold mine. The part got fashionable, you know."

The mention of a lord reminds Leslie—she had forgotten it until now—that the young man beside her is a duke, and she wonders whether she ought to have addressed him as "your grace."

"Now, Miss Lisle," he says, "you've got to play the part of guide, you know. Is it straight on, or how?"

"Straight on, your grace," she says, thinking she will try how it sounds. It doesn't sound very well in her own ears, nor, apparently, in his, for he stops in the act of flicking a fly off the horse's harness and looks at her; but he does not make any remark.

The roads are good, the day heavenly, and as they bowl along Leslie leans back, wrapped in a supreme content. Her father's voice discoursing of "art" floats now and again toward her, the thud, thud of the horses' hoofs makes pleasant music; and if she should tire of the pretty scenery, there is the handsome face of a good-tempered young man beside her to look at for a change.

Leslie does not know very much about driving; but she knows that he is driving well, that the horses, fresh and high-mettled as they are, are thoroughly under his control; and, half-unconsciously, she finds herself admiring the way in which he handles the whip and the reins.

"May one ask what you are thinking of, Miss Leslie?" he says, glancing at her, after a long silence.

"I was wondering which I liked best—sailing or driving," she replies.

"But you haven't driven yet," he says. "Would you like to drive?"

Leslie shakes her head.

"I should drive them into a ditch, or they would run away with me," she says, smiling.

"Not a bit of it," he retorts; "and I know you are not afraid, because you said last night that you never were afraid."

"Did I say that?" she says. "What wonderful things one says in the moonlight!"

"See here," he says. "I'll show you how to hold the reins."

"If I am not afraid, they will be, if they think you are going to transfer these wild animals to my guidance," and she glances over her shoulder.

"Oh, they're all right," he says, carelessly. "Give me your hand. No, the left one. That's it."

He takes it and opens the slim fingers, and inserts the reins in their proper places; and as he does so notices, if he did not notice last night, how beautifully shaped and refined the small hand is.

"That's right. Now take the whip in your right hand, and—how do you feel?"

"As if I were chained to two romping lions, and they were dragging me off the box."

He laughs, the frank, free laugh which Leslie thinks the pleasantest she ever heard.

"You'll make a splendid whip!" he says, encouragingly. "Hold 'em tight, and don't be afraid of them. Directly you begin to think they are getting too many for you, set your teeth hard, hold 'em like a vise, and give 'em each a flick. So! See? They know you're master then."

The ivory white of Leslie's face is delicately tinted with rose, her eyes are shining brightly, her heart beating to the old tune, "Happiness."

"There is a cart coming, and there isn't room. Oh, dear!" and she begins to get flurried.

"Plenty of room," he says, coolly. "You should shout to the man! But I'll do that for you," and he wakes the sleeping wagoner with a shout that causes the man to spring up and drag his horses aside as if Juggernaut were coming down upon him. "See? That's the way! Oh, you'll do splendidly, and I shall be quite proud of you. I'm fond of driving. Do you know, I've often thought if the worst came to the worst that I'd take to a hansom cab."

Leslie stares at him.

"A duke driving a hansom cab would be rather a novelty, wouldn't it?" she says, with a smile.

To her surprise, his face flushes, and he turns his head away. What has she said? At this moment, fortunately for Yorke's embarrassment, the duke remarks with intentional distinctness:

"Are you insured against accidents, Miss Lisle?"

Leslie holds out the reins.

"You see," she says, "they are getting frightened; and not without cause."

But he will not take the reins from her.

"I know you are enjoying it," he says, just as a schoolboy would speak. "You're all right; I'll help you if you come to a fix. Give that off one a cut, he is letting the other do all the work."

"Which is the off one?" she asks, innocently.

He points to it.

"That's the one. So called because you don't let him off."

It is a feeble joke, but Leslie rewards it with a laugh far and away beyond its merits, and he laughs in harmony.

"You seem to be enjoying yourselves up there," says the duke. "Pray hand any joke down."

"It is Miss Leslie making puns," responds Yorke.

"Now you are getting tired," he says, after a mile or two.

"How do you know?" she asks, curiously.

"Because I can see your hands trembling," he replies. "Give me the reins now, and if you are a good girl you shall drive all the way home."

It is a little thing that he should have such regard for her comfort, but it does not pass unnoticed by Leslie, as she resigns the reins with a "Thank you, your grace."

His face clouds again, however, and he bestows an altogether unnecessary cut on the horses, who plunge forward.

"There is St. Martin, and there is the castle," she says, presently. "Is it not pretty?"

"Very," he assents, but he looks round inquiringly. "I'm looking for some place in which to put the cattle up," he explains. "Horses don't care much for ruins, unless there are hay and oats."

"There is a small inn at the foot of the castle," says Leslie.

"That's all right then," he rejoins, cheerfully. "Hurry up now, my beauties, and let's show them what Vinson's nags can do."

They dash up the road to the inn at a clinking pace, and pull up in masterly style.

The landlord and a stable boy come running out and Yorke flings them the reins. Then he helps Leslie down, and goes round to the back to assist the duke.

"I suppose we shall be able to get some lunch here Yorke?" he says, as he leans on his sticks.

"Lunch indoors on a day like this? Not much!" retorts Yorke, scornfully. "Out with that hamper, Grey, and get this yokel to help you carry it to the tower. You can walk as far as that, Dolph? Miss Lisle will show you the way."

At the sound of her name Leslie turns from the rustic window into which she had been mechanically looking.

"Oh, yes. There has been another party here this morning," she adds.

"How do you know that?" asks Yorke.

"Because I can see the remains of their luncheon on the table," she says, laughing.

"Yes, sir," says the landlord. "Party of three, sir; two gentlemen and a lady."

"Thank goodness they have gone!" says Yorke. "You go on. I'll go and see that the horses are rubbed down and fed; I owe that to Vinson, anyhow."

He is not long in following them, but by the time he has reached the tower, Grey has unpacked the basket, and laid out a tempting lunch. There is a fowl, a ham, an eatable-looking fruit tart, cream, some jelly, the crispiest of loaves, and firmest of butter, and a couple of bottles with golden tops.

"Where did you get this gorgeous spread, Yorke?" inquires the duke.

"Oh, I was out foraging early this morning," he says, carelessly. "Now, Miss Leslie, you are the presiding genius. Of course the salt has been forgotten; it always is."

"No, it has not!" says Leslie, holding it up triumphantly. "Nothing has been forgotten. You have brought everything."

"Including an appetite," he says, brightly, and as he opens a bottle of champagne, he sings:

"The foaming wine of Southern France."

"Yes, I wonder how many persons who read that in their Tennyson realize that it is champagne?" says the duke, brightly.

They seat themselves—cushions have been brought from the wagon for Leslie and the duke—and the feast begins.

"Some chicken, Miss Leslie? This is going to be a failure as a picnic; it isn't going to rain," says Yorke.

"And I rather miss the cow which usually appears on the scene and scampers over the pie," says the duke. "I suppose your grace couldn't manage a cow on a tower."

Yorke looks at him, half angrily.

"Oh, cut that!" he mutters, just loud enough to reach the duke.

Mr. Lisle looks round with his glass in his hand.

"I must find a spot for my sketch," he says.

"All right, presently," says Yorke. "Pleasure first always, as the man said when he killed the tax collector. Miss Lisle have you sworn never to drink more than one glass of champagne?"

But Leslie shakes her head, and declines the offered bottle, and her appetite is soon appeased.

"Shall we leave these gourmands, and find a particularly picturesque study for your father, Miss Lisle?" suggests Yorke; "that is if he is bent on sketch——."

He stops suddenly, for a woman's laugh has risen from the green slope beneath them. It is not an unmusical laugh, but it is unpleasantly loud and bold, and the others start slightly.

"That is the other party," says Leslie.

"It is to be hoped that they are not coming up here. If they should, you will have an opportunity of seeing how I look when I scowl, Miss Lisle," he says.

Leslie gets up and goes to the battlements.

"No; they are going round the other side," she says.

"Heaven be thanked!"

"Too soon!" she rejoins, with a laugh; "they are coming back. What a handsome girl!"

Standing talking and laughing beneath her are two men and a girl. The latter is handsome, as Leslie says, but there is something in the face which, like the laugh, jars upon one. She is dark, of a complexion that is almost Spanish, has dark eyes that sparkle and glitter in the sunlight, and raven hair; and if the face is not perfect in its beauty, her figure nearly approaches the acme of grace. It is lithe, slim, mobile; but it is clad too fashionably, and there is a little too much color about it.

She stands laughing loudly, unconscious of the silent spectator above her, for a moment or two; then, perhaps made aware by that mysterious sense which all of us have experienced, that she is being looked at she looks up, and the two girls' eyes meet. She turns to say something to her companions, and at that moment Yorke joins Leslie.

He looks down at the group below.

"That's the party, evidently," he begins. Then he stops suddenly; something like an oath starts from his lips, and he puts his hand none too gently on Leslie's arm.

"Come away," he says, sharply, and yet with a touch of hoarseness, or can it be fear, in his voice. "Come away, Miss Lisle!"

And Leslie, as she draws back in instant obedience, sees that his face has become white to the lips.

At the same moment, a voice—it must be that of the girl beneath, floats up to them, a lively "rollicking" voice, singing this refined and charming ditty:

"Yes, after dark is the time to lark,
Although we sleep all day;
To pass the wine, and don't repine,
For we're up to the time of day, dear boys,
We're up to the time of day!"

CHAPTER IX.

THE PICNIC.

As the words of the music-hall song rise on the clear air, Leslie turns away. No respectable woman could have sung such a song, and she is not surprised that her companion, and host, has bidden her "come away."

She steps down from the battlement in silence, and as she does so glances at him. His face is no longer pale, but there is a cloud upon it, which he is evidently trying to dispel. She thinks, not unreasonably, that it is caused by annoyance that she should have heard the song, and she is grateful to him.

The cloud vanishes, and his face resumes something of its usual frank light-heartedness, but not quite all.

"We'll give those folks time to get clear away before we begin our exploration, Miss Lisle," he says, casually, but with the faintest tone of uneasiness in his voice. "That is the worst of these show places, one is never sure of one's company. 'Arriet and 'Arry are everywhere, nowadays."

"Why should they not be?" says Leslie, with a smile. "The world is not entirely made for nice people."

"No, I suppose not," he assents; "and I suppose you are going to say that they had better be here than in some other places, and that it might do 'em good; that's the sort of thing that's talked now. I'm not much of a philanthropist, but that's the kind of thing that good people always say."

"They seemed very happy," says Leslie.

"Who?" he asks, almost sharply. "Oh, those people? Yes; Mr. Lisle ought to get a good sketch somewhere hereabouts," and he leads her back to the duke and Mr. Lisle.

The duke looks up. Grey has made a "back" for him with the cushions and the hampers, and he's smoking in most unwonted contentment.

"Back already!" he says. "I thought you had gone to prospect?"

"So we had," responds Yorke, "but we were alarmed by savages from a neighboring island." He lights a cigar as he speaks. "We are going to give them time to get away in their canoes, as Robinson Crusoe did, you know. By the way, Miss Lisle, if you will sit down, I will reconnoiter and report."

Leslie sinks down beside her father, and Yorke strolls leisurely to the steps leading from the tower.

He pauses there a moment or two, listening, then goes down. At the foot of the steps on the grassy slope he stops again, and the cloud comes on his face darker than before.

"It must be a mistake," he mutters. "It couldn't be she, and yet——."

He walks on a few paces, and at the foot of the tower comes upon traces of the "savages"—a champagne bottle, empty, of course, and a newspaper.

He takes the latter up mechanically, then unfolds it and turns to the column of theatrical advertisements, and sees the following:

"Diadem Theater Royal. Notice. In consequence of serious indisposition, Miss Finetta will not play this evening."

With an exclamation which is very near an oath, he flings the paper from him and walks on, and as he goes round the base of the tower he is almost run into by one of the gentlemen whom Leslie saw with the dark young lady of the song.

They both stop short and start, then the new-comer exclaims, with a laugh:

"Hello, Auchester! Well, I'm——."

"Hush! Be quiet!" says Yorke, almost sternly, and with an upward glance.

"Eh?" says the other, "what's the matter? Who the duse would have expected to see you here?"

"I might say the same," retorts Yorke, with about as mirthless a smile as it is possible to imagine.

"How did you come here?"

"Why, by boat," responds the other. "Didn't I tell you so? What have you done with my nags?"

"They are all right," says Yorke. "Come this way, will you? Keep close to the tower, if you don't mind."

The young fellow follows him, with a half-amused, half-puzzled air.

"What's it all mean? Why this mystery, my dear boy?" he asks.

Yorke, having got him out of sight and hearing of the three on the tower, faces him, and instead of replying to his question, asks another.

"Was that Finetta with you just now, Vinson?"

"Yes," says Lord Vinson, at once; "of course it was. Didn't you see her, know her?"

Yorke nods curtly.

"Yes. What is she doing here? How did she come here with you?"

"The simplest thing in the world," replies Lord Vinson. "After you'd left me this morning, I was wondering who I should hunt up to come for a sail, when I saw her coming down the street. You might have knocked me down with a feather."

"I dare say. Well?"

Lord Vinson looks rather aggrieved at being cut so short, but goes on good-temperedly enough.

"She spotted me at once, and the first question she asked was, had I seen you?"

"Well?" demands Yorke, as curtly as before.

"Well, I didn't know what to say for the moment, because I thought perhaps you wouldn't care for her to know."

A faint expression of relief flits across Yorke's face, but it disappears at Vinson's next words.

"She saw me hesitate, and of course knew that I had seen you. 'It's no use your playing it low down on me, my dear boy,' she said, laughing—you know her way. 'You couldn't deceive a two-months-old calf, if you tried. You've seen him, and he's here somewhere.' It was no use trying to deceive her, as she said, and I had to own up that I had seen you this morning, and—that you borrowed my rig."

Yorke bit his lip, and nodded impatiently.

"She took it very well, she did indeed. She only laughed and said that she knew you had left town for some fishing; and, being sick of London herself, she had sent a certificate to say she was down with low or high, or some kind of fever, I forget which, and had to run down here for a bit of a holiday with her brother—or her uncle, I don't know which it is."

Yorke looks round with ill-concealed anxiety.

"Oh, it's all right," says Lord Vinson; "they've gone on to the inn. I came back for my stick. There it is. Well, I thought the best thing I could do was to ask them to come for a sail, and it took her ladyship's fancy, and here we are, don't you know."

Yorke stands with downcast, overclouded face, and the young viscount, after regarding him attentively, says:

"Look here, Auchester, I know what it is, you don't want to run against her just now. Got friends up there, eh?" and he nods his head in the direction of the tower.

"No, I do not want to see her, and I certainly don't want her to see me," assents Yorke. "If you can manage to take her away, Vinson!"

He lays his hand on the young fellow's shoulder, and Vinson, who is never so delighted as when doing a service for his friend, nods intelligently.

"I see. All right, you leave it to me." He pulls out his watch. "I'll get her away at once; in fact, it's time we started. Don't you be uneasy."

"Thanks," says Yorke, and his brow lifts a little. "When does she go back?"

"To-night; she plays to-morrow."

Yorke's brow clears completely, and he smiles.

"Off with you, then," he says. "I'm awfully obliged to you, Vinson. You are right; I don't want the—the people I am with to see her."

Vinson looks up at the tower curiously, and rather wistfully.

"No, my dear boy, I'm not going to introduce you," says Yorke, with a smile. "I'm too anxious to be rid of you—and her. See them safe on board the train to-night, and if anything occurs to prevent them going, send me a message to-morrow morning. I'll give you the address——." He stops. "No, never mind. Make them go to-night. Tell her she'll lose her engagement, anything, but see that she goes."

Vinson grins.

"I'll tell her you've gone back to town," he says.

Yorke colors.

"Woodman, spare the lie," he says, with forced levity. "No need to tell her that."

"No, it wouldn't do, come to think of it. She'd find out I'd sold her when she'd got back, and then——." He whistled, significantly. "I like Finetta with her claws in, don't you know. I think you're the only man that's not afraid of her."

Yorke smiles again.

"Well, do what you like," he says. "But go now, there's a good fellow; and for Heaven's sake, don't let her come this way again. We heard her singing!"

Vinson laughs.

"Yes, if you were within a mile of her you couldn't help doing that," he says, dryly. "Well, good-by, old chap. Don't trouble about the nags."

"They are all right," says Yorke. "I'll bring them back safe and sound——."

"When the coast's clear," finishes the young fellow; and with a smile and a nod, he picks up his stick, and goes off.

Yorke Auchester stands where his friend has left him, and looks out to sea, with a troubled countenance; stares so long, and so lost in thought that it would seem as if he had forgotten his own party. It is not often that the young man has a moody fit, but he has it now, and very badly.

But presently there comes down to him the faint sound of Leslie Lisle's soft, musical laugh—how striking a contrast to that of the young lady whom he has just got rid of! and he wakes from his unpleasant reverie and climbs up to the tower.

The duke is leaning back with an amused and interested smile on his face, which is turned towards Leslie, and it is evident that he is happier and more contented than usual.

"Miss Lisle has just been giving me a description of the Portmaris folks. You have missed something, Yorke," he says, with a laugh. "Have the savages disappeared?"

"Quite," says Yorke; "and if Miss Lisle and her father would like to look round, the coast is now clear."

"You go, papa," says Leslie, with her usual unselfishness; "and I will stay with Mr. Temple."

The duke glances at her.

"You will do nothing of the kind," he says. "I am not going to impose upon your good nature, Miss Lisle. Besides, I dare say, I shall take forty winks."

Leslie hesitates a moment, then she gets up and goes for the easel; but Yorke is too quick for her.

"Come along, Mr. Lisle," he says, touching him on the arm, while he stands looking from the edge of the tower absently, and the three descend.

"Now, this strikes me as a good place," says Yorke, setting up the easel. "Don't know much about it you know, but it seems to me that the outline and the——."

"Excellent; yes, very good," assents the artist, eagerly getting out his drawing paper. "Yes, I can make a picture of this. You need not wait," he adds. "You will want to talk and——."

"I see," says Yorke. "Come along, Miss Lisle; we're evidently not wanted."

They stroll away side by side, and slowly descend the grassy slope, which gradually becomes broken by rock, which kindly nature, who has always an eye to effect, has clothed with ferns and moss and lichen.

"I suppose I ought to show you the hermit's cell?" says Leslie. "Everybody sees it."

"By all means," he assents, but rather absently—the loud laugh of Finetta, the music-hall song are still echoing hideously in his ears. "Which hermit?"

"Didn't you know?" she says, lightly stepping from stone to stone. "There was a hermit here once ever so long ago. Here is his cell," and she stops before a cavity in the rocks, a deliciously shady nook, overhung with honeysuckle and wild clematis which perfume the air.

Yorke looks in. Somebody since the hermit's time, had been kind enough to fix a comfortable seat in the little cell, from which a delightful view of the sea and the cliff can be obtained.

"Let us sit down while you tell me about him," he says.

Leslie seats herself, and looks out at the greenery at her feet and wide-stretching blue of sea and sky beyond; and he takes his place beside her, but looks at her instead of the view. "The proper study of mankind is—woman."

"There really was a hermit here ever so long ago," she says, dreamily. "They talk of him at Portmaris even now. He was a very great man in his time, but I am afraid not a very good one. It is said that he killed his best friend in a duel, and, that smitten with remorse for his crime and his foolish life, he vowed that he would never set eyes on mortal man again. So he came and lived in this cell, which he dug out with his own hands, and spent the rest of his life in prayer and meditation. Every day the village folks, and sometimes the pilgrims who visited his shrine, placed food on the ledge of the little window; but though they could hear his voice in prayer or singing hymns, no one ever saw his face, nor did he ever look out upon those who came to visit him."

"He must have been fearfully unhappy," says Yorke, in a low voice, for the soft, subdued tones seem to cast a spell over him.

"No, they say not; for he was often heard, especially after he had been living here for some years, to be singing cheerfully; but that was after he had received his sign."

"His sign?" he asks.

"Yes. He prayed that if Heaven forgave him his sins, and accepted his penitence, it would render the birds tame enough to come at his call."

"And did they?"

"Yes. The pilgrims to the shrine often saw a thin hand thrust through the window with a hedge sparrow or thrush perched upon it, and the rabbits, there were numbers of them, here, would come when he called, and let him feed them with the remains of his frugal fare. One day the village people received no answer when they called to him, not even the *Pax Vobiscum*, which amply repaid them for their pious charity. They waited two days, and then they entered the cell, and found him lying dead on his stone pallet, and a wild dove was resting on his breast. It flew away as they entered, but it was seen hovering about the cell for years afterward, and the Portmaris people say that a dove is always near here, even now."

If Yorke had read the story of the Hermit of St. Martin in a book—he didn't read many books, unfortunately—it would not have affected him at all, but told by this lovely girl, in a voice hushed with sympathetic awe and reverence, it moves him strangely.

"It's a pity there are not more hermits," he says, "a pity a man can't leave the world in which he has made himself such a nuisance, and have a little time to be quiet and repent."

"Yes, your grace," assents Leslie.

He looks at her quickly, and then away to the sea again.

"I wonder whether you'd be offended if I asked a favor of you, Miss Lisle."

"What is it?" she says, lightly. "In the old times the proper reply was, 'Yea, unto half my kingdom,' but I haven't any kingdom."

"Oh, it isn't much," he says. "I was only going to ask you if you would be kind enough not to address me as 'your grace.'"

Leslie looks at him with her slow smile, and a faint blush.

"Is it wrong?" she asks, apologetically. "I didn't know. You see, I have not met many dukes."

He strikes at the sandy pebbles which form the floor of the good hermit's cave, with his stick.

"Oh—oh, it's right enough to call a duke 'your grace,'" he says, hurriedly, "but I'd rather you didn't call me so."

"I'm glad it was right," she rejoins, with an air of relief. "I thought that perhaps I'd committed some awful blunder."

"No, no," he says. "But don't, please. I have a decided objection to it. You see I'm rather a republican than otherwise—everybody is a republican nowadays, don't you know." Oh, Yorke, Yorke! "There will be no dukes or any other titles presently."

"But until that time arrives what should one call you?" asks Leslie, not unreasonably. "Is 'my lord' right?"

"It's better," he admits, "but I don't care much about that from friends, you know. I'm afraid you think it's rather presumptuous of me to call you a friend."

"'An enemy' would sound rude and ungrateful after your and Mr. Temple's kindness," she says, as lightly as before.

"My name is Yorke—one of 'em, and it's the name I like best. I dare say that you have noticed that Mr.—Mr. Temple calls me by it?"

"Yes," says Leslie.

"So it sounds more familiar to me, and—and nicer. I suppose a man has a right to be called what he likes."

"I imagine so," says Leslie.

"Then that's a bargain," he says, cheerfully, as if the matter were disposed of. "This place," he goes on, as if anxious to get away from the subject, "reminds me of Scotland a little bit. You only want a salmon river. I've spent many a day fishing and shooting in a solitude as complete as the hermit's. You get scared at last by the stillness and the silence, and begin to think that all creation has gone to sleep, and are afraid to move lest you should wake it; and then while you stand quite still beside the stream, something comes flitting down the mountain side—something with great antlers and big mournful eyes, and it steps into the water close beside you, and takes a drink, looking round watchfully. Then up you jump and give a shout, and away the stag goes, and all creation's awake again."

It is Leslie's turn to listen now, and she does so with half-parted lips.

"Then at night you go out with a gun, and you lie down flat amongst the bracken, and keep your eyes open, and after a while when you are just feeling tired of it, and thinking what an idiot you are not to be in bed, or at any rate, beside a cozy fire with a pipe, you hear a flap, flap in the air, and a couple of heron come sailing between you and the moon, and you raise your gun carefully and quietly—awfully sharp chap the heron—and down comes one of 'em, and perhaps, if you have any luck, the other with the second barrel.

Then you load up again and wait, and after a time, if your luck holds good, a flush of wild duck come flipperty, flopperty, above your head and you bring one or two of them down. And all the time the stream ripples and babbles on, and the soft wind plays through the pines, and——." He stops with a laugh and that peculiar look which expresses shyness in a man. "I beg your pardon, I forgot; I mean, I must be boring you to death."

"No, you were not," says Leslie, quietly, and with a little sigh.

"I forgot that ladies don't care for sport, except hunting, some of them. They like to hear about London, and all the gossip there."

Leslie shakes her head.

"I'm afraid I'm very singular, then," she says. "For I would rather hear about fishing and shooting, if it is all like that you have been telling me of."

"But it isn't," he says, with a laugh. "Sometimes the birds don't come, and the fish won't rise, and instead of catching any you catch a cold. And then you go back to London, and swear that's it's the best place after all; but after a little while you get sick of it again, and think if you could only get on to a Scotch moor, you'd be happy."

"Man never is, but always to be blest," says Leslie.

"Yes, because men are such fools that they spoil their lives before they know where they are," he says. "I once saw a man try to swim across the Thames, for a wager, with a ten-pound weight round his neck. He would have been drowned, if they hadn't picked him up pretty smartly. It's the same in life ——." He stops suddenly and laughs rather shortly. "We'll get on to a more cheerful topic. There's a hawk, see?" and he points to a bird circling in the vault of blue.

"I was wondering what it was," says Leslie. "You must have good eyes. Do you know all the birds when you see them?"

"Nearly all, I think," he replies. "Horses, and dogs, and birds, I know a little about, but I don't know anything else. I think I should have made a decent gamekeeper or horse breaker; I'm not fit for anything else. But sometimes I console myself with something I read in the paper the other day; the fellow said that there were far too many clever people in the world, and that very soon it would be quite a distinction not to have painted a picture, or written a book, or done something in the scientific way. I'm on the safe road to distinction, Miss Lisle. There isn't a bigger dunce in Portmaris than I am."

So they talk. It is not much. It is neither witty nor wise; it is just the pleasant, aimless chatter of two young people who are almost strangers; and yet so absorbed and interested are they, that they do not note how time flies, that the sun is sinking in the west, and that the shadows are stealing over hill and dale.

Leslie is perfectly at her ease. She has almost forgotten, quite forgotten for the time, indeed, that the young man sitting beside her with his arms folded behind his head, and talking of his fishing and his shooting, and of the strange beasts and birds and fishes he has seen, killed, or captured, is a duke; and he, Yorke, always ready to be happy, to meet the sweet goddess Happiness, half-way, is filled with a strange feeling of peace, that yet is not peace, which at times almost startles him.

In all his life he has not met with a girl like this; so simple, yet so sweetly wise; so good, and yet so bright and winsome. He is beginning to know some of the multitudinous expressions of the beautiful face, to lay traps for the slow heart-winning smile, to set snares for drawing the clear, darkly gray eyes toward his, that he may look into their depths. Her voice makes sweet melody in his ears, and stirs his heart with a vague thrill which will trouble him presently, trouble him very much. It seems to him one moment that he has known her for years, the next that she has just lighted from the clouds, or risen from the depths of the blue sea, and that he shall never know her or get any nearer to her.

And under the influence of these sensations, which summed up as a whole, are as a potent spell, he forgets the dark girl whom he has persuaded Vinson to take away out of sight, forgets the compact that he has made with the duke, forgets that he is sailing under false colors and is deceiving the girl beside him—forgets, in short, everything, save that she is beside him, and that he has the delight of looking at, and talking to, and, ah, best of all, of listening to her.

He would be content to sit there—so that she were by his side—till the end of the world, but a shadow falling across the entrance to the hut rouses Leslie to a sense of the flight of the common enemy.

"Why, it must be late," she says, with the air of one making a great discovery.

"Is it?" he says. "Must we really go? It is very jolly here—it is as jolly as it was last night on the water."

But he gets up and follows her, and they make their way back. As they emerge on the hill-side, they find that the wind has dropped, and is sighing across the downs rather plaintively; and Yorke, looking up, sees a cloud, which, though it is not much bigger than a man's hand, is full of warning.

"Did you happen to bring an umbrella with you?" he asks, with affected carelessness.

Leslie laughs.

“Not even a sunshade. Why?”

“Nothing,” he says, inwardly calling himself opprobrious names for not providing the Englishman’s traveling companion.

“Do you think it is going to rain?” she asks. “Oh, no, it isn’t possible.”

“Everything is possible in this charming climate of ours,” he says. “Well, Mr. Lisle, how are you getting on?” he asks, as they go up to the artist, still hard at work.

He looks up with a start. To him they have only been absent, say, a quarter of an hour.

“It is difficult,” he says. “Very. One needs time—time.”

“We’d better come another day,” says Yorke. “Oh, you have got on famously,” and he keeps his countenance capitally as he looks at the sketch. “I’ll carry your easel,” and he folds it up, and puts it over his shoulder.

They find the duke waiting for them at the bottom of the tower, and seeing them all together, he does not suspect that the two young people have been spending the whole afternoon *tete-a-tete*.

“I was just going off without you,” he says, addressing all three, but looking at Leslie’s face, which wears a rapt and dreamy expression.

“It’s well you didn’t,” retorts Yorke. “You and Grey would never have reached home alive. Miss Leslie and I are the only persons who can manage these nags. But come on,” and he glances upward—that cloud has grown considerably since they left the hermit’s hut—and leads the way to the inn.

“Now, ma’am,” he says to the landlady, in his frank, and genial way. “Got the kettle boiling? Right! Let us have some tea while the horses are being put to.”

Then he goes round to the stable, inspects the horses, and is back in time to hand Leslie a cup of the beverage, which be the hour what it may, is always welcomed by fair women.

“Now up you get,” he says, after surreptitiously tipping everybody—landlord, hostler, rosy-cheeked maid, all round. “Miss Leslie, we can’t get on without you in front, you know,” he remarks, as Leslie is about to go inside; and he helps her to the box.

The horses are fresh and eager for work, and for a time he drives, but presently he puts the reins in her hands.

“According to promise,” he says. “Hold ‘em tight while I,” and he bends down and searches for something under the box seat.

"Oh, how beautifully they go," she says, half to herself. "What is it you are looking for, your gra—Lord Yorke?"

"Never you mind," he says. "You look after your horses."

Leslie laughs, and laughs again as he comes up, red in the face, and with a Scotch wrap in his hand.

"Are you so cold?" she asks.

"Very," he responds. "It's going to snow, I fancy."

"Why, it is quite close," she says, removing her eyes for a moment from the horses to glance at him with smiling surprise. "It seems hotter than it has been all day."

As she speaks, a low rumbling rolls over their heads and a flash of light cuts across the sky.

"That is lightning," she exclaims.

"It was rather like it," he admits, dryly.

"Did you bring any gamps?" asks theduke.

"Nary one," replies Yorke, grimly. "Slang away, I can bear it—and I deserve it," he mutters, glancing at the girlish figure beside him.

Mr. Lisle looks round absently.

"I'm afraid—it—it is going to rain," he says.

In another minute it is raining. Yorke takes the rug in both hands, and deftly wraps it round Leslie.

"Oh, no, please," she says, and she glances behind her. "Give it to him—Mr. Temple."

"It would be more than my life is worth," he says. "I dare not offer it to him. Please let me fasten it. How shall I? Give me a hairpin!"

"You must hold the horses, then," she says.

"I can see one sticking out," he says.

"Well, take it," she responds, innocently and all unconsciously, for she is thinking of her driving far more than the rain or the rug or anything else.

He looks at her intent and absorbed face, and puts up his hand and draws the hairpin from its soft and silken nest, and she, unheeding, does not know that his hand trembles, actually trembles, as he fastens the rug round her.

"Now give me the reins," he says, "and keep your head down; we are in for a regular storm."

As he speaks, the rain comes down with a whiz, as if it meant to wash them off the box.

Leslie laughs.

"After all, it is a proper picnic," she says.

But the next instant her laugh dies away, for the heavens seem to open before them, a peal of thunder roars like the discharge of a park of artillery just above their heads, and the horses, startled and frightened, stop dead short, then rear up on end.

The carriage sways, and for a moment it seems as if it were going over, and Leslie is forced up close against Yorke.

He holds the terrified horses with one strong hand, against him.

"All right," he says, in a low voice. "Don't be afraid, Leslie!" His arm holds her, supports her, presses her to him, perhaps unconsciously. "You are quite safe, dearest, dearest."

Low as his voice is, Leslie hears him, or—she asks herself—is it only fancy?

For a moment, one brief moment, she cowers, nestling to him, her face hidden against his shoulder; then with a start, she draws away, and with her face red and white by turns, looks straight before her.

And through the roar of thunder, and the hissing of the rain, she hears those words re-echoing, "Leslie, dearest—dearest!"

CHAPTER X.

YORKE IN LOVE.

The great changes of our lives come suddenly. Swift as the lightning's flashis the revelation to Yorke that he loves the girl who sits beside him.

Half-unconsciously he had uttered the words which are still ringing in her ears, but he knows that his heart has been saying "dearest" all day long.

He knows now what that strange, peaceful happiness meant which made him feel as if he would be content to pass the rest of his life by her side in the hermit's cell.

And he knows that this is no transient passion which will have its day, and pass, leaving not a wreck behind, as so many passions alas! have passed with him. To every one of the sons of men, it is said, comes once in his life, the great all-absorbing love which wipes out all others, and which shall make of all his days an endless misery or a surpassing happiness; and this love has come to Yorke.

In an instant, as it were, it seems to have wrought a change in him. Gay, reckless, thoughtless, an hour ago, he is serious enough now.

His heart is beating quickly, furiously; his strong hands tremble as he holds the terrified horses, and urges them on with whip and voice; and yet, though apparently engrossed with them, thinking more of the silent girl beside him.

She is so silent! She scarcely seems to move, but sits, with the rug concealing her face, her head bent down.

"What have I said?" he asks himself; in truth he scarcely knows. It is as if his heart had suddenly become the master of his voice and actions, and had made a helpless slave of him.

If she would only speak! He longs past all description to hear her voice, even though it should be in anger and indignation; but she does not speak. He lifts his face to the sweeping rain and almost welcomes it. The storm is in harmony with the tempest of awakened passion which rages in his breast. He does not dare to speak to her, scarcely ventures to look her way, and he sits as silent as herself, while the horses dash along the streaming road and up the Portmaris street.

"We might have come by boat, there is water enough," says the duke, dryly. "Miss Lisle, I am afraid you are wet through. Pray get in at once, or you will catch cold."

She stands up on the box, and Yorke goes to unfasten the wrap, but she is too quick for him, and, taking out the hairpin, lets the rug fall, and stands before his eyes, her slim, graceful figure swayed a little away from him as if she did not want him to touch her.

He gets down, and offers her his hand, but she springs from the box lightly, stands a moment, then with a low-voiced "Good-night—and thank you," follows her father into the house.

The duke looks after her.

"The poor child is wet through and chilled," he says, sympathetically. "It's a pity you didn't think of a mackintosh, Yorke. What are you going to do with the rig and horses?"

Yorke looks down at him as if he scarcely heard or understood, for a moment; then he says, absently, like a man only half recovered from a stunning blow:

"The horses—oh, I'll find a place for them."

"You might take them to the station, your grace; they could put them up there in the good stable," suggests Grey.

"Yes, yes; and look sharp," says the duke. "We'll have some dinner by the time you are back. Will you have a glass of whisky and water before you go?"

But Yorke shakes his head almost impatiently.

"I'm all right," he says, curtly, and he drives off.

He sees the horses made comfortable in the stable at the station, and helps to rub them down and litter them; then he turns back.

But at the top of the street he pauses. He cannot face the duke just yet. There is that in his face, in his voice, he knows, which will reveal his secret.

He turns off to the right, and makes his way along a little used road toward the sea.

He is wet through, but he does not notice it; he scarcely knows where he is going until he stands on the edge of the sea.

"I love her!" he murmurs. "Yes, I love her. There is no woman in all the world like her! So good, so gentle, so beautiful."

He thinks of all the girls he has seen, talked with, danced with, and flirted with; but there is none like Leslie.

"I am a lost man if I do not get her!" he says to himself. "And how can I get her?" He groans, and pushes his hat off his brow, that is hot and burning. "She cares nothing for me; why should she? If I was to ask her to be my wife—my wife! How can I?" And he shudders as if some black thought had swept down upon him, and crushed the hope out of him. "How can I? Oh, what a mad, senseless fool I have been! How we chuck our lives away to find out, when it is too late, what it is we've lost. If I had met her a year ago——." He breaks off, and sighs, as he tramps up and down in the rain. "If I could only wipe out that year! But I can't, I can't, though I'd give ten years of the life that's left in me to be able to do it! What would she think—say—if she knew, if I told her? With all her sweet, childlike ways, and all her innocence and purity, she is a woman, and the very goodness for which I love her would fight against me! She looked and spoke like an angel when she was telling me that story about the hermit. An angel! I'm a nice kind of man to fall in love with an angel, and want to marry her! I might as well fall in love with one of those stars." And he looks up despairingly at the diamond lights that are peering through the rift in the clouds.

"Besides," he mutters, "even if—if that other woman weren't in the question," and he sets his teeth, "how could I ask her to marry me? Even if she'd have me—and why should I dare to think that I could win her love? I'm a pauper and worse. And she thinks me a duke! That's another thing! I forgot that idiotic business! Oh, I've tied myself up in every way, and haven't a chance! And yet I love her—I love her! Leslie!" he repeats the name, as Romeo might have repeated Juliet's, finding a torturing joy in its music. "No, there's no hope! Yorke, my boy, you are badly hit. You've laughed at this kind of thing often enough, but your turn has come. And as there is no hope for you, you have got to bear it. The best thing you can do is to clear out in the morning, and blot Portmaris out of the map of England. I mustn't see her again—never again!"

All his nature protests against this resolve, and his heart aches badly, very badly; but he squares his shoulders and sets his teeth hard.

"Yes, that's the only thing to do; to cut and run. There's one comfort, she won't mind. She won't miss me. God knows what I said when I felt her face against my breast; but whatever it was, I've offended her past forgiveness. She wouldn't see me again, I dare say, if I stayed, and so——." He heaves a sigh, which is very much like a groan, and turns homeward.

He finds Grey alone in the room when he enters; the dinner things are still on the table, and Grey looks at him with a rather grave and startled expression.

"I've saved some dinner, your grace," he says.

"'Your grace' be da—hanged!" says Yorke, almost fiercely.

"Yes, my lord," murmurs Grey. "The duke waited for over an hour, and he has gone to bed; I was afraid of a chill, my lord. And your lordship is wet, very wet, still——."

"All right," says Yorke, as politely as he can. "Never mind. Go and see after the duke, and dinner—oh, yes. Thanks, you need not wait."

He tries to eat, but for once his faithful appetite fails him, and he pushes his plate away and gets his pipe, that great consoler in all times of trouble; and this is the worst trouble Yorke Auchester has ever had.

It is well on into the small hours when weary, but oppressed by a ghastly wakefulness, he goes to bed, and there he lies, open-eyed and thoughtful, until the sun floods the room.

He gets up, and as he looks in the glass after his bath, he smiles grimly.

"Only one night of it!" he says. "And a great many similar ones lie before me before I get over this! I wonder whether she has been thinking of me? Why should she? And if she should have been they wouldn't be pleasant thoughts."

He pulls the blinds aside and looks at the house opposite, wondering which is her window; and as he does so, the lover's heart-hunger for a sight of his loved one assails him.

It has still strong possession of him when he goes down the stairs and into the street; but he fights against it. The best thing he can do is not to see Leslie Lisle, but to drive Vinson's horses back to Northcliffe, and take the train from there to London, and—stop there; stop there till in a round of the folly which has suddenly grown so senseless and worthless in his eyes, he has dulled the pain of this, his first real love.

It is early, but Portmaris is alive and very much in evidence. The fishermen are out on the beach, the women are bustling about, the children are playing in the road-way. Some with a huge slice of bread and butter or treacle in their fists; breakfast is evidently a very movable feast with the entire population.

Yorke stands a moment and looks round with a pang of regret.

"I shall think of this place," he says. "Think of it too often to be comfortable. Why couldn't I have come here—and to her—a year ago? What's that song about 'the might have been'? That's how I feel this morning. Oh, lord!"

He strides on with his head drooping, in an attitude very unlike that of Yorke Auchester's usual one; and without the last night's opera song on his lips as is ordinarily the case; and he is near the station, when he hears the laughter of children ahead of him, and looking up, sees a group that make his heart leap, and the blood rush to his face.

Under a great oak in the pretty lane stands no other than Leslie herself, with a child upheld in her arms, and two others clinging to the skirts of her pretty, simple morning dress. The child borne aloft has pulled off her hat, and the sunlight as it comes through the trees, falls in flecks of light and shadow on her hair and upturned face. She is laughing the soft, sweet laugh, which, though he should live to be as old as the old man walking along on the other side of the road, Yorke will never forget, and—she does not see him.

Shall he turn and go back, go back and leave her forever? Better! But he cannot, simply cannot. So he goes on slowly, and it is not until he is close behind her that she hears him.

She turns, the child still held, crowing and struggling in her arms, and a startled look comes into her eyes, and the color flies to her face, and then leaves it pale.

Yorke lifts his hat.

"Good-morning," he says.

Her lips move, and her head bends over the child now lying in her arms, and staring with blue eyes up at the big man who dares to address "Miss Lethlie." Leslie's lips move; no doubt she says "good-morning," in response, though he cannot hear her.

"You are early this morning," he says, and he knows that his voice falters and sounds unnatural, as surely as he knows that his heart is beating like a steam-hammer, and that the longing to cry to her, "Leslie, I love you!" is almost irresistible.

"Yes," she says. "It is so beautiful after the rain——."

She stops, for the word has recalled that homeward drive, the storm, his words—all that she has been thinking of through the long night.

"Yes," he says, vaguely, stupidly. Then he says, suddenly, "That child is too heavy for you——."

"Oh, no; I often carry it," she falters, bending still lower over the pretty face enshrined in the yellow curls.

"But it is," he says. "Let me take it, if it must be carried."

"She would not let you," she says.

"We'll see," he rejoins, scarcely knowing what he is saying; and he holds out his arms.

The mite stares at him, turns and clutches Leslie for a moment, then, with the fickleness of its sex, swings round and holds out its arms to him.

Yorke laughs, and holds it up above his head.

"Now what shall I do with you?" he says, hurriedly. "Take you to London with me. No?" for the child struggles. "For that is where I am going." He puts the child down, and it toddles off with the other two. "Yes, I am going to London, Miss Lisle," he goes on, trying to speak lightly, carelessly.

"Yes?" she says, with downcast eyes, and she stoops to pick up her hat. As she does so, he stoops too; they get hold of it together, and their hands meet.

But for that sudden meeting, that touch of her hand, he could have gone, and the history of Leslie Lisle would have been a very different one; but it is the link which the Fates have been wanting to make their chain complete.

"Leslie!" he cries, scarcely above his breath. "Leslie!" And he takes both her hands and holds them fast, and looks into her eyes, the dark, gray eyes which she lifts to him with a swift fear—or is it a swift joy? mirrored in their clear depths.

"Let—me—go," she falters, with trembling lips.

"No!" he says, desperately. "Not till I have told you that I love you!"

CHAPTER XI.

AN IMPETUOUS AVOWAL.

"I love you!"

Leslie draws her hands from his grasp, and stands with averted face, her bosom heaving, her breath coming with difficulty.

It is so sudden, so swift, this declaration, that she is overwhelmed. The heart of a pure-minded, innocent girl is not unlike a fortress. It withstands many an attack, and is able to repulse the besiegers until the one comes who cries "Surrender!" and at the sound of his voice, before some nameless magic in his presence, her strength goes, the gate is thrown wide open, and the conqueror marches in.

Leslie had been calm and self-possessed enough when Ralph Duncombe was pleading his passionate love, and was able to withstand his urgent prayer, but to Yorke she can find nothing to say; she can only stand with downcast eyes, her heart beating fast, and the gates beginning to open!

He takes her hand, but again she draws it from him, and sinking on to the trunk of a fallen tree, keeps her face, her eyes, from him.

"You are angry?" he says, his usually light and careless voice deep and earnest enough now. "Well, I deserve that. I—I ought not to have told you so suddenly. But——," he leans against a tree close beside her, and looks down at her—"but—well, I couldn't help it. I was going away this morning." His heart gives a little quiver. "I was going away from Portmaris—and from you. I've been thinking of you all night, and I'd decided that that was the best thing to do. It's sudden and—and startling to you, Leslie—Miss Lisle—but it doesn't seem so to me. You see, I suppose I have been getting to love you ever since I saw you on the beach; that's not long ago, I dare say you'll say, but it seems a long time to me—months, ages."

It is almost as if her own heart were speaking, it is just as she has felt. She listens in a kind of amazement at the subtle sympathy between them.

"I have thought of nothing else but you since I saw you. I know that I shall be the happiest man in the world if—if you'll let me go on loving you, and try to love me a little in return, and the most wretched beggar in existence if—if you can't."

He waits a moment, for a strange sensation comes in his throat and stops his speech, usually so fluent and so free. Then, she still remaining silent, he goes on with the same grave, earnest tone, and with the same half-eager, half-hesitating tremor in his voice.

"I've never seen any one like you; I know plenty of women, but none like you, Leslie—I beg your pardon! You see, I always think of you as Leslie. If I were to try and tell you how I feel, I should make a mess of it. I can only say that I love you, I love you!"

With all his ignorance and lack of eloquence he is wise. "I love you," sums up all a woman wants or cares to hear.

"Of course," he goes on in a lower voice, daunted by her silence, her motionless, downcast face, her hidden eyes. "Of course, I can't expect, don't expect you to understand or—or to care for me even a little. You haven't known me long enough or—or—anything about me. All I want is a little hope. If you don't dislike me, right down dislike me, I'll be glad enough, and I'll try and get you to love me a little. You can't love me as I love you; that isn't to be thought of!"

"Is it not?" she thinks, but she says nothing.

Up above their heads a thrush is singing melodiously, and the liquid notes seem to say quite plainly, "I love you." The sun, as it shines between the leaves of the old oak, and touches Yorke's brave, and eager face, is surely smiling, "He loves you!" The stream rippling in a hollow behind them, as it runs laughing down to the sea, is as certainly murmuring, "Love, love, love!"

"You are angry and—and offended," he says, after a pause, during which she has been listening to this harmony of nature's voices. "Well, I deserve it! I ought to have waited until you knew more of me—but you see, as I said, I could not keep it. I had been thinking of you, dreaming of you, all night, and then I saw you suddenly, and I felt as if I must speak, happen what might. If I hadn't seen you, I dare say I could have found heart enough to clear out, and —and hold my tongue; but when I saw you with that little one in your arms, looking so beautiful and so good, just the Leslie I love so dearly, the words rushed out almost before I knew it—and—and——," he squares his broad chest, and tilts his hat back with a gesture which, unlike most gestures, fits him like a glove, "there it is!"

She does not lift her face, does not open the lips that are trembling—if he could only see it; and he waits a moment before he says, sadly, with the lover's despairing note audible through an affected cheerfulness:

"I'm—I'm sorry that I've made a nuisance of myself, and—and worried you. Don't be upset and think anything of it. I ought not to have spoken. I couldn't help loving you, but I might have had the sense to hold my tongue, and taken myself off without distressing you. Don't—don't think any more of it. I'm not worthy of you, not worth a thought from such as you, and—well, I'll say good-by, Miss Lisle."

He puts his hat straight, and braces himself together, so to speak, for the parting; then he bends down and takes her hand, the hand that lies in the lap of the pretty morning frock like a white flower.

She does not draw it away now, and as he holds it, the passion which raises men to a level with the gods, takes possession of him.

"Leslie!" he says, almost hoarsely. "I can't let you go! I love you too much. Look at me, speak to me! Unless you hate me, I must stay and try and make you love me! I can't lose you! You are the only woman I have ever seen or known that I wanted badly! And I do want you! I can't live without you! I can't leave you, knowing that I may never see you again. I can't. Look up, Leslie—dearest—dearest! Tell me straight, once and for all—I will never come back to worry you—once and for all, will you try and love me?"

He takes her other hand—he has got both now, and lifts her, actually lifts her from the tree. She does not resist him, but lets her hands, trembling, remain willing prisoners, and when her face is on a level with his, she raises her eyes and looks at him.

There must be something in the dark gray eyes, something under the shadow of the black lashes, which contains a potent magic; for at sight of it his heart leaps and the blood rushes to his face, then leaves it pale with the intensity of a supreme emotion, an incredible joy, an amazed delight.

"Leslie!" breaks from him, "Leslie!"

Her eyes meet his, steadily, yet shyly, o'er-brimming with the secret which a maiden keeps, hugs closely, while she can. A secret which she is loth to part with, but which the loved one's eyes read so quickly.

"Leslie—do you—ah, dearest, dearest, you do love me!"

She tries to withstand him, to draw away from him, even now; but his passion is too much for her, and the next instant she is folded in his arms and her head lies on his breast.

Sing on happy thrush; but no music even your velvet throat can make shall compare with the music ringing through these two human hearts. A music which shall not die though these same hearts may be torn apart and wrung with anguish; a music which for joy or pain, weal or woe, shall echo through their lives till Death comes with its great silence.

But it is of life and love and joy, and not death or parting, that they are thinking now.

He draws her arm within his as if she had belonged to him for years, or rather as if he wanted to assure himself that she belonged to him, and they pace slowly along the meadow in the shadow of the trees; her hat swings on her hand, her eyes lift, heavy with love, to his face, as he bends down to her his own, eloquent with the devotion and adoration which fill his heart to overflowing. And yet through all the storm of passion that tosses in his breast, he has sense enough to notice how beautiful she is, how lightly and gracefully she walks by his side, how delicious is the pose of the slender neck, the half averted face. This flower that he has found and plucked to wear in his breast is no common weed, but a rare blossom of which an emperor might be proud.

And she—well, she scarcely realizes yet what this is that has happened to her; she only knows that a supreme happiness, a novel joy, so intense as to be almost pain, is thrilling through her; that at one moment she feels inclined to cry and the next to laugh. He is hers! She is to be his wife!—his wife! Oh, what a singular dream! Shall she wake soon? Wake to find that he has gone, and that all that is now happening is but a phantasy, a vision that will fade and leave her desolate.

She starts presently and looks up at him.

"Papa! He—will miss me—wonder where I have gone," she says. "How long have we been here?" and she looks round as if she expected to see the shades of night falling.

He laughs softly, the laugh of a man so completely happy that time has ceased to be of consequence.

"I don't know. What does it matter? Your father will know you are all right. He will think you have gone to the beach, that you are playing with the children—how fond you are of children, dearest."

"Yes, yes," she murmurs.

"I never saw any one go on with them as you do. No wonder they love you; but I suppose everything and every one does. By the way——." He stops, and a faint shadow falls on his face. "I suppose there have been ever so many fellows who've been in love with you?"

She makes a little gesture of indifference, as if the thought was too trivial to be entertained or spoken of. What does it matter who loved her, now?

"That—that letter and the ring?" he says, inquiringly.

She raises her clear eyes to his.

"Do you want me to tell you about them?" she says, in a low voice, as if he had the right to search her soul, and she were wishing that he should do so.

"No, no," he rejoins.

"But I will. He—he who wrote the letter and gave me the ring——."

His face grows cloudier.

"No, no tell me just this. He is nothing to you, you never cared——."

"Never," she says simply. "He has gone—I will tell you."

He presses her face to his to silence her, and a wave of remorse, of self-reproach, sweeps over him.

"No, no, not a word. That is enough for me. You are mine now and always and forever."

"Forever!" she breathes.

"And—and," he hurries on. "I have no right to ask you about the past—the past that did not belong to me. Besides, if I did you would have the right to ask me, and——." He stops suddenly, pale, and trembled.

She looks up at him.

"I ask nothing," she says, in a low voice. "You shall tell me all you want to tell me; just that, and no more."

"My darling, my dearest!" he says, but the trouble still rings in his voice. Shall he tell her? Now is the time. She would forgive him, love him none the less, if he told her all now. Shall he throw himself upon her great love and mercy?

For a moment Yorke's guardian angel hovers near him and whispers, "Tell her, trust her!" but he thrusts the angel aside and silences her.

"I am not worthy of you, dearest," he says; "I can tell you that much: no man is worthy of you! But the best of us couldn't love you better than I do, Leslie. Leslie! Do you know that when I heard your name it seemed to me the prettiest I had ever heard, and as if it belonged to some one I had loved for years? Have you any other name?"

She shakes her head.

"Isn't one enough?" she says, laughing, softly. "I am not big enough for more than one of two syllables. Why, see, yours is only one, or have you got more names? Tell me them? How strange; oh, how strange! I do not know rightly what you are called, and yet——."

"Yet you love me, and promise to be my wife—why don't you say it right out?" he says.

She shakes her head.

"But your names?"

"Oh," he says, carelessly. "There's a string of 'em. Yorke, Clarence, Fitzhardinge Auchester—"

"And Rothbury," she says, with sudden gravity.

He starts slightly, and colors. This foolish whim of the duke's! What is to be done about it now?

"Duke of Rothbury," she goes on, gravely, and with an almost troubled smile. "I—I had forgotten——."

"Go on forgetting!" he says, drawing her arm closer.

"Yes! I—you will not be angry?"

"At nothing you can say, unless it were, 'I do not love you!'"

"I was going to say that I wish I could—that I wish you were not a duke, and had no title of any kind!"

"So do I if you wish it," he says. "What does it matter?"

"But will it not matter?" she asks, her brows coming together. "Will not the people—your people, all those great folks who belong to you, your relations—be angry with me for—for——."

"Stooping to love such a worthless, useless creature as I? Why should they?"

"I—I don't know. Yes I do. It is not girls like me, girls with no title or anything, poor girls who know nothing of the fashionable world, and have no relations above a plain 'Mr.' who ought to marry noblemen. I know enough for that. They will be right to be angry and—and disappointed!"

"Not they!" he says, lightly, but inwardly chafing against the bonds which his promise to the duke has woven round him. "Let them mind their own business!"

"But it is their business!" she says. "What a duke, a well-known nobleman, does, must be everybody's business, and everybody will be astonished and—sorry."

"Wait until they see you!" he says, confidently.

She looks up at him with eyes dewy with gratitude.

"Do you think everybody will see me with your eyes?" she says, in a low voice.

"I think every man will envy me and wish himself in my place!" he responds, promptly.

She shakes her head.

"No no! They will say when they hear of it that you have done wrong, and say it still more decidedly when they see me. Why, I shall not know what to do." She laughs half light-heartedly, half-anxiously. "I shall not know how to begin, even, to play the great lady; I shall make all sorts of mistakes, and call persons by their wrong names and titles. Why, I did not know how to address you, your grace!" And she looks up at him, with parted lips that smile but tremble a little.

He kisses them tenderly, reassuringly.

"You are only chaffing me," he says. "I can see that. You are the last girl in the world to be frightened by anybody. You'd just take your place in any set as naturally as if you'd known it and been in it all your life. Why, do you think I don't know how proud you are?"

"Am I?" she says, self-questioningly. "Yes; I think I was yesterday—until—until now. But now my pride seems to have melted into thin air, and I amonly anxious. Do you know what I should do if I were to see that you were even the least bit ashamed of me?"

"What would you do? Something terrible?"

"I should die of shame for your sake!" she says, slowly.

"If you wait till you die of that complaint you'll live to be as old as—what's his name, Methuselah!" and he laughs. "Why, I feel so proud of winning you that I'm trying all I know not to swagger."

She gives his arm just the faintest pressure.

"Oh how foolish, how foolish!" she murmurs. "To be proud of me!"

"I dare say, but I am, you see! I know I've got one of the loveliest women in the world for a wife, and I shall get beastly conceited, I expect, and perfectly unendurable. It isn't every man who wins the love of an angel."

"Ah, don't," she says. "An angel! They will not think me that, but only a commonplace girl, who knows nothing, and is not fit to be—a duchess!"

She utters the word as if he did not like it, and he colors again.

"Tell me," she says, after a moment. "Tell me whom I shall have to fear most.

You see, I don't know even if you have a mother—a father. I don't know anything!"

He is silent a moment, mentally execrating the chain of circumstances which compel him, force him, to—yes, deceive her!

"They are both dead," he says, truthfully. "I haven't any near relations—no brother and sister, I mean. I've an uncle, a Lord Eustace and his two sons who's the next to the dukedom—he and they."

"After you?" she says. "I don't understand—how should I?"

"It does not matter," he says, hurriedly.

"Tell me about him then—them. Is he nice? Will he be very angry?"

He laughs.

"No, he's not very nice. He's the miser of the family—you see, and you'll have cause to be ashamed of some of us, dearest! And he won't care the snap of his fingers whom I marry, or what becomes of me."

This would sound singularly improbable to Leslie if she were worldly wise; but she is not. As she says, she simply does not understand or realize.

"I am sorry," she says. "But I don't think it is true."

"You think they are all so proud and fond of me?" he laughs, with a faint tinge of bitterness. "Well, then I've other cousins——."

"Mr. Temple?" she says.

"Yes, Mr.—Mr. Temple," he mutters.

"And what will he say?" she asks, with a smile.

"He? Oh——." He stops. Yes, what will the duke say when he hears that Leslie "has made love," as he will put it, to the supposed duke?

"Look here, dearest," he says, after a pause.

"Why should you or I care a brass farthing what any one thinks or says! The only one I care about is your father."

"Ah, papa!" she murmurs; and she pictures to herself Mr. Lisle's amazement and distress at what he will regard as a "fuss" and disturbance of his placid "artistic" life.

"Are you afraid, Leslie?" Yorke asks.

"I—I don't know. I am all in all to him; and—I do not know what he will say. He will not be pleased; I mean he will see more plainly than I do that I am not fit to be your wife, that I am not suitable for a duchess. And he will say it is so sudden—and it is, is it not? If he had had a little time to—to get used to it ——."

"Let us give him time," he says. "I was going to him now straight away to ask him to give you to me; but if you think it better, if you wish it, it shall be exactly as you think and wish, dearest. I will wait for a little while, until he knows me better, and has got used to me. I suppose it would startle and upset him if I were to go now."

"Oh, yes, yes!" she says. "You do not know how nervous he is, and how easily upset."

"I think I can guess," he responds, thoughtfully.

As he has said, it was his intention to go straight to Mr. Lisle and tell him to go to the duke and announce the engagement; but if Leslie wishes the announcement delayed—well, it will be as well! Will it not be better that he should clear up sundry matters in London before the world hears of his betrothal? Besides, how can he go to Mr. Lisle without confessing that he has been masquerading as a duke and explaining why? Before he can do that he must get the duke to release him from this foolish agreement, which, foolish as it is, still binds him.

"What shall we do, dearest?" he asks, looking down at her.

"Let us wait," she murmurs. "Let us wait for a day or two, till my father knows you better, and—and you have had time to think whether it is well that you should stoop so low——." Her voice dies away. The mere thought of losing him is an agony.

“Yes,” he says, almost solemnly, “we will wait, but not for that reason, Leslie. I don’t want to think about anything of that kind. As to stooping—well, you will learn some day how I love you, and how infinitely above me you are. God grant you will not repent having stooped to me, dearest! Yes, we will wait. After all, it may seem sudden to them, and we will give them a little time to get used to it.”

“And meanwhile,” she says, with a smile, which is half a sigh of regret, “I will try and realize that I am to be a great lady. It will seem rather hard at first. There ought to be a school at which one could learn how to behave. They used to teach girls how to enter a room, and bow, and courtesy, so that they might not disgrace their belongings.”

He holds her at arm’s length, and laughs at her, his eyes alight with admiration, and love, and worship.

“I’ve seen you walk down the street and cross the beach, Leslie,” he says. “You don’t want any lessons in deportment. I’m thinking you’ll give some of ‘em points, and beat them easily. Don’t you ever look in the glass? Don’t you know that you are the loveliest, sweetest woman man ever went mad over?”

“Oh, hush, hush!” she says, putting her finger lightly on his lips, and hiding her crimson face against his breast. “You must be blind! But—oh, stay so, dearest, and never, never see me as I really am!”

CHAPTER XII.

MISS FINETTA.

Two mornings later there rode into the Row at Hyde Park a young lady whose appearance always attracted a great deal of attention. In the first place, she was one of the handsomest, if not the handsomest woman there; in the next, she rode her horse as perfectly as it is possible for a girl to ride; and, lastly, wherever she went, on horseback or on foot, this lady was well known; in fact a celebrity. For she was Miss Finetta.

As she rode in at a brisk canter in the superbly-fitting habit, which seemed an outer skin of the lithe, supple figure, and followed by her correctly clad groom, mounted on a horse as good as that of his mistress, the hats of the men flew off, and the eyeglasses of the women went up, or their owners looked another way. But to smiles or frowns, pleasant nods, or icy stares, Finetta returned the same cool, good-humored smile, the flash of her white teeth and black eyes.

Every now and then London has a fit. Sometimes it takes the shape of hero worship, and down the mob go on their knees to some celebrity, male or female; at others it goes black in the face with hooting and mud-flinging at some object which it has suddenly taken it into its head to hate.

At present all London—all fashionable male London—was in fits of admiration of Finetta; and, strange to say, it had rather more than the usual excuse for its enthusiasm. For she was a remarkable young woman.

Not very long ago she had been playing in company with other girls in the alley in which her father's small coal store was situated; and was perfectly happy when the organ man came into the alley, and she and her playmates danced round that popular instrument.

Her mother wanted her to go to school, or at any rate to help her in the green grocer shop, which was run in conjunction with the coal store; but Finetta—her name at that time was Sarah Ann, by the way—declined to go to school, and confined her ministrations in the shop to stealing the oranges and apples.

Her mother alternately scolded and beat her; her father declared with emphatic and descriptive language, that she would come to no good. And Sarah Ann, taking the scoldings, and the beatings, and the prophecies of a bad end, with infinite good-humor, went on playing hop-scotch, and dancing round the organ, quite happy in her ragged skirts and her black tousled hair, and almost as black face and hands.

But the gods, they say, delight in surprises, and one day an individual happened to come down that alley who was fated to have an immense influence on Sarah Ann's career.

He was a well-known dancing-master, a first-rate one, and a respectable man whose whole life had been devoted to his art and nothing else.

He saw the group of girls dancing round the organ, stood and watched them with an absent, reflective smile, and then, suddenly, his face lit up and his eyes brightened.

Sarah Ann had run out from the green grocer's shop with an orange she had stolen, and as she tore off the peel with her white teeth, set to dancing with the rest.

The dancing-master drew aside a little, and kept his eyes on the lank, angular girl whose dark orbs glowed under the excitement of the dance, which, unlike that of her companions, was in perfect time with the "music," and full of a grace which was as natural as a young Indian's.

Monsieur Faber, he was a Frenchman, went up to her.

"Are you fond of dancing?" he asked.

"Am I! Ain't I?" she retorted, flashing her teeth upon him. "Why, of course I am! Who ain't?"

"So am I," he said. "Would you like to learn to dance properly?"

"Learn! I can dance already!" she retorted, with a toss of her head.

"Ah, you think so!" he said, smiling, with a kind of good-natured pity.

He looked round; the alley was empty, excepting for the children; and he signed to the organ man to go on playing, and as he played, the thin, dapper little Frenchman began to dance. We won't try and describe it. All the world has seen him, and knows what is meant when it is said that it was Monsieur Faber at his best.

He seemed to be made of springs, India rubber springs, to be as light as a thistle down, to tread, float, on air, and to possess the wind and speed of a dervish.

The black-eyed slip of a girl watched him in breathless amazement and delight; and when he finished and came on his toe points as if he had just floated down from the grimy house-tops, she uttered a long-drawn sigh of envy and admiration.

“I couldn’t do that,” she said, looking at him sullenly but wistfully.

“No, not yet,” he said. “And why, my child? Because you have not been taught. One does not know how to dance till one learns. Would you like to learn?”

“Shouldn’t I, just!” she responded.

“Take me to your mother, and we will see,” he said.

She ran, sprang into the shop.

“Mother, here’s a man as dances like—like—an angel,” (she said “a hangel”,) “and he’s going to teach me.”

The poor woman “went for her” with a stick that lay handy, but M. Faber interposed, and entered on an explanation and a proposal.

He would take Sarah Ann as a pupil, teach her to dance, get her an engagement at one of the theaters, and in return, she was to be bound to him as a kind of apprentice, and give him a certain percentage—it was a fair one—of all she might earn for the next five years.

Sarah Ann’s parents hesitated, but Sarah Ann cut the negotiation short by coolly announcing her determination, in the event of their refusing, to accept the offer, to “cut and run,” and, knowing that she was quite capable of carrying out her threat the couple consented.

M. Faber christened her Finetta, and commenced the lessons at once. He had two daughters of his own, but though they worked hard, neither they nor any of the other pupils were half so quick at the enchanting science as Sarah Ann—pardon! Finetta—the daughter of the small coal man.

She worked hard, almost day and night; it might be said that she danced in her dreams. She had a good ear for music; “if you only had a voice, my dear child,” M. Faber would murmur, throwing up his hands, and when she danced it was like a human instrument playing, moving, in accord and harmony with the mechanical one, the violin or the piano.

She would do nothing at home in the alley; would not serve in the shop, or keep the small coal accounts, or wash her face or brush her hair; but she obeyed M. Faber with an eager alacrity which was almost pathetic.

“I want to dance better than any one in the world!” she would say, and her master encouraged her by remarking that it was not unlikely she would attain her wish.

The months passed on. The angular girl—all legs and wings, like a pullet—grew into a graceful young woman, with a face, which, if not beautiful in the regulation way, was singularly striking, with flashing eyes, and rather large but mobile lips.

"There is a great future before that girl," M. Faber would remark to his wife, a good-natured woman, who treated all the pupils as if they were her own children. But he did not hurry. "One does not learn to dance in a day," he would say, when Finetta begged him to get her an engagement, even if it were ever so small a one. "Patience, my good child; and when the time comes, *voila*, you shall see!"

The time came, and Finetta appeared among the ladies of the ballet at a small provincial theater. He kept her in the ranks for two years, then gave her a "solo" part, and lastly obtained an engagement for her at the Diadem.

To dance at the Diadem was the height of Finetta's ambition. Her heart beat that night as it had never beat before, not even on her first appearance at the provincial theater; but it did not deafen the music, or drive her steps out of her mind, and when she had finished, the roar of delight that rose in the theater proclaimed the fact that Finetta had scored a triumph, and that M. Faber had not labored in vain.

This was three years ago. Her popularity had steadily increased. She was now the rage. Her salary exceeded that of a cabinet minister; the percentage alone was a good income for the patient, persevering M. Faber.

When she appeared at night the house roared a welcome, and rewarded her efforts with thunders of applause.

Her photographs were placed among the other celebrities in the shop windows, next those of the Royal Family, the great poets, the eminent statesmen, and sold as well as, if not better than, the rest. Outside the theater hung a huge transparency, showing Finetta in her Spanish dancing-dress; the tobacconists sold a cigarette bearing her name.

All this ought to have turned her head. It did a little, but only a little. To tell the truth, she was a good-hearted girl, and in her prosperity did not forget those near to her. She set her father up in the wholesale coal trade, and put her mother into a nice house in Islington; sent her brother to school, and had her sister to live with her in the pretty house in St. John's Wood, and though the world said hard things of her, she was unjustly accused andcalumniated.

Her manners were not those of Lady Clara Vere de Vere. She gave supper parties at which only gentlemen and ladies of the ballet were present; she talked and laughed loudly; she knew nothing, and cared less, for the proprieties; was fond of champagne, and enjoyed a cigarette; delighted in riding, and driving tandem, and did both surpassingly well; but scandal could find no chink in her armor through which to shoot its poisoned darts, and the worst the world could, with truth, call her was "Finetta, the dancer!"

The men who thronged round her called her "a good fellow!" and when a woman of her class has earned that title, depend upon it, she is not so black as the virtuous paint her.

She knew half the peerage—the male side—but she was as friendly and pleasant to a struggling young journalist as to my Lord Vinson. Men sent her letters, telling her they adored her; she lit her cigarettes with them, and told the writers, when next she saw them, not to waste ink and paper upon her, but to make up a party to take her for a drive and a dinner at Richmond.

Sometimes, very often, they sent her presents—diamond rings, bracelets, pendants, lockets, with their portraits (which she always took out), and she accepted them with a careless *sang froid*, which was amusing—to all but the donors. The horses she and her groom rode were a gift from a well-known turf lord. It was said that the lease of the house at John's Wood had been given to her; but that was not true.

"Why shouldn't I take 'em?" she said to her sister. "They'll only give 'em to some one else who wouldn't look half so well on them, and wouldn't know how to ride 'em."

So that she often danced at the Diadem wearing gems which made the ladies in the stalls envious, and appeared in the row riding a horse which was a better-looking and going one than even Lady Harkaway's, the famous sportswoman.

Sometimes one of the young men who paid her court, fell in love with her—genuine, honest love—and offered to make her his wife. She might have been a countess, had she chosen; but she did not choose.

"No, thank you," she said to one young peer, who implored her, with something like tears in his eyes to marry him. "What would be the use? You'd find out that you'd made a mistake before a month was out; and so should I. Then people would cut me, and I shouldn't like that. Besides, you'd want me to give up dancing and live what you call respectable, and I'm certain I shouldn't like that! No, you go and marry one of your own set, and take a box for my next benefit and bring her, and you'll be able to say: 'See what you saved me from!' You wouldn't? Oh, yes, you would! I know your sort of people too well. You won't take an answer? Well, then the truth is, I've made up my mind not to marry till I come across a man I can really care for, and I've not tumbled on any one yet, thank you."

She knew the world very well, did Finetta.

She sent them away when they got too "foolish," as she said, and wanted to marry her; dismissing them good-temperedly enough. In fact she was not a bad-tempered woman, and it was only at times that her passionate nature revealed itself. At such times, when she let out, it was a revelation indeed. It was almost as safe to brave the tigress in her den at the Zoological Gardens as to affront Finetta; and they who had done it once were satisfied with the attempt, and did not repeat it.

Now, one day, or rather one night, there came Yorke Auchester, and with him a change in the life of Finetta. They were friends at once. She amused and interested him; he liked to see her dance, liked to hear her talk in her cynical, good-tempered way; liked to drop in at the little house in St. John's Wood after the theater, at the little suppers over which she presided with a light-hearted gayety which made them extremely pleasant.

He admired her on horseback, admired her pluck, her coolness, her readiness to give and take in the game of repartee; and so it came about that of all the men, none were so often in her company as Yorke.

We are the slaves of habit. This is by no means a new saying, but it is a painfully true one.

Yorke got into the habit of dropping in at the Diadem for Finetta's great dance; got into the habit of dropping in at St. John's Wood, of driving her down to Richmond, of riding with her in the park or into the country.

And although he seldom gave her presents, never told her that she was the most beautiful, the cleverest, the best of her sex, as most of the other men did, Finetta liked him better than all the rest put together. And so the chain began to be forged.

When she went on the stage her dark eyes would scan the stalls, and if she saw his handsome, careless face and long figure there, a little smile would curve her lips, and she would dance her best.

At the little supper parties she managed, somehow or other, that he would sit beside her. If she were dull before he came, she brightened up when he made his appearance. If she had made an engagement, she would break it if Yorke asked her to ride and drive with him.

He didn't see this marked preference for some time, but the others did. Her quiet little sister who ran the house, once said:

"Fin, you're going soft on that big Lord Yorke," and the next moment had sufficient cause for being sorry that she had spoken.

But it was the truth. Finetta, who had laughed love to scorn, and broken, or cracked, so many hearts, was in a fair way to discover that she had a heart of her own.

Often when he had left her, she would sit perfectly motionless and silent, thinking hard; then she would start up with a laugh, and burst into a music-hall song. But it often ended with a sigh.

She was angry with herself, and she fought hard against the thralldom that was creeping over her; but she could no more help feeling happy when he was present, and miserable when he was absent, than she could help dancing in time, or dropping her 'H's' when she was excited.

Nothing stands still in this world; love grows or decreases. Finetta's love for Lord Yorke grew day by day, until it had reached such a pass that when he went off she needs must throw up her part for the night and follow him, and failing to find him, come back wretched at heart, though outwardly as cool and debonair as usual.

That morning as she was putting on her habit, her sister Polly had ventured to say a few more words of warning.

"That Lord Yorke will make your heart ache, Fin," she said, as she buttoned her sister's boots.

"Oh, will he?" she retorted, with a dash of color coming into her cheeks.

"Yes, he will. And what's the good? He won't ask you to marry him."

"Oh, won't he? How do you know?"

"I've heard them talk about him. He's as poor as a rat."

"But I'm not!"

"No, I dare say; but that won't help you. Besides, he's a good as engaged to that Lady Eleanor Dallas."

Finetta jerked her foot away, and her eyes began to glow dangerously.

"Her? Why she's like a wax doll."

"Oh, no, she isn't," said Polly. "She's as good-looking as most of the swells, and more so; besides, she's rolling in money, and it's money he wants. Take my advice, Fin, and don't let him hang about you any longer."

"And you take my advice, and hold your tongue!" retorted Finetta. "He shall hang about me as much as he likes. Who said I wanted to marry him, or—or that I would if he asked me?"

"I do; if he'd give you the chance," said Polly.

Finetta drew her foot away.

"I'll button the other myself," she said, passionately. But when her sister had gone she sat with the other boot unbuttoned, and kept the groom and the horses waiting for a good half-hour; and when she did go down and mount and ride off, her handsome face was clouded and thoughtful.

But at the sight of the green park and the people, she chased the melancholy brooding out of her dark eyes, and touching the magnificent horse with her golden spur, sent him into the row in her well-known style.

"If he were only here," she thought, and a sigh came to her lips. "Somehow I feel tired and bored without him, and lost if he's away for a day or two. Going to marry Lady Eleanor, is he?"

Almost before the muttered words had left her lips her eyes fell upon a stalwart figure standing against the rails, and the color flew to her face as she brought the horse up beside him.

It was Yorke—Yorke leaning against the rail, with his usually careless face grave and thoughtful, his eyes absent and staring vacantly at the ground, and yet with a strange look in them, which she, with a woman's quickness, noticed in an instant.

"Yorke," she said, bending down.

He started, and looked up, and her name came to his lips, but without the friendly smile which usually accompanied it.

"Why, when did you come back?" she asked, her face, her eyes all alight with life and happiness.

"To-day," he said. "Sultan's looking well——."

"Where have you been?" she demanded, noticing a change in his voice. "Did you get any fishing?

"Not much," he said, and his eyes were fixed on the horse.

"No? Then why didn't you come back? It's been awfully slow without you. Did you know that I had a day off and run down to the country? I was near you, I believe. Why didn't you leave word where you were going? What's the matter with you?" she broke off sharply, her color coming and going, for there had come into his face, into his eyes, a look almost of pity—newly born pity.

He knew now that he himself loved, that this woman loved him, and how she would suffer presently.

"I'll come in after the theater to-night," he said.

"Ride on now, or we shall have a crowd."

Several men had stopped, but waited, as if recognizing Yorke's right to monopolize her.

"Very well," she said, and she turned the horse. "It has come at last!" she murmured, "at last! He is going to be married. I know it! I know!" Her breath came painfully, and her hand stole up to her heart.

At that moment a lady came riding in the opposite direction. She was fair as a lily, and as beautiful, with soft brown eyes that looked dreamily about her; but as they met the dark ones of Finetta they seemed to awake, and the softness instantly vanished and gave place to an expression that in a man would be called hard and calculating.

Finetta's face, pale a moment before, grew white.

"That's her," she muttered. "And he is going to marry her. Polly's right; she's beautiful. Beautiful, and different to me. He'll marry and love her."

Her head drooped and her lips set tightly, and then she rode on. But suddenly she stopped the horse under some trees and looked back.

The beautiful girl with the soft brown eyes had stopped beside the rail, and Yorke and she were shaking hands.

Finetta could see their faces distinctly, and she watched, scanned his eagerly.

A singular expression came into her bold, handsome face.

"It's not her he's thinking of," she said; "not her. There's the same look in his eyes as when he looked up at me. What is it? I'll find out to-night." Her white teeth came together with a click. "I feel like fighting to-day. Going to marry Lady Eleanor, is he? We'll see! Oh, Yorke, if—if——." She looked round at the aristocrats riding past. "There isn't one that could love you as I do."

CHAPTER XIII.

"WHAT A MESS I'M IN!"

Lady Eleanor pulled her horse up beside the railing, as Finetta had done, and smiled down upon Yorke. She had a beautiful smile which, beginning in her brown eyes, spread over her face to her lips, the well-formed, cleanly cut lips, which more than anything else gave her countenance the patrician look for which Finetta—and others—hated her. And she did not smile too often.

"Well, Yorke," she said, and her voice was low and clear, and sweet, with just a touch of languid hauteur in it that was also aristocratic. "What a lovely day. Why aren't you riding?"

She didn't ask him, as Finetta had done, where he had been. That would have been a mistake which Lady Eleanor was far too wise to make.

"Horse is lame," he said.

"Oh, what a pity!" she exclaimed, nodding to some friends who were passing. "Just when you want him, too."

"Yes," he said, "though I am going to sell him."

She turned her eyes upon him, and raised her brown eyes with a faint surprise.

"Going to sell Peter! I thought he suited you so well."

He nodded, and laughed rather uneasily. The announcement that he intended to sell his horse had been a slip of the tongue.

"Oh, he suits me well enough, but I shall sell him all the same. What a lot of people there are here to-day."

"Aren't there!" she said, bowing and smiling to one and another of the men who saluted her. "Nearly everybody one knows. By the way, I haven't seen the duke this morning."

"Dolph's down in the country," he said.

"Oh!"

She would not have asked where, even had she not known; that would have been another mistake of which she would not have been guilty for worlds, but her "oh" gave him a chance to tell her if he chose. Apparently he did not choose, for he changed the subject.

"How did the Spelham's dance go off last night?"

"Very well," she replied. "But it was terribly crowded. The princess was there. I saved a couple of dances for you as long as I could."

"I'm sorry," he said. "I couldn't get back."

She looked quite satisfied with the explanation, or rather want of one, quite satisfied and serenely placid.

"You missed a very pleasant ball," was all she said. "I must go on now. Will you come in to luncheon? Aunt will be very pleased to see you."

"And you too?" he said, as a matter of course.

He always had a good supply of such small change about him.

She smiled.

"And I too, certainly," she said, and with a nod rode on.

Yorke looked after her thoughtfully, and gnawed his mustache.

The last two days had been the happiest in his life. He had spent them with Leslie, had walked with her through the lanes and on the beach, and had driven her to Northcliffe, and every moment of the delicious time his love had increased; it had seemed to him that he had not really loved till now, and that his past existence had been a sheer waste; and he had been happy notwithstanding that he was still deceiving her, that she still thought him the Duke of Rothbury, and that he had come to town to break off with two women who loved him.

It is well to be off with the old love before you are on with the new, even when there is only one old love; but when there are two!

It had cost him a great deal to tear himself away from Leslie, even for a few days, but he had done so. And all the way up to town he had been hard at work forming most excellent resolutions.

He would reform, and reform altogether. He would sell his horse, send in his resignation to two or three of his most expensive clubs, would give up cards and betting, especially betting. He didn't see why he shouldn't do without a man-servant. Fleming, his valet, had been a faithful fellow, and suited him down to the ground; but, yes, Fleming must go.

And then—well, then he would go to Mr. Lisle and ask for that pearl of great price, his daughter,—and marry!

His heart leaps at the thought. Marry Leslie! He pictured her as a bride, drew delightful mental sketches of the time they would have. He would take her to the Continent for their wedding-trip, and then they'd settle down in a cottage. It would have to be a cottage.

"Love in a cottage!" Great goodness, how often he had laughed at the idea, how he had pitied the poor devils who had committed matrimony and gone out of the world to live in respectable poverty with cold mutton and cheap sherry for luncheon!

But cold mutton and cheap sherry didn't seem so bad with Leslie to share them.

He would have to give up a great deal of course, and live within the small income left of his mother's dower. What a fearful lot of money he had spent! He had never thought of it before, but now he went through a little mental arithmetic, and was quite startled. Would anybody believe that gloves, button-holes, stalls at the Diadem, cigars, dinners at Richmond, could run up to such a sum?

What would he give for some of the money now? He took out the duke's check and looked at it. It was a large sum; but he owed all that and a great deal more.

Then he put dull care behind him, and gave himself up to thinking of Leslie, her beautiful face ten times more lovely than when he had first seen it, how that her love for him was shining in her eyes. What eyes they were! Eleanor's were nice ones, Finetta's were handsome ones—but Leslie's!

And her voice, too! He could hear it now calling him, half-shyly, "Yorke!"

He reached town, and went to his rooms in Bury Street, and Fleming had got his London clothes, the well-fitting frock coat and flawless hat, all ready as if he had expected him. And Yorke's heart smote him as he thought that he would have to give that faithful servant notice.

Then he went out, still thinking of Leslie and the dark gray eyes which had grown moist and tender as she said "Good-by!" and then had come Finetta and Lady Eleanor!

Yes, he had got his work cut out for him! But he would do it! He would devote his life to the dear, sweet girl down at Portmaris, whose pure, unstained heart he had won; he would reform, cut London, and go and be happy in a cottage for the rest of his life.

Meanwhile he had promised to lunch with Lady Eleanor, the woman whom the duke and the world at large had decided that he was going to marry; and he had promised to sup with Finetta, who doubtless thought that he should marry her.

He had made love to both these women. It was so easy for him, with his handsome face and light-hearted smile. He had only been half in earnest! if so much had meant—well, what had he meant—by soft speeches just murmured, by tender glances, by eloquent pressures of the hand? But they? How had they taken this easy love-making of his? He knew too well.

"Oh, lord, what a mess I'm in!" he muttered, as he made his way slowly toward Lady Eleanor's house in Palace Gardens.

Lady Eleanor rode home rather quickly, and as she entered the morning-room in which her aunt, Lady Denby, was sitting, there was a brightness in her soft eyes and a color in her cheeks which caused the elder lady to regard her curiously.

"Yorke is coming to luncheon," she said, and Lady Denby at once knew the cause of her niece's vivacity. "I wonder whether they can send up some lobster cutlets; he is so fond of them, you know. At any rate, will you see that they put on the claret he likes, the '73 it is, isn't it?"

"Oh, yes, we will serve up the fatted calf," said Lady Denby, with a smile. "So his gracious majesty has come back?"

"Yes," said Lady Eleanor, moving about the room restlessly, and flicking her habit-skirt with her whip. "Yes, and he looks very well, but——."

"But what?"

"Well, I scarcely know how to put it. He seemed grave and more serious than usual this morning. It isn't often Yorke is serious, you know."

"He has been up to something more reckless and desperate than usual, perhaps," suggested Lady Denby.

"Perhaps," assented Lady Eleanor, coolly.

"You say that with delicious *sang froid*," remarked Lady Denby. "I suppose if he had been committing murder or treason it would make no difference to you."

"Not one atom," said the girl, her color deepening.

"The only crime that would ruin him in your eyes would be matrimony with some one other than yourself."

Lady Eleanor started, and bit her lip, then she forced a laugh.

"I don't know whether even that would cure me," she said. "I should hate his wife, hate her with an active hatred which would embitter all my days; but I would go on caring for him and hoping that his wife might die, and that I might marry him after all."

Lady Denby shrugged her shoulders, and looked at the proud face, with its tightly drawn lips, and now brooding eyes.

"Yours is about the worst case I think I have ever met with, Eleanor," she said.

"Oh, no, it isn't," responded Lady Eleanor. "Only I'm not ashamed to admit how it is with me, and other women are. But you needn't be afraid on my account. I only wear my heart on my sleeve for you to peck at. I keep my secret from the rest of the world."

"Or think you do," said Lady Denby. "And how is it going to end?"

"God knows!" exclaimed Lady Eleanor, with an infinite and pathetic wistfulness. "Sometimes I wish I were dead, or he were——."

"What?"

"Yes! I'd rather see him dead than the husband of another woman!"

"My dear Nell!"

"You are shocked. Well, you must be so. It's the truth. Sometimes I wake in the night from a dream that he has married, and that I am standing by and see him put the ring on, and I feel——," she stopped, and laughed with a mixture of bitterness and self-scorn. "What weak, miserable fools we women are! There is not a man in the whole world worth one hundredth part of the suffering we undergo."

"Certainly Yorke Auchester does not!"

Lady Eleanor swung round on her with a kind of subdued fierceness.

"What have you to say against him? I thought he was a favorite of yours!"

"So he is; but I'm not blind to his faults——."

"His faults! What are they?"

"He is selfish, for one thing——."

"Selfish. He would give away his last penny——."

"I dare say; he hates coppers——."

"Would go to the end of the earth to save a friend. Is truth itself. And where is there a braver man than Yorke Auchester?"

Her voice softened and faltered as she spoke his name.

"Or a more foolish and infatuated girl than Eleanor Dallas," said her aunt. "There!" and she stroked the golden head which Eleanor had let fall on her hands; "you can't help it, I suppose, and we must make the best of it. I'll see that he has what he likes for luncheon. Thank Heaven, if we know nothing more about men, we know the nearest way to their hearts."

Lady Eleanor put out her hand to stop her aunt for a moment.

"I—I saw that woman this morning," she said, in a low voice.

"You mean Finetta?"

"Yes, she had come into the park to meet him, I believe, I saw them talking together. She is a beautiful woman—very."

"She is that."

"I don't wonder at his being—fond of her and liking to be with her."

"I hear they are seldom apart," said Lady Denby, gravely. "That ought to cure you, if anything would, Eleanor."

Lady Eleanor shook her head.

"It only makes it worse," she said, with her face hidden. "Jealousy doesn't kill love——."

"But wounded pride should do so!"

"No, no! It's true I'm proud enough to the rest of the world, but it all goes, slips away from me when—when I am near him! Oh, dear! Why, this morning when I saw him my heart——! And he looked up at me as if he had seen me only an hour or two ago! But there, what is the use of talking! I hope they will have some of these cutlets!"

Lady Denby shrugged her shoulders, and shook her head.

"It's a pity that Yorke does not know what is good for him. He could have lobster cutlets and '73 claret for the rest of his life, and all manner of good things, if he would only throw his handkerchief in the right direction."

Lady Eleanor smiled up at her almost defiantly.

"It is of no use your taunting me," she said. "You are right; if he threw his handkerchief, as you put it, I should be only too glad to go on my knees to pick it up."

A servant came to the door, with a card on a salver.

Lady Denby took it, and glanced at it.

"It is Mr. Ralph Duncombe," she said.

"I cannot see him this morning. Say that I am not at home."

Lady Denby signed to the footman to wait.

"Ought you not to see him?" she said in a low voice. "It may be important business."

"Oh, very well. Show Mr. Duncombe into the library."

"That's right," said Lady Denby, approvingly, "You can't afford to offend such a man as this Mr. Duncombe. There are not too many men who are willing to work for you for nothing. I suppose he has come about those mines?"

"I suppose so," assented Lady Eleanor, bitterly.

"I will go and see."

Ralph Duncombe had been a friend of Lady Eleanor's father. The late earl had been fond of dabbling in the city and had met the successful young merchant there and found him extremely useful. It had been chiefly owing to Ralph Duncombe's advice and counsel that the late earl had made the fifty thousand pounds which he had left to Lady Eleanor. He had done nothing for some years before his death without consulting the keen man of business, and Lady Eleanor had followed her father's example.

She would not have been a particularly rich woman with fifty thousand at three per cent., but Ralph Duncombe had invested it for her in such a way that it had brought in sometimes ten and fifteen. He had bought shares and sold them again at a big profit; had dealt with her money as if it had been his own, and had been as lucky with it. The greatest and latest piece of good fortune had only just turned up. He had purchased some land on the coast, calculating to dispose of it to a building company, but while negotiating with them discovered traces of copper; and it was on the cards that he had by one of those flukes which seemed to come so often to Ralph Duncombe, found a large fortune for her.

"How do you do, Mr. Duncombe?" she said. "What a shame that you should have to come all this way from the city."

"It does not take long by the Underground," he said, in his grave voice, as he shook hands; "and I have some important news for you."

"Yes," she said, and she motioned him to a chair.

As he sat down she noticed that he looked graver than usual, and that there was a tired and rather sad expression in his eyes.

"Is it bad news?" she said.

"Bad?" He looked at her with faint surprise.

"I thought you looked graver than usual, and rather disappointed," she explained.

He flushed slightly and forced a smile.

"We business men seldom look elated," he said, with something like a sigh. "Money making is not an exhilarating pursuit, Lady Eleanor."

"I should have thought otherwise," she said; "but I don't know much about it. I only know that it is very kind of you to take so much trouble over my affairs."

"Not at all. It comes natural to me," he said, with a slight smile. "I was your father's adviser—if I may put it so—for so long and so intimately that it seems a matter of course that I should continue to be his daughter's. But about this copper, Lady Eleanor. We were not mistaken; the indications are particularly distinct, and there is every reason to believe that the land contains a vast quantity."

"Yes," she said; "that is good news. I suppose it will make me very rich?"

He nodded.

"Yes, immensely so. The thing to decide now is how to work it. I have a plan which I should like you to consider," and he went on to explain it to her.

She listened not very attentively.

"I leave it all to you," she said, when he had finished. "I suppose you will think that is very cool of me; but I don't know what else I could do. That is, if you will undertake the business for me."

He nodded.

"I will do so, and not altogether disinterestedly, for I shall ask your permission to take some shares in the company."

"Why, yes, of course," she said at once. "I consider that it belongs as much to you as to me; you found it."

He shook his head, with a smile.

"Scarcely that," he said; "but I shall have an interest in it. We shall get to work at once, and I think I may say, positively, that you will be, as you put it, very rich, before many months are out."

"Very rich," she murmured; "thank you."

It was rather a strange way of accepting the information, but she was thinking of how little use the money would be if a certain person refused to share it with her.

Ralph Duncombe glanced at his watch and got up.

"You will stay to lunch?" she said....

"Thank you, Lady Eleanor, not this morning.

"I have to attend a board meeting, and shall be late as it is."

"I am sorry."

She gave him her hand, and as he held it she said, as if at a sudden thought:

"Did you—did you get those bills I asked you about?"

"Lord Auchester's?" he said, and he noticed that her hand quivered. "Yes, I bought them up." He looked at her gravely. "It cost rather a larger sum than I expected."

"You mean that he was very much in debt?" she said, in a low voice, and with downcast eyes.

"Yes, very much," he replied, laconically.

She bit her lip softly, and still evaded his keen gaze.

"Tell me," she said. "You know I do not understand such matters; but—but, supposing that you were to compel him to pay these bills, what would be the result?"

"You mean try to compel him?" he said, with a smile. "You cannot get water from a dry well, Lady Eleanor, and from what I hear, Lord Auchester is a very dry well. If you forced him to take up those bills, you would ruin him."

"Ruin him!"

"Yes. That means that you would make a kind of outcast of him. A man who cannot meet his engagements is dishonored; he would have to give up his clubs and leave London. I don't know where such men go now; to some corner of Spain, I believe. Any way, he would be ruined and thoroughly finished."

She drew a long breath.

"And I—and I could do that?" she said, in a very low voice.

"You could do that, as I hold the bills for you, certainly," he replied.

"Thank you," she said, with a laugh that sounded forced and unnatural; "I only wanted to know. I'm afraid you must think me sublimely ignorant."

"Not more so than a lady should be of business matters," he replied, politely.

There was a moment's pause. He took up his hat and gloves. Then, suddenly,

Lady Eleanor said:

"Do you know a place called Portmaris, Mr. Duncombe?"

CHAPTER XIV.

"NOW, YORKE!"

The carefully brushed, exquisitely shining, and glossy hat—the city man's god, as it has been called—fell from his hands, and he flushed and then turned pale; but that, perhaps, was at his clumsiness. At any rate, whatever the cause, he was able to look Lady Eleanor steadily in the face when he recovered his hat.

"Portmaris?" he said, smoothing it with his sleeve. "Yes, I know it. It is a small fishing village on the west coast. Why do you ask?" and his keen eyes grew to her face.

"Oh, I only heard of it the other day," she said.

"A friend of mine, the Duke of Rothbury, has gone down there, and——," she paused a moment—"and Lord Auchester has been there."

"Lord Auchester?" he said, and his brows knit thoughtfully. "It is a strange place for a man about town, like Lord Auchester, to stay at."

"He has been fishing."

"There is no fishing there," he remarked, and he put one glove on, and took it off again, the frown still on his face.

"He has been to see the duke. You may know that the duke and he are great friends. They are cousins."

He shook his head, with an impatience strange and unusual with him—the cool, self-possessed, city man.

"I know very little about such persons, Lady Eleanor," he said, gravely. "Your father, the late earl, was the only nobleman I ever knew, and—I don't mean to be offensive—I ever wanted to know."

Lady Eleanor looked at him with faint, well-bred surprise; then she smiled.

"If reports speak truly, you are likely to be a nobleman yourself some day, Mr. Duncombe. You have only to enter Parliament——."

He shook his head by way of stopping her.

"I have no ambition in that direction, Lady Eleanor," he said, almost gloomily. "I am a man of business, and care nothing for titles. I was going to say and for little else; but I suppose that wouldn't be true. I do care for money; I've been bred to that. Is there anything else you would like to say to me?" he broke off abruptly.

His manner was so singular, so unlike his usual one, that Lady Eleanor was startled.

"Thank you, no," she said; "except—except that I should be glad if you could get any other bills or debts of Lord Auchester's."

He nodded.

"Certainly." He brushed his hat slowly, then added, "Excuse me, Lady Eleanor, but will you allow me to ask why you are purchasing—and at a heavy price—Lord Auchester's liabilities? I am aware that I have no right to ask you the question——."

"Yes, you have," she said, quickly, and struggling with the color that would mount to her face. "You were my father's friend, and have been and are mine; and you have every right to ask such questions. But I find it difficult to answer. Well, Lord Auchester is a friend of mine, and I would rather that he owed me the money than a lot of Jews and people of that kind."

Ralph Duncombe inclined his head with an air of, "You know your own business better than any one else."

"Good-morning, Lady Eleanor," he said; "I will do as you wish. And please, say nothing about this mining scheme of ours."

He got outside the house, and drew a long breath.

The mere mention of the word "Portmaris" had stirred his heart to its depths, and recalled Leslie and his parting scene with her.

He might aspire to nobility, might he? What would be the good of a title to him, when the only title he longed for was that of Leslie Lisle's husband? And so this Lord Auchester had been at Portmaris. Had he seen Leslie? Had he spoken to her? It was not unlikely! Such men as this Lord Yorke Auchester would be sure to discover a beautiful girl like Leslie, and make acquaintance with her.

Ralph Duncombe spent a very bad half-hour on the Underground on his way back to the city; very bad!

Five minutes after the man of business had left Palace Gardens, Yorke, the man of pleasure, arrived there, and was welcomed as if he were the great Lama of Thibet.

"I haven't had time to change my habit, Yorke," said Lady Eleanor.

"You couldn't put on anything prettier," he said, with that fatal facility of his, and he looked at her admiringly.

Lady Eleanor never appeared to greater advantage than in the dark green habit, upon which Redfern had bestowed his most finished art.

"Come in to luncheon at once," she said; "it is the only way of stopping your compliments. Here is Aunt Denby in a complete quandary as to whether there is anything fit to eat. You know we women don't care what we get, but it is different with you men."

But the luncheon was perfect in its way. Clear soup, a fish pie, salmi of fowl, and—oh, wonderful cook! lobster cutlets; and the famous '73 claret.

Yorke did full justice to the good fare, and rattled away for the amusement of the two women. He talked of the opera, of the next meeting at Sandown, of anything and everything which would interest two women moving in the ultra-fashionable circles, and made himself so pleasant that Lady Denby—who always suspected, while she liked him—relaxed into a smile, and Lady Eleanor was beaming.

"Never get cutlets like these anywhere else," he said, helping himself to a second serve with a contented sigh.

"Not at Portmaris?" asked Lady Eleanor.

He held his fork aloft, and looked at her with sudden gravity.

"Eh! Oh, Portmaris. No. No lobster cutlets down there. I rather think they eat the lobsters raw."

"What an outlandish place it must be!" said Lady Eleanor. "I wonder how you could stay there, you and Dolph."

"Oh, anything for a change," he said, carelessly, but with his mind apparently fixed on his plate, at the bottom of which he could see Leslie's face as plainly as if she were standing before him.

The lunch was over at last. It had seemed interminable to Lady Eleanor, and Lady Denby had, with a half-audible murmur of an afternoon drive, taken herself away and left the coast clear.

"You want to smoke?" said Lady Eleanor. "Come into the conservatory. Aunt doesn't mind it there, as it kills the insects."

He lit a cigar, and lounged against the doorway, and she sank into a seat and absently picked the blossoms nearest to her.

"Now is the time," he thought, "to tell her everything," but at the moment he remembered the bracelet which the duke had given him for her, and he put his hand in his pocket and drew it out.

"By the way, Eleanor," he said, carelessly, "you had a birthday the other day."

"Yes, I think I had," she said, smiling up at him. "Do you remember it?"

"Well, I shouldn't, if it hadn't been for Dolph," he said, honestly. "Dolph always remembers, you know."

"Yes, I know."

"And so—so——." He took the morocco case from his pocket and opened it. "And so—well, I know it isn't worth your acceptance, but if you care to take it, here's a trifle—Dolph gave me," he added, honestly and he held out the bracelet.

She took it, and her face brightened, brightened with a soft glow which made it look inexpressibly tender and grateful.

"How good of you! How pretty it is! And it is just the size, see," and she unbuttoned the habit sleeve and slipped the bracelet on. "How does it fasten?"

"Eh?" he said. "Oh, like this, I expect," and he closed the spring and fastened it over her slender, milk-white wrist, and the touch of his hand sent a thrill through her, though he performed the operation in a most business-like way.

"How very good of you!"

"Say, rather of Dolph," he said. "It was he who gave it to me for you."

"But it was you who gave it to me," she said, in a low voice.

"I told him you wouldn't care for it," he said. "You who have no end of presents."

"But none I value more than this," she said, her voice singing, so to speak. "I will always wear it."

"Don't," he said. "Better wear the bracelet that goes with your diamond set. That's more suitable to a rich person than this—though that's hard on Dolph, who chose it and paid for it, isn't it?"

She was silent a moment, then she said:

"That reminds me, Yorke. Do you know that I am likely to be richer even than you think?"

"Oh? Well, I'm very glad," he said, with friendly interest and pleasure. "What will you do with so much coin; roll in it?"

She sighed softly, and lifted her eyes to his for a moment, with a look that said, "I would like to give it to you, and you can roll in it, or fling it in the Thames, or play ducks and drakes with it, or anything." But he was not looking at her, and did not see the appeal of the soft brown eyes.

"There is one thing I can do with it," she said. "I can buy your horse, if you really mean selling it, Yorke. But you don't?"

"But I do," he said, quickly, and with a touch of red showing through his tan. "I'm going to cut down my establishment—big word 'establishment,' isn't it? —as low as it can be cut, and the horse has got to go."

"Then I will buy it," she said, her face flushing, and then going pale.

Why was he selling it? What was he going to do? Surely nothing rash; he was not going to marry. No! she drew a long breath—that was impossible. He couldn't marry with those debts hanging round his neck, and those awful bills which she held, unless he married an heiress, and in that case he would not want to sell his horse, an old and loving favorite.

"You?" he said. "Why should you buy it? You've got enough already. Besides, he's not altogether safe."

"Thank you," she said, laughing a little tremulously. "It is the first time my horsemanship has been called in question. I'm not afraid of Peter. Besides, I —I should like to have him."

"To put under a glass case?"

"Yes, that I might look at him and recall the many jolly rides we have had together. No, no one shall have Peter but me. You can't prevent my buying him, you know!"

"No," he said. "And I'd rather you had him than any one else. I should see him occasionally, and I think I could make him quiet enough for you. Perhaps," he laughed, "you might feel good-natured enough sometimes to lend him to a poor chap who can't afford a nag of his own."

"Yes," she said. "I could do that. Is there anything I wouldn't lend or give you, Yorke?" and her voice was almost inaudible.

He started and looked at his watch. How was he to tell this beautiful woman, whose eyes were melting with love, whose voice rang with it, that he had no love to return, that he had indeed given his whole heart to another woman? And yet, that was what he meant doing this morning!

"I—I must be off," he said, almost nervously.

She rose, and as she did so the bracelet, which he must have fastened insecurely, fell to the ground. He stooped and picked it up, and she held out her arm.

"That's a bad omen, isn't it?" she said, with a wistful smile.

"Oh, no," he replied, as lightly as he could. "That kind of thing only applies to rings; wedding ones in particular. Let's see, how does this clasp go, once more?"

She put her disengaged hand to show him, and their fingers met, touched and got entangled, and he laughed; but the laugh died away as he saw her lips quiver as if with pain, and her soft eyes fill with tears.

He got outside and took off his hat, and drew a long breath.

"I could as soon have struck her as told her," he muttered.

And that was how he was 'off with the old love' No. 1.

He went down to the club, and sauntered from reading-room to reception-room, and at last consented to play a game at billiards with a man with whom he had often played, and always at an advantage.

Yorke was good at most games of strength or skill, and the men, hearing that he was playing, dropped in and sat round to while away the tedious hour before dinner.

But that afternoon Yorke could not play a bit.

"Completely off color," remarked a young fellow, in tones of almost personal resentment. "Never saw such a thing, don't-yer-know. There! That's the second easy hazard he's missed, and bang goes my sovereign."

"And why on earth does he keep on smoking like that?" inquired another in an undertone. "Looks as if he were mooning about something. He can't be—be——."

The first young fellow shook his head.

"No, Yorke Auchester doesn't drink, if that's what you mean; it isn't that, but hang me if I know what it is. Yorke!" he called out, "you can't play."

Yorke gave a little start in the middle of one of the reflective smiles.

"Eh? No. I'm making a fool of myself, I know."

"You must have been to bed early wherever you've been for the last week," suggested one of the men, and they were all surprised to see him flush, "like a great girl, by Jingo!"

"Yes, I have, and it hasn't agreed with me in a billiard sense," he said, good temperedly, as he put on his coat and sauntered out. He went to his chambers and dressed, and the faithful Fleming also noticed the singular fit of abstraction which had fallen upon his beloved master.

"Seems to have something on his mind," was his mental reflection. "And it doesn't look as if it was bills or anything unpleasant of that kind."

"Shall I wait up to-night, my lord?" he asked, as he put on the perfectly cut dress overcoat, and handed the speckless, flawless hat.

He had to put the question twice, and even then Yorke did not seem to catch the sense of it immediately.

"Eh? No, don't sit up; I may be late. And, by the way, I may be off to the country to-morrow morning, so have some things packed."

"Something up at that outlandish place he's been staying at," was Fleming's mental comment, and he watched his master go slowly down the stairs with the faint flicker of a smile on his handsome face.

Yorke dined at the club and for once seemed quite indifferent as to what he ate, and when the footman brought the wrong claret, took it without a word of reproach. Some of his friends watched him from an adjacent table, and shook their heads.

"Somebody's gone and died and left him a hatful of coin, or else he's won a big wager. Never saw Yorke Auchester go dreaming over his dinner in his life before," was the remark.

About nine o'clock he lit a cigar, and walked down to the Diadem.

The attendants, box-keepers, even the men in the orchestra knew him, and people pointed him out to each other as his stalwart figure made its way to his stall; and when Finetta sprang onto the stage in her dainty page's dress of scarlet and black satin, the man who always "knows everything" about the actors and actresses whispered to a country cousin, "That's Finetta. Look! You'll see her glance toward him and perhaps give a little nod. They say he's spent every penny of an enormous fortune in diamonds for her; got some of 'em on to-night," etc.

As a matter of fact, Finetta saw him without any direct glance, and saw nothing else.

It was said that she danced her best that night, and the house stamped and cheered with delight.

But as Yorke looked at her, and clapped, he thought:

"Poor Fin. It won't be hard to leave her."

And the remembrance of the laugh he had heard at St. Martin's Tower rose, and made him shudder. He lit a cigar after the theater, and set out to walk to St. John's Wood.

As the page opened the door—Finetta had two men-servants, both as well appointed and trained as any of Lady Eleanor's—Yorke heard the sound of laughter and music in the dining-room; and above it all, Finetta's laugh; it made him shudder once more.

Supper was nearly over—a dainty supper with ice puddings and the best brands of champagne and some one at the piano was dashing out with the true artistic touch, the popular song from the late comic opera, and some of the guests were singing it.

There were three or four men—Lord Vinson was among them and—and as many ladies. At the head of the table sat Finetta. She was magnificently dressed in a cream silk, soft and undulating.

A crimson rose was her only ornament, and that worn in the thick, glossy hair; she knew Yorke's taste too well to smother herself in diamonds, and she knew also that the soft cream and the rich red rose showed up her dark, Spanish complexion as no other colors could do.

Her eyes lit up as he entered, and she signed to him to take a chair next her.

"I knew you'd come," she said, in a low voice. "You never break a promise. Polly, give Lord Auchester some gelatine—or what will you have?"

He took a biscuit and a glass of wine, and joined in with the talk.

It was not very witty, but it was not dull. The men talked of the theater, the turf, and talked a great deal better and more fluently than they did at "respectable" dinner parties, and every now and then one of them was asked to sing, and did so cheerfully and willingly, and as a rule sang well, and the rest made a chorus if it was needed.

With the exception that no one looked or was bored, and all tried to make themselves pleasant and agreeable, it differed very little from the dinners and suppers which we, the most respectable of readers, so often yawn over.

Finetta said but little, sang one song only, and was so silent and quiet and subdued, that Lord Vinson, as he rose to take his leave, whispered to Yorke on passing:

"Look out for squalls, old fellow! She's most dangerous when she's like this, don't you know."

When they had all gone but Yorke, and Polly had retired to a corner of the inner room, and taken out some lace of her sister's to mend, Finetta lit a cigarette for Yorke, and then, going to the piano, began to play—she had learned to play a little—the air to which she danced her great dance. Then she moved way and as if she were thinking of anything but the silent young man with the far-away look on his face, and humming the air musically enough, glided into the dance itself.

Surely since Taglioni there has been no more graceful dancer than Finetta, and even Yorke, with his heart soaring miles away to the flower-faced girl who owned it, could not but look and admire.

"Bravo, Fin," he said, almost involuntarily. "No wonder they encore that every night! Don't leave off," for she had stopped suddenly right in front of him, her dark eyes flashing into his, her lips apart.

"Yes," she said. "I am not going to dance any more to-night. I am going to sit here and listen while you tell me everything! Now Yorke!"

CHAPTER XV.

FINETTA LEARNS THE TRUTH.

"Now tell me everything," repeated Finetta, and she drew an amber satin cushion from the sofa, and seated herself at his feet, her hands clasped round her knees, her dark eyes turned up to him.

Now here was the way ready made for him; but what man ever answered such an appeal at once and fully? Yorke took the cigarette from his lips and looked down at her with a troubled surprise.

"What do you mean?" he said. "How do you know there is anything to tell?"

She laughed, almost contemptuously.

"How do you know when it's going to rain? By the clouds, don't you? Do you think I'm blind, Yorke? I'm not clever like some of your swell friends, but I'm not a fool. I've got eyes like other women, and perhaps they're sharper than some, and I can see something is the matter. I saw it the moment I rode up to you in the park to-day, and I've been watching you all the evening."

"You'd make a decent detective, Fin," he said, trying to speak banteringly.

"I dare say," she assented. "Most women would, especially if they knew the man they were after as well as I know you."

"Yes, we are old friends, Fin," he said.

"That's it," she said. "And that's why I ask you what's the matter, what's happened? Some men would push me off or give me the lie, but you aren't like that sort."

"Thanks," and he laughed.

"No, you always go straight, and that's one of the reasons why—I like you, don't you see?"

"I see," he said. "And so you thought I looked this morning as if I'd got something on my mind?"

She nodded.

"Yes, when I came up you were leaning against the rail, looking at nothing, as if you were dreaming; and while you were speaking to Lady Eleanor——."

He moved slightly.

"You don't like me to speak of her?" she said, with a woman's quickness. "All right, I sha'n't hurt her by mentioning her name."

"Don't be foolish, Fin," he said, coloring at the truth of her insight; he did not like to hear her mention Lady Eleanor's name.

"Oh, I'm not foolish. I was saying that you looked at her ladyship just as you looked at me, as if you didn't see either of us, as if you were looking right away beyond us, and it's been the same to-night. You haven't heard half that was going on, but have just been mooning and dreaming, and so I ask you what it is? Wait a minute. If you're going to tell me that it's money matters, you needn't, for I shouldn't believe you. If the bailiffs were in the house you wouldn't let it trouble you, you know."

He laughed.

"I am afraid I shouldn't," he admitted.

"Very well," she said, "then it isn't that—though you are hard up, and pretty deep in debt, eh, Yorke?"

"Of course," he said. "Always have been, and shall be; everybody knows that."

"And so you're used to it, and don't mind it," she went on. "It isn't that then. What is it?"

He was silent, struggling hard for courage to tell her.

"You don't like making a clean breast of it," she said, slowly. "And you think it's like my cheek to ask you. But I'm an old friend, am I not? I'm only Finetta, the girl that dances at the Diadem, but I've got a feeling that I'm a better friend to you than many of your swell ones. I dare say they think I'm a bad lot, and that I've done you no end of harm. Perhaps I have. I've let you come here when you liked, and take me about riding and driving, when you ought to have been with them; but I don't know, after all, that I've hurt you much. I dare say I could if I liked. You'd have given me things like Charlie Farquhar, if I'd let you; but I didn't. I was a fool, perhaps, sometimes I think I am. But—but, you see, I liked you. I didn't care for the others, they were nothing to me and it wouldn't have mattered if they'd spent their last shilling in rings and flowers and things. But with you it was different. I don't know quite why," and her eyes sank thoughtfully. "Perhaps it was because you always treated me like a lady, and didn't bother me to run off with you or—or marry you."

Her voice softened, and a dash of color came into her olive cheeks.

"You'd have made a poor bargain if I had and you consented, Fin," he said, gravely.

"I dare say," she assented. "Anyhow, you didn't and don't mean to. Don't deny it. I know how you've always thought of me. I've been just Finetta, of the Diadem, and it's been pleasant and amusing to take me about and come and have supper, and—and that's all."

She raised her eyes to his face with a smile, a brave smile that did not hide her aching heart from him.

"And we've been such very good friends," she went on after a pause, "that I speak out straight and plain when I see that something is the matter, and I ask you what it is, and if you take my advice, you'll tell me. Who knows, I might be able to help you, if you want any help. Don't laugh. What's that story about the lion and the mouse? I'm only a mouse I know, and you are no end of a lion, but you may find yourself in a net some day, don't youknow."

Her tone was slangy, but there was an earnestness in it, and in her dark eyes, which touched Yorke.

He was silent for a moment or two, then he said in a voice inaudible to Polly, who stolidly stitched and stitched in the inner room:

"You are right, Fin. Something hashappened——."

"I knew it," she said, quietly.

He screwed his courage up.

"The fact is, Fin, I am—going to be married," he said, almost in a whisper.

She did not start, did not move a muscle for a moment, then she got up.

"Wait a minute, I want a cigarette."

She crossed the room to an inlaid cabinet, and took out a silver box—of course a present—and got a cigarette from it, and her hand shook so that for a moment she could not hold the match straight.

But when she glided back to her place at his feet her hand was steady, and seeing that his face was rather pale, she showed no sign of emotion, either of surprise, or anger, or resentment.

"Going to be married?" she said, leaning back. "To Lady Eleanor, I suppose?"

"No," said Yorke, emphatically. "Why should you think that?"

He was relieved, greatly relieved by the quiet way in which she had taken the announcement, and, man like, was completely deceived.

"Oh, I don't know. Everybody said you were going to marry her. She has plenty of money and is a swell. So, it's not her?" she said, slowly, her eyes downcast.

"No, it is not," he responded. "And there's no reason why people should say ——." He stopped, conscience-smitten.

"Oh, they say it because you and she are so much together, and you've made love to her; but that means nothing with you, does it?" she said, shooting a glance up at him.

Yorke colored.

"If a man's to marry every girl he flirts with——," he said, half-angrily.

"All right, I don't mind. You've flirted with me and I haven't asked you to marry me. And so it's not her ladyship." A faint smile curved her lips, which looked drawn and constrained. "What other swell is it? I know 'em all—by sight."

"She is not a 'swell' at all," he said. "And you do not know her. I only saw her the other day down in the country."

"Where you have been this last week?" she said, in a low voice, perfectly steady and under control.

"Yes, I saw her, met her, by chance, quite by chance."

"And—and you fell in love with her right off?" she said.

"Yes," he said, looking straight before him and speaking as if in a dream. "I loved her at first sight."

"She must be very good-looking."

He smiled, absently. "Good-looking" was so poor a phrase by which to describe his Leslie.

"Yes, she is good-looking, as you call it, Fin," he said.

"What is she like? Is she tall and fair—I suppose so, that's the style that fetches most men."

"N-o," he said. "She is not fair—not what one would call fair."

"Dark?" and she flashed her brilliant eyes up at him, and then at a mirror opposite her.

"N-o, not dark, I think; I can't tell. Her hair is dark."

"As mine?" she asked.

He looked down at her as if he had forgotten the color of her hair, and she felt the look like a dagger stab.

"Yes, but she has blue or gray eyes."

She nodded.

"I knew," she said, shortly, as if it cost her something to speak. "I know the sort of girl. I've seen 'em. Dark hair and bluish-gray eyes. Yes! And you fell in love with her at first sight. And—why don't you go on? I want to know all about her," and she laughed.

In his abstraction he did not detect the tone of agony, of jealousy, in the laugh, and only thought how well Finetta was behaving, and what a brick she was.

"There's not much more to tell," he said. "I—I told her that I loved her, and—and——." He paused, recalling the tender, the precious confession of his darling. "Well, we're to be married, Fin, as soon as we can. I'm as poor as a church mouse, and we sha'n't have much to live upon; but I dare say we shall get on somehow or other. Anyhow, I've made up my mind, and——." He stopped.

"No one, not the devil himself, could stop you," she finished, not passionately, but in a slow, steady voice. "And so you've come to me and told me like—like a man, Yorke."

"We are old friends, Fin," he said, "and I felt you ought to know."

"I see," she said. "It will make a difference to us, won't it? Good-by to our acquaintance now. No more dinners at Richmond, or suppers at the little house in St. John's Wood. It wouldn't do for a man who is going to be married to be friends with Finetta, eh? Oh, I understand, and I'm much obliged to you——."

"Fin——."

"Wait. I'm speaking the truth. I am much obliged to you. Some men would have kept it to themselves; would have cut me straight away without a word, and left me to find out the reason by reading the accounts of the wedding in the newspapers. But you aren't that sort, are you, Yorke—or I suppose I ought to say Lord Auchester now?"

He colored and bit his lip.

"Hit away, Fin," he said. "I deserve it."

"No," she said. "I won't hit you, though I dare say Lady Eleanor and the heaps of other ladies you've made love to will, and pretty hard. But I am not a lady, you see, and that makes a difference. And this—this young lady? You say she's not a swell?"

He laughed.

"Not what you call a swell, Fin," he said. "She is the daughter of an artist, and not a first-rate one at that."

"An artist?" The full lips writhed into an expression of amazement and contempt which he did not see. "An artist, one of those fellows who paint pictures."

"And awfully bad ones," said Yorke, with a rueful laugh.

"And they're poor?"

"They are certainly not rich," he said.

"And you'll be poor, too, you and she, when—when you're married?"

He laughed rather ruefully again.

"I know the sort of thing," she said, with all the scorn of one who has passed from squalid poverty to luxury and wealth. "You'll have to live in a small house with one or two servants, you won't be able to afford a valet or a horse ——."

"Excepting a clothes-horse."

"Well, you'll want that, as I dare say she—your wife—will have to do the washing, and you'll have to dine like a workman, in the middle of the day, and drink cheap ale, and wear shabby clothes. I should like to see you in seedy clothes, Yorke; you'd look funny," and she laughed bitterly. "And she'd wear cheap things, turned dresses, and that sort of thing, and she'd get dowdy and ill-tempered, and you'd ask yourself what on earth you ever saw in her that you should go and ruin yourself by marrying her. Oh, I know!" and she leaned back and puffed at her cigarette with a contempt that was almost imperial.

Yorke colored.

"A good deal of what you say is true, but not all, Fin," he said, almost gently. It would be base ingratitude to be angry with her after the admirable way in which she had received the news. "For one thing, Leslie would never be dowdy. You'd understand that if you knew her, had seen her. I suppose she wears cheap clothes, now. If so, all I can say is that she looks as well, as refined and lady-like, as—as anybody I know."

"As Lady Eleanor?" she put in, with a flash of her dark eyes.

"Well, yes," he assented; "and for another thing, she wouldn't get ill-tempered; it isn't possible."

"Oh, isn't it?" with another curl of the lip.

"No," he said, quietly, earnestly; "I'll go bail for that much. And I'll stake my life I shall never ask myself why I married her! But you're right about a great deal of it, Fin; and we shall have to put up with it. After all, you know, you can't have everything you want in this world. Did you ever notice that the rich people, the people with hatfuls of money, generally look the most wretched? I have. They want something they haven't got, you may depend upon it; something they value ever so much higher than their coin. Well, we shall want money, but we shall have a good many other things——."

She laughed, a dry, harsh laugh.

"Don't mind me," she said; "I can't help smiling. It's as good as a play to hear you talking like the leading juvenile in a sentimental piece. Love, love, love! That's what you're thinking of. Well, perhaps you're right. God knows! I dare say you're right."

She was silent a moment, then she said:

"And when's the wedding to be?"

"Soon," he said, dreamily; "as soon as possible. It's a secret. I mean our engagement."

She looked up sharply.

"Oh, it isn't in the papers or known yet?"

He shook his head.

"No, no. We've reasons for keeping it quiet for a little while."

"But you came and told me," she said, broodingly. "Well, it was straight and kind of you, as I said, and—and I'm much obliged."

He put out his hand to her in acknowledgment. She looked at it for a moment as if she doubted whether she would take it; then she put her own into it, and hers burned like a red-hot coal.

She took it away instantly, and rose and walked slowly up to the table, poured out a couple of glasses of champagne, and brought him one and raised the other to her lips.

"Here's luck to you—both!" she said, with a laugh. "May you be happy ever afterward, as they say in the story books," and she looked over the rim of the glass at him, with her dark eyes flashing under the thick brows.

"Thanks, Fin," he said. "You are a good sort, and——." He rose.

"But you don't want to know any more of me," she broke in. "I understand.

Oh, don't apologize. I'm cute enough to see why you've told me, why you've come to me first of all. There's to be an end to our friendship——." Her voice broke for a moment, then she hurried on with forced gayety and indifference. "And you're quite right. A man who's going to settle down, doesn't want such acquaintances as me. Well, good-by."

She held out her hand.

Yorke, feeling as a man must feel under such circumstances, when he cannot contradict and would like to do so, hung his head for a moment, then he took her hand, and holding it, said:

"I'm not much loss, Fin. As I told her, I'm a bad lot, and dear at any price, and—there, good-by!"

Then he did a foolish thing. He raised her hand to his lips and kissed it.

She quivered, almost as if he had struck her; her eyes closed, and she leaned heavily against the edge of the table.

Yorke, feeling unutterably miserable, dropped her hand and left the room. He gave the page who helped him on with his coat a sovereign, and got outside.

"Poor Fin!" he muttered, standing on the pavement and staring about him. "Poor Fin!"

And so he got off with the old love number two.

Finetta stood where he had left her for a second, then sprang forward with her magnificent arms stretched out.

"Yorke, Yorke!" broke from her white lips. But the door had closed, and he did not hear her.

She stood erect for a moment, then staggered and fell face downward upon the sofa.

Polly ran to her—locking the door on her way—and raised her head. She had fainted.

Polly poured some wine through the clenched teeth and bathed the set face, and presently Finetta came to; but it was to pass from a swoon into an awful torrent of weeping.

"He's gone! He's gone! Forever!" she moaned. "I shall never see him again! Why did I let him go like that? Why didn't I ask him on my knees to let us be friends still? I should have seen him now and again, and that would have been something; to speak to him, hear him laugh and talk, and call me 'Fin;' but it's all over now. He'll never come back! Oh, I wish I were dead, dead, dead!"

"Hush, hush," implored Polly, trying to soothe her. "He's better gone. There was no good in his staying."

"No, no! I know that! He never cared for me. I only amused him, and directly he left me he forgot me. They're all alike. No, he was different. Look how he came and told me—like a man! Oh, Yorke, Yorke! Oh, he little guesses how I ——." Her lips shook, and she hid her face even from her sister.

"Where's your pride, Fin?" whispered Polly, almost as Lady Denby had said to Lady Eleanor.

"My pride!" retorted Finetta. "Ah, you can talk like that, you who don't know what I feel! I haven't any. I'd have followed him round the world like a dog, grateful for a kind word—or a blow! I'd have worked for him like a slave. Poor! He needn't have been poor if he'd married me. He should have had every penny, and I'd have been content to go in rags so long as he had the best of everything; and I'd have made him happy, or die in the trying."

"You'd most likely have died," remarked Polly, with a woman's insight.

"I dare say. Well, I could have died. But it's all over."

She hid her face in her hands and shook like a leaf for a full minute, then suddenly her mood changed, and she started up—in a fury.

The tears dried up in her burning eyes, her face became white, her lips rigid; and as she stood with clenched hands and heaving bosom she looked like an outraged goddess, a tigress robbed of her cub, a woman despised and deserted —and that is a more terrible thing than the outraged goddess or the bereaved tigress, by the way.

"He's a fool!" she panted. "A fool! To leave me for such as her! Says she's pretty!" She strode to the glass and stood erect before it. "Is she better looking than I am? I don't believe it. And what else is she? Nothing. She's poor—she isn't a swell even. And he's left me and that other, that Lady Eleanor, for her! Yes; I could have borne it better if it had been Lady Eleanor; if it had been one of her sort it would be more natural; but a mere nobody, the daughter of an artist!"

In her ignorance poor Finetta regarded the painters of pictures and gate posts as equals.

"A common painter! Why, he'd better have married me!" and she drew a long breath. "I'm as good as she is, and she'll be a lady. I'd make as good a lady as she would."

"You never saw her," ventured Polly, timidly.

The tigress swung round upon her, dashing the wine glasses to the ground in the movement.

"Saw her! I don't want to see her, to know what she's like! I can guess. A dowdy, simpering, doll-faced chit of a girl that caught his fancy! And she'll be his wife, while I——." She raised her clenched hands above her head, and laughed a wild, discordant laugh. "It makes me mad!"

She fell to pacing the room. Her hair had become unfastened, and fell in a black torrent over the creamy satin. Her lithe figure, erect and quivering, looked six feet high. A magnificent spectacle for a painter or sculptor, but not for the man or woman who had offended her.

"I'm flung aside as not fit for him to know, and she'll be his wife. I wish she were here now; I'd kill her! Oh, if I could only do something to separate them! If I could only come between them!"

She flung herself on the sofa, and hid her face on the cushion.

Polly went up to her.

"You're wearing yourself out, Fin," she said. "You'll suffer for this to-morrow. Better come to bed. Besides, what's the use of it? You can't bring him back, or stop his marrying the other girl."

Finetta raised her head, and looked at her as if she did not see her.

"Can't I?" she muttered between her closed teeth. "Can't I? I don't know! Such things have been done. Sometimes there's a way." She put her hand to her brow, and drew a labored sigh. "I can't think; my head's like lead and on fire, and my heart's aching. When did he say the wedding was to be?"

"Soon," said Polly. "What's the use——."

Finetta held up her hand to silence her.

"Go to bed," she said, hoarsely.

"You come too——."

"Go to bed; get out of my sight. I want to be alone, to think. To think! There must be some way to stop it, and—and I'll find it out. Go away——," with a flash of her somber eyes—"Go away and leave me. I'm best alone."

Polly, awed and frightened, crept to the door; but as she paused a moment and looked back she heard the hoarse, broken voice still muttering:

"There must be some way!"

CHAPTER XVI.

THE FOOLISH NOTE.

Yorke walked all the way from St. John's Wood to Bury Street, and it was not altogether a pleasant walk.

There is a popular parlor game called "Consequences," and, after a fashion, he was playing that game as he strode along smoking vigorously.

It is an easy and pleasant amusement running into debt; but there are consequences. It is also an easy and pleasant matter to make love to two women; but the consequences have to be reckoned with, and the reckoning, whether it come sooner or later, is a serious matter.

He had never loved Lady Eleanor, but he respected and liked her. He had certainly never loved Finetta, but he had liked her—liked her very much; and as he made his way through the silent streets his heart—it was by no means a hard one—was filled with pity and remorse.

"It was playing it very rough to go and tell her that I should have to cut her, that she wasn't fit company for me any longer, but what else could I do? I couldn't cut her without a word, without saying 'Good-by,'" he mused. "And how well she took it. No scene! no fuss! no reproaches!" It was well that he was unable to see Finetta at that moment; or perhaps it would have been better for him if he could. "She bore it like a brick. She is a brick! Most women of her class would have raised a duse of a row, and made it hot for me all round. Yes, Fin's behaved well. What a fool I have been! What fools we men all are! Why did I want to strike up a friendship with Finetta of the Diadem? And yet that's scarcely the fair way to look at it, for in a way she's as good as I am. And she'd have gone a hundred miles to do me a service; yes, and have shared her last penny with me. I know that! Poor Fin! Thank Heaven, it's over! I'll begin a new life from to-night, please God. A life devoted to my darling. My darling! Heaven! It scarcely seems true that she is mine. I wonder whether she is asleep. Perhaps she is looking up at these small stars, and——. Yes, I hope she is thinking of me. Jove! It's like having a guardian angel all to one's self to be loved by such a woman as Leslie. I wish I were more worthy of her. I wish I'd met her years ago! What a time I seem to have wasted!"

He had forgotten Finetta long before he reached home, and was wrapped up heart and soul in Leslie, and looking with impatience toward the hour when he could return to Portmaris.

He would have gone back the next day, but the duke had asked him to do one or two things for him; and he, Yorke, was anxious to pay some bills.

He went out after breakfast, and his first call was at a grimy office in a dark and dingy court leading out of Lombard Street. This was the parlor of a certain money-lending spider called Levison, and Lord Yorke was not the first fly that had found its way into it.

Mr. Levison was a grimy man with a hooked nose and thick lips, an unctuous smile, and decidedly Israelite accent. He was dressed in the height of fashion, wore a scarlet necktie in which shone an enormous diamond horse-shoe pin, a thick gold cable albert across his waistcoat, and innumerable rings upon his fingers, which called unkind attention to the fact that the latter were dirty.

This young gentleman greeted Lord Yorke with a mixture of respect and familiarity which made Yorke—and most other persons—feel an almost irresistible longing to kick him.

"And 'ow's your lordship?" said Mr. Levison, with a smile that stretched his flexible lips from ear to ear. "It ain't often we see you in the city, my lord; more's the pity for the city!" And he laughed and rubbed his hands. "What can I have the pleasure of doin' for your lordship? A little accommodation, I s'pose, eh?"

Yorke shook his head.

"Thanks, no, Mr. Levison," he said.

Mr. Levison appeared to be surprised.

"No? Oh, come now, my lord! Not want a little money? You're joking!"

"Strange as it may seem, I am serious," said Yorke as pleasantly as he could. "I don't want any money; in fact, I've come to take up that bill for two hundred and fifty pounds."

And he took out his pocket-book, in which were lying snugly the bank-notes for which he had cashed the duke's check.

Now, it is generally and not erroneously supposed that a Jew is always ready and glad to receive money; but Mr. Levison, singular to relate, looked neither ready nor glad. He stared at Yorke with widely opened eyes, and his face grew first red and then pale.

"You don't mean to say that you want to pay off that two hundred and fifty, my lord?" he said at last and in a tone almost of dismay.

"Startles you, doesn't it?" said Yorke, with a smile, for the Jew's consternation amused him. "It is rather an unexpected and extraordinary proceeding on my part, I'll admit; but——. Get the bill, Levison," and he began to separate the notes.

The Jew gazed at them, and then up at the handsome, careless face, and lastly at the ground.

"Look here, my lord," he said, thickly. "There really ain't any neshesity for you to go and inconvenience yourself, there ain't, indeed! Besides," he had turned to the grimy desk and consulted a grimy account book, "the bill ain't due! There's no call to pay it for some time yet."

"I know, at least I thought so," said Yorke, carelessly; "but I've got some money, and I thought I'd like to clear off something of what I owe you. Why!" and he laughed, "you don't seem inclined to take it. What's the matter? You haven't—" his face grew grave, "you haven't parted with the bills to any one else, Levison?"

Mr. Levison's oily face grew almost pale—say yellow.

"What! Me go and part with the bills of a customer like you! Not me, my lord! 'Tain't likely! I know better what's due to a swell like yourlordship."

"Very well, then," said Yorke. "Take my money, and let me have it, please."

"Yesh, yesh, certainly. If your lordship insists; but upon my sacred honor, I'd rather lend you another two-fifty than——. Well, well!" And he went to a safe and fumbled in his pocket.

"Tut, tut!" he exclaimed. "Blessed if I haven't left my keys at my brother's. Excuse me half a minute, will you, my lord? 'Ave a glass of sherry and a smoke while you're waiting——."

"No, no, thanks," said Yorke, who had once been prevailed upon to taste Mr. Levison's sherry, and had smelled the cigars while Mr. Levison had been smoking them. "Look sharp, my cab is waiting."

"Not more than 'arf a minute," said Mr. Levison, and he darted out, down the street, and full pelt into Messrs. Rawlings and Duncombe.

Ralph Duncombe, cool, grave, collected, a contrast to the flurried Israelite, looked up from his writing-table.

"Mishter Dunkombe, sir!" gasped Levison. "Here's Lord Horchester come to take up that bill of two-fifty. Wonderful, ain't it? Let's have it sharp. Moses! I wouldn't have him know I'd sold it to you for twice the money, and he 'arf suspects something a'ready."

Ralph Duncombe looked down at the letter he was writing; finished it, as if he had scarcely heard, then drew a book toward him, looked at it, and said:

"The bill isn't due. Why should Lord Auchester want to pay money before it is wanted?"

"'Ow do I know? Mad, p'raps! Anyhow, he does!"

Ralph Duncombe thought a moment, then he pushed the book from him, and looked straight at the anxious face before him.

"He cannot have the bill," he said.

Levison gasped.

"What?"

"He cannot have it. It suits me to stick by it till it is due."

"Oh, Mishter Dunkombe, sir! What's the meaning of that? What am I to say to him?"

"A mere whim on my part—perhaps," said Ralph Duncombe, coolly, impassively. "What are you to say? Say anything. Offer to lend him more money. I will take any bill he gives you. Good-morning."

He struck the gong standing at his elbow, and Levison, feeling too bewildered to expostulate or argue, was shown out.

He went back slowly, wiping the perspiration from his face. If it were known that he had parted with Lord Auchester's bills he would probably get a bad name with the other 'swells,' and lose half of them as customers; his business would be ruined!

He forced a grin as he entered the office, and threw up his hands with a beautiful gesture of amazement.

"Heresh a go, my lord!" he exclaimed. "Brother's gone off to see a client in the country, and took them confounded keys of mine with him. But there, it don't matter for a day or two, does it? I'll send the bill, or call on your lordship——."

Yorke put his pocket-book back.

"Very well," he said. "Mind, I want to pay the money—while I've got it. You see?"

The Jew grinned.

"I see; before it melts; eh, my lord? But there, as I said, why pay at all? Why not let me lend you——."

Yorke shook his head and laughed.

"No, thanks, Mr. Levison. I don't mean to trouble you in that way again, if I can help it. Good-morning." And with a pleasant nod he went out of the grimy parlor, leaving the spider staring after him with unfeigned surprise.

"Don't want to borrow any more money!" he gasped. "Why, what in the name of Moses has come to him. He—he must be going off his 'ead!"

Yorke dismissed the little incident from his mind, guessing nothing of its significance, or the effect it would have on his future, and had himself driven to Bond Street.

He had commenced the morning by doing his duty—or trying to do it—and now he was going to reward himself by buying a present for Leslie.

He had pondered over what he should get, and had at first, naturally, thought of a ring; but he had remembered that she could not wear it without attracting notice and question, and had decided on a locket.

The man showed him some, and Yorke selected a plain one with the initial 'Y' prettily worked in bas-relief.

While he was paying for it, the shopman, who knew him quite well, brought forward a tray of diamond ornaments.

"The newest designs, my lord," he said.

Yorke shook his head, but even as he did so Finetta flashed across his mind. He looked at the bundle of notes; he had plenty of money; she had behaved remarkably well; she deserved a present, a parting gift; he would give her one.

He knew Finetta's passion for diamonds, and comforted himself with the reflection—a wrong one, as we know—that they would console her for the loss of him.

He was not long in choosing—not half as long as he had been in selecting Leslie's simple locket—and purchased a pendant. It cost him a hundred and thirty pounds.

"Shall I send them, my lord?" asked the man.

"No," said York. "I'll take 'em. Put them up, singly, in a box. I'm going to send them through the post."

The man inclosed them in a couple of wooden boxes, and bowed Lord Auchester out.

York went home, and straight to a drawer in which he kept odd things, and after some amount of rummaging found a *carte de visite* portrait of himself. He sat down, lit a cigar, and, as neatly as he could, cut out the head of the portrait and fitted it in the locket; wrote on a slip of paper, "From Yorke," and laid them aside.

Then he took a sheet of paper, and dashed off in the charming scrawl which boys acquire at Eton—and never lose—the following note:

> "DEAR FIN.—Will you accept the inclosed and wear it for the sender's sake, and in remembrance of the many delightful times we have spent together? I thought of you nearly all the way home last night—it was awfully late!—and shall never forget how good you have always been to me. Think of me sometimes when you wear this trifle, and don't think too unkindly!"
>
> "Yours,
>
> "YORKE."

It was a foolish note. But he would be a wise man who could write a wise one under such circumstances. Of course, a wise one wouldn't have written at all; but Yorke was not famous for prudence.

He laid this note beside the beautiful diamond pendant, wrapped, like the locket, in tissue paper, and was putting them in their respective boxes when Fleming came in.

"Lord Vinson, my lord," he said.

Yorke looked up with a shade of annoyance on his face.

"Oh——. Ask Lord Vinson to wait a moment," he said, hurriedly. "There's a midday post for the country, isn't there?"

"Yes, my lord," said Fleming. "Can I help your lordship?" for Yorke was hunting about for string and sealing wax.

"No! Yes. Here, wrap these boxes up in thickish paper, and seal the string. Mind! This, No. 1, goes in this one, and that, No. 2, in that! Understand?"

"Yes, my lord," said Fleming, and no doubt he thought he did. But when he brought them back from the side table at which he had been packing them, and Lord Yorke asked him which was No. 1, Fleming, the usually careful and correct, handed him No. 2!

And so it happened that when, a few minutes later, Fleming walked off with them to the post-office, the locket with the portrait, but with Finetta's letter, was directed to Finetta, and the diamond pendant to Leslie!

CHAPTER XVII.

A WORD OF WARNING.

To Leslie the days seemed to go by like a dream during Yorke's absence. She thought of him every hour, but she had yet scarcely realized all that had happened to her.

If Francis Lisle had not been utterly unlike the ordinary run of parents, he would not have failed to see the change that had come over her; but he was too absorbed in his painting to notice the difference; and, indeed, if Leslie had appeared at breakfast in a domino and mask, or sat during the meal with an umbrella up, he would very likely have failed to see anything extraordinary in the occurrence; and it rather suited him than otherwise that Leslie should sit beside him perfectly silent, with her hands folded in her lap, eyes fixed on vacancy, with a dreamy smile on her lips.

But if Francis Lisle was blind, the duke was not.

His keen eyes noted the change in the expression of the lovely face, the soft light of a newly born joy in the gray eyes, and he guessed the cause.

"Like the rest!" he thought, with the bitter cynicism produced by his pain. "Like the rest! Well, it will afford me a little amusement; it will be a *petite comedie* played for my special benefit."

And yet at times, when he was free from pain, and he looked up at Leslie as she stood beside his chair, he felt doubtful and uncertain as to the accuracy of his judgment of her.

"She has the eyes of an angel," he muttered, when they were together one morning, the second after Yorke's departure for London. "One would say that they were the clear windows of a soul as pure as a child's."

His muttering was almost audible, and Leslie, awakened by it from a dream, bent down to him, and asked:

"What did you say, Mr. Temple?"

"I was saying—and thinking—that you are very good-natured to keep a crusty, irritable invalid company on such a delightful morning."

"Did you say all that?" she said, with a soft laugh.

"Well, if I didn't say it, I thought it," he responded. "You must find it dull work, but you are used to sacrificing yourself for others, are you not?" and he glanced at the painter who was at work at a little distance on the beach.

"It is not much of a sacrifice to stay with those one likes," she said, half absently.

The duke looked up at her sharply, and yet with a touch of color on his face.

"Thank you. I am to take it that you rather like me than otherwise, Miss Leslie?"

She blushed, and eyed him with sweet gravity.

"I should be very ungrateful if I did not," she said. And mentally she added, "And how could I help liking you; you are his friend?"

"I see," he said. "Well, it is very kind of you to keep me company. I should have missed my cousin—the duke—very much, if you had not been here. I am afraid mine is dull society after his, and that you miss the pleasant drives and sails."

"They were very pleasant, yes," she admitted, a little confusedly.

How hard it was that she should be obliged to deceive this kind-hearted friend of Yorke's, and how she longed for the time when he and her father should know her and Yorke's blissful secrets, when all concealment should be at an end, and her great happiness proclaimed. And yet it was sweet, this secret of theirs; it seemed to make their love more precious and sacred.

"Yes," said the duke. "Yorke is capital company. He is a great favorite wherever he goes."

"Yes," she murmured.

"He's so light-hearted," went on the duke. "And light-hearted people are extremely rare nowadays; but after all it isn't very much to his credit; I mean that it is easy to be joyous when you are young, in perfect health, and are ——," he paused a second, "a duke."

"Are dukes so much happier than other people?" she said, with a faint smile.

He winced. She had unconsciously struck home.

"No," he said, laconically. "Most of those I know are very much less happy than the rest of mankind, but it is different with the Duke of Rothbury. He is, as I say, young and in splendid health——," his lips moved and he sighed cynically, "but if he weren't he would still be very popular and always welcome everywhere."

"Why?" said Leslie, looking at him with her guileless eyes.

He met their glance for a moment, then lowered his keen, suspicious ones.

"Is it acting?" he asked himself, and he gnawed at his lip.

"Why? Because he is a duke. If he were old and ugly, and—and twisted as I am, he would still be run after by all sorts and conditions of men—and women," he added, but in a lower voice, as if he were half ashamed of his cynicism.

Leslie understood, and her face flushed for a moment; but it was not with guilt, but the indignation of a pure-hearted girl.

"You mean that they—women—would pretend to like him because of his rank?" she said, quietly, but with gentle gravity.

"That's what I meant," he assented, eyeing her attentively. "There isn't a woman in the world whose heart doesn't leap at the thought of becoming a duchess."

"It is not true!" she said, her eyes flashing down at him with purest indignation. "It is—but you are only speaking in jest, Mr. Temple," and she smiled at the warmth she had been hurried into.

He looked hard at her.

"I am not jesting," he said; "but stating the solemn, shameful fact."

She gazed down at him almost pityingly.

"Ah, you do not know women at all," she said. "No," with a shake of her head, as he opened his lips. "You may know a great many, and they may be very great ladies, and a few of them may be as worldly as you say they are, but not many. I will not believe that."

He fingered his chin with restless fingers, and looked from right to left.

"If she is not acting then—then she is on the brink of a great misery," he thought. "If I could only believe her!"

"You mean that it would make no difference to you whether a man were a duke or not?" he said.

Her face went rather pale.

"Yes, it would make a difference," she said in a low voice. "I would rather not make the acquaintance of a duke, or any one so far above me in rank; and there are thousands of women who feel the same."

"Oh," he says, curtly. "I never was fortunate enough to meet any. Seeing that that is your feeling, it was very kind of you to honor me—I mean my cousin," he corrected himself sharply, "with your friendship, Miss Leslie," and he smiled.

Leslie's cheek burned, and she turned her face from his keen eyes.

"An actress," he muttered. "And yet I'll give her a word of warning, though she doesn't deserve it."

"Did the duke happen to say when he was coming back, Miss Leslie?"

"No," she said. "He said that he might be two or three days."

He laughed.

"I shouldn't be surprised if Portmaris never saw him again."

He saw Leslie start slightly, then a faint smile flashed over her face, a smile of perfect faith. Yorke not come back! She remembered his last word to her. I shall count every moment while I'm away from you, dearest, every moment till I am back with you.

"My cousin is rather erratic," said the duke, casually and indifferently. "He is a very nice fellow, good-hearted and the rest of it; but—well, a little fickle; at least, that's the character the ladies give him."

"Fickle," she said, smiling still.

"Y-es," he said, languidly. "What's that song in 'The Grand Duchess,' 'A butterfly flits from flower to flower?' One mustn't blame the butterfly, you know. 'It's its nature to,' as Dr. Watts says; and, like the butterfly, Yorke is what is called very susceptible. He is always falling in love——."

She moved slightly, and the smile died away from her lips; but the clear eyes met his steadily, unflinchingly.

"And, fortunately, falling out of it again. He's like the man in the play who was in the habit of proposing to some woman every day; and if she accepted him he rode off, and she saw him no more, and if she refused him he asked her to be a sister, an aunt, or something of that kind, and rode off just as easily."

She opened her lips slowly.

"I thought you were a friend of the Duke of Rothbury's, Mr. Temple?" she said, in a very low voice.

The duke flushed.

"Eh? Oh, I see. You think it very base of me to speak ill of him behind his back?"

"That's what I meant," she assented, gravely.

"Oh, but the world wouldn't consider that I had spoken at all ill of him."

"The world!" she said. "How wicked and heartless it must be, this world of yours, Mr. Temple!"

"It is," he said, curtly. "As heartless as a flint."

"Or as the Duke of Rothbury, if he were what you have painted him," she said very softly.

"You don't believe me, then?" he asked, looking up at her from under his thick brows.

She shook her head.

"Not the very least!" she said, actually smiling.

"You forget that I have known him all his life, and that you have only known him five minutes!"

She still smiled.

"But in five minutes one may know——." She stopped, and her face flushed, and the tears arose to her eyes. "No, I don't believe it," she said, her voice tremulous. "There may be some men who are as false and heartless as you say, but not the Duke of Rothbury."

He looked at her gravely, almost pityingly.

"Don't be too sure of that, Miss Leslie!" he said, with a touch of warning in his tone. "He is a good fellow, a charming companion, but——." He was stopped by the expression of pain which shone in her eyes.

"Oh, please let us talk of something else!" she said, quickly. "See, here is the postman."

"I hope he has brought my medicine," said the duke. But the postman, tugging at his cap, handed a small parcel to Leslie.

"For me!" she said, with surprise. "Why, what can it be? Are you sure it is for me and not papa? It is like one of the boxes they send the colors in."

"A sample of a new scent or pearl powder," said the duke, leaning back languidly.

"Why should they send it to me?" she said, laughingly.

She tore off the outer paper as she spoke, and with the pleasant excitement which is always produced by the receipt of a parcel whose contents are unknown, she opened the little wooden box.

The duke heard an exclamation, a cry of amazement, of admiration, of delight, and looked up sharply.

"Is it scent or pearl powder?" he asked, with an amused smile.

She looked at him as if she scarcely heard him. Her eyes were shining, her lips apart.

"It is neither," she said, and without another word, with the little box fast clasped in her hand, ran toward the house.

CHAPTER XVIII.

STRANGE TALK.

She ran up the street and into the house, and up the stairs to her own room, her heart beating fast. Locking the door first, she opened the little wooden box, and took out the pendant, a glimpse of which she had caught as she stood beside the duke.

But though the glitter of the diamonds pleased her as it will every woman, the few words in his handwriting were more precious to her than the costly gems.

Can any one ever tell what her first love letter means to a young girl who is in love with the writer?

Leslie gazed at one line in Yorke's awful scrawl as a Moslem might regard a verse from the Koran, and not once or twice only did her sweet lips kiss the scrap of paper. Then she examined the pendant more minutely, and though her experience of jewelry was of a very limited character, she knew that the gift was an expensive one.

"It is too good, too grand for me," she said, and yet with a sensation of pleasure in its worth. "I should have been as pleased if he had sent me a bunch of flowers bought in the London streets. But, oh, how good of him! And, after all, it is not too grand for his wife. He would think nothing too rare, too costly for her. Oh, my love, my love! If I were only more worthy of you!"

She found a piece of ribbon and put the pendant on it, and hung it around her white throat, and the fire and glitter of the diamonds almost startled her.

"It is just as well that I may not wear it openly—yet," she said to herself with a soft, shy laugh. "I should feel as if every one was staring at me. I wonder whether I shall ever get used to wearing beautiful things like this? He would say 'Yes,' but I feel now as if I never should be able to do so without being conscious of my splendor. But I must hide you for the present, you beautiful thing," and she arranged the pendant so that it nestled over her heart, and buttoned her dress over it, and there it seemed to glow with a soft, consuming fire, as if it knew that it had come from the hand of the man she loved.

Several times during the day she stole up to her room and drew the pendant from its hiding-place, and looked at it with glistening eyes; and if Francis Lisle had not been blind to everything but his awful pictures, he could not but have been startled by the expression on her face after one of these visits.

But if her father was blind the children were not, and as they clustered around her they looked up at her, frank wonder in their wide-open orbs, and one mite lisped:

"What makth 'oo sthmile so, Mith Lethlie. Have 'oo been a dood girl, and got a penny diven 'oo?"

"Yes, I've got a penny given to me, Trottie," said Leslie, taking the child up in her lap and kissing it. "Such a beautiful shining penny."

"Thow it me," said the little one.

But Leslie put her hand on her bosom with a jealous smile.

"No, no; I can't show it even to you, Trottie," she said; "not to any one. And I am not going to buy anything with it, but going to keep it as long as ever I live."

She did not see Mr. Temple again that day, and did not even think of him or the hard, unjust things he had said of Yorke; and if she had, it would only have been to laugh at them. Yorke fickle and false! With that gift of his rising and falling on her heart, she would not have believed an angel if he had come to tell her anything against her beloved.

The duke missed her all that afternoon, missed her very much. He had got used to having her standing or sitting by his chair, and her sweet, low-pitched voice had been as a soothing balm in his moments of pain. And yet he could not wholly trust her, or believe that she was better and less mercenary and self-seeking than the rest of her sex.

His keen eyes had seen the change in her face when he had spoken of Yorke, and he had told himself that what he had prophesied was coming true; this artless-looking girl with the clear, guileless eyes was already aiming at a ducal coronet. It did not occur to him that she might love Yorke for himself alone; or, if it did, he put the thought away from him and hugged his old cynical mistrust of her sex.

The next day passed and no Yorke appeared, but on the morning of the following one he got into the train at Paddington on his way to Portmaris.

As he did so, with a sigh of relief and expectant happiness, he noticed a tall lady dressed in black with a veil over her face pass his carriage and enter the next, and he was struck in an absent kind of way by the grace of her figure; but she disappeared from his mind the moment she passed the window, and he gave himself up to picturing his meeting with Leslie.

A few hours, and then——. He lit a cigar, and stretched his long legs on to the opposite seat and thought.

The few days he had been absent from her had taught this young man how very completely he was in love, and he was actually asking himself why they should not be married at once!

"What's the use of waiting?" he mused; "I shall never be better off. We might just as well be married now——." Then a reflection cut across his roseate visions, and, as Hamlet says, 'gave him pause;' he was fearfully in debt, and though Mr. Levison hadn't turned up with the bill, and seemed more inclined to lend him more money than take any from him, he, Yorke, knew the reason. The money lenders all depended upon his marrying an heiress, and he knew—and his face flushed as he thought of it—that they one and all expected him to marry Lady Eleanor Dallas, and relied upon it.

The moment they heard that he had married what they and the rest of the world, in its language of contempt, would call a pauper, they would swoop down upon him like a flock of kites, and——.

He sat up in the railway carriage and rubbed his forehead.

Couldn't he ask Dolph to lend—give—him the money to pay his debts? Well, he could ask him, and no doubt the duke would do it—if he approved of Yorke's marrying Leslie. But would he approve? Somehow Yorke felt doubtful.

"I might try him," he thought, and he pondered over it until the train reached Northcliffe, and then suddenly an alternative course occurred to him, an idea which flashed upon him suddenly, and sent the blood rushing to his face.

Why shouldn't he and Leslie be married secretly? They might go away, leave England, and settle down in some Continental place quietly until he had screwed enough money out of his income to pay his debts, and then they might proclaim their marriage to the whole world.

His heart beat hopefully, and he was so absorbed in his plans and schemes that he did not notice that the tall lady in black got out at Northcliffe; indeed, he could not have seen her unless he had looked back— which he did not do—for she did not get out until the rest of the passengers had alighted, and then kept in the background until the station was clear.

Yorke got a fly at once and had himself driven to Portmaris, and as the ancient vehicle rattled down the street he looked eagerly at the windows of Sea View. But Leslie was out, and with a little pang of disappointment Yorke ran up the stairs of Marine Villa.

The duke was sitting in his chair, his head resting on his hands, and Yorke saw at once that it was a 'bad afternoon' with the invalid. The duke raised his head, with a transient smile of welcome on his pale face.

"Well, Yorke, back again," he said, holding out his hand. "I was just on the point of telling Grey to pack up."

Yorke started.

"What, tired of Portmaris already, Dolph?" he said.

The duke sighed.

"About five minutes is long enough for me anywhere. There is only one place I shall not get weary of—the grave. But this isn't a very cheerful greeting, Yorke. What's the news?"

"Oh, nothing! I saw Lang"—this was the duke's agent—"and told him what you wanted done, and——."

"Oh, thanks!" said the duke, indifferently; "and you have had a pleasant time, I hope? Did you see Eleanor?"

Yorke nodded.

"Yes, oh, yes; had luncheon there. She's very well. What a lovely sunset to-night! 'Pon my word, this is a jolly little place."

"Jolly, is it?" said the duke, eyeing him keenly.

"Hem! Well, perhaps it's jollier when you are here. It's been dull enough without you, any way. As I said, we have missed you very much, young man."

"'We'? Meaning you and Grey?" said Yorke, standing at the window and watching the opposite ones anxiously.

The duke smiled grimly.

"Well, I dare say Grey has missed you; but I was thinking, when I spoke, of—Miss Lisle."

"Oh, Miss Lisle," said Yorke, flushing like a schoolgirl. "I—I hope she is all right."

"Yes, I think so. The fact is, I have not seen very much of her since yesterday morning, when in the course of conversation I ventured to hint that your grace ——."

Yorke started.

"Your grace was not quite perfect."

Yorke laughed uneasily, and kept his back carefully turned to the duke.

"She seemed to think that you were more divine than human, and put out her claws in your defense like a woman—and a cat."

A spasm of pain shot through him and he groaned faintly, and so, though all Yorke's soul arose in horror at hearing his beloved likened to a cat, he held his tongue.

"In short," continued the duke, wearily, "I was quite correct in my surmise as to what would take place. The girl is dying to marry your grace and become a duchess."

Yorke bit his lip.

"It's time that bit of nonsense came to an end," he said, with angry impatience. "I didn't like it from the first, Dolph, and I like it now less than ever."

The duke waved his hand with tired indifference.

"It was an idiotic idea," he said; "but it has served my purpose. I have been left alone here, and the rest and quiet have done me good. You can tell the Lisles, and whom else you like, at once if you choose. Stay," he said; "wait till to-morrow evening. I shall have gone by that time."

"Gone?" said Yorke. "You mean going?"

"Yes," said the duke, impatiently; "I am tired of it. I'll go and hide myself at Rothbury, I think; and I think you had better go, too."

"Why?" asked Yorke, but his voice faltered slightly.

"Well," responded the duke, grimly, "I've an idea—don't trouble to contradict me, it isn't worth while—that Miss Leslie has succeeded in making an impression on your grace——."

"And that would be such an awful calamity, wouldn't it?" said Yorke, feeling his way.

The duke laughed cynically.

"No, I suppose not. You would ride away, like the man in the ballad, and leave her weeping. Not that the youngest and most unsophisticated girls weep much now, I believe; they dry their tears and look out for the next man."

"Dolph, for a man who loves and respects women—and I know you do——."

"Oh, do you?" snarled the duke, or, rather, the demon of pain that had got possession of him.

"Yes," said Yorke. "For one who loves and respects them, you talk strangely."

"Well, well. We don't want to squabble about women in general or this young woman in particular. All I mean to say is that, though usually I think they are well punished for their mercenary scheming, I've a sneaking fondness and pity for Leslie Lisle, and I don't want you to let her think that she has a chance of being a duchess. In short—well, of course, you have been flirting with her; you always do, you know. Well, leave her alone, and go back to London." He sighed. "That's good advice. We'll let her off this time."

Yorke stood motionless, with stern face.

"If I were the duke I have been masquerading as," he said, "I could not find a better woman or one——."

"More fitted by nature to adorn, etc. I know," interrupted the duke with peevish irritation. "But, unfortunately, you aren't the duke—I wish to Heaven you were, or anybody were but I!—and as you are not, and only Yorke Auchester, with not enough to keep yourself upon, to say nothing of a wife, you can't afford to do more than flirt with her. There! The subject is played out. You have got to marry Eleanor Dallas, my dear fellow. She is made for you, and you will be as happy as a man ever can be in this beastliest of all beastly worlds."

"You dispose of me very easily," said Yorke, his throat dry, his eyes flashing, but his back still turned.

"Yes, because I care for you, and am anxious for your future and happiness."

"Thanks," said Yorke, in a softer voice. "But—well, we are arguing. Suppose I do not care for Eleanor?"

The duke laughed quietly.

"My dear Yorke, no man could be loved by such a beautiful creature as Eleanor and, marrying her, help falling in love with her within the first fortnight. Oh, how tired I am! Don't let us spoil the pleasure I get out of your return by wrangling. Do as I say; leave this little girl with the gray eyes and dark hair—what eyes they are, by the way!"—and he sighed—"leave her alone. You can't marry her, and though you could punish her for wanting to marry you by flirting with her—well, I don't somehow want to see her punished. Seriously, Yorke, I ask you to do this as—as a favor."

Yorke left the window.

"You release me from my promise, from our arrangement regarding the title?" he said, quietly, and with a tone of decision in his voice which the duke would have remarked if he had not been in such intense pain.

"To-morrow—not till to-morrow," he said. "I'll tell Grey we are going to-morrow, and then, just before we go, you can tell the Lisles, explain the reason—anything. I care nothing. I shall be out of reach of the fuss the story will make even in this outlandish place."

"Good," said Yorke, and he drew a long breath. "I'm going out for a stroll—dinner as usual, I suppose?" And the duke heard him going down the stairs two steps at a time.

The duke's few decided, querulous words had fired Yorke. He was to marry Lady Eleanor, was he? Ha-ha! He laughed almost grimly. There was only one woman in the world he would marry, and, if she would have him, he would make her his wife at once.

He strode down the street, and on to the quay, and at a little distance on the beach saw Mr. Lisle, painting as usual.

He looked up impatiently as Yorke came crashing over the stones, and accosted him.

"Oh, how do you do—how do you do, your grace?" he said, in his thin voice, and with a hasty glance at him as if he begrudged every moment from his picture.

"Is—is Miss Lisle out with you?" said Yorke, trying to speak with nothing warmer in his voice than conventional politeness.

"Leslie?" looking around absently. "Yes, she was here a moment ago; but she has wandered off somewhere." And his manner and tone plainly added:

"And I wish to goodness you'd wander off, too."

"How is the picture getting on?" asked Yorke, looking at the daub which Lisle had painted over and over again, making it worse at each stroke.

"Very well—very well, I think," was the reply. "You like it?" and a faint red came into the pale thin cheeks. Somehow Yorke fancied that they had grown thinner and paler during the last few days. "I am going to make a masterpiece of it. I am working hard, very hard. Isn't it very hot and close this morning? I have a stupid headache——. Yes. Would you mind standing out of the light? Thank you."

Yorke left him; he knew it would be of no use to ask the dreamer in which direction Leslie had gone.

"Poor old fellow," he thought. "We'll take him with us, and look after him together. Give him his painting tools, and he'll be happy enough!"

He walked along the beach and on to the cliffs and suddenly he came upon Leslie. She was sitting in a cleft of the rocks, a book on her lap, but it was lying face downward, and she was looking out to sea. He stole behind her, and bent down and kissed her. She started, but not violently, and the blood rushed to her face.

"Yorke!" was all she said, but all her love, her joy on his return breathed in the single word.

He took both her hands, and sat down beside her.

"I startled you, dearest!" he said.

How lovely she looked! How sweet, and, ah, how pure and good! Not Eleanor herself could look more refined, more *spirituelle* than this love of his—his Leslie.

"No!" she said, with a faint smile, and a little shyness in her voice and eyes. "I ought to have been startled, but I was not. Perhaps it was because I was thinking of you. When did you come back?"

"A few minutes ago, dearest," he said. "Has it seemed long to you? I thought, perhaps, that you would have forgotten me."

She smiled at him.

"Well, I might have done so," she said, with delicious archness; "but you provided against that, did you not?"

He did not understand for a moment, then he laughed.

"You got it all right?"

"Ah, yes," she said, with a little sigh of gratitude and content. "I wish you could have seen me when it came! I was standing beside Mr. Temple when the postman brought it, and I cried out—well, like a schoolgirl!"

He looked at her, wrapt in delight at herdelight.

"It was a happy thought of mine, then?" he said.

"Yes, but why did you send me so grand a present," she said in a low voice. "Anything would have done; but that——." She laughed and colored. "It was too rich, too costly for such a simple person as I am!"

He laughed. So she thought the plain little locket rich and costly. What would she have considered the diamond pendant he had sent to Finetta? "God bless my darling! My modest pearl!" he thought.

"And you were pleased with it?" he said. "It occurred to me that you might like it; for a minute or two I feared that you might consider me conceited in sending it, that a ring——."

She shook her head.

"It is beautiful—beautiful!" she said. "Its only fault is that it is too good, too costly. The merest trifle would have served to tell me that you had not—forgotten me! And, indeed, I did not need anything."

"You trusted me so completely, dearest?" he said.

"Yes," she said simply, with a faint wonder in her voice at the earnestness in his.

"You trusted me," he said, as earnestly as before. "And how if I were to ask you to trust me still, to trust me in a greater degree, Leslie?"

She looked at him, still smiling.

"What is it?" she asked; and the question was a good reply to his.

"It is just this," he said, taking her hand in both his and holding it tightly. "See, dearest, I hesitate to tell you—it is so much to ask you! And the worst of it is that I cannot give you the reason——."

Her face paled, but she looked at him bravely.

"Are—are you going to leave me again? If you must go——."

The love in her voice, in her eyes, made his heart actually ache.

"Leave you?" he said. "Well, yes; but it will be only for a few hours a day, if —if you consent to do what I am going to ask you?"

"What is it?" she asked, still calmly.

"I want you to marry me—at once, Leslie?" he said in a low voice, and almost solemnly.

She started, and her hand quivered in his.

"Marry—you—at once!" she whispered, her bosom heaving, her long dark lashes trembling.

"You are frightened, dearest?" he said, drawing her nearer to him.

She was silent a moment.

"No," she replied in a whisper, "not frightened, I think, but——."

"And that isn't all," he said almost desperately. "I want our marriage to be a secret one."

She started now, and drew her hand from his, turning her pale face to him with almost pained surprise.

"Listen, Leslie," he said, getting her hand back again. "There are reasons why it is necessary—do you understand, my darling, necessary—that no one should know of our engagement. The other day, when—when I told you I loved you, and asked you to be my wife, I did not think of those reasons; I didn't think of anything but you. But they came home to me when I was in London. It sounds strange, almost incredible——."

"No, not incredible," she murmured.

"You would believe anything I told you, you mean?" he asked, with bated breath.

Her clear eyes met his with her assent in them as plainly as if she had spoken.

"My darling! And I cannot tell you——. But, Leslie, in a word, I am not free —I mean that I am not my own master——."

A faint smile chased the slightly troubled look from her face.

"It sounds so strangely," she said. "A duke and not your own master——."

He reddened, and his eyes dropped before hers.

"Heaven and earth!" broke from him almost passionately. "Leslie—I beg of you not to—to call me that again——."

"Not——." She looked at him questioningly.

"Yes. Yes—I do beg of you, dearest. Not, we will say, for another day. After that——," he drew a long breath, and brushed the hair from his forehead impatiently. "I will explain then why I ask you, dearest. I will explain everything. Don't—don't—be frightened, dearest! Don't think there is any real mystery! You will—yes, you will laugh, when you hear what it is!"

"Shall I?" she says, trustfully. "I am not frightened, I am not even—I think—very curious——."

"Oh, my darling! And you do not even ask me why this secrecy, this concealment, is necessary?"

"No," she says, after a pause, and placing her other hand in his. "If you say so I am content. I suppose——," she averts her face a little—"I suppose you do not wish your people to know that—-that you are going to marry one so far beneath you, one so unfit to be a duchess——."

He stifles a groan.

"It is not that," he says. But for his promise to the duke he could tell her all. Tell her that he is not a duke with lands and gold galore, but a poor man so incumbered and crippled by debt that he dare not let it be known that he is not going to marry a fortune! "Leslie, I cannot tell you! I am not free to tell you, till—yes, to-morrow! Will you not trust me?"

Her breath comes fast for a moment as she looks out to sea, then she turns to him.

"I cannot but trust you," she says almost piteously. "I could not doubt you if I tried."

"My angel, my dearest!" he says, fervently, reverently. "You shall never regret having trusted me, never! Now, listen, Leslie! There is one person, of all others, who must not know what we are going to do—Mr. Temple."

"Mr. Temple?" she says, not suspiciously, not even curiously but with faint surprise.

"Yes," he says. "He suspects, or half-suspects, already that I love you. It must be kept from him. You will understand why when I tell you all—when I clear up the mystery. Now, see——." He stops and laughs. His face is flushed with excitement, and his eyes sparkling. "To-night I will go up to town——."

"To-night——," she breathes.

"Yes," he says. "There is no time to be lost—you will see that when you know all. To-morrow I will get a special license, and that same day you must come up to London——."

She trembles.

"Alone?" she asks in a still voice.

"No, no," he says. "You must persuade your father——. Stay! I will manage that! I will get a well-known dealer I know to wire to him; some question about his pictures, something that will bring him up."

She trembled still.

"The moment you arrive you must telegraph your address to me. I will tell you where to wire——." He takes out an old envelope, and writes:

"Lord Auchester——."

Then with an exclamation tears it up, and on another piece of paper, writes:

"YORKE,

"Dorchester Club,

"Pall Mall."

"Mind, dearest! Send the telegram at once, and at once I will come to you, and—the rest you must leave to me. You will?"

"I will!" she says, almost inaudibly, and as solemnly as ever marriage vow was whispered.

Her great love and trust overwhelm him, and something like tears—yes, tears—dim his bright eyes.

"My darling, if I ever forget your love and trust, your goodness to me, may Heaven forget me!" he says in a voice that makes her thrill. "I will make you happy, Leslie, happier than any woman ever was before! Every hour of my life——." His voice breaks. "Oh, my darling, what have I done that Heaven should send me such an angel!"

The tears are in her eyes now.

"I've made you cry!" he says. "Ah, I know! You are thinking of your father, Leslie!"

She starts guiltily. For the first time in her life, the life devoted to him, she has forgotten her father.

"Do not fret about him. He shall go with us; he shall belong as much to me as to you. What! do you think I would separate you——."

They sit hand in hand for—how long? At last he tears himself away.

"Remember, dearest!" are his last words. "Send to me directly—the moment—you reach London. And, Leslie, fear nothing! Why, when one thinks of it," and he laughs, "what is there to fear?"

He is gone at last. She stands and watches him as he makes his way—with many a backward glance—along the quay; then she sinks on to the rock again.

Her heart is throbbing, a mist is floating before her eyes; she cannot think, cannot see. So unconscious of everything around her is she that, when half an hour later the dark, graceful figure of a woman passes near her nook, she does not heed or notice it. She is in Love's land, and rapt in Love's dream.

CHAPTER XIX.

FINETTA'S WAY.

After a time Leslie got up, but she wanted to be alone a little longer; she felt that she could not talk even to her father just then; she wanted to be alone to think over all Yorke had told her. She walked a few yards toward the quay, and saw that Mr. Lisle was still painting; then she turned, and slowly paced in the direction of Ragged Point, which stretched out dark and sullen in the sunlight.

As she had said, not a doubt of Yorke's truth and honor cast a shadow over her happiness. If he said that it was necessary that they should be married at once and secretly, it must be so—it should be so! He was her lover, her master, her king. She had given herself to him absolutely; she trusted him because she could not help herself.

She had almost reached the point, and would have gone on, but she remembered that the tide was coming in, and that there would not be time to get round before the sea rose above the narrow ledge of rock at the foot of the cliffs, and she was turning back when she caught sight of something dark above a rock at the very foot of the point.

For a moment she thought it was a bird, then she saw that it was a hat—a woman's hat. Someone was sitting there. In an instant it struck her that it might be a stranger, unacquainted with the conformation of the coast line, and that if she sat there for a few minutes longer she would be unable to get back or to turn the point.

Leslie looked at the tide, and was startled to find that it had run up quicker than she had thought. There would be barely time to reach the woman behind the rock and warn her. She ran forward as quickly as she could and shouted at the top of her voice, but the voice of the incoming waves beating against the rocks drowned hers.

She looked round, hoping to see a boat or a fisherman, but no one was in sight; and she and the unknown, sitting there in all unconsciousness of her peril, were alone in the grim place.

Most women would have paused and thought of her own safety, but Leslie and selfishness had not yet made acquaintance, and she hurried on, running where there was a bare bit of sand, and scrambling over the rocks that lay in her path. At last she reached the one behind which the woman she had come to warn was sitting, and stood before her breathlessly.

"Oh, quick! Quick!" she cried pantingly. Then she stopped, and recoiled a little. It was a girl, seated in an attitude of weariness and lassitude, her elbows on her knees, her head bowed. Even in this first moment Leslie noted the grace and sorrowful abandon of the figure; but it was the uplifted face that made her recoil, for it was that of the woman she had seen below St. Martin's Tower—it was the woman who had sung the disreputable music-hall ditty.

There was no reckless gaiety in the face now, but a misery and despair so eloquent that even as she recoiled, Leslie's heart ached with pity forher.

The dark eyes looked at Leslie vacantly for a moment, then flashed with sudden anger.

"Who are you, and what do you want?" she asked, half sullenly, half defiantly.

Leslie flushed at the tone in which the greeting was conveyed.

"I—I saw you sitting here," she said quickly, and a little tremulously, for the dark face disquieted her, and inspired her with a vague uneasiness. "I saw you from the beach yonder, and I thought that perhaps you were astranger."

"I am a stranger. Yes, what of it?" said the woman, as sullenly and suspiciously as before.

"And you do not know that this is Ragged Point, and that the tide is coming up fast, very fast," said Leslie quickly.

"Is it? What does it matter?" was the dull response.

"Oh, do you not understand?" said Leslie earnestly. "When the tide comes up here, where you are sitting, you will not be able to go on or turn back. You see how the point stretches out?"

The dark eyes looked wearily to right and left.

"I see," she said. "No, I didn't know it. I don't know how long I've been sitting here." She looked up at the sky. "The tide comes up here, does it?"

"Yes, yes!" said Leslie hurriedly. "Pray come away at once!" for the girl had made no attempt to get up. "We have only just time to get round the point, even if we run. Come at once!" and in her eagerness she held out her hand to help her to rise.

The girl disregarded the outstretched hand, and rose wearily, sullenly.

"I suppose I should have been drowned if you had not seen me?" she remarked listlessly.

"Oh, I hope not; I hope not!" said Leslie. "But I am very glad I did see you. I only caught sight of the top of your hat. You had better take my hand. I am used to getting over the rocks and stones."

"I can get on all right," said the girl sullenly, refusing the proffered assistance. "I'm as young as you are, and as strong," she added, glancing out of the corners of her dark eyes at Leslie.

"I am glad you are strong," said Leslie gravely, as she looked at the swiftly, surely incoming sea; "for we shall have to run."

Her companion stopped and looked seaward too, and with a strange expression.

"Oh, why do you wait?" demanded Leslie. "Do you not understand that there is not a moment to lose?"

The girl laughed a reckless, miserable laugh, which was a grotesque reflection of the laugh which Leslie had heard on the tower when she had last seen her.

"I was thinking if it was worth while," she said moodily.

Leslie stared at her.

"Worth while!" she echoed unconsciously.

"Yes. I'm not sure it wouldn't be better and easier to stop here and let the water come up. It would save a lot of trouble." She laughed again.

With a faint shudder, Leslie turned away from the dark eyes and seized the speaker's arm.

"You must come at once!" she said firmly.

The woman drew back for a moment; then, as if yielding against her will, allowed Leslie to draw her forward.

They hurried over the rocks in silence for a moment or two, the waves splashing against their feet; then Leslie stopped and uttered an exclamation, her eyes fixed on the cliff before them, her face suddenly pale.

"What is the matter? Are we too late?" asked her companion dully and indifferently.

"Yes, we are too late!" replied Leslie in a low voice. Then she caught her breath and forced a smile. "Do not be frightened. We may get round the other way; the ledge of rock is wider there, but it is more difficult to get over. We must go back. Follow me."

She turned and sprang quickly from rock to rock, and her companion followed her example. They gained the spot where the girl had been sitting, but it was now covered by the sea, and they had to wade ankle deep.

Leslie caught the girl's hand.

"Hold fast!" she said in a quick whisper. "If we gain that point there, where the rock sticks out——."

Even as she spoke a spurt of foam covered the spot indicated, and the waves dashed over it. She stopped and looked round her, her face white and set.

"We are too late here, too," she said with a smothered sob. "Too late!" and she covered her face with her hands.

The other girl leant against the cliff and stared dully at the angry waves, creeping, creeping like some wild beast towards them.

"You mean we are going to die," she said in a low, harsh voice. "Going to die like rats in a hole. Well," and she shrugged her shoulders, "I don't care much, myself. You see, when you came up just now, I was wishing I was dead."

Leslie shuddered, and put up her hand as if to stop her. Death was too near to be spoken of so lightly.

"Yes, I was. You're shocked, I dessay. I'm sorry for you. It's a pity you didn't stop where you were. You're not tired of life, judging by your face."

"Tired of life!" panted Leslie; "oh, no, no!"

"So I should say," said the other sullenly. "So you don't understand what I mean, and what I feel?"

"No, I don't understand," said Leslie, scarcely knowing what she was saying. "But it is dreadful, dreadful to hear you, and at such a moment. Hah!" She broke off with an exclamation of horror, and drew her companion back close to the face of the cliff, for a wave had dashed at their feet and wet them to the waist.

"It's coming up pretty fast," said the girl. "It won't take long to——. Isn't there any chance for you? I don't care about myself."

Leslie screened her eyes with her hand.

"A boat might be passing," she said faintly. "Oh, to think that they are so near—that there are people just round that bend, who, if they knew—only knew!—would risk their lives to save us," and she sank at the foot of the cliff and hid her face in her hands.

"I'm sorry," said the other. "It's rough on you to lose your life for me, a stranger, too."

Leslie sprang up, her eyes wild with despair.

"We will not die!" she cried. "We will not! Do you hear? Oh, I cannot die; I cannot leave him—like this!" and she beat her hands together.

"You're thinking of your husband—who?" asked the other, eyeing her half pityingly. "It's always a man. That's where I've got the pull of you," and she laughed. "My man wouldn't care whether I lived or died. He's left me already."

The anguish in her voice, the reckless despair, went to Leslie's heart. She shuddered as she looked at the dark eyes.

"Left you!" she breathed. "Oh, now I understand! Ah, yes; I know now why you want to die."

"Yes," was the bitter response. "That's where we women are such fools. We care. Men don't. You think your husband, or sweetheart, or whoever he is, will break his heart for the loss of you!" she laughed mockingly. "Not he! They don't break their hearts so easily! He'll get over it and marry another woman almost before you're—cold in your grave, I was going to say."

Leslie shrank back from her as far as she could, and put her hands up to her ears.

"Oh, hush, hush!" she panted. "It is not true! It is wicked and false! I will not listen to you. Oh, forgive me!" she broke off, her indignation and horror softened by the misery on the white face and dark eyes staring so hopelessly at the angry sea. "How you must have suffered, how you must have loved him to be so wretched, so indifferent."

"Oh, yes, I loved him. I loved him—well, as much as you loved the man you're thinking of——."

"When—when did it happen—when did he leave you? Why? Tell me," said Leslie. "Let us talk—try and forget that it is coming nearer and nearer, that we have only a few minutes—"

"Yes, we haven't long," was the response. "I've been watching that rock there, almost in a line with us. You could see the top a moment ago; it's covered now. When did he leave me? Only a few nights ago. Why? The old story. He got tired of me, I suppose. Anyhow, he met someone else."

"And—and you were to have been his wife!" breathed Leslie pityingly. "And you loved him! Oh, how could he be so cruel, so heartless?"

The other looked down at her, and laughed harshly.

"Why, men are like that, all of them."

"No, no! Not all! They are not all so base, so vile."

"You think so. You wait! Perhaps your turn will come. But I forgot," she laughed again. "Your man won't have the chance to leave you—there, I beg your pardon," for Leslie had shrunk away from her. "Don't mind me or what I say. I'm half out of my mind. I've had no sleep since—since he left me, and I've come a long journey, and eaten nothing. Yes, I'm half mad. I was a fool to follow him. I ought to have stayed at home; but I've got my punishment."

"You came after him? He is here, then?" asked Leslie in a pitying whisper, watching the waves as she spoke.

"Yes," said she; then with a sigh, "Yes, and I've seen him. I meant to speak to him, to—to—try and get him back; but my heart failed me, and I crept out here to be alone. It wasn't only to see him that I came. I wanted to see her."

"Her?" repeated Leslie, half absently.

"Yes. The woman that stole him from me. But it doesn't matter now. Nothing matters to us two, does it? How much longer?"

The question almost drove Leslie frantic with agony, the anguish of despair. It was all very well for this poor creature, abandoned, deserted by the man she loved, to take death so coolly; but she, Leslie, was not deserted and unhappy. Her lover, her Yorke, was going to make her his wife; in a few days, a few hours, he would be waiting for her. Yorke, Yorke! Her heart called to him. And though the name did not leave her lips, the voice within her seemed to give her courage, to fill her with a fierce, almost savage, determination to live.

She looked up at the cliff with straining eyes. It was almost perpendicular and smooth just above them, but a little further along there were a few scrubby bushes projecting from the surface. It was just possible, if they could reach those, that they might at least gain some few inches of foothold. Just possible, though the mere thought of the attempt made her tremble.

"What are you staring up there for?" asked her companion. "You couldn't climb it, if you tried."

"No," panted Leslie. "But we will try!"

The other shook heir head, but Leslie seized her by the hand.

"Come!" she gasped hoarsely. "Better to try and—and fall, than stand here to wait for death. I cannot wait! Come, hold my hand tightly. We will escape or die together."

As if she had caught something of Leslie's frantic desire of life, the other girl gripped Leslie's hand.

"Come on, then," she said. "Though you'd have more chance alone."

"No, no! Together or not at all," cried Leslie, and she plunged into the water.

For a moment or two it seemed as if they would be carried off their feet, as if they had rushed into the arms of the death from which they had been shrinking; but they were both young and strong, and they accomplished together that which would have been impossible if they had been separate.

Gasping for breath, half blinded by the spray, deafened by the roar of the waves, they stood on a narrow ledge of rock, clutching at the bush above their heads, the water rushing nearly to their knees.

CHAPTER XX.

"I'M GOING TO LIVE, AND SO ARE YOU."

"We shall hold on here for about two minutes," said the woman grimly, "if the bush don't give way before that."

Leslie turned her face to the wall, and shut her eyes.

"And he will be waiting for me!" she murmured. "He will not know, will think I have mistrusted him. I shall never see him again, never hear his voice! Oh, why did we part to-day; why didn't I ask him, pray him to take me with him. Never to see him again——." She broke off with a sob that shook her. "My arm is numbed, I am falling!" she said with a wail. "Tell him—tell him —oh, God, and I love him so!"

The agony in her voice seemed to go straight to her companion's heart. The dark face flushed red, her eyes shone with a kind of pity.

"Hold on!" she said, almost hissed between her white teeth shut fast. "You shan't die! You tried to save me, you risked your life for me, and I'll save you. Put your arm round my neck. Don't be afraid. I'm strong. I can dance for hours; my ankles are like steel. Cling to me, I say, with one hand, anyhow."

Scarcely knowing what she was doing, Leslie released the bush with one hand, and put her arm round her companion's neck.

"If I'd only a drop of brandy!" muttered the woman. "How cold your arm feels; you're not going to faint! For God's sake don't do that, or we're both lost; for I don't mean to let you go now. Die! Who says we're going to die? I want to live now! After all, he's not quite lost—my man, I mean! He may come back. I'll get him back. I'll best this other woman or know the reason why!"

Her face was flushed, her voice husky with excitement.

"No use, no use!" moaned Leslie.

"No use! What do you mean! Am I ugly, hump-backed? Do you mean she's better looking than I am! I don't believe it! He's been caught by a new face. That isn't what you mean? You're going to fall? Not you! Hold on tight now, for I'm going to have a shy at the bush above. There's a bit of a path." She laughed fiercely, defiantly. "Old Faber had us do gymnastics. I used to hate 'em; but I'm much obliged to him now. Put your foot against the rock and spring—not too hard, mind—when I do. Once let me get a grip of that bush up there, and I'll hang on or fight my way till my arms drop off. Die! Why should I? I was a fool! I'll get him back, you see if I don't! No, we won't die. You shall have your husband again! Now!" she breathed between her clenched teeth. "If you've got any pluck in you, if you want to see your husband again, put your heart into it! Now!"

She made a spring; they both sprang at the same moment, as if they were one body inspired by the same will, and the woman got hold of the bush, and clung with the strength and tenacity of a leopardess.

"Ah!" she gasped. "We've done it! Cling on to me! We'll wait while I count twenty, and then we'll go for the path."

"No—no!" panted Leslie. "I could not, I could not! Let us stay here till——."

"Till this bit of ledge crumbles under us with our weight, and lets us drop like poisoned flies! No, no! I don't feel like that. It isn't convenient to die now; it was just now! I'm going to live, to live! And so are you!"

She counted the twenty, then put her arm around Leslie's waist.

"Now! Put your hand on my shoulder and cling with the other to the bits of bush and stump, and don't look down! Mind that, or you'll drop, as sure as fate."

Leslie shuddered. Her heart was beating wildly, but a grand hope was creeping over her. Was it possible that she should live and see Yorke once more?

Slowly she felt her way along the surface with her hand, till she got hold of the dry but firmly rooted scrub, then she drew herself up and along the narrow ledge, which was a fissure in the rock rather than a path. No one, in cold blood, could have maintained a footing there for more than thirty seconds, but these two were fighting for dear life, and their blood was burning at fever heat, and they managed, almost miraculously, to creep, crawl, drag themselves upward and still upward.

Below them roared the angry waves, as if with mocking rage at their attempts to escape their voracious maw. Above their heads whirled the gulls, screaming weirdly. Every now and then a stone, displaced by their feet, rolled and sprang from point to point, and ultimately bounded into the gulf below them; and each time Leslie felt that in a moment she would be bounding and falling like the stone, to the hideous death.

For some minutes neither spoke. They could hear each other's breath coming in thick, labored gasps; and Leslie, who was in front, now and again felt her companion's breath striking, like that of a hot furnace, on her neck.

"Keep on! Hold tight!" she heard her say presently. "Keep your eyes up; the path's broadening. If—if we can hold on another minute or two—or a year, for that's what it seems like!—we're saved!"

Leslie could not reply; her tongue cleaved to the roof of her mouth; her lips, dry and stiff, would not move. But still as she climbed her heart's voice murmured "Yorke, Yorke!" and she drew courage from it. It was worth fighting for, this life of hers, this life which his love had made so precious, so beauteous. If she lived she would be his wife. His wife! Yes, she would live, she would fight on while there was breath in her body, while there was strength in her fingers to clutch an inch of even the moss on the cliff's surface.

In such moments Time is not. It is swallowed up in the agony, the suspense, the mingled hope and despair which rack and wring the heart and brain. She scarcely knew how long they had been making their awful journey through the valley of the shadow of death, scarcely realized that they were saved, when she saw the edge of the cliff just above her, and with one great effort raised herself above it—above it!—and threw herself upon the level ground, gripping the short turf with her hot fingers as if she dreaded that something would drag her back again, and hurl her into the awful sea whose voice still howled faintly in her ears.

She lay thus for a minute or two, her companion lying at her elbow, panting, beside her; then, with a great sob, Leslie rose to her knees and poured out her heart in thanksgiving to Him who had restored her to life—and to Yorke!

The woman stood and eyed her with a pale face and half lowered lids.

"Where are we?" she said at last.

Leslie rose and turned to her with both hands outstretched.

"Oh, what can I say, how can I thank you?" she exclaimed in great agitation. "You have saved my life!"

The woman wiped her lips and forced a smile.

"That's a rum way of putting it," she said, her voice shaking a little. "If I did, you saved mine first. It was a narrow squeak for both of us."

She looked round almost impatiently.

"Where are we?" she repeated. "I—I want to get back to London as soon as I can. I——'ve been half out of my mind, I think, and this—this affair has pulled me round. Don't you take any notice of what I said about—about him, the man I spoke of. I don't believe I've lost him, after all. I can get him back." She laughed discordantly, and flushed, as if half ashamed of the new hope that the escape from death had seemed to give her. "He's—he's no worse than the rest. They're all alike, easily taken with a new face. And—and I know he likes me. He was sorry for going directly after he'd left me, and—yes—" she pushed the black hair from her face—"yes, I'll bet my life I get him back."

Leslie looked at her with a smile of sympathy and encouragement.

"Yes," she said, "I hope so; ah, yes, I hope so! It was dreadful to see you and hear you when we were—down there!" and she glanced with a shudder at the edge of the cliff.

"Yes, I was pretty low then," said the other. "It was a hard fight, wasn't it? You and I ought to be friends; but—" she paused and looked hard and almost shyly at Leslie's face—"but perhaps you wouldn't care for that. You're a lady—a swell, I can see, and I—well, I'm not fit——."

Leslie put out her hand to stop her.

"You must not talk like that now—now, just when we have escaped death together. And I hope—ah! yes, I hope that you will be happier, that he—" she blushed, and her voice grew low; love was so sacred a thing to her—"that he you love will come back to you. If he does you must forgive him, and take him back——."

She stopped, for the tall, graceful figure in front of her swayed and staggered; and the dark eyes grew suddenly heavy and closed.

Leslie uttered a cry of alarm.

"Oh, what is it? You are ill, faint——."

The other opened her lips as if to speak, then fell heavily forward on Leslie's arm.

Leslie knelt beside her on the grass, and looked round anxiously. The solitude was as intense as that which they had just left. They were still alone together with no help near.

Leslie remembered that a small spring ran from a cleft on the cliff, and, though the thought of going near the edge made her heart quake, she gently set the woman's head down, and, stooping over the cliff, wet her handkerchief in the rill, and, returning, bathed the white face with one hand while she unfastened the bosom of the lifeless woman's dress with the other.

As she did so her hand came in contact with something hard, though for a second or two she was too intent upon watching for some signs of returning consciousness in the face on her knee to look to see what it was; but presently her eye caught a plain gold locket.

"Poor girl!" she thought. "It is the gift of the man who has deserted her. And she wears it near her heart. Poor girl, poor girl!"

At that moment the white lips parted, and the dark eyes opened.

"Yorke!" she breathed. "Is it you, Yorke? Have you come back to me?"

The words struck upon Leslie's ear at first without any significance. She scarcely heard them or took them in for a space during which one could have counted fifty.

Then, gradually it came upon her, gradually, slowly.

"Yorke! Is it you, Yorke? Have you come back to me?"

She repeated them mechanically, as one repeats a phrase in a foreign language, the meaning of which one does not understand. Then she began to tremble, and a faint, sick dread fell upon her.

All the time she bathed the white face and lips and brushed the dark hair from the low, handsome forehead; doing it mechanically, absently.

Yorke? Had this girl said Yorke, or, was she mistaken?

She waited, breathless, the sick feeling weighing on her heart; and presently the full lips opened again, and again the name—the beloved name—was breathed. There could be no mistake this time. Leslie heard it plainly.

It was Yorke.

Her hand trembled, the beautiful face on her lap grew dim, and seemed to fade away. Then she made an effort and forced the dread from her heart, and a smile to her lips.

What if this girl, the beautiful girl, had called upon Yorke? Surely there was more than one man of that name in the world, the great big wide world; and this woman's Yorke was not, could not be, hers, Leslie's.

She could have laughed at her wicked, worse than wicked, foolish fears! Could have laughed if it had not been for the stress of circumstances.

How could she suspect for a moment that he Yorke—the Duke of Rothbury, her lover, so good and true and stanch—should be the Yorke whom this woman loved, and who had, by her own account, deserted her!

"Oh, I wrong him cruelly, wickedly, even by this momentary doubt!" she told herself. "He would not have doubted me as I have done him, though only for a second!" And her face flushed.

But though she reproached herself, her mind was at work, and, against her will, she remembered how she had first seen this girl.

She recalled the scene, the incident, at St. Martin's Tower. Yorke had stood beside her looking down, and he had started—yes, and turned pale, white to the lips, as the woman's voice had floated up to them.

Did he know her?

All her being rose in revolt at the idea, the suspicion. And yet——. She remembered his face as it had looked at that moment. She had thought that he had turned pale with anger that such a song should have been sung in her presence, and had loved him for his anxiety on her account.

She tried to thrust the dawning suspicion from her as if it were some insidious demon whispering in her ear, but still she could not forget that this woman had told her that she had come down here to Portmaris, had followed the man she loved to this place; and Yorke had come down here, had come down——!

The rays of the setting sun struck the two figures, the white face lying on Leslie's lap adding a lustre to the dark hair that swept across Leslie's dress.

How beautiful she looked, Leslie thought in a dull, vague way; how beautiful! Any man might well lose his heart to such a woman, even though she were not a lady, and capable of singing such a song as she had heard these lips sing. Any man, even——. No, not Yorke! He would not, could not have loved her. It was she, Leslie herself, whom he loved, not this woman!

Even as she laid the flattering unction to her soul, her eye fell again upon the locket.

It was lying open, face downward, upon the woman's snow-white breast.

A desire, an overwhelming desire to take it up and see what face was enshrined in it seized upon her. One glance, and this vague, unjust suspicion of hers would be set at rest for ever. She knew, knew, that it would not be Yorke's, her Yorke's, face she should see.

She fought against the desire, the craving. Love was a sacred thing to her, and it would seem like sacrilege to touch this trinket which this poor girl wore, doubtless the gift of the man she loved so dearly, the man whose desertion had caused her to weary of life, to desire death.

"No, no, I cannot, I will not!" Leslie breathed pantingly, but even as she spoke the words her hand stole towards the locket upon which the rich sunlight was falling. Once, twice, her hand approached it and drew back, but at the third time she took it up, raised it slowly, and then swiftly turned it upwards.

Then still holding it, her eyes riveted upon it with a gaze of horror and agony, she cried—

“Yorke! It is Yorke!”

CHAPTER XXI.

"IT IS FALSE—I WILL NOT BELIEVE IT."

It was Yorke!

Leslie gazed down at the locket lying in the palm of her hand, for the moment too benumbed by the sudden shock to feel anything.

Yes, it was his face, the handsome face whose every line, every expression, were engraved on her heart. For a second or two the portrait, as it smiled up at her with Yorke's characteristic devil-may-care look in its eyes, gave her a kind of pleasure; then she began to realize where she had found it, lying on the bosom of this woman!

She dropped the locket as if it had suddenly burnt her, and shrank back as far as she could without displacing the woman's head from her knee.

Yorke's portrait in a locket in the possession of another woman! How could it be! There must be some mistake, some hideous mistake. It could not be his face, but that of someone, some relation closely resembling him.

She took the locket up again, and as she did so remembered that the woman had murmured Yorke's name. Yes, it was Yorke. She laid the locket down again—gently this time—and bent over the white face of the woman with a strange confusing throbbing in her heart, a loud singing in her ears. The earth seemed to rock beneath her, the sky to be falling.

She was faint with physical exhaustion, with the terrible struggle for life, and this discovery coming so closely upon all she had endured almost crushed her.

Was she really awake, or asleep and dreaming? Delirious, perhaps? Yorke, her Yorke's face lying there on this woman's heart! It was incredible.

All this had passed through her mind, her heart, in a few seconds; one can crowd an awful amount of misery, anguish, joy, into a minute; and by this time the woman had recovered.

"Where am I?" she breathed, staring up at Leslie.

Leslie did not answer, but continued to gaze at her with wide open eyes, in which a horror was growing more intense each moment.

"Where am I? Have I been ill—ah——." She drew a deep breath. "I remember. Are we safe? Why don't we go? What are we staying for?"

She raised herself on her elbow, and half sat up, pushing the black hair from her face and passing her hand across her eyes. Then she looked down and saw the locket, and her hand flew to it.

Leslie's eyes followed the hand.

"Whose—whose portrait is that?" she asked almost inaudibly.

The woman looked at her, and a dull red stole into her face.

"What's that to you?" she retorted, half defiantly. "You've looked at it, haven't you?"

Leslie moistened her lips; they were so hot and dry that she could scarcely speak.

"Yes, I have looked at it," she said. "I know——."

"You know who it is?" As she spoke she closed the locket hurriedly, and buttoned her dress over it. "You know—. Who are you? What is your name?" And the dark eyes scanned Leslie's pale face with suspicious scrutiny.

"My name is Leslie, Leslie Lisle," said Leslie slowly.

"Leslie—," the woman sprang to her feet. "What! You are the girl he left me for," she breathed.

Leslie shuddered and her lips quivered.

"Oh, there must be some mistake!" she almost wailed. "It cannot be he— And yet you spoke his name—Yorke——."

"Yorke! Yes, that's his name! And this is his portrait," was the sharp response. "And you are the girl he's fallen in love with! And I never guessed it! I must have been a fool not to have thought of it, jumped at it! It's lucky for you that I didn't," she added between her teeth. "I'd have killed you down there!"

Leslie shrank back, and instinctively put out her hand as if to ward off an attack.

"What—what is your name?" she asked.

"My name?" The full lips curled with bitter contempt. "You must have been out of the world not to know it," she said. "My name's Finetta; I'm Finetta of the Diadem."

"Finetta—Finetta of the Diadem," Leslie repeated mechanically.

Was it all a hideous dream? Who was Finetta of the Diadem? And how could she talk of Yorke as if he belonged to her—how did it happen that she wore his portrait on her heart?

"Yes, Finetta of the Diadem," said Finetta defiantly. "I should have thought everybody knew me. But I suppose he hasn't told you about me. No, that wasn't likely!" and she laughed hoarsely. "What are you staring at me like that for, as if I was a—a wild animal?"

Leslie put her hand to her brow with a piteous little gesture.

"I—I——. It is all so sudden. Give me time. I do not wish to anger you. I only want to ask you a—a question—one or two questions. Why do you wear that portrait in that locket?"

Finetta looked at her a moment in silence, then with a flash of her eyes and a discordant laugh she replied—

"That's a question to ask me, if you like. What do you think I wear it for?" The red deepened on her face, then left it pale. "What does a woman usually wear a man's portrait for? I'll be bound you've got one of his, too?"

Leslie's hand went to her bosom, to the sparkling pendant, and she shook her head with a strange feeling of injury; he had sent her diamonds, but he had given this woman something far more precious!

"No!" she breathed almost unconsciously. "Did he give it to you? Oh, answer me quickly, and—and truthfully! I will tell you why I ask. I will tell you all. I—I am to be his wife—I was to be his wife——."

At the change from "Am to be" to "was to be" Finetta's eyes flashed, and she lowered her lids.

"Sit down," she said, pointing to a piece of rock.

Leslie sank down upon it, and waited with averted face; she could not bear to look upon the dark defiant face, beautiful with the beauty of a fallen angel at this moment, a face distorted and lined by conflicting passions.

"You were to be his wife, were you?" said Finetta slowly, with a breath between each word. "So was I!"

"You!"

The word dropped from Leslie's white lips unconsciously; it seemed to sting Finetta.

"Yes, me!" she flamed out. "Why not? You speak and you look at me as if—as if I was some monster! I'm—I'm as young and as good looking as you——."

Leslie put up her hand deprecatingly.

"Yes, yes," she murmured. "I did not mean to anger you. Go on! Oh, go on!"

"Why shouldn't he marry me as much as you!" continued Finetta. "I've known him longer than you have! I've been more to him than you have——."

Leslie shuddered.

"I'm as good as you are. Who are you? You're no more of a swell than I am! And you're poor, too, ain't you? And I'm not poor. I can earn thousands a year——." She stopped, panting.

Leslie glanced at her shrinkingly.

"And if it comes to caring for him, I reckon I care for him quite as much as you do! You know that, for you heard me talk down there, when I thought it was all over with us. And as for him—well, I'd wager everything I've got that in his heart he likes me as well as he likes you, or anyone else!"

She laughed bitterly, and with self scorn and contempt.

"No, no," broke from Leslie's quivering lips.

"But I say yes, yes," retorted Finetta. "He's just like the rest. None of 'em could stick to one of us alone to save his life. You must have lived with your head buried in the sand not to know that! What! You think that you're the only one he has made love to; or that I'm the only other one!" She laughed again. "Ask him whether he knows Lady Eleanor Dallas! See how he looks when he hears her name, and hear what he says!"

Leslie looked at her with half dazed eyes, and listened with ears in which the wild sea seemed roaring.

"It is false, false!" she cried hoarsely. "I will not believe——." And she put up her hands as if to cover her ears.

Finetta laughed.

"Well!" she said with a sneer. "He's deceived you easily enough, anyone could see! And if I wasn't so sorry for myself I could find it in my heart to be sorry for you!"

Leslie shuddered. To be pitied by this woman, this terrible woman!

"Look here," said Finetta after a pause. "Don't mind my hard words; it's my way, when I'm put out. I can see you don't believe half I say, and that's only natural; I shouldn't if I were in your place, and didn't know him so well. If you doubt that we are both talking of the same man, take this locket and look at it again." And she held it out.

Leslie turned her head from it.

"No, you don't want to look at it again. I daresay you knew his face directly you saw it. Now, do you think he'd have given it to me if he hadn't cared for me? Answer that!"

Leslie looked at her, a sudden wild hope springing into her bosom.

"It—it was a long while ago!" she breathed, "a long while ago——."

Finetta broke in with a discordant laugh.

"Not a bit of it! It was three days ago. He sent it after spending an evening with me, as he's spent many a score——."

She saw a look of unbelief crossing Leslie's face, and, snatching a letter from her pocket, thrust it under Leslie's face.

"Read that, and believe!" she said.

Leslie took the note and looked at it. The lines swam before her eyes, but she saw a word here and there, and with a low cry, which broke from her notwithstanding all the efforts to suppress it, she held out the note from her.

Finetta took it and restored it to her pocket, then stood and looked down at the motionless figure in silence for a moment or two.

"You believe now," she said in a low, harsh voice. "You see I am telling you the truth, and not a pack of lies. And now, what are you going to do? Wait a minute. Let's see how the land lies. Here am I who've—who've cared for him for years, who would have been his wife if—if he hadn't happened to have seen you; and, mind, I'm just as fit to be his wife as you are. Why, come to that, he'll tire of you ever so much sooner than he would of me, because you haven't any money and I have, and can go on earning enough to keep him amused. Don't you see? We've been fond of each other for ever so long. Why, there's been scarcely a day for months past that we haven't been together! And even when he's smitten by you he doesn't throw me over, you see. He sends me his portrait and a sweetheart's note with it; yes, and just after he's left you, too! Now, that's how I stand; and now, where are you? You've only known him a few days; you can't care for him half—half? no, not one-tenth as much as I do! That's only natural. And it's only natural and right that you should give him up. Think it over. After all, Miss Lisle," she went on, with a kind of sullen insinuation, "he's behaved very badly to you; he has indeed. He never meant to throw me quite over; he'd have come back to me sooner or later."

Leslie half rose from the rock and put out her hand as if to put the words, the insinuation, from her, then sank back and covered her face with her hands.

"He'd have come back to me, and then you'd have been a good deal worse off than you are now."

Leslie did not move, and Finetta, watching her closely, allowed a minute to pass in silence that her words might sink in.

"Come, now, Miss Lisle; there's no occasion for you and me to quarrel. Why, when you think of it, you and me have saved each other's lives, haven't we? And we ought, we really ought, to act square and straight by one another. I'm the one that's been badly treated, because he loved me first, and would have married me but for you. Just think of that! From what I've seen of you, I should say that you were a kind-hearted lady and one that wouldn't injure a fellow woman. I should say you were too proud to rob a poor girl of the man she's loved."

Leslie sprang up panting, and for a moment breathless.

The horror, the humiliation, were driving her mad.

"Oh, be silent, be silent! Let me think!" she breathed. "Every word you speak stabs me." She put her hand to her bosom with a passionate gesture that awed Finetta. "It is all so sudden that—that I cannot realize it; can scarcely believe—oh, do not speak! I believe all you say. You have shown me the note, the portrait is his, and I cannot but believe. And I trusted him! Ah, how I trusted him!" Her voice broke for a moment and her eyes swam with tears; but she dashed them away with her hand and hurried on, with every now and then a break between the words. "But what you say is true. He—he belongs to you more than to me! He has wronged us both; but he has wronged you the more cruelly. And—" she stopped and put her hand to her throat as if she were suffocating—"and I—I give him back to you. Yes, I give him back to you!"

The blood rushed to Finetta's face, then left it pale to the lips.

"You—you throw him up?" she said, as if she could scarcely believe her ears.

Leslie raised her head and looked at her steadily, with a look that would have melted the heart of anyone but a rival.

"He belongs to you, not to me," she said in a low voice, as if every word cost her a heart pang. "I—I will never see him again if I can help it. Do not—" she paused, and a sigh broke from her white lips—"do not let him know; do not tell him that I have seen you. I—I have loved him, and would spare him the shame——."

There was silence for a second, Finetta gazing on the ground with set face and hidden eyes.

"If—if he should ever know that we met, and that you told me what you have told me, tell him that I—yes, that I forgive him. That I have forgiven and forgotten him. That is all."

Her head sank for a moment, then she raised it again and looked at the dark face with a shrinking kind of reluctance.

"You—you say that you care for him?"

Finetta's lips moved.

"Yes, and I know that you do. Be good to him. Do not let the thought that he deceived himself into thinking he cared for me come between you. He must love you very much to give you his portrait, to write you that note; try—try and make him happy."

Her voice broke, and she turned her head away.

Finetta stood with clenched hands, her teeth gnawing at her under lip; then she sprang to Leslie's side and took her hand.

"Miss Lisle——."

Leslie shook her hand off with a little cry, a shudder.

"Don't—don't touch me, please."

Finetta froze instantly.

"I—I beg your pardon," panted Leslie. "But I cannot bear any more. If you would go now. That road leads to Portmaris."

She sank on the stone, and sat with her head erect and face set hard as the stone itself.

Finetta drew her jacket round her and fumbled with her gloves.

"I understand," she said in a low voice. "You've done the right thing, and you won't be sorry for it."

"It is nearly two miles to Portmaris," said Leslie in a dry, expressionless voice. "There is an evening train; you can catch it if you walk quickly."

"I'm going," said Finetta, biting her lips. "Good-by, Miss Leslie. I'm sorry—well, good-by."

Leslie sat motionless and with averted face until the graceful figure of the dancing girl of the Diadem had disappeared below the hill; then with a cry she rose, her arms above her head, and fell full length upon the turf.

CHAPTER XXII.

"FAME HAS COME TO ME AT LAST."

Leslie lay unconscious while the sun sank below the horizon, and the delicious summer gloaming came softly upon the moor; lay like a flower struck down by some rude hand, and the evening star shone pale in the sky before she came back to life and her great sorrow.

For a while it seemed to her that the whole scene through which she had passed was a hideous dream, and when its reality came crushing down upon her she uttered a low cry and shivered as if with cold. The sudden destruction of her joy and happiness left her stunned and bewildered. A few short hours ago and she and Yorke had been sitting hand in hand, heart to heart, talking of their marriage, and now——. Now he was hers no longer. In a sense he had never been hers, but all the time he had been wooing her, forcing her to love him, he had been in honor bound to this other woman.

As she thought of her, this Finetta, this woman with the bold eyes, a feeling of shame and humiliation was added to the misery of Leslie's loss. That he, Yorke, her idol, her king, should ever have stooped to love such a woman seemed to her unspeakably base and terrible. She had set him on so lofty a pedestal, had regarded him as so noble and high-minded, that the knowledge of his falseness—to both of them!—hurt her like a physical blow.

She sat for some time, waiting for strength to enable her to reach home; and as she sat and looked round it seemed as if something had gone out of her life, as if a weight which no power nor time could lift had fallen upon her heart.

Before her she saw stretching in a dull grey, hopeless vista, the many years she would probably have to live; the long life without Yorke, and haunted by the memory of these few happy days.

"If I had never seen him! If I had not loved him so dearly!" was the burden of her heart's wail; "or if I had only died down there before I saw the locket or heard the woman's story!"

She had fought Death hard enough a little while ago, now she would have welcomed him.

She rose at last, and went slowly and draggingly towards Portmaris. Her dress was still heavy with the salt water, she was weak with physical and mental weariness, and the two miles across the moor were surely the longest that ever woman journeyed.

When she reached the villa and entered the parlor, she found her father pacing up and down in the dusk before his easel.

He looked up, but fortunately for her, did not see her white weary face, or notice how she held the door as if to support herself.

"Where have you been, Leslie?" he asked in a kind of irritable excitement. "I have been wanting you. Mr. Temple has sent the notes for the picture, the fifty pounds."

She leant against the door, and drew a long breath as she thought of this added humiliation.

"He is going to-morrow, it seems, and wished to—er—pay for the picture before he left. His departure is rather sudden, I think, but I fancy he is erratic in his movements. I want you to send him a receipt, and—er—to ask him to allow the picture to be exhibited."

"Yes; to-morrow, papa," she said faintly.

"Why not to-night?" he asked testily.

"I—I am tired, very tired," she said, going to him and leaning her head on his shoulder.

"You've walked too far," he said in a tone of complaint. "You'd better go to bed at once. The receipt and the letter must wait till to-morrow, I suppose. Oh, there was something—oh, yes; did you see the duke? He came up to me on the beach and inquired for you."

She turned away from him, a lump rising in her throat and threatening to suffocate her.

"Yes."

"Did he say anything about that sketch of St. Martin's?"

St. Martin's! How the name brought back the memory of that happy, happy day.

"I don't quite know about that sketch," he went on with an air of importance. "I may be too much engaged on important pictures to—er—spare any time for small sketches. However, that matter can rest for the present. The duke has gone back to London to-night, they tell me. By the way, I wish you would prepare a fresh canvas for me."

"Not to-night, oh, not to-night, dear!" she said in a low voice. "I will go to bed as you said, for I am very, very tired. To-morrow——."

She left the sentence unfinished, and crept up to her own room.

To-morrow! What an awful line of dreary to-morrows stretched before her, was her thought. As she took off her dress the diamond pendant flashed in the candlelight, each gem seeming to glitter mockingly in derision of her love and faith and trust. She covered the sparkling thing with her hand and bowed her head over it. The very day he had sent it to her, he had given his portrait—his portrait—to that other woman! She took the pendant off the ribbon, and wrapped it in a piece of soft paper and put it away out of sight in a small box, and as she did so she saw Ralph Duncombe's ring.

One's own misery recalls to us that of other people, and in this the hour of her trouble Leslie remembered Ralph Duncombe, and for the first time she realized something of what he had suffered. With a rush his passionate avowal came back upon her, and she took the ring in her hand and looked at it with a double misery. He had sworn to help her if she ever should be in trouble, had sworn to help her if ever she suffered wrong. How feeble had been his vow! Neither he nor anyone else could help her in this strait; and as to vengeance, she wanted none. Alas, alas! false as he had been, she loved Yorke still.

She fell asleep at last from sheer exhaustion, and did not awake until past nine. Then it all came throbbing, crowding back upon her, in that first awful moment of waking. Surely to the wretched and unhappy, there is no more awful hour in the twenty-four than that which follows the morning awakening. Sorrow seems to have had time to sharpen her arrows during the night, and plunges them with fresh vigor into our aching hearts.

While she was dressing, Leslie went over the whole of the incidents of the previous day, bit by bit, and suddenly, with the sharpness of a flash of lightning, a gleam of hope shot across the darkness of her misery. Suppose this woman had lied! Such women as she would find no difficulty in stooping to untruth and deception. Suppose she had got possession of Yorke's portrait, had forged the letter, had concocted the whole story? The supposition seemed far-fetched and improbable, but it sent a thrill of hope through her, and she finished dressing with feverish haste, and hurried downstairs.

All through the breakfast she felt like one in a dream, as if she were suspended between life and death, and waiting for the verdict. Her father talked of his picture, of all he meant to do, now that he was on the high road to Fame, and his voice sounded in her ears like that of someone speaking afar off.

Yorke, her Yorke, might prove to be hers still! Oh, blessed hope. How mad, how wicked, how foolish she had been to put any trust in the woman who had slandered him!

The revulsion of feeling was so great that it sent a hectic flush to her face, and a feverish light to her eyes.

"That receipt and note, Leslie," said her father. "Tell Mr. Temple that I would rather not sell the picture, that I would rather return his money than forego the right of exhibiting the picture."

"Yes, yes, papa," she said at random. "Yes, it will all come right. It was wicked, foolish, to doubt him, to believe her."

He stared at her with irritable impatience.

"What are you talking of, Leslie?" he said peevishly. "You seem very strange this morning, and so you were last night."

"I know, I know, dear!" she broke in with something between a sigh and a sob. "Don't mind me. I am not very well. You want the receipt?" she sprang to the writing table. "There it is, and the note. Yes, yes! It will come right. I know it will; and—and—oh, how hot it is! I must have air, air!"

She caught up her hat, and with the receipt and note in her hand, ran to the door.

"I shall see Mr. Temple, papa, and I will give him these."

"And tell him," he called after her, "that I make it a condition that the picture shall be exhibited; mind that, Leslie!"

"Yes, yes!" she responded, and ran out.

She drew her breath hard as she paused for a moment on the doorstep, then she hurried to the quay.

A fisherman was drying his net in the sun, but there was no one else there, and she walked up and down, the note in her hand, repeating to herself the formula of hope; the woman, Finetta, had lied to her and deceived her. All would be well. Yorke would be her Yorke still!

She had not been walking thus very long before the bath chair, wheeled by Grey, was seen coming on to the quay.

She hurried toward it, and the duke motioned to Grey to stop.

"Good morning, Miss Leslie," he said, peering up at her. "It is a fine morning, isn't it." Then he paused and scanned her face curiously and earnestly. "Is anything the matter?"

"The matter?" she repeated with a laugh that sounded in her ears hollow and unnatural. "What should be the matter? I have brought you my father's receipt and a note, Mr. Temple."

He took it and glanced at it.

"Humph," he said. "Oh, yes, I'll do anything your father wishes. And there is nothing the matter, Miss Leslie?" and he peered up at her curiously from under his thick brows.

"Nothing, nothing," she responded feverishly. "But I wanted to ask you—the duke, the Duke of Rothbury——."

His pale face flushed, and he motioned to Grey to withdraw out of hearing.

"I thought so!" he said. "Miss Leslie, sick men, like me, acquire a kind of second sight. Directly I saw you just now, I knew that you had learnt the truth."

She looked down at him, and her face, which had been flushed feverishly, paled.

"The truth?" she faltered.

"Yes," he said in a tone that suggested remorse. "You have been cruelly deceived!"

"Deceived!" she echoed the word as if its significance were lost upon her. "Deceived!"

"Yes. Cruelly. But you must not blame him altogether.

"Blame him. Whom?" she said slowly.

"Yorke, Yorke," he said in a low voice. "It was as much my fault as his. I ought to have told you. We have both deceived you wickedly, inexcusably."

Leslie put out her hand and caught the chair, and stood looking down at him.

"Blame me more than him," he went on. "Blame us both. We ought to have told you, at any rate, however we kept other people in the dark. But he was not free, and I—well, I held my tongue."

"He was not free?" she murmured mechanically.

"No! I don't ask you to forgive us; you'd find it too hard. I don't expect you even to understand the motive."

She put out her hand to him.

"Wait—stop! Let me think. He has deceived me, then?"

"He has, and I have, yes," he said, averting his eyes from the misery in her face. "Is it so hard and bitter a blow, Leslie?" he said after a pause.

"Yes," she responded almost unconsciously. "I hoped that—that——. But it does not matter. Nothing matters, now."

He fidgeted in his chair, and peered up at her curiously, strangely.

"Anyway, you know the truth now."

"Yes! I know the truth now," she echoed faintly. "Why," hoarsely, "why did he do it?"

The duke bit his lip.

"It was more my fault than his. I ought to have told you. I did not know—did not know that you would take it so much to heart. For God's sake don't look so wretched, so heartbroken," he burst forth. "Leslie, you make me feel like a criminal!"

She turned her white face to him.

"You let me—love him, go on loving him, knowing all the while——."

He hung his head and plucked at the edge of the shawl across his knees.

"I did!" he said in a low voice. "I tell you so."

"God forgive you!" she panted. "God forgive you—and him!"

She stood a moment as if struggling for breath, and turned and walked swiftly away.

The duke sat for a full five minutes, staring at the front wheel of his chair; then he jerked his hand up and called to Grey.

"Take me home!" he snapped. "What the devil are you waiting for? Take me home and back to London as soon as possible."

Leslie sped along the quay, and staggered rather than walked into the sitting room, and a moment afterward her father hurried in.

"Leslie, Leslie!" he cried. "Where are you?"

She lifted her head from the sofa cushion with dull, blinded eyes.

"Here's a telegram! A telegram from one of the large dealers. He wants to see me in London at once! At once, do you hear? Why do you stare at me like that? There is no time to lose. We must go up to London at once. At once!

Run upstairs and pack our things!"

She rose and staggered to her feet.

"No, no! It is—it is——," she paused and clutched his arm, laughing hysterically. "Don't believe it, papa. It is not true. I can explain!"

"Explain? Not true? What are you talking about, Leslie! I tell you it is from one of the first dealers in London. Fame, fame, has come to me at last! Get ready at once! We will go by the first train we can catch!"

CHAPTER XXIII.

GOOD-BY, AND NOT ADIEU.

Leslie's heart seemed to stand still as she listened to her father's excited words. What should she do? she asked herself. Should she tell him that she had deceived him, that the message from the picture dealer was a mere subterfuge, a trick to get him and her up to town?

But she could not tell him this without explaining fully, without disclosing the whole story of her love for Yorke and the deceit he had practiced on her, and she shrank from the ordeal as one shrinks from fire.

She stood pale and trembling, her hands writhing together, her brain swimming, watching her father as he hurried to and fro picking up some article and putting it down again in another place under the impression that he was packing.

"Oh, papa," she faltered out at last, "don't go! Do not go. Write and—and ask. Oh, I implore you not to go!"

Francis Lisle stopped in his flurried fidgeting about the room, and stared at her with impatient annoyance.

"My dear Leslie, have you taken leave of your senses?" he exclaimed. "You look half distraught."

"I am, I am! Ah, if you only knew!" she almost sobbed.

"Knew what?" he demanded irritably. "What is it you are talking about! Any one would think we were going to—to Australia instead of only to London! And not go? Good heavens, why should we not go? I tell you this is one of the first dealers in London, and—and it is the great opening I have been waiting for, expecting all my life——."

It was unendurable. She went to him and put her arm round his neck and let her head fall on his shoulder.

"Oh, papa, papa! Do not be too confident, too hopeful. You—you may be disappointed! Life is full of disappointment——." Her voice broke. "You may be sorry that you have gone up. Write—let me write to this dealer——."

He put her from him almost roughly.

"You are talking nonsense!" he said. "Sheer nonsense. Why should this dealer write to me and ask me to come up at once—at once, mind—unless he had some important commission for me?"

She knew why, but she could not answer. She dared not. She dreaded the effect of the shock which the disclosure, the disappointment would cause him. He was trembling with excitement as it was, and the reaction would be more than he could endure.

"There," he said with an attempt at soothing her, "I can understand your being upset and unnerved. It is only natural. I—even I—am a little—er—flurried. But do collect yourself, and get ready. We shall go up by the evening train. Take all our clothes, for we may be up some time. I can't tell what this dealer may want, or—or where he may send me. There, do collect yourself and get ready. Wait; give me a little brandy and water. The suddenness of this—this change in our fortunes has agitated me."

She got him some weak brandy and water, and she noticed as he drank it how his hand shook.

Then she stole up to her own room and began to pack, mechanically, like one in a dream.

Gradually she began to realize that after all it was better perhaps that they should leave Portmaris. Yorke—the mere passing of his name across her mind caused her a pang—might come down after her when he found that she had not gone to London and sent him her address, and she felt that a meeting with him would nearly kill her. At all costs that must be avoided. In her heart throbbed only one prayer; that, while life lasted, she might be spared the agony of seeing his face, hearing his voice again.

She finished her preparations for herself and her father, and went downstairs and helped him pack the absurd and worthless canvases; then she went out to say good-by to the old place.

Something, a presentment as strong as certainty, told her that she was indeed saying good-by and not adieu.

She wandered along the quay and stood looking sadly at the breakwater against which she had sat when Ralph Duncombe had declared his love and given her his ring; on which Yorke had been lying the night she and he had gone for a sail. Was it only a few weeks, or years ago that all this had happened to her?

There were some children on the quay, the children who had learned to love her, and amongst them the mite she had held in her arms the morning Yorke had asked her to be his wife. They clustered around her as usual, and she had hard work to keep the tears from her eyes—they were in her voice—as she kissed them.

"'Oo coming back soon, Mith Lethlie?" lisped Trottie, her favorite; and Leslie murmured, Yes, she would come back soon.

When she got back to Sea View, she found her father ready to start, and in an impatient anxiety to do so.

"We are going to London on important business, Mrs. Merrick," Leslie heard him saying to Mrs. Merrick, "Most important business. I—er—anticipate a change in our circumstances; a great change. The world has at last awakened to the fact that my pictures are not—er—without merit," he laughed with a kind of bombastic modesty. "Oh, yes, we shall come back to our old friends, Mrs. Merrick. We shall not forget Sea View, and—er—if I am not mistaken the world of art will not forget it. Some day, possibly, Sea View will become celebrated as the temporary residence of one of England's first artists; eh, Leslie?" and he smiled at her with a childish conceit.

Mrs. Merrick, not understanding in the least, smiled and curtseyed.

"I'm sure we're very sorry to lose you, sir, and Miss Leslie especially. I don't know what Portmaris will do without her, that I don't. We shall be quite dull now for a bit, for Mr. Temple, the crippled gentleman, has gone off to-day. You will be sure and send me your address?"

"Yes, yes," said Francis Lisle, "and—er—if we hear of anyone wanting clean and comfortable sea-side lodgings, we shall certainly remember to recommend you, Mrs. Merrick."

He went off in the broken down fly like a prince with his canvases piled round him, and oblivious of everything but them.

During the journey up to town he spoke very little, but sat in his corner looking out of the window, a smile of self-satisfaction every now and then passing over his thin, worn face.

"I shouldn't be surprised, Leslie," he said once, "if this should prove to be the last time we travel third class. I shall ask, and no doubt obtain, a fair price for my pictures, and we shall at last—at last—be rich enough to afford a little luxury. They say that everything comes to him who can wait, and I think I have waited long enough, long enough!"

Leslie's pale face flushed, and her conscience tortured her, but she could not summon up courage to tell him the truth.

They reached town late in the summer evening, and Leslie calling a cab told the man to drive to a house in Torrington square, at which they had stayed on previous visits to London.

Torrington Square is a quiet secluded spot in the great metropolis. It is central, and yet retired. Nearly every house is let in apartments, and the square is the favorite residence of the journalists and artists who pay occasional visits to London.

The landlady of No. 23 received Leslie and her father as if they were old friends instead of transient lodgers, and she expressed her concern at the appearance of Mr. Lisle.

"He don't look well, Miss Lisle," she said in a stage whisper, as they went in with their baggage. "Been in the country, too! Ah, I often says there's no place like London for health. And you, too, begging your pardon, miss, don't look too rosy. What you want is brightening up, and there's no place like London for brightening up, that I will say."

Leslie smiled sadly. She knew that she looked pale and wan, but it hurt her to hear that her father was not looking well.

She got him to bed early, but directly after breakfast he was all anxiety to go down to the picture dealer who had brought him to town.

"Can I not go alone, dear, while you rest?" she said. But he scouted the suggestion.

"No, no, I will go. Women are all very well, but a man is needed for business of this kind. Get some of the best of my pictures together, and we will go in a cab."

Leslie got ready, and all the time she was putting on her outdoor things she thought of the arrangement with Yorke. She was to have sent him her address to the Dorchester Club. He was waiting for it now, expecting it every minute. She could imagine his impatience, could picture to herself how he would walk up and down fuming for the telegram.

With a heavy heart she tied up the least ridiculous of her father's pictures and sent out for a cab, and told the man to drive to Bond Street, to the picture dealer's.

A hectic flush burned in Francis Lisle's thin cheeks, and Leslie saw his lips move as if he were speaking to himself, telling himself that Fame and Prosperity were awaiting him. Oh, what a tangled web we weave when first we practice to deceive! If she had not consented to deceive her father she would not now be in this awful strait; she was actually leading him to the bitterest disappointment of his life.

There are picture dealers and picture dealers. Mr. Arnheim, of Bond Street, is one of the best known men and the most respected. Many an artist now famous and wealthy owes his first step up the ladder to Mr. Arnheim. He will buy anything that shows promise, and for great works will give as much and more than a private purchaser. His judgment is almost infallible, and to be spoken well of by Arnheim is to have a passport to artistic fame. The cab drew up at his house, which was near the corner in one of the turnings out of Bond Street, and had nothing about it to indicate the nature of his business save and excepting a very small brass plate with "H. Arnheim" on it.

A page boy opened the door in response to Leslie's ring, and, on learning her name, ushered her and her father upstairs into a room hung round with pictures, and, giving them chairs, disappeared through a door in a partition which seemed to screen off a kind of office.

Leslie's heart beat apprehensively, and her face grew paler, but Francis Lisle looked round with a kind of suppressed exultation.

"There are examples of some of our best known artists here, Leslie," he said in a voice quavering with excitement. "There's one of so-and-so's," he mentioned the name, "and that is Sir Frederick's. This Mr. Arnheim is one of the first, the first dealers in the world, and never makes a mistake. Never! He would not have sent for me unless he had seen some of my pictures, and meant taking me up, as they call it."

"Oh, do not be too buoyed up, papa," she murmured in an agony of shame and remorse. "If it should not be so, if there should be some mistake. Oh, if you had let me come alone."

"Mistake? What can you mean, Leslie?" he responded almost angrily. "There is no mistake, can be none. Anyone would think you doubted my—my ability, my artistic capacity."

"Hush, hush!" she whispered, for he had raised his voice unconsciously, and she heard footsteps approaching.

The next moment the door in the partition opened, and a short, stout man with closely cropped hair of silvery white, and small shrewd eyes, entered the room or gallery.

He bowed and looked at them keenly, and it seemed to Leslie that his glance rested longer upon her than on her father.

"Mr. Lisle?" he said.

Francis Lisle rose and held out his hand in a stately kind of way, as if he were Peter Paul Rubens receiving a deputation.

"That is my name, sir," he said, with a kind of kingly affability, "and I am here in obedience to your summons."

CHAPTER XXIV.

"MAD AS A HATTER!"

Mr. Arnheim looked rather puzzled for a moment, then he looked as if he remembered.

"Oh, yes, yes, Mr. Lisle," he said, with a slightly foreign accent; he was German. "I remember——."

"You sent for me, doubtless, to make arrangements for the inclusion of some of my pictures in your coming exhibition," said Francis Lisle in a nervously pompous voice, which quivered with suppressed excitement and importance.

"Not exact——," began Mr. Arnheim, but he happened to glance at Leslie, and something in her pale, wan face stopped him. He was a shrewd man, and the anxiety of the daughter of the half pompous, half frightened creature before him touched him.

"Possibly, possibly, Mr.—er—Lisle," he said. "But my reason for communicating with you was the fact that I had been requested by—" he was going to say Lord Auchester, but he glanced at Leslie's face again, and seeing the imploring expression on it, faltered a moment, then went on suavely—"by a valued client of mine to procure a work by your hand."

Francis Lisle's face fell for a moment, then it brightened again.

"A commission?" he said. "Yes, yes. May I ask the name of your client?"

Mr. Arnheim opened his lips to give the name, but once again met the imploring gaze of the sweet eyes, and kept the name back.

"It is not usual to give our clients' names, Mr. Lisle," he said with an affectation of shrewdness. "We dealers are business men pure and simple, and are never too ready with information that may injure us. I hope you will consider it sufficient that a gentleman has made inquiries after some work of yours, and—er—be prepared to come to terms with me. Of course, I only act as the agent."

Francis Lisle flushed and bit his lip, but a gratified smile was creeping over his thin, wan face.

"I understand, Mr. Arnheim," he said pompously. "I am very busy just at present; indeed, I have only just finished a picture for—er—a patron, for which I have received a fairly large sum, and I have a number of studies in hand; but—er—I think I may say that I shall be willing to paint a picture for you—or your unknown client, if you prefer to put it in that way; but I can only do so on one condition, Mr. Arnheim."

The dealer bowed.

"And what is that condition, Mr. Lisle?" he asked gravely.

"That your client permit any picture he may purchase of me to be exhibited at the Royal Academy Exhibition."

"Certainly, certainly. I'll undertake that he shall accord that permission," said Mr. Arnheim.

"Very good," said Francis Lisle. "And now I should like to show you some of my pictures. We have brought a few—the best, in my judgment; but there are several others, if you would like to see more. Leslie——."

Leslie rose and took up a couple of the canvases, and as she did she looked at the keen, shrewd face of the dealer. It was the look with which she had appealed to Mr. Temple, and it said as plainly as if she had spoken—

"Spare him; oh, spare him!"

Francis Lisle took one of the pictures from her hand, and nervously, excitedly, placed it on an empty easel which stood ready for the purpose.

"A seascape, Mr. Arnheim," he said, waving his hand. "It would savor of impertinence to point out its merits to you who are so experienced and able a critic; but I may venture to hint that there is something in the treatment of that sky which you will not meet with every day."

For a moment the eminent dealer's face expressed a wide gaping astonishment, then it seemed to writhe as if with the effort to suppress a burst of laughter, but lastly it turned to an impassive mask, and, carefully avoiding the anguish in Leslie's eyes, he said, shading the view with his hand:

"Remarkable, very; very remarkable, Mr. Lisle."

"I thought you would say so," said Francis Lisle, with a triumphant glance at Leslie, who had stood with downcast eyes. "But if you think that worthy of notice, what do you say to this?" and he replaced the canvas by another. "'View of Cliffs by Moonlight.' Remark the shadows, the foam on the rocks, the birds, Mr. Arnheim!"

"Yes, yes, yes," said Mr. Arnheim in a kind of still voice. "Most—most singular and admirable!"

He glanced at Leslie, and an expression of pity and sympathy came into his shrewd face.

"And here is another," said Francis Lisle, catching up a third picture. "'The Wreck.' I spent months—months, Mr. Arnheim, over this; and if I may be permitted to say so I consider it one of my masterpieces," and he waved his hand to the fearful daub in a kind of ecstasy.

Mr. Arnheim stood speechless with what the unfortunate painter took to be admiration; and Leslie, trembling and pale, came forward and took the canvas from the easel.

"We—we must not take up any more of Mr. Arnheim's time, papa," she faltered, with an appealing glance at the dealer.

"No no, certainly not," responded Lisle. "But it is only right that Mr Arnheim should have an opportunity of judging of my work. You may be surprised, sir, that I am still, so to speak, an unknown artist. I may say that that surprise is shared by myself. But no one can be better acquainted with the fact that fame and fortune do not always fall to the deserving. No! Art is a lottery, and the best of us may, and, alas! too often do, only draw blanks. But I am confident that now you, who have so many opportunities of directing the attention of the world to what is most worthy of notice in art, have become acquainted with my pictures, that—that—in short——." He put his hand to his head and looked round confusedly.

"Yes, yes!" said Mr. Arnheim soothingly. "I quite understand. You will hear from me—I will see my client."

"Yes, certainly," cut in Francis Lisle. "I—I leave the whole of the negotiations to you. I have perfect confidence in you, Mr. Arnheim."

Mr. Arnheim bowed, and assisted Leslie's trembling hands to repack the pictures, but the artist stopped them by a gesture.

"Wait, wait, Leslie. I am content to leave these works with Mr. Arnheim. He will like to place them in this gallery with his other masterpieces."

The expression on Mr. Arnheim's face at this proposition beggars description, but he mastered his emotion, and managed to bow and mumble out some unintelligible words, which Francis Lisle mistook for expressions of gratitude.

"Do not mention it, my dear sir," he said, waving his hand. "I commit them to your care with every confidence, assured that they will receive every consideration and appreciation from you. Come, Leslie, as you said, we must not take up too much of Mr. Arnheim's time. Good morning, sir. I leave you to conduct all negotiations with your client. I have every confidence in you. Good morning!"

He gave his hand to Mr. Arnheim with the air of a painter-prince, and with a glance round the room as if he already saw his pictures placed among the other gems, stalked nervously out.

Leslie hesitated for a moment, then held out her hand. For a moment she seemed incapable of speech, then her trembling lips parted, and she faltered:

"You have been very good, and—and patient, and forbearing, sir, and I am grateful, very grateful."

"Don't mention it, Miss Lisle," he said, touched by her loveliness and sadness. "I quite understand—that is—well, I can't quite understand!"

Leslie's face burnt like fire.

"Why his—his grace——," she faltered.

Mr. Arnheim looked puzzled.

"His lordship!" he corrected her, but Leslie was too agitated to notice the correction.

"I cannot explain," she said in a troubled voice. "But—you will see him?"

"Yes, certainly," assented Mr. Arnheim.

"Will you tell him, please—" her voice broke, and her hands clasped and unclasped—"will you tell him that I came here against my will—that I was obliged to come, and that—that I wish him to forget everything that has passed. That neither my father nor I wish to see him again. That we wish to pass out of his life as if we had never seen, never known him. Will you tell him this? You—you think it strange, unbecoming, that I should give you this message, Mr. Arnheim but—" her voice broke—"but, perhaps you have a daughter of your own, and—and thinking of her you will not refuse——."

She broke down, and covered her face with her hands.

Mr. Arnheim had a daughter, as it happened, and he did think of her.

"I don't understand, quite, Miss Lisle," he said, in a low voice; "but I understand enough to convey your message."

Leslie gave him her hand without another word, and hurried after her father.

She found him descending the stairs slowly, and he stopped as she reached him, and nodded at her.

"One moment, Leslie," he said, in nervous accents. "I forgot to ask Mr. Arnheim if his gallery is insured. Such works as I have left with him are—are priceless!"

Before she could stop him, he had turned and reascended the stairs, and re-entered the gallery. Leslie followed him. The gallery was empty, but voices were heard behind the partition, and Mr. Arnheim could be heard exclaiming in mingled indignation, pity, and amusement:

"The man is as mad as a hatter!"

Leslie laid her hand upon her father's arm.

"Come away, dear!" she implored; but he shook her hand off, and put his finger to his lip warningly.

"Hush! Be silent! I want to hear what he is saying! These men never express themselves fully about the pictures in the presence of the artists. Now, listen, and you will hear what he really thinks. Hush! It is quite fair, quite!" and he chuckled confidently.

Leslie, turned to stone with apprehension and dread, stood still and waited.

"Mad as a hatter!" continued Mr. Arnheim to some one behind the partition. "The pictures he raves about are simply daubs! The daubs of a lunatic who has had access to paint and brushes. Look at this! He called it a seascape! Look at it! Why, a schoolboy of fourteen would blush to have painted it! In fact, no human being in possession of his senses could have produced it! Did you ever see anything like it? I never did, and I've had some queer experiences in the course of business. If it hadn't been for that sweet creature, his daughter, I should have burst out laughing. But something—dash me if I know what—kept me quiet. Look here, it's a dashed shame, that's what it is. He told me to write for the man, and I thought it was all on the square. But it's my opinion he's got some game in hand with the daughter. I might have guessed that, seeing the sort of man he is. These swells are all alike. Yes it's a dashed shame! She's too good to be made a fool of and deceived. But did you ever see such an awful lunatic daub as this, and this, and this!" the speaker's voice rose in crescendo as he evidently showed each of Francis Lisle's pictures. "There was never anything like 'em out of a madhouse!"

The voice ceased, for lack of breath, and Leslie, horror-stricken, turned to her father. He was leaning against the wall, his face white, livid, his jaw dropped, his eyes staring vacantly.

"Father! father!" she cried in a low voice.

He did not seem to hear her, but his lips moved and she could hear a faint, horrible echo of the words that had been spoken behind the screen.

"Come away, dear!" she implored him. "Come away!"

He dropped his eyes to her face and tried to smile; but it was a hideous grimace.

"Yes, yes," he said, hoarsely, almost inarticulately, "let us go home. Let us ——."

She took his hand, drew his arm through hers, and led him down the stairs. He went with the docility, the helplessness of a child, and sank into a corner of the cab with his eyes dull and lifeless, but his lips still moving.

Presently he beckoned to her. "What—what did he say?" he asked tremulously, his face working.

"It—it does not matter what he said, dear," she said soothingly. "Do not think of it. Try to forget it! Lean against me, dear!"

But he put her from him, not with his old impatient irritability, but with a gentleness that was quite new with him; and lying back in the cab stared at the floor, his lips moving, and Leslie could hear him still repeating the words they had heard from Mr. Arnheim.

It seemed an age before the cab reached Torrington Square, and when it did so the man Leslie helped out was an older man by twenty years than he who had left it that morning.

She helped him up to his room and tried to cheer and comfort him; but, for the first time in her life, her loving flattery proved of no avail.

He listened with vacant eyes and wan, hopeless face, and at last, he suddenly flung his hands before his eyes and uttered a low cry of despair, and awakening.

"God help me!" he cried. "I am a fraud and a lie! I see it all, now. A fraud and a lie! The man was right; I cannot paint!" He caught up a canvas that lay against the wall, and gazed at it. "It is a hideous daub, as he said. It is the work of a madman. I have been mad. Oh, God, if I could have remained so."

"My dear, my dear!" she murmured, kneeling beside him and gently drawing the picture from his weak, trembling hands. "Don't think of what—what he said."

"Not think of it!" he cried, shaking with emotion. "I must think of it, for he spoke the truth. I have been mad, mad! But my eyes are open now. Take them away from me," he motioned to the pictures, "take them away. I cannot bear the sight of them. And—and yet I have been so happy, so hopeful!" and he hid his face with his hands.

Leslie watched beside him till he fell into a deep, deathlike sleep; then she stole downstairs and sent for a doctor. A young man from one of the neighbouring squares came, and though he was young he was not foolish. A glance at the sleeping man told him the sad truth.

“Have you—has your father any relations, any friends who—whom he would like to see?” he asked gently.

Leslie, kneeling beside the bed, looked up at him with sharp and sudden dread in her eyes.

“Do you—do you mean——? Oh, what is it you mean?” she moaned.

The doctor laid his hand upon her shoulder. “The truth is always best, always,” he said gently. “Your father has suffered a severe shock; the heart ——.” He stopped. “For his sake try and be calm, my dear young lady.”

Leslie knelt beside him all through the night, and all through the long hours her conscience whispered accusingly, “It is you—you, who have done it. But for you he would have gone on dreaming and living; but for you—and Yorke!”

Toward dawn Francis Lisle awoke. The doctor was standing beside the bed, Leslie on her knees.

He raised his wan, wasted face from the pillow and seemed to be looking for something; then his eyes rested on her anguished ones, and he knew her and forced a smile.

“Is—is that you, Leslie?” he said, in so low a voice that she had to lay her face against his to hear him. “Is that you? I have had a singular dream. Most singular!”

“What—what was it, dear?” she said at last.

He smiled again.

“I dreamt that my picture had been refused by the Academy. Absurd, wasn’t it? Fancy them refusing one of my pictures! Mine! Francis Lisle’s! Ridiculous as it is, it—it upset me. I—I must be out of sorts. There is only one thing for that kind of complaint: Work. Get—get a fresh canvas stretched for me, Leslie, and I will commence a new picture. Let me see, what did we get for the last? Three thousand pounds, wasn’t it?”

“Yes, yes, dear!” she murmured.

“A large sum, a large sum, but not half what we shall get. Fame, fame and fortune at last, Leslie! I always told you it would come.”

He put out his wasted hand and smoothed her hair lovingly—and, alas! patronizingly. “Always knew it would come, Leslie! Art is long and—and life is brief. I must work hard now fame and success have brought me the victor’s laurels. How dark it is—” the sunlight was streaming through the window —“how dark! Too dark to commence to-day; but to-morrow, Leslie dear, to-morrow——." His voice grew fainter and ceased. The doctor bent over him, then stood upright and laid his hand upon Leslie's shoulder with a touch that told her all.

Francis Lisle had gone to the land where to-morrow and to-day are swallowed up in Eternity.

CHAPTER XXV.

"FORGOTTEN ME, HAS HE?"

If ever a man was in earnest, Yorke, Viscount Auchester, was. He was going to marry Leslie! The thought dwelt with him all the way up to town, hovered about him as he lay awake throughout nearly the whole night, and came to him in the morning with a joy exceeding description.

To marry Leslie!

What had he done to deserve such happiness, such bliss, he asked himself as he hurried through his tub and dressing? And while he ate his breakfast in a feverish, restless kind of haste, he pictured and planned out their future; a future to be spent side by side till Death, and Death alone, parted them.

They would leave London immediately, after the marriage, and cross the Channel. Perhaps they'd stay for a while in Paris; but only for a few days. It would be too big and noisy for such bliss as theirs. No, he would take her to some quiet spot in Normandy; perhaps to Rouen, that delightful old-world town with its magnificent churches and historic streets. Why, he could see themselves standing arm in arm in the vast cathedral, listening reverently to the grand service; he could see Leslie's face with the sweet gravity in her lovely eyes, and the half pensive and yet happy smile on her pure lips. He fancied her by his side looking up at the carved gables of the quaint houses; or seated at one of the little marble tables at the Cafe Blanc, with its shining copper vessels and glittering glass. Then they could go on into Germany; up the Rhine. How delightful to have her beside him as the steamer toiled against the stream and the delicious panorama unfolded itself mile by mile! Then, if they chose, there were Switzerland and Italy. There was Lucerne, for instance. How she would delight in Lucerne, with its marvelous lake, in which old Pilatus shadows himself, with its famous bridge spanning the emerald Reuss; with its snug cathedral in which the wonderful organ surges and wails as no other organ can surge and wail, save that of honored Milan.

Happy! He would make her happy or know the reason why! He would devote every hour of his life, every particle of his by no means gigantic intellect to the effort to prove how dearly he loved her.

He sat for a little while after breakfast making a mental plan of his procedure. He would have to act prudently and warily. No hint of what he was about to do must be allowed to get out. If his numerous creditors, Jew and Gentile, had the least suspicion that he was about to marry a penniless angel instead of Lady Eleanor Dallas, the heiress, they would swoop down upon him. No, he would be very cautious.

He had gone round to Mr. Arnheim, the dealer, on the evening before, immediately he had reached London, and was very cautious with him; giving him to understand that he merely wanted a small picture of Mr. Lisle's, and asking Mr. Arnheim in quite a casual way to write and ask Mr. Lisle whether he would accept a commission.

"Don't mention my name, please," he said; and Mr. Arnheim had smiled and shaken his head.

Yorke went away quite confident that the vaguest of letters from the great dealer would bring Francis Lisle post haste to London; and, as we know, he was right.

Then he went down to Doctors' Commons, and inquired about the license.

He knew no more about the business than the veriest schoolboy; but he had a vague idea that you could buy a license somewhere in that strange locality, and that armed with that he could marry Leslie right away at once. At once! The thought sent the blood rushing to his handsome face, and made St. Paul's Cathedral, hard by which is Doctors' Commons, waver before his eyes.

A seedy-looking gentleman led him to the Faculty office where the mystic license was to be obtained, and a grave and sedate clerk got off a high stool at a desk and put several questions to Yorke, who for the first time in his life—or the second, perhaps, for he was nervous when he had asked Leslie to be his wife—felt embarrassed and agitated.

"Is it an ordinary license you require, or a special?" asked the clerk.

Yorke looked doubtful.

"What is the difference?" he asked, almost shyly, and struggling with an actual blush.

The clerk eyed him with cold superiority.

"By an ordinary license," he explained, "you can marry in the church of the parish in which one of the parties resides; and only there. And he or she must have resided there fifteen days. With a special license you can marry in a particular church without having resided in the parish fifteen days; but you would have to give sufficient reasons for requiring this special license."

Yorke stared at the dingy floor while he thought the matter out.

He knew of a quiet little church near Bury Street—a "little church around the corner," so to speak, to which he and Leslie could go, the morning after her arrival in London; and with no one but the parson, the clerk, and pew-opener the wiser. Yes, an ordinary license would do, he said.

The clerk inclined his head—just as if he were a shopman selling gloves!—and went off to another clerk at another desk, and presently appeared with an affidavit.

"What's this? the license?" said Yorke.

"No. You will have to swear this. I shall have to ask you to accompany me to the next office, to a solicitor. You have to swear that the parties are of age, and that one of you has resided in the parish fifteen days. You are prepared to do so, I presume?"

It is to be feared that Yorke was prepared to do anything to obtain his Leslie, and he was led off—he felt like a criminal of the deepest dye—to another dingy office, and there repeated the oath gabbled out by the solicitor. Then he returned to the proctor's office, and, after waiting a quarter of an hour, the clerk handed him a document.

"What have I got to pay?" asked Yorke, prepared for a demand, say, of fifty pounds. "Only two pounds two and sixpence!" he said, with a surprise that made even that solemn clerk smile.

Only two pounds two and sixpence for the privilege of marrying Leslie! He stood and gazed at the mystic document, and laughed aloud, so that the seedy man who had conducted him to the office eyed him rather fearfully, and pocketing the half-sovereign Yorke gave him, scrambled off, fully convinced that the young man was mad.

And indeed he could scarcely be considered in full possession of his senses that day. Nearly every hour he took out that precious license and read it through or gazed at the imposing coat of arms at the top, and the Archbishop's signature at the bottom; and every time put it away again in his breast coat pocket. He patted the coat to feel that the document was there safe and sound.

From Doctors' Commons he walked to the Dorchester Club.

Everybody knows that aristocratic institution. It is not so magnificent as some of the modern political clubs; some of them are palaces compared with which those of the Caesars were very small potatoes; it had no marble entrance hall and oak-paneled dining-room, and its smoking-room was not as vast as a church; but it was snug and comfortable, and excellent to a degree. You had to have your name down on the list of candidates full fifteen or twenty years before you could hope to be balloted in, and some fathers put their sons down when they were eighteen months old.

Yorke was well known at the club, and the hall porter in his glass box bowed to him with a mixture of respect and recognition which he accorded to a very few of the members.

"There are no letters for me, Stephens, I suppose?" said Yorke.

"No, my lord, none."

"Ah, well, I expect one or a telegram directly," said Yorke, trying to speak casually. "If it comes just send into the smoking-room, or dining-room, or drawing-room, in fact and see if I'm in the club. I want it directly it comes, you understand."

"Certainly my lord," was the response. "If your lordship is in the club when the letter arrives I will see that you have it at once."

Yorke sauntered into the drawing-room and took up a paper; but he did not see a word of the page he gazed at. He was calculating how soon that letter could possibly reach him.

Then he went out, and making his way to Regent Street examined the shop windows carefully, and ultimately made several purchases.

He bought a lady's ulster, a wonderful garment of camel's hair, soft as lambs' wool and as warm, with cuffs that could be let down over the hands, and a hood that could be drawn completely over the head.

No lady with this marvelous ulster on could be cold, even while crossing the Channel, where, as everybody knows, it is possible to be frozen even on a summer's night. He also bought a traveling rug of Scotch tweed.

Then he sauntered into the park till lunch time, when he went back to the club. He knew that no letter could be waiting for him, and yet he could not help glancing inquiringly at the porter, who faintly smiled and respectively shook his head.

One or two acquaintances dropped in while he was eating his lunch at a side table, and they gathered round him and plied him with eager invitations to join them in a driving trip to Richmond; but he shook his head.

"Better come, Auchester," said one young fellow. "Jolly afternoon! Besides, a friend of yours is of the party."

"Who is that?" asked Yorke with polite indifference.

Drive to Richmond when he wanted to be alone to think of Leslie and all that license in his breast coat pocket meant! Not likely.

"Why, Finetta," said the young fellow. "She has promised, if we get her back in time for the theater."

Yorke shook his head, and while he was doing it Lord Vinson strolled up.

"What's that about Finetta and Richmond?" he inquired. "Afraid you'll be disappointed. Just been up there," he drawled. "She's vamoosed the ranche, sloped off somewhere, and isn't going to dance to-night. Know where she's gone, Auchester?"

"No," said Yorke, and he answered very quietly. Poor Fin! was she taking the breaking off of their friendship to heart after all?

"Strikes me Mademoiselle Fin is playing it rather low on an indulgent public!" grumbled the young fellow who had arranged the outing, and as he sauntered off with the rest he remarked in a low voice, "Shouldn't be surprised if Auchester had arranged to take her somewhere; they're awfully thick, you know, and she'd throw over anything for him."

After lunch Yorke went to Bury Street, and with his own hands packed a portmanteau or two.

Then he went back to the club, for though he knew no telegram could have arrived, he felt constrained to be there in waiting, so to speak, and dined quietly and in solitude, and afterwards he walked by the park railings to Notting Hill and round the quiet squares, and was happy thinking of Leslie and the days that lay before them, the delicious, glorious days when they two should be one—man and wife. Man and wife!

He went to bed early that night and slept soundly, so soundly that he was rather later than he meant to be at breakfast, and he hurried over that meal and made his way to the Dorchester with a fast-beating heart.

There might possibly be a telegram for him. But the porter said no, nothing had come for his lordship, and Yorke, too disappointed to make a pretense of looking at the papers, went out and stood on the broad steps and stared up and down Pall Mall.

Arnheim had promised to wire the night Yorke had seen him; there had been time for the Lisles to get up to London, time for Leslie to wire. Well, he would be patient and not worry. But, Heaven and earth, what should he do with himself while he was waiting for that telegram! He was so wrapped up in the thought of meeting his darling that he could not endure the distraction of even exchanging greetings with his acquaintances. He could not go to Finetta's—never again!—or Lady Eleanor's. He wanted to be alone, alone with his thoughts. What should he do? Was there anything else he could buy? As the question crossed his mind the answer flashed upon him and made him almost start. Why, there was the ring! He had not bought that yet. What an idiot he was. Even with a license, you could not be married without a ring. He went straight off to Bond Street, to the jeweler's of whom he had purchased the diamond pendant and the plain gold locket, and stood for a minute or two outside looking at the things in the window.

He would have a keeper as well as a plain wedding ring. He would get the prettiest and 'solidest' they'd got. He gazed at the rows of diamond ornaments, for the first time in his life covetously. Ah, if he were only the Duke of Rothbury, as she thought him, what things he would buy for her! Notwithstanding that, if he were the duke he would have the great Rothbury diamonds, those gems which were supposed to rank next to the Crown jewels, and they would be hers, his duchess's; yet, all the same, he would buy her all sorts of pretty things. As the heathen loves to deck his idol, so he, Yorke, would love to deck his idol with all that this world counted good and precious.

Regarding that masquerade of his, that sailing under false colors, he thought that Leslie would neither be very disappointed nor angry.

"It is me she loves," he told himself with a proudly swelling heart. "And it will not matter what I am or am not. But all the same I wish that idea had not occurred to poor old Dolph."

All this was passing through his mind as he was standing outside the well-known shop in Bond Street. Everybody knows it, and everybody knows that the street is rather narrow just where the shop is situated, and at that moment it happened that one of the many blocks of the day occurred, and that a neatly appointed brougham was brought to a standstill very nearly opposite the jeweler's shop.

It was a charming little brougham, one of those costly toys which only very wealthy people can indulge in. The interior was lined with Russian leather, the cushions of sage plush; there was a clock in ormolu and turquoise and a delightful little reading lamp, fan and scent case, and china what-not basket.

It was the brougham which took the celebrated Finetta to and from the Diadem; the brougham of which the newspapers have given an elaborate account, and in it was no less a personage than Finetta herself. She was leaning back against the eiderdown cushions, her handsome face pale, with purplish rings round her dark eyes. She looked as if she was half worn out by excitement and physical fatigue.

She had been lying with closed eyes till the block and stoppage came, then she opened her eyes and asked listlessly:

"What is it?"

"It's a block," said Polly who sat beside her. "There's a carriage and a butcher's cart in front, a swell carriage——."

Finetta leant forward listlessly, then her listlessness changed, fled rather.

"It's—it's Lady Eleanor Dallas," she said between her teeth.

"Oh," said Polly; "is it? Well, I wish they'd get on, and—oh!" The exclamation escaped her lips unawares, and Finetta, following the direction of Polly's eyes, saw Yorke standing gazing in at the shop window.

She uttered a faint cry and fell back, clutching Polly's arm.

"It's him!" she breathed.

"Lord Auchester. I know it is!" said the matter-of-fact Polly. "Well, you needn't start as if you'd got the jumps."

"What is he doing there, what is he going to buy?" said Finetta in a low and agitated voice.

Polly jerked down the blind.

"Don't make a perfect fool of yourself, Fin," she ventured to remonstrate. "What's it matter to you what Lord Yorke is doing or going to buy? He and you have done with each other——."

"Have we!" between the set teeth. "Much you know about it!"

"Well, if you haven't, you ought to have done. Oh, I wasn't deaf the other night when he was telling you about the girl he had fallen in love with and was going to marry; I heard enough to put two and two together. And I tell you what it is, Fin: you are making yourself a perfect idiot over that young man, and all for no good. Why, you've been away from the Diadem for two nights, and though I suppose you think I don't know where you've been, why I can guess. You've been dogging him down in the country somewhere——."

"Hold your tongue," said Finetta, her eyes still fixed, through a chink beside the silk blind, on Yorke.

"Yes, I can hold my tongue; but I'm talking for your good. Here you've been away for two days, goodness knows where, though I can guess, as I say, and you come back looking more dead than alive, and no more fit to dance to-night than I am."

"What is it he is buying? Something for her?" said Finetta almost to herself.

"What's it matter to you? You and he have done with each other, I tell you," said sensible Polly. "You let Lord Auchester alone, and forget him. You bet your life he's forgotten you by this time," and she ventured on a short laugh.

Finetta turned on her.

"Forgotten me, has he? What did he send me his portrait in a locket and that letter for, then? You hold your tongue! Tell the man to drive to Piccadilly and then back again!"

Her face was flushed, her eyes shining with feverish light in their purple rings.

"Well, if anyone had told me that you—you, Fin—would make such a fool of yourself over a man, I'd have given them the lie," remarked Polly after she had delivered the directions to the coachman.

Finetta fell back.

"Sneer on," she said in a low voice. "You don't understand, and, what's more, you never will. Is there any one in the carriage opposite? Is—is Lady Eleanor in it?"

CHAPTER XXVI.

A WEDDING RING.

Polly peered out.

"I can't see," she said, "the blinds are down."

But though she could not see her, Lady Eleanor was in the carriage, and she was looking, as Finetta was, at the stalwart young man in front of the jeweler's window. And her face was quite as pale as Finetta's. Should she open the window and call him? She longed to do so, and yet something, some vague presentiment, kept her from doing so. She watched him, her heart beating with love, until the block had melted away and the carriage had moved on, then she pulled the check string and, when the footman got down, said:

"Drive to Oxford Street, and then come back here, please."

Meanwhile, all unconscious that these two women were watching him, Yorke went into the shop.

"I want to look at some rings," he said to the man who bowed to him with an air of respectful recognition. It happened to be the same man who had served him the other day.

"Fancy rings my lord?"

"No, no," said Yorke, trying to speak in the most ordinary and casual way, and feeling very much as he had felt while procuring the license. "Er—wedding and keeper rings."

"Certainly, my lord," said the man, without the faintest change of countenance, and he placed a couple of trays on the counter.

"What size, my lord?"

Yorke looked up with a start of perplexity.

"Size?" he repeated, vaguely as he mentally called himself an idiot for not having measured Leslie's finger. "Oh, a small size. I don't quite know. Yes quite a small size. Here, I'll take two or three. They're all alike. I suppose!"

"Some heavier than the others, my lord."

"All right; give me the heaviest. And the keeper—isn't that what it's called?"

"Yes, my lord; it keeps the wedding ring in its place, you see."

"I see," said Yorke. "Well, I'll have one or two of these, the smaller ones; put this one in," and he picked out one set with pearl and turquoise. "I'll send back those I don't keep."

He tried to slip them on his little finger, but they would not go farther than the first point, and he laid them down with a smile. In a few hours, perhaps, he would be placing them on his darling's finger; his wife's!

The shopman put the rings in a box, and Yorke stowed them away carefully, very carefully, in an inner pocket, and went out, still dreaming of the hours when he should stand before the altar of the quiet little church in St. James'.

Two or three minutes afterward the dainty brougham pulled up to the shop door, and Finetta entered.

She was as well known to the jeweler as was Lord Auchester, and, if possible, he made her a more respectful and elaborate bow; she was a good customer, and, like most people in her position, she liked a great show of respect. So he leaned forward and placed a chair for her, and with another bow asked what he could have the honor of doing for her. Finetta's large, dark eyes wandered over the counter with a feigned indifference and listlessness.

"I only want a small present," she said.

"Yes, madam. For a gentleman?" and he made for a tray of silver cigarette cases and similar articles. Finetta looked at them, but kept the corners of her eyes fixed on the trays which had been on the glass counter when she entered.

"What pretty rings!" she said, taking up a jeweled keeper. "They almost tempt one to get married."

The man smiled sympathetically.

"I suppose the bridegroom always chooses the rings," she said, with seeming carelessness. "Now, I wonder which of these most men would choose?"

The man fingered the rings lightly.

"Some one, some another, madam," he replied. "The gentleman who has just gone out chose one like this."

Finetta's face was pale already, but it seemed to blanch, and the ring rolled along the counter.

"Lord Auchester was buying a wedding ring and keeper!" she said involuntarily.

As the words left her lips, a lady had entered the shop, and she heard them as plainly as if they had been addressed to her; and they took an instantaneous and extraordinary effect. She let the door slip, and put her hand to her heart, and so stood gazing with a strange expression in her eyes from Finetta to the man.

It was a dramatic moment. The two women stood silent and motionless, regarding each other with a world of meaning in their eyes. Finetta, still eyeing Lady Eleanor, went on:

"It was Lord Auchester who bought the ring?"

The jeweler smiled deprecatingly.

"Well, as you saw him, madam, it is no breach of confidence. It was his lordship." Then he looked toward Lady Eleanor, and, bowing, placed a chair for her.

Finetta rose; her face was still white, her full lips pale and trembling.

"I—I will come in again," she said, and moved toward the door; then she stopped, and swaying forward rather than stepping, leaned toward Lady Eleanor.

"I want to speak to you," she said abruptly and hoarsely.

Lady Eleanor shrank back and eyed her haughtily. "I—

I—" she began, but her voice seemed to fail her.

"You'd better not refuse, for—for your own sake!" said Finetta, hissed it, rather. "You—you know me——."

Lady Eleanor tried to look a denial, but the effort failed as the effort to speak had.

"And I know you," went on Finetta, still in the low, husky, agitated voice. "What I have to say concerns you. You'd better not refuse!"

Lady Eleanor looked round as if seeking some means of escape, then rose, hesitated a moment, her white teeth catching her lip, and followed Finetta to the end of the long shop, the jeweler discreetly keeping out of earshot, and respectfully waiting until his customers had finished their conference. He saw that something was happening; but his well-trained face was absolutely impassive.

Lady Eleanor stood turned sideways to Finetta, her haughty lips half lowered, but her lips trembling. If anyone that morning had told her that Finetta of the Diadem would dare to address her, and that she would consent to listen to her for one single moment, she would have laughed the idea to scorn. And yet here she was actually waiting for what the woman had to say.

Finetta's bosom was heaving with the effort at self-control. She could not help admiring Lady Eleanor's self-possession, while she hated her; and she tried to imitate her.

"You heard what the man said," she said at last, in a low, shaken voice.

Lady Eleanor's haughty lids moved slightly in assent.

"Well!" said Finetta, with a kind of gasp, "it's true!"

Lady Eleanor made the faintest movement with her hand. It seemed to say:

"If it is, what is it to do with me—or you?" and Finetta understood her.

A hot flush passed over her handsome face.

"You mean it's no business of mine. Well—" she drew a long breath, "perhaps it isn't. But it is of yours, or people make a great mistake when they say he is going to marry you."

Lady Eleanor's face crimsoned with humiliation, and she made as if to leave the place at once; but Finetta put out her hand, and Lady Eleanor stepped back as if the touch would contaminate her.

"I—I cannot listen to you—I have nothing to say," she said in a labored voice. "You have no right to speak to me—I do not know you—have no wish——."

Finetta's teeth came together with a click.

"Very well, go then!" she exclaimed vindictively. "Go! Do you think it's any pleasure to me to speak to you? Do you think I'd have spoken to you if it hadn't been for his sake?"

Lady Eleanor winced.

"You treat me like the dirt under your feet, you won't stoop to listen to what I've got to say, though it should save him from ruin. And you call yourself his friend! A pretty friend! I've heard you swells have got no heart, and I should think it's true, judging by you!" Her breath came fiercely. "Go! Why don't you go?"

Lady Eleanor looked at the door and then at the white, working face and flashing eyes; and remained.

She drew her light wrap round her and held it with a clenched hand.

"Say what you have to say quickly," she said, and her voice was thick and husky. "You are right; I am a friend of Lord Auchester's, if it is he whom you mean."

Finetta eyed her with a touch of scorn in her flashing eyes.

"You know it is him. Friend! I should think you were! Do you think I didn't see you start when you came in, and do you think I don't see how you're trembling and shaking? Bah! with all your acting you wouldn't be worth much on the stage. I tell you what the man said is true. Yorke Auchester has bought his wedding ring, and he'll use it unless you can prevent it!"

Lady Eleanor's face was like a mask, but her eyelids quivered.

"I've done my best—or worst," went on Finetta, and she laughed harshly. "I've seen the girl and tried to put a spoke in her wheel, and I thought I'd succeeded; but it seems I haven't——."

"You have seen her?" escaped Lady Eleanor's lips.

"Yes!" said Finetta. "Did you think it was me he was going to marry?" Her lips twitched. "It's a young girl down in the country, at a forsaken place called Portmaris."

"Portmaris!" Lady Eleanor breathed.

"Yes. Quite a young girl, a country girl, a mere nobody, and not a swell like you; though she's what you call a lady," she added.

Lady Eleanor sank into a chair and sat with tightly clasped hands. The shock of this sudden news had caused her to forget that the woman who was speaking to her was Finetta, the dancing girl at the Diadem, the girl with whom Yorke Auchester had been so intimately friendly.

Finetta looked down at her with a bitter smile. She had brought this haughty aristocrat to her knees, at any rate.

"How she must love him!" she thought. "How we both love him!" and she ground her teeth.

Lady Eleanor, with her eyes downcast, asked after a pause:

"What is her name?"

"Leslie Lisle," replied Finetta. "She's as pretty and—and fresh as—as a flower; and when I told her that—that—"

Lady Eleanor looked up.

"What did you tell her?" she asked, in a low, husky voice.

Finetta flushed sullenly.

"Well, it doesn't matter. I thought that what I'd told her would break it off between him and her; but it hasn't, or he wouldn't be buying the wedding ring. They are going to be married secretly, and at once; and now what are you going to do, my lady?"

Lady Eleanor looked before her vacantly. Her heart was aching, burning with jealousy and the terror of despair. She shook her head.

"I daresay you wonder why I spoke to you, why I tell you this, seeing—that it can't matter to me who he marries?" said Finetta, with a flush.

Lady Eleanor glanced at her.

"Yes; why did you speak to me?" she said indistinctly.

Finetta bit her lip.

"I don't know, and that's the truth," she admitted. "The news knocked me over, and—and I was flurried. And besides—well, two heads are better than one, and——."

Lady Eleanor understood. This dancing girl meant that she was not afraid of Lord Auchester's marrying her, Lady Eleanor, but that she was terribly afraid that he would marry this girl in the country, this Leslie Lisle.

She rose.

"I can say nothing. I am not Lord Auchester's keeper. If he chooses to marry a dairy maid—or worse—it is his business."

Finetta watched her keenly.

"But all the same, you'll do all you can to prevent it," she said sharply, and with an air of conviction. She had caught a significant gleam in the proud eyes.

Lady Eleanor turned pale, stood a moment as if waiting to see if Finetta had anything more to say, then with a slight inclination of her head passed out of the shop.

She walked proudly and haughtily enough to her brougham, but when she got inside her manner changed, and she covered her face with her hands, and cowered in the corner, trembling and moaning.

Yorke going to marry! Going to marry and beneath him, too! He had passed her over for some country wench, some nobody beneath him in rank, utterly unworthy of him. It tortured her. What should she do? What could be done? She asked herself this as the carriage rolled on homeward, and for a time no answer came; then suddenly she started and pulled the check string.

"The nearest telegraph office," she said to the footman.

There was only one person who could help her, even if he would, which was doubtful. She sent a telegram to Ralph Duncombe.

"Can you come and see me at once on important business?"

Meanwhile all unconscious of the strange meeting between his two old loves, Yorke betook himself to the Army and Navy Stores, and whiled away the time by buying a lady's portmanteau, one of the latest and most expensive kind, and ordering the initials "L. A." to be painted on it. This afforded him a subtle delight. "Leslie Auchester." How well it sounded, "Leslie, Viscountess Auchester!" Take the peerage all through, and there wouldn't be a more beautiful, charming woman than this wife of his! He bought one or two other things—traveling luxuries, which should add to her comfort on their journey, then went back to the club.

"Any telegram for me?" he asked, almost confidently.

"No, my lord," was the reply.

Yorke's face clouded, then it cleared.

"Look here," he said, "I forgot to tell you that it would be addressed to Yorke."

The porter looked in the 'Y' pigeon-hole and shook his head.

"Nothing for that name either, my lord."

Yorke stood at the door of the porter's glass box and stared at the man as if he could not believe his ears. Then he swung round, and jumping into a cab, told the man to drive to Arnheim's.

He met the dealer coming down the stairs.

"Oh, good morning, my lord," he said. "I have written to you."

"Yes, yes! Mr. Lisle—has he been here?"

"Yes, my lord," said Arnheim, looking at the handsome and palpably agitated face curiously. "He has been here."

"With——."

"With his daughter, Miss Lisle. Yes. And he has left some pictures. Of course, your lordship knows best, but I am bound to tell you, it's only right, that the pictures are utterly——."

"I know, I know," Yorke broke in quickly. "That's all right. I mean it doesn't matter. I'll explain afterward. What I want now is their address!"

"Port——."

"Yes, yes, I know; I mean their London address, where they're staying."

The dealer thought a moment, while Yorke looked at him as if he could tear the answer from him.

"I—well, the fact is, I don't know it. I did not think to ask it!" said Arnheim.

Yorke flushed a dark red.

"Oh, nonsense! They must have given you their address, some place to write to!"

"You'd naturally think so, but as it happens they didn't!" said Arnheim. "I admit I ought to have asked Mr. Lisle, but—well, I didn't! I suppose I expected him to call again. And," with a faint smile, "of course he will do so, the man is an enthusiast——."

"I know all about him, thanks," said Yorke sternly. "What I want is Lisle's address." He thought a moment, then said slowly and impressively—"When he calls next—he may do so to-day, any hour—be sure and get the address. Wire it to me at the Dorchester, and at once."

"Certainly, my lord," said Arnheim; "and about the pictures?"

"Buy two or three, give him his own price for them. But, mind, keep my name out of the business!" and he ran down the stairs and jumped into the cab again, telling the man to drive back to the club.

"I'll stick there till Leslie's telegram comes," he said between his teeth, "if I stay there till doomsday."

He was consumed by anxiety. Leslie in London, and he did not know where! Good Heavens, could the telegram have miscarried? Was anything wrong? He tried to remain cool and confident, but he looked as he got out of the cab like a man oppressed by a terrible presentiment.

On the steps of the club stood Grey.

"Hallo!" said Yorke. "Grey!"

Grey touched his hat.

"I've been to Bury Street, my lord, and Fleming sent me here. His grace is back, and would be glad if you could come and see him."

Yorke hesitated, and was on the point of sending a message to say that he would come presently—to-morrow; then it occurred to him that the duke had come from Portmaris, and that he might have some news of the Lisles.

"All right," he said, "I'll come at once. Keep the cab."

He ran up the steps to the porter.

"That telegram?"

"Nothing, my lord, for you as yet."

With something like a groan Yorke went slowly down the steps again and into the cab.

Leslie! Where was she? Why—why had she not wired as she promised?

CHAPTER XXVII.

"GONE, AND LEFT NO ADDRESS."

The ducal house in Grosvenor Square was not seldom referred to as an instance of the extreme of luxury which this finish of the century had attained to. It was an immense place, decorated by one of the first authorities, with ceilings painted by a famous artist, and walls draped by hangings for which the Orient had literally been ransacked. The entrance hall was supposed to be the finest in the kingdom. It was of marble and mosaic; a fountain plashed in the center, and the light poured through ruby-tinted glass and warmed with a rose blush the exquisite carvings and statuary. At the end of the hall rose broad stairs of pure white marble, in the centre of which was laid a Persian carpet of such thick pile that footsteps were hushed. Stately palms stood here and there, relieving the whiteness of the marble and 'breaking the corners.' The staircase led to the first corridor, which ran round the hall, and upon the walls of this corridor hung pictures by the great English masters. The family portraits were at Rothbury. The state rooms were on the ground floor, and were on a par in the way of luxury and magnificence with the hall. Altogether it was a very great contrast to Marine Villa, Portmaris.

Yorke followed Grey to the hall, and was ushered into a room behind the state apartments.

It was a small room, and, compared with the rest of the house, plainly furnished in oak. There were bookshelves and a large writing table, and one of those invalid couches which are provided with bookrests and an elaborate machinery which enables one to move the couch by merely pressing a lever.

On this couch lay the Duke of Rothbury. Though the day was warm, a fire burned in the grate, and a superb sable rug was tumbled on the couch as if the invalid had pulled it off and on restlessly. Three or four books lay on the floor, but he was not reading, and he looked up sharply as Yorke entered, and did not speak until Grey had closed the door upon them.

Then, as he held out his hand and his keen eyes scanned Yorke's face, he said:

"Do you think I have sent for you to crow over you, Yorke?"

Yorke stood and looked down at him for a moment without replying; then he said vaguely:

"Crow over me? What do you mean, Dolph?"

The duke raised himself on his elbow.

"Sit down," he said; "you look tired and knocked up. Is anything the matter?"

Yorke sank into a chair and avoided the keen eyes.

"Matter? What should be the matter?" he said evasively. "You don't look quite the thing; but I suppose the journey took it out of you?"

"Yes, it was the journey," said the duke dryly.

"Isn't it rather a pity that you left Portmaris?" said Yorke after a slight pause. "It was a pretty place, and healthy and all that, and I thought you rather liked it than otherwise."

"It's a pity I ever went there," responded the duke grimly.

Yorke looked up suddenly and caught the eyes fixed on him half pityingly.

"Why so?" he asked. "I should say you were the better for the change——."

"And I should say I was so much the worse," broke in the duke. "And now we have fenced with each other and beat about the bush, Yorke, don't you think we'd better be open and above board?"

"What do you mean?"

The duke raised himself a little higher, and worked the lever of the couch so that he brought himself facing Yorke.

"Why do you look as if you were waiting for a sentence of life or death, Yorke?" he said quietly. "You look as anxious and harried and worn as a man might look who stood on the brink of ruin. Have you heard from her?" he added quietly but sharply.

"Heard from whom?" said Yorke with averted eyes.

"From Miss Lisle—Leslie," said the duke.

Yorke raised his eyes quickly.

"You know——?" he said.

"Yes, I know all," said the duke gravely, almost sympathetically. "And—yes, I am sorry for you, Yorke! No, I don't mean to crow over you, though my prophesy has come true, and my estimate of her—and her sex generally—has proved the correct one. I am not going to indulge in the delicious luxury of remarking, 'I told you so!' I'll spare you that. Indeed, I haven't the heart to do it, for to tell you the truth I had been hoping all along that my prophesy would be falsified, and that your faith in her would be established. But it wasn't to be. Who is it says that a woman can be beautiful, lovable, magnanimous, clever, everything—but true?"

Yorke looked at him with a harassed and perplexed frown.

"What the devil are you talking about, Dolph?" he said.

The duke sat up and scanned the face before him in silence for a moment or two, then said:

"Is it possible that you don't know?"

"Don't know what?" demanded Yorke impatiently. "What are you talking about? I beg your pardon, Dolph, but—but I'm rather worried and upset about—something, and I'm short-tempered this morning. I've been expecting an important telegram for the last two days and it hasn't turned up, and—there, don't mind me, but go on and explain what you were saying about Les—Miss Lisle. I can't make head or tail of it!"

"From whom are you expecting a telegram, Yorke? Shall I make a guess and say the young lady herself?"

Yorke thought a moment, the color mounting to his face, then he looked the duke straight in the eyes.

"Yes, it was from her, Dolph," he said. "I'd better make a clean breast of it. You'd get it out of me somehow or other if I didn't own up, for I'm too worried to keep on guard. It is from Leslie I'm expecting that telegram, and—and—Well, look here, Dolph, take it quietly. I've asked her to be my wife, and—and she's consented."

He waited a moment, expecting to see the duke start up and fly into one of his paroxysms, but the duke leant upon his elbow and looked at him with a grave and pitying regard.

"I know that," he said.

"You—knew—that—that I had asked her, that she had agreed to come up to London and marry me on the quiet?" exclaimed Yorke, staring at him. "She told you?"

"No, she did not tell me that you had arranged a clandestine marriage," said the duke quietly, "but she confessed that you had asked her to be your wife. And so you were going to marry her secretly? Was that—was that straight of you, Yorke?"

There was a touch of gentle reproach in the tone that made Yorke wince.

"Put it that way, it wasn't, Dolph," he said. "But look how I am placed. I am up to my ears in debt. Yes, I know I ought to be ashamed of myself, but there it is, you see! And if it got out that I was marrying without money the blessed

Jews would be down on me, and—and—I knew you wanted me to—to marry someone else, and that I couldn't count on you; and so—and so I thought Leslie and I would get spliced quietly and wait till things had blown over, and ——."

The duke dropped back on the couch, but kept his eyes fixed on the harassed, anxious face.

"My poor Yorke! You must love her very much."

Yorke flushed red.

"Love her—!" he broke out, then he pulled himself up. "Look here, Dolph, I love her so much that if I knew that by marrying her I should have to drive a hansom cab or sweep a crossing for the rest of my life, I'd marry her!"

He got up and strode to and fro, his eyes flashing.

"I tell you that life wouldn't be worth living without her. Why, why," his voice rang low and tremulous, "I cannot get her out of my thoughts day or night. I see her face before my eyes, hear her voice always. It's Leslie, Leslie, and nothing else with me! I know now, I can understand now why a man cuts his throat or pitches himself off the nearest bridge when he loses the woman he loves. I used to laugh at the old stories, at the Othello and Romeo and Juliet business, but I understand now! It's all true, every word of it! I'd rather die any day and anyhow than lose her. And—and there you are! You see, Dolph," with a kind of rueful smile, "I'm as far gone as a man can be; just raving mad. But it's a madness that will last my life."

"I hope not," said the duke gravely. "Yorke, I am sorry for you. I did not know that the thing had gone so far. I have bad news for you."

"Bad news!" echoed Yorke.

"Yes. As I said, I was right in my estimate of Leslie Lisle, and you were wrong. She knows all, Yorke, and——." He paused and shrugged his bent shoulders.

"She knows all?" said Yorke, almost stupidly. "What do you mean?"

"She discovered the deceit, the trick, we had played upon her. How, I do not know. Perhaps she came across a peerage, or a society paper referring to the 'crippled Duke of Rothbury,' or Grey may have let slip a word in her hearing which revealed the secret. Who can say? After all, it was wonderful that we succeeded in keeping up the deceit so long. She was bound to discover the truth sooner or later."

Yorke gazed at him with a troubled face.

"You mean that she discovered that you were the duke and not I?" he said.

The duke nodded.

"Yes. She came to me early in the morning, so pale and changed, so thoroughly overwhelmed with disappointment——."

"Hold on," broke in Yorke. "Disappointment? Do you mean that she was disappointed that I was not the duke, that she was cut up, that she cared one straw?"

"My dear Yorke, if you had seen her you would have been as astonished and as full of remorse as I was—though the trick was not yours, but mine. I told her so, I took all the blame, but it was of no use to plead for you. She was broken down with the agony of disappointment. If, as you say, you had arranged a secret marriage with her, she looked upon herself as already the Duchess of Rothbury, and to have the cup dashed from her lips! My dear Yorke, one must make all allowance for her. Human nature is human nature all the world over, especially feminine human nature——."

Yorke's face went from white to red and from red to white again.

"You are talking rot, utter rot, Dolph!" he said. "Leslie—Leslie Lisle—cut up and knocked over because she was not going to be a duchess! Ha, ha!" and he laughed scornfully. "How well you know her! she wouldn't care a pin; I've told you so half a dozen times! Why, she was shrinking from the idea of being a duchess; would have refused me for being what I thought I was, if—if—well, if she hadn't cared for me as she does, God bless her!"

He turned his head away and his eyes grew moist.

The duke watched him gravely.

"You doubt my word, Yorke?"

"No, no! But I say you are mistaken. There was something else."

"What else, what other cause could there be? No, I tell you that it was the agony of disappointed ambition——."

Yorke laughed again.

The duke flushed.

"Come," he said, "you will not credit my statement, or rely on my judgment. Perhaps you are right. A man should have faith in the purity and single-mindedness of the woman he loves. But facts are stubborn things."

"Facts?"

"Yes! She had arranged to come up to London to you—to send to you. I don't know what plans you made, but I can imagine them. I know how I should have arranged in your case. Well, she is in London, or has been, and has she sent to you, has she met you as she promised?"

Yorke gazed at him with a half doubtful, half scornful expression.

"No," he said at last. "But—but there has been some mistake, blunder, on somebody's part. The telegram has miscarried. She may not have been able to send it. You know how closely she waits upon her father; she may not have been able to get out——."

The duke shook his head.

"My dear Yorke, her last words to me were a distinct farewell to me and to you. I've not the least doubt in the world that the person who informed her that you were not the duke had also told her that you were heavily in debt, and in Queer Street generally, and that she saw how foolish it would be to throw herself away and ruin her whole life by making an imprudent marriage."

Yorke uttered an oath.

"By heaven, Dolph, if it were anybody else but you who talked of her like this I'd—I'd make him take his words back!"

The duke sighed.

"Even if I were your equal in strength, and we bashed each other, it wouldn't alter the truth a hair's breadth," he said sadly and wearily. "And the truth is as I prophesied weeks ago and state now. Leslie, learning that you were not the Duke of Rothbury, has thrown you over!"

"The truth! It's a foolish and cruel lie!" exclaimed Yorke, his eyes blazing, his hands clenched. "You always misjudged her, you were prejudiced against her, from the first——."

The duke put his hand as if to stop him, but the passionately indignant voice rang out:

"From the first! She is as pure and high-minded as—as an angel, but you had made up your mind that she was a mercenary schemer, and not even the being with her, and knowing her, and seeing her every day, disabused your mind and opened your eyes to the wrong you were doing her! Yes, you were against her from the first. You'd made your mind up. That ridiculous idea of yours that all women are greedy and hungry for wealth and a title has become a monomania with you, and your mind has got as twisted as your body!"

He stopped aghast and breathless. The words—the cruel words—had slipped out on the torrent of his indignation before be scarcely knew or realized their cruel significance.

The duke sank back, and put his hand to his eyes, as if Yorke had dealt him a physical blow.

Yorke hung his head.

"Forgive me, Dolph," he said in a low voice. "I—I did not mean——."

The duke dropped his hands from before his face.

"Let that pass," he said in a low voice. "You did not mean it. It is the first unkind word you have ever——. But no matter! You say that I was prejudiced, that I wronged her. Yorke, you have forced my hand, and to show you that you have wronged me, I must tell you all. Yorke——," he paused, and his eyes dropped, then he raised them, and looked steadily into Yorke's —"I loved her!"

Yorke started.

"You!"

The duke plucked at the sable rug for a moment to silence, then he went on—

"Yes! I should not have told you, should never have confessed it, even to myself, but for—what you said. It is the truth. I loved her! What!" and he leant forward, his thin, wasted face flushed, his lips trembling. "Do you think that it is given to you only to appreciate such beauty and grace and sweetness as Leslie Lisle's? You remind me that I am crooked, twisted, deformed——."

"Dolph!"

"But do you think, because I am what I am outwardly, that I have no heart? God, who sees below the surface, knows that there beats in my bosom a heart as tender, as hungry for love, as quick to love as yours! Ah, and quicker, hungrier! And I loved her! Loved her with a love as strong and passionate as yours!" He stopped for want of breath.

Yorke sank into a chair and turned his face away.

"And you did not guess it? Well, that is not surprising, for I strove hard to hide it from even myself. I knew that it was madness to hope that I might win her love! But I knew that if I had offered myself in my right colors she would have accepted me, bent, twisted, deformed, mockery of a man as I am!"

Yorke groaned.

"And—and—" he stopped, and seemed to be struggling with something —"and I was tempted! Yes, I was tempted the morning she came to me and told me that she knew, was tempted to tell her that she might still be a duchess, that I loved her and would marry her!"

Yorke sprang to his feet.

"Sit—sit down," said the duke hoarsely, and Yorke sank down again. "But I resisted the temptation. I left her without a word, without a look or sign by which she could know the truth. I had to bear it. It is a burden which crushes, which tortures me! Even since I left the cursed place the temptation has assailed me at intervals, and once or twice I have almost resolved to write—to go down to her—and offer her that upon which she has set her woman's heart—the ducal coronet—for which even a Leslie Lisle will sell herself!"

Yorke opened his lips, but the duke by a gesture stopped him again.

"Now you know the whole truth. If you have to suffer, so also have I. And my lot will be worse than yours. You—" he looked at him, not enviously, but with a sad admiration—"you will get over this—will forget her——."

"No, no!"

"Yes. There are other women whose love you may win. There is one already." He paused. "Yes, if one nail drives out another, so one love may drive out, wipe out all remembrance of another. And so it is with you. But I!" He dropped back and covered his face with his hands. "For me there can be no such hope. The door of love, the gates of the earthly paradise are shut against me, and will remain shut while I live. To me the Fates say mockingly, 'Rank, wealth, station, we give you, but the love of woman, that supreme gift of the gods to man, thou shalt never know it!'"

There was silence for a moment, then he raised himself on his elbow.

"Yorke, you must bear your burden. Forget her. It will be hard. Don't I know how hard? To forget Leslie—those sweet gray eyes, with their melting tenderness, that low, musical voice! But you must forget her. As I said, there are others. There is one. Eleanor——."

Yorke sprang to his feet.

"Forget her! Forget Leslie! What are you talking about? We must be mad, both of us; you to talk as you have done, and I to listen! She's as true as steel! I shall find a telegram waiting for me at the club, and—and all will turn out right."

The duke regarded him gravely.

"Go and see," he said quietly. "If you do not find a message from her, what will you do?"

Yorke looked at him.

"Though my body's twisted, my brain is straighter and more acute than yours," said the duke with a smile, "and I will tell you what to do. Wire to the landlady at the house they lived in, Sea View. What was the woman's name?"

"Merrick," said Yorke.

"Yes, Merrick. Ask if the Lisles are there, and if not, for their address. Pay for the return message and all charges. But I can tell you the result at once."

"The result? What?"

"You will not find her. She does not intend that you should. With all her beauty and grace and sweetness, she, even she, even Leslie! being a woman, is too worldly wise to marry Yorke Auchester now that he is a duke no longer."

Yorke caught up his hat and laughed hoarsely.

"I'll soon prove you wrong!" he said.

"And if you do not? If you prove that I am right?" asked the duke, looking at him steadily.

Yorke stopped at the door and looked over his shoulder.

"Then—then—" he stopped and swore—"then you may do what you like with me; marry me to whom you please, when you please, send me to the devil——."

He strode through the marble hall and called a cab. He ran up the steps of the Dorchester and confronted the patient Stephens.

"There's a telegram for me now, Stephens. Name of 'Yorke,' you know.

"No, sir, nothing for you," was the reply.

He turned at once, and going straight to the telegraph office in Regent Street, sent the following telegram to Mrs. Merrick:

"If Miss Lisle is not at Portmaris, send her address to Yorke, Regent Street Post Office. Reply, paid, at once."

"I'll wait," he said.

"It may be an hour, sir," said the young ladyclerk.

"I'll wait if it's ten hours," he said.

He waited for an hour and a half, and then they handed him this:

"Mr. and Miss Lisle have gone and left no address."

He walked from the post office to Grosvenor Square with the telegram crushed in his hand, and went straight to the duke's room. He was still lying on the couch, and he did not lift his head as Yorke entered.

"Well?" he said. "But I need not ask. You are convinced?"

Yorke flattened out the telegram and dropped it into the duke's hand.

"No address! Here in London, and I do not know where to look for her!" he said hoarsely.

"Convinced! No! No!"

Then his voice broke, and he sank into the chair by the table and dropped his head upon his arms.

The duke sighed.

"My poor Yorke! Oh, woman, woman! God sent you as a blessing, and you have proved a curse!"

CHAPTER XXVIII.

"I WOULD DO ANYTHING TO SAVE HIM."

Lady Eleanor reached Palace Gardens and went straight to her boudoir and flung herself on a couch.

To women of her class come very few such adventures as that which had happened to her this morning. From their cradles, through their girlhood, and indeed all through their lives, they are so hedged in and protected from the world outside the refined and exclusive circle in which they move, that there is little chance of their coming in contact with other than their own set.

She had seen Finetta on the stage of the Diadem, had heard of her, read of her, knew that Yorke Auchester's name was in some way connected with her, but she had never dreamed that a meeting with her would be even possible, much less probable.

And now she had not only met with her, but talked and listened to her.

The fact that she had done so filled her with shame and confusion. What would her friends and relatives think if they knew? What would Godolphin, the duke, say if he were told that she had not only engaged in conversation with this Finetta, but actually entered into a kind of compact and conspiracy with her.

But she soon dismissed this part of the case and allowed herself to think only of the information Finetta had given her.

Yorke going to be married!

She would almost as soon have heard that he was going to die. Indeed, death would not more completely remove him for her, would not set up a more surmountable barrier between them than a marriage. For if he were to die, she could still think and dream of him as hers; whereas, if he married, he would belong in this world and the next to another woman.

And such a woman! Finetta had spoken of this Leslie Lisle as if she were an uncultivated, half-educated country girl.

Lady Eleanor could imagine what she was like; some simpering, round-faced girl, just a step above a laborer's daughter. One of these girls who blushed with timidity and fright when they were spoken to, who spoke in a strong provincial dialect, who dressed like a dowdy and looked just respectable; something between a servant and a shop girl.

She was pretty, no doubt; but to think that Yorke, Yorke the fastidious, should be caught by a pretty face! Why, she, Lady Eleanor, was pretty! She looked at her pale, agitated face, and a kind of indignant rage consumed her for a moment. She was the acknowledged belle of many a ballroom. She might have been a professional beauty if she had cared to be one. She was accomplished, was in his own rank and class, a fitting mate—yes, she told herself with inward conviction, a fitting mate for him.

With her by his side, as his wife, he could have filled a conspicuous place in the world, their world, the upper ten thousand, the rulers and masters.

And he had passed her by and was going to marry a half-educated, uncivilized, uncultivated country girl, with pink cheeks and a simpering smile.

The thought drove her half mad. Finetta had said that she had tried to prevent it, and that it now rested with her, Lady Eleanor, to make an attempt.

Lady Eleanor shuddered and reddened with shame at the idea of being a conspirator with such a one as Finetta of the Diadem. And yet was not the object to be attained worthy of even such means?

She would not ask herself why Finetta desired to stop the marriage; she put that question away from her resolutely, and told herself that it was of Yorke and Yorke's welfare alone that she was thinking.

A servant came up to announce visitors, but Lady Eleanor answered through the locked door that she wasn't at home.

"I will only see Mr. Ralph Duncombe," she said, and she longed for his presence with a feverish impatience; though she had no fixed plan in her mind, nothing but a vague idea that Ralph Duncombe, the cute city man, might be able to help her.

About six o'clock the servant announced him, and she had him shown up to her boudoir. She had had time to collect herself and regain composure, to change her dress for a tea gown and do her hair; but her face was pale and still showed traces of the terrible agitation which she had suffered, and Ralph Duncombe as he took her hand looked at her inquiringly.

"I am afraid you have found the heat trying, Lady Eleanor. I hope you are well," he said, in his grave, sedate voice.

"Thank you, yes," she said; "I am well, quite well. But I am—what is the term you city men use when you want to say that you are worried? Pray sit down," and she pointed to a chair so placed that she could see his face while hers was against the light.

“We find ‘worried’ good enough for us, Lady Eleanor; but we are worried so often that we think little of it and take things very much as they come.”

“Ah, then I envy you!” she said with a genuine sigh. “I am afraid you will think me very inconsiderate in sending for you, you who have so much to occupy your time and energies.”

“I am always glad to be of some slight service to you,” he said with grave courtesy, “and can always spare time to come to you when you send for me. Is anything the matter? Are you anxious about the Mining Company? You have no cause to be, for everything is going on remarkably well, and succeeding beyond my expectations. Some of the best men in the city have joined us, and, as I wrote to you, the shares already stand at a high premium. You have made a very large sum of money, Lady Eleanor, and are on the way to making a still larger.”

“Money, money!” she exclaimed. “It is always money. You talk as if it were the one and only thing desirable and worth having! And, after all, what can it buy? Can it buy the one thing on which one’s heart is set? Have you found it so all-powerful that you set such store by it?”

His face flushed and a singular look came into his eyes.

“I—I beg your pardon!” she said hurriedly and almost humbly. “I did not mean to be impertinent or obtrusive; but just now I am in trouble in which I think even the all-powerful money will be powerless.”

“Tell me what it is,” he said in a low voice, and rather absently, as if the hasty words she had just spoken were still haunting him. “That is, I suppose you sent to consult me about it?”

“Well—yes,” said Lady Eleanor more calmly, but with her color coming and going. “I sent to you because you are the only friend I have whom I should care to consult about this—this trouble. Because I feel that you will understand, and, what is more important, not misunderstand me, or—or my motives.”

“I will do my best to understand and sympathize, Lady Eleanor,” he said, watching her, yet without seeming to do so.

“You remember,” she said after a pause, during which she was seeking for some way of beginning the subject as if it were not of much importance after all. “You remember Yorke Auchester, Lord Yorke Auchester?”

He inclined his head, suppressing a look of surprise.

“Certainly,” he said. “That is, I remember—I could not fail to do so—that I have purchased his debts, to a very large sum, on your behalf.”

"Yes," she said nervously, "and I daresay—I know—that you have wondered why I have done so."

He kept silence, but raised his eyebrows slightly.

"Well," she went on, "it was to save him from trouble. He is a great friend of mine; his cousin, the duke, and I are great friends. But you know all this! And now I want to do something more for—for Lord Auchester."

He looked up. Her face was red one moment and pale the next, but she kept her eyes—the half-proud, half-appealing eyes—upon his.

"He is in great trouble and—and danger. A worse danger than a monetary one."

He smiled.

"Can there be worse?" he said with a city man's incredulity. "We live in a prosaic age, Lady Eleanor, from which we have dismissed the midnight assassin and all the other romantic perils which made life and history so interesting in the middle ages; and the only dangers we run now are from a railway or steamboat accident——."

She tried to listen to him patiently.

"It is not that kind of danger I was thinking," she said. "Is it not possible for a man to—to ruin and wreck his life in—many ways, Mr. Duncombe?"

He looked at her still half smilingly.

"Oh, yes, a man may enlist as a common soldier, or forge a check, or marry his cook; but I do not imagine that there is any risk of Lord Auchester committing any of these—shall we say, follies?"

"Of all the things you have mentioned, it seems to me that the last is the worst," said Lady Eleanor bitterly.

"Yes?"

He raised his brows again.

"At any rate it is punished more severely than the others," she said.

"Yes," he assented thoughtfully. "But," and he smiled, "Lord Auchester does not contemplate marrying his cook, does he?"

"His cook? No; but he is in danger of marrying almost as far beneath him!" The retort flashed from her with hot hauteur. "Mr. Duncombe, when a man of Lord Auchester's station marries beneath him he is as utterly ruined, his life is as completely wrecked, as if he had committed forgery or enlisted as a common soldier."

He leaned back and listened with sedate politeness, wondering whither all this was leading, and what it was she would ask him to do.

"A man of Lord Auchester's rank has only one life—the social one. He has no business, no profession to fall back upon, to employ his thoughts, to engross and solace him. He must mix in the world to which he belongs, and he can only do so as an equal with his fellows. When he marries he is expected to take for a wife a lady of his own rank, or at any rate, a lady who is accepted as such in the circle to which he belongs. She must be one whom his friends can receive and visit, one of whom neither he nor they will be ashamed. His life may then continue in its old course; he will still have his friends and relatives round him, still have his place in the world, his niche, be it a high or a moderately high one, and all will be well with him."

She paused for breath, and put her hand to smooth back the delicate silken hair from her fair forehead.

"But if he should so far forget himself and all he owes to society as to marry beneath him—then, as I say he is utterly wrecked and undone. His friends will not receive his wife, or if they do it is with a coldness which she and he cannot fail to notice and resent. He sees them look pityingly, scornfully upon the woman he has made his wife, and he feels that he cannot take her amongst them. So he drifts from his own class, and either sinks into the one below it—where he is wretchedly miserable, or lives like a hermit. In the latter case he has plenty of time in which to get tired of his life and of the woman who has, in all innocence, severed him from all his old associates and, still in all innocence, has degraded him. The result, be it quick or slow in coming, is invariably the same. He is always thinking of the sacrifice he has made in marrying her, she is always conscious that he is so thinking, and sooner or later they grow to weary of and hate each other. She has ruined him, wrecked his life, and both know it! I am not speaking by theory; I have seen it, seen it in half a dozen cases, and I say that a man had better throw himself into the Thames than marry beneath him."

She dropped back in her low chair and put her hand to her head. She had talked swiftly, passionately, and her brow was burning.

Ralph Duncombe looked up.

"All you say is very true, no doubt, Lady Eleanor. And Lord Auchester——."

"Is thinking of making such a match," she said in a low voice.

Ralph Duncombe looked at the carpet.

"It scarcely seems—pardon me—scarcely seems credible. I do not know Lord Auchester, but from what I have heard of him I should think he would be the last man to be blind to the consequences of contracting a marriage with a lady who was considered his inferior in the social scale."

"Ah, yes!" she said with a sigh. "So anyone who knew him would have said; but—but—in this matter even the wisest men are fools."

He smiled gravely.

"Yes, fools!" she said bitterly; "they are caught by a pretty face, a look in the eyes, a curve on the lip, a dimple in the cheek——." She rose and took one or two paces, as if her impatience would not permit of her sitting still any longer. "At any rate, Lord Auchester has been so caught!" she wound up suddenly.

"And you wish——?"

"Ah, I scarcely know," she answered, stretching out her hands. "He is doing this thing secretly. He is keeping it from his friends. From the duke, from—from me, from all of us."

"Then he is half ashamed of it?" he suggested.

"Perhaps so," she said. "Perhaps so. But if he has made up his mind to do it he will go through with it, in spite of all arguments and attempts to dissuade him. Yorke—" she used his Christian name unconsciously—"Yorke is one of the sweetest tempered men—you can lead him with a silken thread, until he has resolved to do anything; then——." She had turned to him and looked at him beseechingly. "Can you help me, us; his friends, I mean, generally? He is so popular, so much liked. It would be a shame and a sin that such a one should be wrecked and ruined. In such a case a man should be saved in spite of himself. Can nothing be done? I sent for you, because you have always helped me, have always been so kind——." She stopped and turned her head away.

Ralph Duncombe regarded her with grave surprise.

"I am very sorry," he said slowly, as a lawyer speaks to a client to whom he has been listening patiently. "But I do not see how you can act in the matter. You might try persuasion——."

She shook her head.

"Ah, you do not know Lord Auchester!" she said.

"I scarcely see what else you can do. He's of age, and his own master, and the lady is of age, I presume. You could scarce bring any pressure upon her?"

Lady Eleanor shook her head scornfully.

"It is scarcely to be expected that she would be induced to release him. In these cases the woman is generally a low-bred schemer, or some simple girl who believes that she and the man she is ruining are in love. Oh, no; nothing can be done with her! Besides, I know—" she was going to say, "I know one who has tried and failed," but stopped suddenly.

"Well, then," said Ralph Duncombe, "I fear that I can suggest nothing. After all, if Lord Auchester is resolved upon committing social suicide——."

"Oh, it is terrible, terrible!" she exclaimed in a low, agitated voice; "and I thought you would be able to help me."

"I am very sorry at being so useless," he put in.

"I thought that perhaps these bills you hold for me—that they would give you some power over him," and she colored and cast her eyes down.

He smiled.

"There is no longer arrest for debt, Lady Eleanor," he said. "They say there is no longer imprisonment, but that is not true. They imprison still, but they call it for contempt of court. Ah, it is a pity we are not living in the dark ages! We could have set an ambush for Lord Auchester, seized him bodily, and cast him into a dungeon below the moat until he had come to his senses; but there is an absurd prejudice against that kind of thing nowadays."

She drew a long breath, and, taking her silence as an acceptation of the fact that he could be of no use to her, he reached for his hat and prepared to go.

"I suppose it is the usual thing," he said sympathetically. "Some girl of the lower middle class has attracted him, and she and her parents have succeeded in obtaining a promise of marriage from him. It is not an uncommon case."

Lady Eleanor had sunk into the chair again, and answered languidly, for the excitement was beginning to tell upon her.

"I do not know the details of the affair. It is very probable. The girl's name is Lisle, Leslie Lisle——."

"What!" The exclamation broke from him with the suddenness of a gunshot.

Lady Eleanor looked up, but he had turned and stood at a little distance with his back to the window; and, though pale as usual, his face was set and calm.

"I—beg your pardon, I did not quite catch the name," he said. He spoke very slowly, enunciating each word distinctly, as if he were uncertain of his voice. "I did not quite catch the name."

"Leslie Lisle," said Lady Eleanor. "He met her at a place called Portmaris. You may remember that I mentioned it to you when you were here some weeks ago."

“Yes—I—remember,” he said, in just the same slow, mechanical voice. He put his hat down and sat with tightly set lips and eyes fixed on the carpet.

Lady Eleanor looked at his grave, set face, waiting.

“Have you thought of anything, any plan by which the marriage could be prevented?” she asked anxiously.

He was silent for a moment or two, then, without looking up, he said:

“And they are to be married secretly?”

“Yes,” and her face flushed and paled.

“And at once?” he asked, and she thought his voice was strangely hoarse.

“At once, I—I am told.”

“At once,” he repeated, as if to himself. “Lady Eleanor, I see a carafe of water on that side table; will you allow me——.” He rose and crossed the room and drank nearly a glassful of water, while Lady Eleanor pressed him to allow her to ring for wine.

“No, no. Water, I prefer water. I am almost a teetotaler. Thanks, thanks,” he waved his hand impatiently, almost imperiously. “And is that all you know? Do you know the place they are going to be married at?”

“No,” she said. “Lord Auchester is in London,” she added after a moment; “I saw him this morning.”

He leant his head on his hand so that his face was almost completely concealed from her.

“In London. To be married at once,” he repeated. He looked up. “I am thinking, Lady Eleanor——.”

“Oh, yes, yes,” she breathed, leaning forward. “I know if you will only think you will find some way. It is a shame to bother and trouble you——.”

He smiled grimly.

“Don’t mention it. Let me see.” He put his hand to his forehead. “He is fearfully in debt. Some of those bills are long overdue. Do you think he means to leave the country?” He asked the question suddenly, with a flash.

“I—I don’t know. He must, I should think.”

“I see—I see,” he said. “Say, don’t be too hopeful, too sanguine. But—well, the law has long claws still, though we have pared them down pretty considerably. And in the city its claws are longer than elsewhere. That’s an anomaly, but it’s true. In a city court of law you can do strange things. For instance, if a man owes me money and I go and swear that I have reason to believe that he is intending to leave the country—to abscond, in short—the court has an almost forgotten power to stop that man. The machinery is antiquated and rusty, but—but it may be made to work." He rose. A strange light was burning in his eyes, a hectic flush on his pale and rather hollow cheeks. "Lady Eleanor——."

"What is it?" she asked, almost frightened by the change in his manner, by the subdued eagerness and earnestness where a few minutes ago was only polite indifference.

"Lady Eleanor, if I consent to help you, I can do so on one condition."

"Yes! What is that?" she asked, trembling a little.

"That you follow my instructions to the letter. That you leave the whole matter to me, and offer no opposition to anything I may direct or do. I see—mark me!—I see a small chance, a slight hope of saving Lord Auchester from this," he smiled scornfully, "ruinous marriage. It is but slight, and to do anything with it I must have a free hand. Will you give it me?"

"I will," she said. "I would do anything—anything to save him."

"And so would I!" he muttered, but so low that she did not hear him.

CHAPTER XXIX.

THE NEW LODGER.

Some blows which Fate deals us are so severe and crushing that, for a time, they deprive us of the power of feeling; and of such a nature was the bereavement which Leslie had suffered. She was simply crushed and powerless to feel or to act. Fortunately the landlady of the London lodging-house, and the young doctor, were kind-hearted persons, and they came to her aid.

Francis Lisle had quarreled with and separated himself from his people years ago, and Leslie scarcely knew his relations by name, but she found the addresses of one or two, and the doctor wrote to them.

It is a hard world. One can forgive one's relations many sins, but that of poverty is the unpardonable one; and those of her kin to whom the doctor wrote doubtless regarded this sudden death of Francis Lisle as an additional injury dealt to them by that eccentric and unfortunate man.

One brother wrote a letter to Leslie expressing the deepest sympathy, and regretting that a severe attack of the gout would prevent him attending the funeral, but desiring her to be sure and let him know if he could do anything for her. A cousin sent his secretary with a ten-pound note—if it should be needed; and another relative wrote to say how sorry he was, and that he should, of course, attend the funeral, and that he hoped and trusted "poor Francis" had left his daughter well provided for. He added, incidentally, that he himself had a large family, and had had a great deal of sickness that year; also that he would have been glad to have taken her into his house if it had not been so small and already overcrowded. The head of the family wrote her a short note from a German watering place, saying that he was in such a wretched state of health that he could not come to England, excepting at the risk of his life, and that it would probably not be long before he joined her father in the realms above.

"Ain't it dreadful, sir?" said the landlady to the doctor. "They don't seem to have a heart amongst 'em."

He shook his head. He had seen similar cases.

"I am afraid Miss Lisle is not very well off," he said. "If she had been an heiress her relatives would have flocked round her, overflowing with sympathy and offers of assistance. It is the way of the world, Mrs. Brown. I fear Miss Leslie will feel this neglect and cold-heartedness very keenly. We must do all we can for her."

"Yes, sir, that we will," said the woman, with moist eyes. "As to feeling it, I don't think dear Miss Lisle feels anything at present. I could scarcely rouse her to see about her mourning, and it makes one's heart ache to go into the room and see her sitting there in her plain, black dress—she would have it so simple and no crape, though I told her that crape was always worn for a father—sitting there and just looking before her as if she was too weak and overcome even to think. It's my opinion, sir, that she scarcely realizes what has happened to her yet. Since the day he died she hasn't shed a tear. And such a sweet young soul as she is, and so grateful for the littlest thing one does for her. But there, she was always the nicest young lady that I ever took in, always; and if her relations is too proud or too heartless to look after her, why she shan't want for a friend while Martha Brown has got a shilling."

The landlady's graphic description of Leslie's condition was a fairly truthful one. Day after day Leslie sat with her hands lying listlessly in the lap of her black dress, her eyes fixed on the trees in the square, her sorrow too great for thought.

If she had overheard the landlady and the doctor discussing her future she would have listened with perfect indifference. What did it matter what became of her, or whether she lived or went to join the poor, weak soul whom she had loved and cherished, and yet—ah, what bitterness was in the thought!—deceived! If she had not listened to Yorke's proposal, had not consented to his plan of bringing her to London, her father might be alive now! It was true that the doctor had assured her that the weakness of the heart which had been the immediate cause of death had been latent for some time, and that her father had been a doomed and sentenced man for years past, and that any shock would have been sufficient to cause his death; but even this assurance scarcely softened the poignancy of her remorse.

It was of her father and his loss that she thought entirely during the days immediately following her bereavement, and it might be almost said that she had forgotten Yorke and her great love for him. Almost, but not quite. It was lying in the centre of her heart, buried for a time under the load of her anguish and sorrow, but it needed only a sight of him, only the sound of his name, to arise, like a giant, and reassert all its old influence over her.

After a while she began to recover sufficiently to be able to think, to realize her position, and to look vaguely and indifferently towards the future.

The doctor, and the secretary of the great man, had gone into Francis Lisle's affairs, and discovered that a portion of his small income had died with him, and that what remained amounted to only a few pounds a year—not enough, by itself, to keep body and soul together. There was a little money in hand, but the largest part of that sum consisted of the fifty pounds paid by Mr. Temple for the picture he had bought; and Leslie, directly she was able to think, resolved that she would return the money, though it, and it alone, should stand between her and starvation.

There was something else also that she must return—the diamond pendant which Yorke had given her.

That, too, must go back. She could not summon up sufficient courage to take it from its hiding-place as yet; and, indeed, she did not know where to send it, unless she addressed it to the Dorchester Club, and it seemed to her that it would be wrong to send so valuable an article to a club; that she ought to send it to the duke's residence.

A woman of the world would have been aware that the address of so well-known a personage as the Duke of Rothbury could be found in a London directory; but Leslie was anything but a woman of the world, and felt helpless in her ignorance.

There was another article which lay in her box beside the diamond pendant; Ralph Duncombe's ring.

She remembered that, in a weary, listless way. He had said, when he placed it in her hand, that if ever she needed a friend, a helper, an avenger, she had but to send that ring to him and he would come to her side. But, though she were in the sorest strait in which a woman could be placed, she would not summon Ralph Duncombe to her aid; for to do so would be tantamount to engaging herself to him. The mere thought made her wince and shudder; it was an insult to the love that lay dormant in her bosom—her love for Yorke.

One day she got out her money, and spread it on the table and counted it. With the strictest economy it would not go very far, and it was all that stood between her and the grim wolf, destitution; for she felt that she would rather die than appeal for assistance to her father's relatives.

"In the struggle for life we forget our dead," says the philosopher; and the problem of what was to become of her gradually drew her away from the sad brooding over her bereavement.

What should she do? She could not dig, and to beg she was ashamed. The question haunted her day and night as she sat by the window or walked up and down the room, or lay awake at night, listening to the multitudinous London clocks striking the hours. One afternoon she summoned up strength enough to go out, and in her plain black clothes, with her veil closely drawn over her face, she walked through the squares into Oxford and Regent Streets. She felt weak and giddy at first, and soon tired. The vast thoroughfares, and their eager, busy crowds confused and bewildered her. It seemed to her as if every one was looking at her, as if every individual of the throng knew of her trouble, her double loss, and was pitying her; and she turned homewards, faint in body and spirit.

As she reached No. 23 she saw a cab standing at the door; the cabman was carrying a modest box into the house, and as she passed into the narrow hall a young lady, who was talking with the landlady, made room for her.

Leslie concluded that it was a new lodger, and went up to her own rooms to take up the perpetual problem. What should she do?

She recalled all the novels she had read in which the heroines had been left alone in the world, and sought some help from their experiences and course of action. But most, if not all, these heroines had been singularly gifted beings, who had at once stepped into fame and fortune as singers, actors, painters, or musicians; and she, Leslie, knew that she was not gifted in any of these directions.

"There is nothing I can do!" she told herself that night as she undressed herself wearily and hopelessly. "Nothing! I am a cumberer of the ground!"

She had tired herself by her walk, and slept the whole night, for the first time since her father's death; but she dreamed that she was married to Yorke, and that she was surrounded by a crowd—the crowd she had seen in Regent Street—and that they called her 'Your Grace' and 'Duchess.' And she woke to a sense of the reality with a heart that ached all the more bitterly for the pleasant dream.

Was it years ago, that drive to St. Martin's, when he had sat beside her and shown her how to hold the reins? Or did it never happen, and was it only a phantasy of her imagination?

So great a difference was there between then and now, so wide a gulf, that only the present seemed real, and the past a vision of a disordered mind! She unlocked the small box, and took out the diamond pendant and looked at it, and the scrap of paper with the precious words "From Yorke" written on it, until the tears blotted them from her sight; but they had recalled all the joy, the delight, the sacred ecstasy of the past all too distinctly.

It was true. She, Leslie Lisle, helpless, friendless, with only a few pounds between her and want, was the Leslie Lisle who had looked on that short sunlight of happiness.

She thought she would make another attempt to go out that morning, and after dressing slowly, and putting off the dreaded moment of leaving the house and facing the outside world, she went down the stairs. As she did so the door of one of the rooms on the floor below hers opened, and the girl she had seen in the hall yesterday came out.

She stepped back as she saw Leslie, and seemed about to beat a retreat back into her own room again, then hesitated, and made a slight bow.

Leslie returned the bow absently and went out; and it was not until she had got into the crowded streets that she thought of the girl; then she remembered that she, too, was dressed in black, and that though not more pretty, she was modest, and looked like a lady, and wore eyeglasses. She thought no more of her than this, and after a weary walk returned home, and rang the bell for some tea.

When the door opened she was surprised to see the girl instead of Mrs. Brown; and her surprise must have shown itself in her face, for her visitor colored and stopped at the threshold.

"I—I beg your pardon," she said. "I hope you will forgive me, but Mrs. Brown has sprained her wrist, and she asked me—that is, I offered—to come instead of her——."

Leslie rose and looked at her with the half startled expression which indicated her condition of mind.

"I—I wanted some tea; but it does not matter," she said in a low voice.

The new-comer colored.

"Oh, but I will get it for you," she said. "I will get anything for you; that is, if you don't mind my doing it instead of Mrs. Brown."

Leslie looked at her more attentively, and saw a pleasant, amiable face with eyes beaming softly through eyeglasses perched on a tip-tilted nose.

"You are very kind," she said in a low, musical voice. "But I do not think I ought to trouble you."

"Oh, it is no trouble, Miss Lisle," said the girl, still standing on the threshold as if she dared not venture further.

"You know my name?" said Leslie, with a faint smile.

"Yes," said her visitor, with a nod half-grave, half-smiling, and wholly friendly and propitiatory. "Mrs. Brown told me, and—and about your trouble. I am so sorry! But," as Leslie winced, "I won't talk of that. I'll see that you have some tea."

"Will you not come in?" said Leslie.

The girl came into the room timidly, and took the chair which Leslie drew forward for her.

"I think I saw you in the hall yesterday," she said. "You are a lodger, like myself?"

"Yes. Oh, yes," replied her visitor, nodding. "And I saw you. I asked Mrs. Brown who you were, and she told me. I hope you don't think me inquisitive?" and she colored timidly.

"No. Oh, no. It was a very natural question," said Leslie. "Will you tell me your name?"

"Oh, yes. My name is Somes. Lucy Somes."

"And you are paying a visit to London?" said Leslie, trying to interest herself in this pleasant looking girl who had from sheer kindness acted as the landlady's substitute.

"A visit?" said Lucy Somes, doubtfully. "Well, scarcely that. I'm here—" she hesitated—"on business. But I must not keep you waiting for yourtea."

"My tea can wait until Mrs. Brown can get it," said Leslie.

"Oh, but I am going to get it for you, unless—" she hesitated, but, encouraged by Leslie's faint smile, she continued—"unless you wouldn't mind coming down to my room and taking tea with me. I have just got mine; and I should be so pleased if you would come."

Leslie did not respond for a moment or two. Trouble makes solitude very dear to us. But she fought against the desire to decline.

"Thank you," she said simply; "I shall be very pleased."

Lucy jumped up.

"Come along, then," she said with evident pleasure.

Leslie followed her downstairs, and Lucy Somes ushered her into the tiny room which served for bedroom and sitting room.

"I hope you don't mind," said Lucy, with a sudden blush on her pleasant face. "But you see I am not rich enough to afford two rooms, and so——."

"Why should I mind?" said Leslie, in her gentle voice.

"Oh, I can see you have been used to something better than this," said Lucy, bustling to and fro as she spoke, and adding another cup and saucer and plate to the tea things on the small table. "I laughed to myself when Mrs. Brown said you were a real lady—persons like her make such mistakes—but I see that she was right. But a lady does not contemn poverty, does she?" and she laughed as she cut some bread and butter.

"Especially when she is poor herself," thought Leslie, but she only smiled.

"And so I thought I would venture to intrude upon you," continued Lucy Somes. "I was half afraid, for you looked so—so—I want a word! it isn't proud; so aristocratic and reserved I'll say—that I quite trembled; and it was only by saying, 'she is only a girl and no older than yourself and all alone and in trouble,' that I plucked up courage to go up to you."

"Am I so very terrible?" said Leslie, with the smile that all Portmaris—and Yorke—had found so irresistible.

"Not now when you look like that," replied Lucy Somes, "but when you are grave and solemn, as you were when you passed by me yesterday, you are very—very—stand-offish. Will you have some sugar in your tea? I've made some toast. Papa—" she stopped suddenly, then went on in a subdued voice —"papa used to say that I made toast better than any of the others. He is dead," she added after another pause; and Leslie saw the eyes grow dim behind the spectacles.

She put out her hand and laid it on the girl's arm.

"Did he——?"

"Three months ago," said Lucy Somes, sadly, yet cheerily. "He was a country clergyman down in Wealdshire. He caught a fever visiting a parishioner. There are seven of us—and mother. I'm the second."

She poured out the tea while she was speaking, and was obviously fighting with her tears.

"Seven of us! Just fancy! Poor mother didn't know what to do! So I came up to London to fight my way in the world. And I mean to fight it, too! What awful stuff the London butter is, isn't it? I don't believe there is a particle of cow's milk in it; do you? Seven of us! Three boys and four girls. And we're as poor as poor can be. Won't you take some milk, if one can call it milk?"

"And you are going to fight the world," said Leslie, with tender sympathy for this young girl who could be so cheerful under such circumstances. "What are you going to do?"

Lucy Somes laughed as she put a fresh piece of toast on the rack.

"I'm going to be a governess."

"A governess!" said Leslie. "In a gentleman's family?"

Lucy Somes shook her head emphatically.

"Oh, no, thank you! I know what that means! Six young children to teach, all the mending to do, and heaps of other things for twenty pounds a year; less than they give their cook! No, no! I am going to be the mistress of one of the country schools."

"Yes?" said Leslie vaguely.

"Yes, I am going to try and get the mistressship of a Board or Voluntary school in some country place; I couldn't live in London. I don't seem as if I could breathe here. Every morning I wake and fancy I have been shut up in a coal mine. Did you ever notice how the smuts come into the room when you open the window? And that's what London folks breathe all the time."

"It does not seem to disagree with them," said Leslie, with a faint smile.

"It disagrees with me," retorted Lucy, laughing. "Oh, no, no, give me the country, with plenty of space to move about, and the flowers and the birds, and butter that isn't manufactured from fat, and milk that isn't a mixture of chalk and water. Don't you think it will be very nice to be the mistress of a school in some pretty village? There is always a nice little house for one to live in, and perhaps I could afford to keep a young girl for a servant, and—and—be able to save some money to send to mother to help her with the rest of us."

Leslie listened, and her conscience smote her. Here was this girl, no older than herself, alone in London, and so bravely ready to fight the great battle; thinking little of herself, and so much of those dear ones she had left behind.

"Of course I am rather afraid of the exams," went on Lucy, knowing somehow that the best thing she could do for this sweet, sad-looking girl was to talk of herself, and so coax Leslie from dwelling on her own sorrow. "They are rather dreadful, but I have been working hard, and I think I shall pass. I'll show you some of my books, shall I—may I? But you must have your tea first, quite comfortably. It was so kind of you to come down to me! I was feeling so dreadfully lonely and—and friendless. London is such a big place to be alone in, isn't it?"

"Ah, yes!" said Leslie.

"I tried to make friends with the sparrows," said Lucy, laughing. "I put some crumbs on the window-sill as breakfast, and they come and eat them. But they are not like the country sparrows; they look, somehow, so—disreputable. I suppose it's because they sit up late, like everybody else in London. All the animals are different; the very horses look knowing and sharp. Now you shall sit in that easy-chair while I show you my books." And half timidly she put Leslie in the chair, and arranged a cushion for her as if she were a great invalid.

Leslie's tender heart melted under all this gentle sunshine, and when Lucy, kneeling beside her, opened her books, Leslie found, with a vague kind of surprise, that she was interested.

"You see? It is a great many subjects to get up, isn't it? But I'm not afraid. I should get on faster if some of the girls were here to hear me repeat some of the most difficult passages; and if—papa were here to explain things I don't quite understand. He was so clever! There was nothing he did not know," she added with simple, loving pride.

"Let me see," said Leslie, taking up a book. "Why should I not help you, Miss Somes?"

Lucy colored furiously.

"Oh, indeed, indeed," she said imploringly. "I did not mean that! I could not think of allowing you. But how kind of you to offer! Oh, no, no!"

"But the kindness will be on your part if you will let me try and be of some help," said Leslie, with gentle insistence. "I, too, am all alone, and I have nothing to do—" she smothered a sigh—"and the time seems very long and weary. I could hear you repeat what you have learned as well as one of your sisters. I could do that, at least. Let me see. I am very ignorant; you will soon see that. But I remember something of this book. I had it at school."

Lucy would not hear of it for some time, but at last Leslie overcame her scruples, and with a little blush repeated some of the paragraphs she had got off by heart.

CHAPTER XXX.

THE ENCOUNTER.

Reading for an exam, even a little one, is awful work. If it were only one or two subjects which one had to master it would not be so bad; but when there are six or a dozen then the trouble comes in. As fast as one subject is learned it is driven out of its place in the memory by a second, and the second by the third, and so on. Then one has to go back and begin all over again, until they all get mixed up, and one feels it will be impossible to ever get them properly sorted and arranged.

The more Leslie saw of this pleasant-faced, kind-hearted girl, the more she admired and wondered at her patience and courage.

They lit the lamp and worked through the evening, though Lucy over and over again protested that it was both wicked and cruel to take advantage of Leslie's good nature; and at last she swept all the books together, and declared that Leslie should not touch another.

"But if you knew what a help it has been to me!" she exclaimed gratefully.

"And to me," said Leslie with a smile. "It is I who ought to be grateful—and, indeed, I am, for I should have been sitting upstairs alone with nothing to do but think, think!"

"Ah, that is the worst of it," said Lucy gravely. "That is why I am so glad I am obliged to work! You see I haven't the time to think; I keep on and on, like the man who climbed the Alps—what was his name, Excelsior?"

The next morning Lucy knocked at the door. She had got her outdoor clothes on, and had a bunch of flowers in her hand.

"Oh, I beg your pardon," she said, blushing timidly, "but I have been for a run. I always go into Covent Garden, and—and I brought some flowers. I thought you would not mind, would not think it intrusive; but I am so fond of flowers myself——."

Leslie made her come in and sit down, while she got a glass for the flowers. Lucy looked round and saw the easel. Leslie had put the pictures out of sight.

"Are you an artist, Miss Lisle?" she asked timidly.

"No, oh no. It was my father——."

"Yes, yes. I see," said Lucy quickly. "It is so hard to paint or draw, isn't it?

That is where I shall fail, I expect. You see, I have never been able to get any tuition. I suppose you can draw?"

"Yes, a little," said Leslie.

"And play? But of course!"

"Yes," said Leslie.

Lucy sighed, not enviously, but admiringly.

"It is a pity that it is not you who are going up for the exam instead of me. It would be so easy for you. They think so much of drawing and playing and accomplishments generally, I'm told."

Leslie looked at her half-startled.

"You think I—I could pass, that I could get a place in a school!" she faltered.

Lucy laughed confidently.

"Oh, yes! Why, easily. But you do not want it, fortunately."

Leslie looked at her in silence for a minute, then she took out her purse and turned the money out on the table.

"That is all I have in the world," she said with a quiet smile.

Lucy crimsoned, and then turned pale.

"Oh, I—I beg your pardon. Please—please forgive me!" she said. "I did not know, I thought——."

"That I was a princess, a millionairess," said Leslie, smiling. "No, as you see, I am very poor, and quite—quite alone. I would give something for a mother and six brothers and sisters, Miss Somes."

"Oh, don't! Call me Lucy!" Lucy implored timidly. "I am—it is very wicked! —but I am almost glad that you are not well off! It draws us nearer, and—and you will not mind? But I like you so much! You are not angry?"

Leslie bent down and kissed the resolute little forehead.

"No, I am only grateful, Lucy," she said in her sweet, irresistible way. "We two, who are alone in this big London, ought to cling together, ought we not? You must call me Leslie, and try and think that I am one of your sisters."

"That won't be hard," responded Lucy, fervently. "But let me think! You say ——." She paused. "Oh, but you would not like it. It—it would not be good enough——."

"What would not be good enough, Lucy?"

"Why, a place like that I am trying for," said Lucy timidly.

Leslie sighed.

"It would be too good to hope for," she said gently.

Lucy sprang up eagerly.

"Oh, that is nonsense!" she exclaimed in her half-proud, half-impetuous fashion. "Why, you could pass easily, and——! Yes! I see it as plainly as possible! You shall go in for the exam. We will work together! No, don't shake your head! We should both stand a better chance if we tried together, for there may be things that I could help you in, and I know that you could help me. There's the drawing, for instance! Oh, I can see it all beautifully! and only think, Leslie, perhaps we might get into the same school! It might be managed! Mother has some influence, for poor papa's people are well known, and can help us once we have passed. Now, you shan't say anything against it or shake your head. Wait!"

She ran out of the room, and before Leslie could recover from the varied emotions, the hope, the fear, which Lucy's suggestion had aroused, Lucy was back with her books and papers.

"Look here, Leslie dear," she exclaimed, panting, "here is the list of subjects and the books and everything, and we will start at once. Yes, at once."

Leslie still hesitated, but Lucy drew her down to a chair beside the table, and gently forced her to examine the papers.

Lucy and her scheme came just in the nick of time, and once Leslie had commenced she worked with a feverish eagerness which Lucy declared required the brake.

"I was just like that myself when I started, though I don't think I was quite as bad as you are, Leslie dear; but you soon find that the pace is too fast, as my brothers would say. You can't keep it up, and you have to slow off into regular work, with regular rests. Come, you must go out now; it is two days since you left the house, and you must come out with me. You would soon break down if you kept on at this rate."

Leslie put down the book she was working at reluctantly, and with a sigh.

"I am not tired, I do not care to go out," she said. "While one works one cannot think, and not to think——."

She broke off and turned her face away.

"I know," said Lucy; but she didn't, for she thought Leslie was only trying not to think of her father. "I know. But if you kept on driving it off by constant working you would find that you would get no sleep, and lie awake all night and think, and that is worse than thinking in the daytime. Come, dear, we will go for a nice long walk, and come back fresh to the tiresome books."

"Blessed books, say rather!" said Leslie. But she went and put on her outdoor things submissively. The two girls had by this time entered into a kind of partnership. Fate had thrown them together in the whirlpool of life, and they had decided to cling together to this spar; the chance of a misstressship in a country school, and to sink or float together. They joined housekeeping and ate their meals together, and worked with an amity and friendliness which did credit to both their hearts. Leslie's was the quicker brain, but Lucy had been working for some months, and could stick to her task with a dogged perseverance which Leslie envied, whereas Lucy regarded Leslie with an admiration and affection which almost amounted to worship. To her Leslie seemed the epitome of all that was beautiful and sweet and graceful, and if Leslie had permitted it Lucy would have become a kind of Lady's-maid as well as fellow-student.

The afternoon was a hot one, but Leslie wore her veil down, walking along with absent preoccupied eyes, and only half listening to the bright, cheery chatter of the brave-hearted girl at her side.

"After all, London is not bad," said Lucy. "One gets fond of it, stupidly fond of it, without knowing it. It doesn't seem so hard and cold-hearted after a while, and I—yes, I really think it is more friendly than the country. The shops are so bright and cheerful that they seem to smile at you and tell you to cheer up; and then there's the noise. I didn't like it at first, but I don't mind it so much now. It seems like company. Do you know what I mean, Leslie?"

"Yes," said Leslie absently. She was thinking of what Yorke had said about London, and how good it was to get away from it. Where was he now? she wondered.

"Yes, if I were a rich woman I would have a house in London—not for the season, oh, no! Fancy all rich and fashionable people leaving the dear delicious country just when it is beginning to look its very best, and coming up here into the hot streets and stuffy houses! Though the parks are pretty, I will admit that. No, I would come up when the days draw in, and the country lanes are muddy, and the roads dark. Then London is at its best, with the lighted streets and the theaters and the warm houses. Yes, Leslie, if I were rich ——." She laughed. "How strange it must seem to anyone who becomes suddenly rich! One hears of girls marrying wealthy men, and stepping from poverty to luxury. I suppose it must be confusing and bewildering at first; at least, to most girls. I don't think it would be to you, Leslie," she added, glancing up at her with a reflective smile. "I think if you were to marry a duke you would take it quite calmly and as a matter of course. Somehow when I am looking at you, when you are bending over the books, or, better still, when you are standing at the window with your arms folded and that strange far-away look in your eyes, I think what a pity it is that you are not a great lady. You are so tall, and—and—what is the word?—distingué, that I fancy you dressed in white satin with a long train, and hear you being called 'your grace.'"

Leslie bit her lip.

"I am not distingué or so foolish as to believe all you say, Lucy," she said, scarcely knowing what she said, for the aimless chatter had set her heart aching; not for the loss of the dukedom, but the man. "Where are we?"

Lucy laughed with a gentle triumph.

"If I don't know half so much of other things as you do, I know London better," she said. "We are coming out into St. James', and we will walk into the Park and through Pall Mall, and then take a bus, your grace."

Leslie stopped and laid her hand on Lucy's arm.

"Don't—don't call me that," she said, so gravely, almost sternly, that Lucy looked up half frightened.

"I beg your pardon. I am so sorry, Leslie, if I——."

"No, no," broke in Leslie, ashamed of the agitation into which Lucy's idle badinage had thrown her. "Call me what you like, dear."

Lucy looked up at her timidly and wonderingly, and was silent; and Leslie had to force herself to talk to restore her companion's peace of mind.

They went into the Park, talking of the future and their chances.

"It will not be long now," said Lucy. "Oh, how I long for the day when we shall hold those certificates in our hands! I shall be so proud and glad that I shall scarcely be able to contain myself. I shall have to telegraph to mother; it will cost eighteenpence, for they are two miles from the telegraph office; but I don't care. And you'll wire, too, Leslie——."

Leslie shook her head.

"I have no one to tell," she said; "at least I shall save the eighteenpence," and she smiled gravely.

"You will have me, at any rate," murmured Lucy gently, and Leslie pressed her hand gratefully.

They wandered in the Park—what a host of memories it calls up to him who knows his history of London, that same Park!—until the twilight came, and then turned homewards.

As they passed down Pall Mall they met the broughams and cabs rolling home to the West, and Lucy, regarding them with a pleasant interest, remarked—

"They are all going home. It is their dinnertime; see, some of the women are in evening dress. Yes, it must be nice to be rich and great; but we are happy, we two, are we not, Leslie dear?"

"Yes," said Leslie, and she tried to speak the word cheerfully.

"These are the famous clubs, are they not?" said Lucy, looking up at the stately buildings, through the windows of which the lights were beginning to glimmer.

"Yes," said Leslie.

"How strange it seems that there should be so many people who have nothing whatever to do, who have never worked, and who have so much money as to find it a nuisance, while others have to work every day of their lives, and all their lives, and have never a spare penny. Look, Leslie, there are some gentlemen going into that club—I suppose it is a club. How grand and nice they look in their evening dress! It must be nice to be a rich gentleman instead of——."

She broke off suddenly, alarmed by a sharp cry that seemed to force itself through Leslie's lips.

They had come within a few yards of the club into which the men Lucy had noticed had disappeared, and Leslie's absent, preoccupied eyes had fallen upon another man who was coming towards them.

He was a tall man, with broad shoulders, but he was walking with a slow, listless gait, and his head was bent as if he neither knew nor cared where he was going.

Leslie knew him in a moment. It was Yorke.

And yet could it be? Could this weary-looking, listless man with his hands thrust into his light overcoat pocket, with his drooping head, be Yorke with the straight broad shoulders, the figure upright as a dart, the well-poised head, the handsome face with its cheerful devil-may-care look in the bright eyes? Oh, surely not Yorke, not her Yorke as she remembered him in the street at Portmaris, on the beach, beside her on the tower at St. Martin's?

After that one cry she made no sign, but drew back a step so that Lucy could screen her from him if he chanced to look up.

He came towards them like a man walking in a dream, and as he reached their side he raised his head and looked at them. Leslie had hard work to keep the cry that rose in her heart from escaping her lips.

It was Yorke's face; but how changed! How weary and sad and hopeless—and, yes, reckless! There was that in the dark eyes which she, an innocent girl, did not understand; but instinctively a pang went through her heart, and she trembled, she knew not why.

His eyes, with that strange, awful look in them, rested on their faces for a moment, then dropped again and he passed on. He went up the steps of the club, but turned and stood just outside the door, and Leslie, almost sinking with agitation, hurried on.

"What is the matter? Leslie dear, you frighten me!" said Lucy. "Are you ill?"

"No—yes!" said Leslie.

She walked swiftly and yet tremblingly up a side street, and stood there, out of the reach of those eyes, shaking like a leaf.

"You are ill!" said Lucy, catching her arm. "We have walked too far—you are tired. Oh, what is it, dear?"

"Yes, I am tired," said Leslie when she could command her voice. "That is it. We—we must have a cab. Stay! Not here, come farther up the street——."

Lucy called a cab, and Leslie sank back, her hands clasped tightly, her face white as death behind her veil.

"You frighten me, Leslie!" said Lucy, holding her hand. "And you look so frightened yourself. What is it, dear? You look as if you had seen a ghost."

"Yes," said Leslie, but in so low a voice that Lucy could not hear her. "Yes, I have seen a ghost."

Yorke stood on the steps of the club with downcast face and moody eyes for some half minute, then the eyes lit up with a sombre light, and going down the steps he crossed the road and laid his hand sharply on the shoulder of a man who was lounging against a post. The man looked up, but he did not appear surprised.

"You're watching me!" said Yorke, and his voice matched his face—it was hard and stern. "You have been watching me for the last two days. Don't trouble to deny it!"

The man, whose appearance was like that of a respectable servant out of livery, a butler out of place, for instance, touched his hat.

"Lord Auchester, I think, sir?" he said coolly, yet not disrespectfully.

"You know my name well enough," said Yorke a little less sternly, as if he were too weary to be resentful. "Who are you and what do you want? I have seen you following me for the last two days. Why do you do it? What is it?"

The man took a paper from his pocket, and just touched Yorke's arm with his finger, as if he were going through some form.

"I am a sheriff's officer, my lord," he said, "and this is my writ."

Yorke looked at him and at the paper.

"What writ?" he said, not angrily, but with obvious indifference.

"A matter of five bills overdue, my lord. Judgment has been signed a week ago——."

Yorke shook his head.

"You might as well talk Arabic, my man," he said listlessly. "I know nothing about the law——."

"Certainly not, my lord," said the man, as if he would not insult his lordship by suggesting such knowledge. "It isn't to be expected. But your lordship has had the former summonses——."

Yorke shook his head.

"Delivered at you rooms at Bury Street, my lord——."

"I see," said Yorke. He had not opened a letter that looked like a business one since—since the hour he had learnt that Leslie had "jilted" him. "I see. What do you want me to do?"

"Only to go home, my lord, and put in an appearance to-morrow, at the court, you know."

"I don't know," said Yorke. "Why have you watched me?"

"Well, my lord, we had information—in fact, we've sworn it—that you intended leaving the country——."

"I did," said Yorke.

"Just so, my lord, and I was keeping my eye on you. I could have arrested you—it's a City process—if you'd attempted to leave one of the English ports."

Yorke smiled grimly.

"You must have had some trouble," he said.

The man smiled and nodded.

"Indeed I have, my lord. You nearly walked me off my legs. I never shadowed such a restless gentleman, begging your lordship's pardon. I must have walked—oh, law knows how many miles, following you, and it's a wonder to me we ain't both knocked up."

Yorke gave him a sovereign.

"Go home," he said. "You need follow me no longer. I will attend the court, wherever it is. Stop, what is the name of the man who does all this, the man I owe the money to?"

"Mr. Ralph Duncombe, my lord."

Yorke repeated the name vacantly.

"I don't know him. I never heard of him," he said. "But it does not matter. I owe a great many persons money, and he may be one of them. Good-night," and he walked away, his head down again, his hands in his pockets.

The man looked after him with a puzzled countenance, and turned over the sovereign Yorke had given him.

"One of the right sort he is," he muttered. "But ain't he down on his luck? I've seen a good many of 'em in Queer Street, but none of 'em looked half so bad as that. If I was his friends I should take his razors away!"

Yorke reached Bury Street, but before he could ring, the door opened, and Fleming with a scared face stood before him.

"Oh, my lord!" he began. "Better not come up—go to the club, my lord, and I'll bring your things——."

Yorke put him aside gently and went slowly up the stairs.

A man—own brother in appearance to the man in the street—was sitting on the sofa. He got up as Yorke entered, and touched his forehead.

"Well?" said Yorke.

"I'm the man in possession, my lord," said the man respectfully enough.

CHAPTER XXXI.

CLEANED OUT.

A man in possession! Yorke looked at him half vacantly.

"Do you mean that you are going to stop here?" he said—"that you have got to stop here?"

"Yes, my lord, I'm sorry to say," said the man. "Somebody's got to be here to see that none of the things is removed."

Fleming, standing behind his master, groaned. Yorke turned to him quite coolly.

"Give the man something to eat and drink and make him comfortable. He can't help it, poor devil! Bring me some cigars and my letters into the dressing-room."

He sat down and lighted a cigar, and opened the letters which had been lying disregarded for weeks, and as he looked through them he saw that he was in a worse mess than he had ever before been. All his other money troubles were trifles and child's play compared with this.

There was not a worse business man in London than Yorke, and he did not understand half the legal documents, the summonses, the orders of the court which he opened and stared at; but the prominence and frequency of one name in the whole business struck him.

"Who on earth is Ralph Duncombe?" he asked himself. "Levison I know, and Moses Arack I know, and this man, and this. I remember having money from them; but Ralph Duncombe—" No, he could not recall the man's name. But after all it did not matter. It was evident that his creditors had all combined to swoop down upon him at once, and the avalanche would crush him unless he got some help. And where should he turn? It would be useless to attempt to borrow money through the usual channels. No doubt the news that he was going to marry a penniless girl instead of the rich heiress, Lady Eleanor Dallas, had leaked out, and all the money-lenders, who hung together like bees, would refuse to lend him a silver sixpence.

Dolph! He almost started at the thought of him, for two days ago the duke, who had been seriously ill, had started for the Continent, and Yorke did not even know in which direction; for, to tell the truth, Yorke had avoided the duke and every other friend and acquaintance since the day he had been convinced that Leslie had thrown him over.

No doubt the duke would lend him the money—would give him twice as much as was necessary, though the sum-total was a large one—but the money must be forthcoming at once. The man had said he would have to appear in the court in the city to-morrow—or was it the next day? Good heavens! appear as a common defaulter in a public court!

He smiled grimly. So far as he was concerned, he felt, in the humor he was then in, that he did not care a button what became of him. When you have reached the point at which life is a burden and a nuisance it does not matter whether you are ruined or not. But there were other people to think of. There was Dolph and Lord Eustace and all his other relatives. How would they take it when they opened their newspapers and read of the appearance of Lord Yorke Auchester, "cousin of the Duke of Rothbury," in a debtors' court in the city? Lord Eustace, who was always talking of his 'nerves,' would have a fit.

Now, most men would have gone to a lawyer, but Yorke knew that it would be of little or no use troubling a lawyer with this business. What was wanted was money, and no lawyer would lend it to him without security; and as for security—why, there was already a man in possession of the few things he owned in this transitory world.

Fleming knocked at the door, and in answer to a cold "come in," entered.

"Did you ring, my lord?" he said.

"You know I didn't," said Yorke. "What is it? You look upset, Fleming," and he smiled the smile which is not good to see on the lips of any man, young or old, simple or gentle.

"Beg pardon, my lord," said Fleming, who was genuinely attached to his master, and who had watched the change in him with sincere grief and regret, "but I thought you would want to send me somewhere, perhaps."

Yorke smiled.

"The best thing I could do for you would be to send you about your business!" he said.

"Oh, don't say that, my lord," remonstrated Fleming. "I'm—I'm afraid something is wrong, my lord—"

"Yes," said Yorke, grimly. "Something is very much wrong, Fleming. The fact is I am up a tree; cleaned out and ruined."

"Ruined?"

"That's it," assented Yorke, coolly. "I've been hard up, once or twice before—

you know that, Fleming?"

"Oh, yes, my lord."

"But this is the finale, the climax, the wind up. But don't let me stand in your light. Look here, you have been a deuced good servant—yes, and a friend to me, and as it won't do you any good to be mixed up in this beastly mess you had better go at once. Lord Vinson has often told me that if I wanted to get rid of you he'd be glad to take you on. So you go to him—I'll give you a letter and—"

For the first time in his exemplary life Fleming was guilty of vulgar language.

"I'm damned if I do!" he said. "I beg your pardon, my lord, I humbly beg your lordship's pardon, but I'm not that kind of a man—I'm not, indeed;" and there was something very much like water in the honest fellow's eyes. "I shouldn't think of leaving your lordship while you were up a tree, as your lordship puts it. I should never look myself in the face again. I'm much obliged to Lord Vinson; but no, my lord. I'm not the man to desert a good and kind master in misfortune. I beg your lordship's pardon, but I thought—" He hesitated respectfully.

"Think away," said Yorke, lighting another cigar and tilting his hat back. "Perhaps your thinking will be more valuable than mine. I've been thinking, and can see no way out of the mess."

"The—the duke, my lord," suggested Fleming. "I'm sure he—"

"So am I, Fleming; but the duke has left for the Continent, and I don't know where he has gone, and this paper says that I've got to show up at the court in the city at once."

"And it will all be in the newspapers!" said Fleming aghast. To be 'in the newspapers' was the direct disgrace and calamity in the eyes of that worthy man.

"Just so," said Yorke, knocking the ashes off his cigar. "You see, Fleming, I am in a hole out of which it is impossible to pull me. Never you mind; after all, it doesn't matter."

"Doesn't it matter, my lord?" echoed Fleming, startled. "You—you who are so well known to—to appear in court!"

"And get six months—is it six months or six weeks? I don't know—I don't know anything; but I suppose I shall, and pretty quickly. Never mind. Look here; see that man in the next room has all he wants."

"Oh, yes; all right, my lord," said Fleming, with a touch of impatience, "All he wants is beer, and I've given him half a dozen bottles."

Yorke laughed and leaned back in the chair.

"All right. Bring any letters that may come; I should like to know the worst."

Fleming went out, but appeared again in a few minutes.

"Will you want me for half an hour or three-quarters, my lord?" he said, in a thoughtful, troubled kind of way.

"No. Going after that place, Fleming? Better."

Fleming colored and opened his lips; but he did not say anything; and Yorke, left alone again, leaned his head on his hand and gave himself up to gloomy reverie.

A man in possession in the next room, a summons to appear in a debtors' court, his name in the newspapers as a ruined man! It was all bad enough, but he scarcely felt it. He had endured the maximum of suffering when he had become convinced that Leslie had jilted him, and this—well, this was, so to speak, almost a relief and a diversion. And yet the disgrace! He passed a very bad half hour in that dressing-room—a half hour in which there rose the specter of an ill-spent past in which follies marched in ghostly procession before him, and all, as they promenaded by, whispered hoarsely, "Ruin!" And yet, through it all he saw more plainly than anything else the sweet face of Leslie, the only woman he had ever loved—the woman who had seemed to him an angel of truth and constancy, but who had deserted him the moment she had heard that he was not a duke.

Fleming, meanwhile, had put on his hat and sallied into the street. He had left his beloved master utterly reckless and indifferent, and therefore it rested with him, the devoted servant, to display all the more energy. That he should sit still and see Lord Yorke drift into utter ruin and destruction was simply impossible.

"Something's got to be done," he said to himself, "and I've got to do it. He isn't going to appear at any court; not if I know it! What! my guv'nor, the cousin of a duke, to come up before a beak—some miserable city alderman?" Fleming's ideas of the city law courts were, like his master's, hazy. "Certainly not—not if I have to move heaven and earth! Now, if the duke was at home I could see Mr. Grey, and we could arrange this little matter between us; but as he isn't, why, the thing to do is to go to the next person, and that is, naturally, Lady Eleanor Dallas. It isn't likely that she'd see Lord Yorke in such a hole as this without helping him out; and she's rich, and richer than ever lately. I'll try her!"

He called a hansom and had himself driven to Kensington Palace Gardens.

“Anyhow, her ladyship can only refuse to see me,” he said to himself. “But I don’t think she will;” and “he winked the other eye.”

Oh! my friends, do you think our servants are deaf, and dumb, and blind? They know all our little secrets and our little difficulties; all our little entanglements. There is scarcely a letter we receive that, unless we lock it up securely, they do not read. No friend ever visits us but they know all about him and his, and whom his daughter is engaged to, or why the engagement is broken off.

Therefore let us be grateful to a kind Providence for the servants who are also devoted and trusty friends, such as was Fleming.

When Fleming reached Kensington Palace Gardens he was told by one of the footmen that Lady Eleanor was engaged.

“You’ve come with a message from Lord Auchester, Mr. Fleming, I suppose?” said the footman.

Fleming was an ‘upper servant’ and was always addressed by those beneath him as ‘Mr.,’ and he was very much respected on his own account as one who had saved money and was in ‘good society.’

“Well, no, I haven’t,” said Fleming, gravely, and a little pompously. “I’ve come on business of my own.”

The footman took his name into the boudoir where Lady Eleanor was sitting with no other than Mr. Ralph Duncombe.

She flushed slightly.

“It is Lord Auchester’s valet,” she said.

Ralph Duncombe looked up with a slight start.

“I do not wish him to see me, Lady Eleanor,” he said.

“No, no; oh, no! I understand,” she said nervously.

“And yet I should like to know what he has to say.”

Lady Eleanor pointed to a large four-fold Japanese screen which cut off one of the corners of the room.

“He will not be here many minutes,” she said.

Ralph Duncombe went behind the screen, and Lady Eleanor rang the bell and told the footman she would see Fleming.

He came in, looking rather nervous and embarrassed, for it was a bold thing he was going to do, and he knew that Lady Eleanor could look and speak haughtily and sternly when she was displeased.

"You want to see me, Fleming?" she said, graciously enough. "Is it a message from Lord Auchester?"

"No, my lady," he said, and like a man of the world he went straight to the point. "No, my lady, his lordship does not know that I have come, and if he had known I was coming I'm sure he would have forbidden me; but I ventured to intrude on your ladyship, knowing that you and my master were old friends, if I may say so."

"Certainly you may say so, Fleming," said Lady Eleanor, pleasantly, and looking as if she were expecting anything but bad news.

"Well, my lady, my master is in a terrible trouble," he said, plunging still further into the business.

"In terrible trouble?" echoed Lady Eleanor; and her face flushed. "What do you mean, Fleming?"

"It's money matters, my lady," said Fleming, gravely, and looking around as if he feared an eavesdropper. "His lordship—I'm obliged to speak freely, my lady, or else you won't understand; but it's out of no disrespect to his lordship, who has been the best of masters to me—"

"Say what you have to say quite without reserve," said Lady Eleanor, in a low voice.

"Well, my lady, I was going to say that his lordship has always been hard up, as you may say. There's always been a difficulty with the money. It's usual with high-spirited gentlemen like Lord Yorke," he said, apologetically. "They don't know, and can't be expected to know, the value of money like common ordinary folk, and so they—well, they outrun the constable."

"Lord Auchester is in debt?" said Lady Eleanor, guardedly.

"It's worse than that, my lady," said Fleming. "That would be nothing, for ever since I've been in his service he has been in debt. But now the people he owes money to want him to pay them."

He gave the information as though it were the most extraordinary and unnatural conduct on the part of any creditor of Lord Auchester that he should want payment.

"People who owe money must pay it some time, Fleming," suggested Lady Eleanor.

"Yes—ah, yes, my lady, some time," admitted Fleming, "but not all at once. It seems as if the people my lord owes money to had joined together and resolved to drop upon him in a heap. There's a man in possession in Bury Street, my lady."

"A man in possession!" repeated Lady Eleanor, as if she scarcely understood.

"Yes, a bailiff, my lady, sitting there in his lordship's sitting-room; and I daresn't throw him out of the window."

Lady Eleanor looked down.

"And—and Lord Yorke, Fleming—I suppose he is in great trouble about this?"

Fleming hesitated.

"Well, my lady, he is in great trouble; but if you mean is he cut up about this money matter, I can't say that he is. He don't seem to care one bit about it, and takes it as cool and indifferent as if—well, as if nothing mattered. But he is in great trouble for all that, and he has been for weeks past—"

He hesitated.

Lady Eleanor looked up.

"You had better tell me everything, I think, Fleming," she said, in a low voice.

"Well, my lady, it's just thus: His lordship had a blow—a disappointment of some kind. It isn't money, it isn't betting, or card-playing, or I should have heard of it, for his lordship generally makes some remarks, such as 'I've had a good day, Fleming,' or, 'I'm stone broke, Fleming,' so that I know what kind of luck he's had; it isn't that. It's something worse—if there is anything worse," he put in philosophically. "A little while ago his lordship was in the very best of spirits; I never saw him in better, and he's a bright-hearted gentleman, as you know, my lady. I'm speaking of the time when he came back from that place in the country where he and his grace the duke were—Portmaris."

Lady Eleanor leaned her head on her hand so that her face was hidden from him.

"Then all of a sudden a change came, and his lordship got bad, very bad. It was dreadful to see him, my lady. Eat nothing, cared for nothing; scarcely even spoke. Nothing but smoke, smoke, all day, and wander in and out looking like the ghost of himself. And he, who used to be so bright and cheerful, with the laugh always ready! I'd have given something to have spoken a word, and asked him what was the matter; but—well, my lady, with all his pleasantness, my master's the last gentleman to take a liberty with."

"You don't know what it was, this terrible disappointment?" said Lady

Eleanor, almost inaudibly.

Fleming hesitated and glanced at her; then he coughed discreetly behind his hand.

It was sufficient answer, and Lady Eleanor's face grew red.

"Whatever it was that made him so happy and cheerful, it was knocked on the head and put an end to, my lady," he said. "And so it is that this regular smash-up of affairs—I mean these summonses and man in possession—don't seem to affect him. You see, my lady, he was as low down as he could be already. Sometimes—" He stopped, and looked down at the carpet very gravely and anxiously.

"Well?"

"Well, my lady, it isn't for me to say such a thing, but I've been almost afraid to let him out of my sight in the morning, and I've been truly thankful to see him come in at night."

Lady Eleanor drew a long breath and shuddered.

"You mean—"

"Men, when they're down as low as my master, they do rash things sometimes, my lady," said Fleming, in a solemn whisper.

Lady Eleanor's face went white, and she put her hand to her delicate throat as if she were suffocating.

"You—you should not say—hint—at such terrible things, Fleming," she panted.

"I—I beg your ladyship's pardon," he said, humbly, "but it's the truth and—and I thought I ought to tell you, being his lordship's friend."

"Yes—yes, I am his friend," she said, as if she scarcely knew what she was saying. "And I will try to help him."

Fleming's face brightened.

"Oh, my lady!" he said, gratefully.

"Stop!" she said. "Your master, Lord Yorke, must not know;" and her face grew crimson again.

"Oh, no, no, my lady! Certainly not! Why, if his lordship ever knew that I'd come to you—" He stopped and shook his head.

"I understand," said Lady Eleanor. "No, Lord Yorke must never know—no one must know—"

"I should have gone to the duke, my lady, but his grace is abroad, as no doubt your ladyship knows."

Lady Eleanor turned her head aside. She and Ralph Duncombe had timed the attack on Yorke for the moment when the duke should be beyond reach.

"His grace would have helped my master, I know; and I'd have made bold to write to him, but there isn't time."

Lady Eleanor shook her head.

"No, no," she said. "He must not know—no one must know. You need not be anxious any longer, Fleming. You were right in coming to me and—and—" She sunk into the chair.

Fleming heaved a sigh of relief.

"Very well, my lady. I don't know much about it, but the person who seems the principal in this set upon his lordship is a man named Duncombe—a money-lender, I expect. They take all sorts of names. I wish I had him to myself for a quarter of an hour. I'd teach him to put a man in possession—begging your ladyship's pardon," he broke off.

Lady Eleanor's face reddened, and she glanced toward the screen.

"You had better go back now, Fleming," she said, "and—and don't leave Lord Auchester more than you can help. And, remember, not one word that might lead him to guess that you have been to me."

"You may be sure I shall be careful for my own sake, my lady," said Fleming, with quiet emphasis; and, with a bow in which gratitude and respect were fairly divided, he left the room.

Ralph Duncombe came from behind the screen and stood looking down at Lady Eleanor, whose proud head was bowed upon her hands.

"What are you going to do?" he asked.

She looked up. "Set him free—at once—at once!" she responded with feverish impetuosity. "Did you not hear the man? That he actually feared his master would—" She shuddered. "This must come to an end at once. It will drive him mad!"

Ralph Duncombe smiled grimly.

"I heard the man say that it was not the money trouble that was affecting Lord Auchester," he said. "It seems to me, Lady Eleanor, that we have taken a great deal of trouble for nothing. This marriage which you so much dreaded was broken off before any plans to prevent it were put in operation. The—the young lady had disappeared—"

She looked up suddenly as he stopped and bit his lip.

"Disappeared? How do you know?" she exclaimed breathlessly.

His face was as pale as hers, but was set and stern.

"Well, I thought I had better run down to this place, Portmaris, and see for myself how matters were going," he said, in a kind of business-like coolness and indifference, "and—and I found that Miss—what is her name?" he asked, as if he had forgotten.

"Lisle—Leslie Lisle," said Lady Eleanor.

"Ah, yes! Miss Lisle had flown."

"Flown?"

"Yes, flown and disappeared. Disappeared so completely that all my efforts to discover her track failed."

He still spoke calmly and with affected indifference, but if she herself had not been so agitated she would have noticed the pallor of his face and the restless movement of his hands.

"What—what do you think it means?" she asked, in a whisper.

He shrugged his shoulders.

"A lovers' quarrel—but no; it is more shame than that. Yes; I should say that the engagement was broken off for some reason or other, so that you have had all this trouble and expense for nothing, Lady Eleanor."

"And you can not find her?Disappeared?"

He took up his hat.

"Disappeared," he repeated, grimly.

"And that is why he is wretched and unhappy," she said, with a sigh. "How—how he must love her after all!" and her head drooped.

Ralph Duncombe moistened his lips.

"Yes," he said. "But perhaps she did not care for him. Any way, you see it is she who has left him, not he who has left her."

"Yes," she said, and she pushed the hair from her fair forehead with an impatient gesture. "Oh, I cannot understand it! The engagement broken off! Disappeared! But there must be an end to these law proceedings now, Mr. Duncombe."

"There can be only one way of terminating them," he said.

"And that?"

"Is by paying the money into court," he said. "The thing has gone too far."

"I see," she said. Then she held out her hand. "I will send or come to you in the morning. I am too confused and—and upset even to think at this moment."

Fleming hastened back to Bury Street and found Yorke sitting as he had left him, with the formidable-looking letters and papers littered aroundhim.

Fleming picked them up and put them away, and got out Yorke's dress clothes.

"Don't trouble, Fleming, I shall dine at home," said Yorke; but Fleming went on with his preparations.

"Very sorry, my lord, but the kitchen grate is not in order." He didn't intend that his master should eat his dinner in company with a man in possession. "Better go and dine at the club, my lord, if I may make so bold."

Yorke got up with a grim smile.

"Perhaps you're right, Fleming," he said, listlessly. "I suppose they never have anything the matter with the kitchen grate at Holloway, or whatever other quod it is they send people who can't pay their debts. And what about these clothes, Fleming? Perhaps our friend in the next room will object to my walking out in them."

"I'd punch his head if he was to offer a remark on the subject," said Fleming, fiercely. "I beg your lordship's pardon—if I might say a word, my lord, I'd implore your lordship not to take this business too much to heart; I mean not to worry too much over it. You never can tell what may turn up."

Yorke laughed drearily as he allowed Fleming to dress him.

"I won't," he said. "To tell you the truth, I don't feel so cut up as you'd imagine, or as I ought, Fleming. I feel"—he stopped and looked round absently—"well, as if I were another fellow altogether, and I was just looking on, half sorry and half amused."

"Yes, that's right. Keep feeling like that, my lord," said Fleming, cheeringly. "Depend upon it, it will come out right."

Yorke shrugged his shoulders.

"I dare say," he said, indifferently. "Don't sit up for me. I may be late."

He came in a little after two in the morning, and Fleming could have been almost glad if his beloved master had showed signs of having spent a 'warm' night; but Yorke was 'more than sober,' and looked only weary and sick at heart, as he had done for weeks past.

"Oh, by the way, Fleming," he said, as he took off his coat, and as if he had suddenly remembered it, "you must call me pretty early to-morrow. I have to be down in the city, you know."

That was all.

CHAPTER XXXII.

BOUGHT AND PAID FOR.

A city law court is not exactly the place in which to spend a happy day—unless you happen to be a lawyer engaged in a profitable case there—and Yorke, as he entered the stuffy, grimy, murky chamber, looked round with a feeling of surprise and grim interest.

Upon the bench sat the judge in a much-worn gown and a grubby wig. A barrister was drowsing away in the 'well' of the court, and his fellows were sleeping or stretching and yawning round him.

The public was represented by half a dozen seedy-looking individuals who all looked as if they had not been to bed for a month and had forgotten to wash themselves for a like period. There was an usher, who yawned behind his wand, one or two policemen with wooden countenances, and two or three wretched-looking individuals, who were, like Yorke, defendants in various suits.

The entrance of this stalwart, well-dressed and decidedly distinguished and aristocratic personage created a slight sensation for a moment or two; then he seemed to be forgotten, and he stood and looked on, and wondered how soon his case would be heard, and whether he would be carried away to jail forthwith.

He waited for a half hour or so, feeling that he was growing dirty and grimy like the rest of the people round him, and gradually the sense of the disgrace and humiliation of his position stole over him.

Great heavens, to what a pass he had come! He had lost Leslie. He was now to lose good name and honor—everything! Would it not be better for himself and everybody connected with him if he went outside and purchased a dose of prussic acid?

The suspense, the stuffy court, the droning voice of the counsel began to drive him mad.

He went up to the usher. "Can you tell me when my case comes on?" he said.

The man looked at him sleepily.

"Your case—what name?" he asked, without any 'sir,' and with a kind of drowsy impertinence, which seemed to be in strict harmony with the air of the place.

"Auchester!" said Yorke. "I am the—the defendant."

"Horchester? Don't know. Ask the clerk," said the man.

With a sick feeling of shame Yorke went up to the man pointed out by the usher and put the same question to him.

"Auchester? Duncombe versus Auchester; Levison versus Auchester; Arack versus Auchester?" said the clerk, in a dry, business-like way.

"Yes, I dare say that's it," said Yorke, hating the sound of his own name.

The clerk looked down a list, then raised his eyes with the faintest of smiles.

"Scratched out," he said, curtly.

"Scratched out?" echoed Yorke, blankly.

"Yes, sir—my lord," said the clerk, who, while looking at the list, had come upon Yorke's title. "The cases have been removed from the list. Settled."

"Settled? I don't understand," said Yorke, staring at him. "I've only just come down—I've paid nothing."

"Some one else has, then, my lord," said the clerk. "Wait a moment till this case is heard; it will be over directly, and I'll explain."

Yorke, feeling like a man in a dream, stepped into a corner and waited. Presently the court adjourned for luncheon, and the clerk came toward him.

"This way, my lord." He led Yorke into an office. "Now, my lord. Yes, all the cases have been discharged from the list—been settled this morning."

"This morning?" echoed Yorke, mechanically, still with a vast amazement. "But—but who—I don't know who could have done this. I have not, for the best of all reasons. I came down here prepared to go to prison, or wherever else you sent me."

The clerk raised his brows and shook his head gravely.

"Yes, you would have been committed, my lord, for a certainty," he said. "You see, you let things slide too long. But there is no fear now. The money, all of it, has been paid. You are quite free, quite. I congratulate your lordship."

"But—but"—stammered Yorke, and he put his hand to his brow—"who can have done it—paid it? Is it the Duke of Rothbury?"

Could Dolph have heard of it in some extraordinary way and sent the money?

The clerk went into the inner office for a few minutes, then he came back with a slip of paper in his hand.

"I don't know whether I am doing right, my lord," he said, gravely, and even cautiously. "Perhaps I ought not to give you this information, but I trust to your lordship's discretion. You won't get me into a scrape, my lord?"

"No, no!" said Yorke, "who is it?"

The clerk handed him the slip of paper.

It was a check on Coutts' for a large—a very large—sum, and it was signed "Eleanor Dallas."

"Eleanor!"

The name broke in a kind of sigh from Yorke's lips, and his face reddened. But it was pale again as he handed the check back to the clerk.

"Thank you," he said.

He stood and looked vacantly before him as if he had forgotten where he was; then he woke with a start.

"Then I can go?" he said.

"Certainly, my lord," said the clerk. "As I said, you are quite free. There are no actions against you now; everything is squared—paid."

Yorke thanked him again, wished him good-day, and got outside.

Everything paid—and by Eleanor!

He repeated this as he walked from the city to the west; as he tramped slowly, with downcast head, across Hyde Park.

He told himself that he ought to be grateful; that he could not feel too grateful to the woman who had come to his aid and saved him from ruin and disgrace.

But he knew why she had done it, and he knew what he ought to do in return. The least he could do would be to go and kneel at her feet, and ask her to accept the life which she had snatched from disgrace. And why shouldn't he? The only woman he had ever loved had proved false, and mercenary, and base, and there was nothing now to prevent him asking Lady Eleanor to be his wife; and yet, alas! he could not get that other face out of his mind or heart.

He thought of her—she haunted him as he walked along; the clear gray eyes, so tender one moment, so full of fire and humor the next; the dark hair, the graceful figure, the sweet voice. "Oh, Leslie, Leslie! if you had but been true!" was the burden of his heart's wail.

He looked up and found himself close upon Palace Gardens; unconsciously his feet had moved in that direction. He rang the bell of Lady Eleanor's door.

Yes, her ladyship was at home, the footman said, and said it in that serene, confident tone which a servant uses when he knows that his mistress will be glad to see the visitor.

Yorke followed the man to the small drawing-room.

Lady Denby was there tying up some library books.

She started slightly as she saw his altered appearance, but she was too completely a woman of the world to let him see the start.

"Why, Yorke!" she said, "what a stranger you are! We were only speaking of you this morning at breakfast, and wondering where you were. Have you been away? Sit down—or tie up those tiresome books for me, will you? They slip and slide about in the most aggravating way. I'll go and tell Eleanor; I fancy she was going out."

She met Lady Eleanor in the hall, and drew her aside.

"Yorke is in there, Eleanor," she said.

"Yorke!"

Lady Eleanor repeated the name and started almost guiltily, almost fearfully.

"Yes, I came to tell you, and—well, yes—prepare you. I don't want you to do as I did—jump as if I'd seen a bogey man. He has been ill, or up to some deviltry or other, and he looks—well, I can't tell you how he looks. It gave me a shock. I thought I'd prepare you."

Lady Eleanor touched her hand.

"Thank you, dear. No, I won't look shocked. He looks very ill?"

"Very ill, oh! worse than ill. Like a man who has robbed a church and been found out, or lost everything he held dear."

Lady Eleanor put her handkerchief to her lips. They were trembling.

"I don't mind what he has been doing," she said.

"Oh, my dear Eleanor!"

"No, I don't. I'll go in now. Don't let any one disturb us. He—he may have come to see me to talk about something."

She went into the room, and Yorke turned to meet her. It was well that she had been forewarned of the change in his appearance. As it was, she could scarcely suppress the cry that rose to her lips.

"Well, Yorke," she said, with affected lightness, "tying up aunt's books? That is so like her. No one can come near her without getting employed. What a shame to worry you!"

"It doesn't worry me," he said.

He leaned against the table and looked down at her. There is a picture of Millais's—it is called, I think, 'A Hot-house Flower'—which Lady Eleanor might have sat for that morning, so delicate, so graceful, so refined and blanche was her beauty. She wore a loose dress of soft cashmere, cream in color, almost Greek in fashion. Her hair was like gold, her eyes placid yet tender, with a touch of subdued sadness and anxiety in them. A charming, an irresistible picture, and one that appealed to this man with the storm-beaten heart aching in his bosom.

She glanced up at him, saw the haggard face, the dark rings round the eyes, that indescribable look which pain and despair and utter abandonment produce as plainly as the die stamps the hall-mark on the piece of silver, and her heart yearned for him, for his love—yearned for the right to comfort and soothe him. Ah! if he would only have it so—if he would only let her, how happy she would make him! All this, and much more, she felt; but she looked quite placid and serene—like a dainty lily unstirred by the wind—and said in her soft voice:

"We were thinking of advertising for you Yorke. Have you been away?"

He might have answered: "Yes, I have been in the Valley of Sorrow and Tribulation, on the Desert of Dead Love and Vain Hope," but instead he replied:

"No, just here in London; but I have been busy."

She looked up and smiled.

"Busy! That sounds so strange, and so comic, coming from you!"

"And yet it is true," he said. "I have been busy thinking." If there was a touch of bitterness in his voice she did not notice it. "And that's hard work for me—it's so new, you see."

There was silence for a moment. He held the string with which he had been tying up the books in his hands, and fidgeted with it restlessly. Lady Eleanor dropped into small-talk. Had he been to the chrysanthemum show at the Temple? Had he noticed that the Duchess of Orloffe was not going to give her autumn ball? Did he—

He broke in suddenly as if he had not been listening, his voice hoarse and thick:

"Eleanor, why did you do it?"

"Why did I—do what, Yorke?" she said.

"Why did you fling so much money away upon a worthless scamp?" His face went white, then red.

"Who told you?" she breathed.

"They told me down at the court where I had gone to be disgraced," he said, "and you saved me! How can I thank you, Eleanor? How can I? And you would have done it in secret, would have kept it from me?"

"Yes, oh, yes," she murmured, her head drooping. "Don't—don't say anything about it. It was nothing—nothing!" She looked up at him eagerly, pleadingly. "Yorke, you will not think badly of me because I did it? Why shouldn't I? I am rich—you don't know how rich—and what better could I do with the stupid money than give it to a—a friend who needed it more—ten thousand times more—than I do or ever shall! Don't be angry with me, Yorke."

"Angry!" The blood flew to his face and his eyes flashed. He drew nearer to the chair in which she sat, he knelt on one knee beside her.

"Eleanor, I am utterly worthless—you know that quite well. I was not worth the saving, but as you have saved me, will you accept me? Eleanor, will you be my wife?"

Her face went white with the ecstasy which shot through her heart. Ah, for how long had she thirsted, hungered for these words from his lips! And they had come at last!

"Will you be my wife, Eleanor? I will try to make you happy. I will do my best, Heaven helping, to be a good husband to you! Stop, dear! If you act wisely you will send me about my business! There are fifty—a hundred better men who love you; you could scarcely have a worse than I, but if you will say 'yes,' I will try and be less unworthy of you. All my life I will never forget all that I owe you—never forget that you saved me from ruin and disgrace. Now, dear, I—"

She put out her hand to him without a word; then as he took it her passion burst through the bonds in which she thought to bind it, and she swayed forward and dropped upon his breast.

"Yorke, Yorke, you know"—came through her parted lips—"you know I love you—have always loved you!"

"My poor Eleanor!" he said, almost indeed, quite pityingly. "Such a bad, worthless lot as I am!"

"No, no!" she panted. "No, no; the best, the highest to me! And—and if you were not, it—it would be all the same. Oh, Yorke, be good, be kind to me, for you are all the world to me!"

They sat and talked hand in hand for some time, and once during that talk he said:

"By the way, Eleanor, how did you hear I was in such a mess—how did you come to know?"

It was a very natural question under the circumstances; but Lady Eleanor started and turned white, absolutely white with fear.

"No, no; not one word will I ever say or let you say about this stupid money business!" she exclaimed. Then she took his hand and pressed it against her cheek. "Why, sir, what does it matter? It was only—only lending it to you for a little time, you see. It will all be yours soon."

Lady Denby came in after a discreet cough outside; but Lady Eleanor did not move or take her hand from Yorke's.

"Oh!" said Lady Denby.

"Eleanor has made me very happy, Lady Denby," he said, rising, but still holding Lady Eleanor's hand.

"Oh!" said Lady Denby again. "What do you want me to say? That you deserve her? No, thank you, I couldn't tell such an obvious fib. What I'm going to say in the shape of congratulation is that she is much too good for you."

"That is so," he said with a grim smile.

"You'll stay to dinner?" murmured Lady Eleanor. "You will stay, Yorke?"

"Yes," he said, bending down and kissing her—"yes, thanks. But I must go and change my things. I'm awfully dirty and seedy."

She went with him to the door, as if she begrudged every moment that he should be out of her sight, and still smiled after he had left her and had got half-way down the Gardens. Then suddenly he stopped and looked round him with a ghostly look.

And yet it was only the face of Leslie that had flashed across his mental vision. Only the face of the girl who had jilted him!

"My God! shall I never forget her?" he muttered, hoarsely. "Not even now!"

CHAPTER XXXIII.

A LITTLE SUNSHINE.

The announcement of the engagement between Lord Auchester and Lady Eleanor Dallas had appeared in the society papers a month ago, and the world of 'the upper ten' had expended its congratulations and began asking itself when the wedding was to take place, for it was agreed on all hands that so excellent and altogether desirable a match could not take place too soon.

"He has been dreadfully wild, I'm told, my dear," said one gossip to another, "and is as poor as a church mouse. But there is plenty of money on her side; indeed, they say that lately she has become fabulously rich, so that will be all right. Of course she might have done better; but everybody knows she was ridiculously fond of him—oh! quite too ridiculously. Gave herself away, in fact; and she goes about looking so happy and victorious that it is really quite indecent!"

"That is more than can be said of the bridegroom-elect," remarked gossip number two, "for he looks as grave as a judge and as glum as an undertaker. The mere prospect of matrimony seems to have taken all the spirits out of him. Not like the same man, I assure you, my dear."

It was autumn now. The greenery of the trees had turned to russet and gold; a mystic stillness brooded softly over the country lanes; the yellow corn waved sleepily to the soft breeze; the blackberries darkened the hedge-rows, and on the roads lay, not thickly as yet, but in twos and threes, the leaves of the oak and the chestnut. An air of repose and quietude reigned over the land, as if nature, almost tired of the sun and heat and the multitudinous noises of summer, were taking a short nap to prepare itself for the rigor and robust energy of winter.

In one of the loveliest of our country lanes stood a village school. It was a picturesque little building of white stone and red tiles. The tiny school-house adjoining it was so overgrown by ivy as to resemble a green bower. There was a window at the back, and an orchard in which the golden and ruddy apples were almost as thick as the blackberries in the lanes. Everything in and about this school was the picture of neatness. The curtains of white and pink muslin were exquisitely clean and artistically draped behind the diamond-paned windows.

The door-sills were as white as marble; the diminutive knocker on the school-house door shone like a newly minted sovereign. Not a weed showed its head in the small garden, which literally glowed with single and double dahlias, sweet-scented stocks and many-colored chrysanthemums. There was a little gate in the closely cut hedge, which was painted a snowy white—in short, the tiny domain made a picture which Millais or Marcus Stone or Leslie would have delighted to transfer to canvas.

From the open door of the school there issued a hum and buzz which resembled that which proceeds from the door of a bee-hive, for afternoon school was still on, and the pupils were still at their lessons.

The village—it was rather more than half a mile from the school—was that of Newfold, a quiet, sleepy little place, which not even the restless tourist seems to have discovered; a small cluster of houses, with an inn, a church, and a couple of shops lying in the hollow between the two ranges of Loamshire hills. A Londoner would tell you that Newfold was at least five hundred years behind the times; but, if it be so, Newfold does not care. There is enough plowing and wood-cutting in winter, enough sowing and tilling in spring, enough harvesting in autumn to keep the kettle boiling, and Newfold is quite content. Some day one of those individuals who discover such places will happen on it, write an article about it, attract attention to it, and so ruin it; but he hasn't chanced to come upon it yet, and oh! let us pray that he may keep off it for a long while; for Newfolds are getting scarcer every year, and soon, if we do not take care, England will become one vast, hideous plain of bricks and mortar, and there will be no place in which we can take refuge from the fogs and smoke of the great towns.

In another quarter of an hour school would 'break up,' and the girls were standing up singing the evening hymn which brought the day's work to a close. In the center of the room stood a pleasant, fair-haired young lady, whose eyes, mild and gentle as they were, seemed to be looking everywhere. On a small platform stood another young lady with dark hair and gray eyes. These were the two mistresses of the Newfold village school, and their names were Leslie Lisle and Lucy Somes.

Life is not all clouds and rain, thank God; the sun shines sometimes, and the sun of good luck had shone upon Leslie and Lucy. It was good luck that they should pass the much-dreaded examination, that ordeal to which they had looked forward with such fear and trembling; it was good luck that there should be two appointments vacant; but oh! it was the superlative of luck that these appointments should be to the same school, and that the school should be here in peaceful Newfold!

It seemed to Leslie as if misfortune had grown tired of buffeting her, and had decided to leave her alone for a time. She could scarcely believe her eyes when Lucy Somes ran into her room at Torrington Square with the news that they were to be sent to the same school, and in her beloved county. Of course influence had been used at headquarters by Lucy's people, but Lucy persisted that luck had more to do with it than anything else, and that Leslie had brought the good fortune; and it did not lessen Lucy's happiness that Leslie, having obtained the most marks at the exam., was given the post of head-mistress, and that she, Lucy, was to be her subordinate. "It is quite right, dear," she said, brightly and cheerfully. "Of course, you ought to be the first; any one could see that at half a glance. You are ten times quicker and cleverer than I, and, besides, if we are to be together—and oh! how delightful it is to think that we are!—I would a thousand times rather you were the principal!"

"We will both be head-mistress, Lucy!" Leslie had said, as, with tears in her eyes, she had put her arms round the good-natured girl, and kissed her.

They had only been four days at the school, but short as the time had been they had grown fond of it—fond of the work and the children, and who can tell how fond and proud of the little house that nestled against the school building!

Lucy was like a child in her unrestrained joy and delight, and if Leslie took their good fortune more quietly, she was not lacking in gratitude. In this new life she would not only find peace, please God, but work—work that in time might bring her forgetfulness of the past. And the forgetfulness, for which she prayed nightly, was as much of happiness as she dared hope for.

The lily that has been beaten down by the storm may live and bloom still, but the chances are that it will never again rear its stately head as of old.

The evening hymn was finished; Leslie struck the bell on the desk before her, and in her sweet voice said "Good-afternoon, children," and with an answering "Good-afternoon, teachers," the children trooped out.

Lucy went and stood beside Leslie, and watched the happy throng as it ran laughing and shouting to the meadow.

"How happy they are, Leslie, and how good, too! I am sure they are the best children in the world! And many of them are so pretty and rosy; and they are all healthy—all except two or three. I should hate to have a school full of sickly, undergrown children, all peevish and weary and discontented; but all ours are cheerful and willing."

"They would find it hard to be otherwise where you are, Lucy," said Leslie, looking at the happy face with a loving smile.

"Oh, I—oh, yes; I'm cheerful enough," said Lucy, laughing and blushing. "I'm just running over with happiness and contentment; but I'm afraid that they couldn't get on very fast if I were quite alone with them. They wouldn't mind me enough. Now you—"

"Are they afraid of me?" said Leslie, smiling.

"No, no!" Lucy hastened to respond. "Afraid? no, no! But they look up to you, and think more of your good opinion already. Oh, I can see that, short as the time has been. They were quite right up in London in making you the head-mistress, dear. Are you tired, Leslie? It has been rather hot for the time of year, and the children, good as they are, make a noise. Does your head ache? I'm afraid you will find it rather trying at first."

"I am not tired, and my head doesn't ache in the least," said Leslie, "and why should I, more than you, find it trying, Lucy? and, dear, I want you to let me have the English history class. You have got more than your fair share. Did you think that I should not notice it? I believe you would take all the work if I would let you, you greedy girl."

Lucy blushed—she blushed on the slightest provocation.

"I don't want you to work too hard, Leslie," she said. "You are not strong yet, not nearly so strong as I am, and you felt the awful grinding for that exam. more than I did because you were not used to it, and had to do it in a shorter time; and so I am going to take care of you."

Leslie laughed.

"Why, I could lift you up and carry you round the room, little girl!" she said, in loving banter; "and it is I who have to take care of you. But we'll take care of each other, Lucy. And now let us go in to tea."

They went into the little house, and the small maid who was house-maid, parlor-maid, and cook rolled into one, had set out the tea in the cosy parlor, fragrant with the musk and mignonette which bloomed in the window-box. Lucy looked round with a sigh of ineffable content.

"Isn't it delicious, Leslie?" she exclaimed with bated breath. "I feel like Robinson Crusoe!"

"Robinson Crusoe with everything ready made for him and all the luxuries?" said Leslie, laughingly.

"Yes, that's what I mean," assented Lucy naively. "All through I looked forward to something like this, but my dreams never reached anything half so delightful. For one thing, I never dreamed that I should have you for a companion and friend. I thought that there would be sure to be a thorn in my bed of roses, and that that thorn would probably take the shape of a disagreeable head-mistress—some horrid, middle-aged, disagreeable person who would be always complaining and scolding. But you! Mother writes that I must have exaggerated just to please her when I described the school and told her what you were like; but I didn't exaggerate a bit. Oh, Leslie"—she stopped with a slice of bread and butter half-way to her mouth—"do you think we are too happy—that something will happen to spoil it all?"

Leslie smiled.

"I think not," she said. "It is only those who don't deserve to be happy whose happiness doesn't last. Now you, Lucy—But give me some more tea, and don't try and croak, because you make the most awful failure of it."

Lucy's face wreathed itself in its wonted smile again.

"I wonder whether there are two happier girls in all the world than you and I, Leslie?" she said. "What shall we do this evening—go for a walk? You haven't been into the village yet. Will you come? It is such a pretty, quaint little place, with the tiniest and most delightful church you ever saw! Isn't it strange that we should be pitchforked down here into a place we know nothing about and never heard of? It is like Robinson Crusoe again. I hope the natives will not be savage!"

Leslie looked up from the copy-book she was examining.

"We shall have very little to do with the natives, savage or friendly, Lucy," she said.

"Of course not," assented Lucy, cheerfully. "I suppose the clergyman's wife will call—Oh, I forgot! He said the first morning he came to read prayers that he wasn't married. But the squire's lady will drive up in a carriage and pair, and walk through the school with her eyeglass up. But no one else will come to bother us. You see," she ran on, jumping up to water the flowers in the window, "school-teachers are supposed to be neither fish, flesh nor fowl—and not very good red herring. People don't visit them."

"That is good news for school-teachers, at any rate," said Leslie, smiling.

"Yes; we don't want anybody, do we, dear? You and I together can be quite happy without the rest of the world. And now about our walk. Shall we go, Leslie?"

"I don't think I will this evening, Lucy. I will stay and go over these books. But you shall go on a voyage of discovery, and bring back a full and particular account of your adventures."

"No, no! I'll stay," began Lucy. But Leslie looked up at her with the expression Lucy had learned to know so well. "Very well, dear," she said, gently. "I will just run into the village and order some things we want and come straight back; and mind, you are not to do all those copy-books, or I shall feel hurt and injured."

Leslie worked away at her exercise books for some little time; then she drew a chair up to the window, and, letting her hands lie in her lap, enjoyed the rest which she had earned by a day's toil, but not unexpected toil.

As she sat there, looking out dreamily at the lane, which the setting sun was filling with a golden haze, she felt very much like the Hermit of St. Martin. She had refused to go down to the village with Lucy from choice, and not from any sense of duty toward the exercise books. She felt that she and the world had, so to speak, done with each other, and she shrunk from encountering new faces and the necessity of talking to strangers. If fate would let her live out her life in this modest cottage she would be contented to confine herself to the little garden surrounding it, and perhaps the meadows beyond.

With her children and her flowers she was convinced that she could be, if not happy, at any rate not discontented. She had lived her life, young as she was. Fate could give her no joy to equal that which Yorke's love—or fancied love—had given; nor could it deal out to her a more bitter sorrow than the loss of Yorke and her father. So let Lucy act as a go-between between her and the outer world, and she (Leslie) would work when she could, and when she could not, would live over again in her mind and memory that happy past which had been summed up in a few all too brief days.

Of Yorke she had heard nothing. She had never read a society paper in her life, and was not likely to have seen one during the last busy month, so that she knew nothing of the engagement between him and Lady Eleanor Dallas. And if she had known, if she had chanced to have read the paragraphs in which the betrothal was announced and commented on, she would not have identified Lord Auchester with Yorke, "the Duke of Rothbury," as she thought him. Sometimes, this evening, for instance, she wondered with a dull, aching pain, which always oppressed her whenever she thought of him, where he had gone, and whether he still remembered, whether he regretted the flirtation "he had carried on with the girl at Portmaris," or, whether he only laughed over it—perhaps with the dark, handsome woman, the Finetta to whom he had gone back!

The sun had set behind the hills, and the twilight had crept over the scene before Lucy came hurrying up the path.

"Did you think I was lost, Leslie?" she said, with a laugh.

Leslie looked round, and though it was nearly dark in the room, she saw that Lucy's eyes were particularly bright, and that there was a flush on her cheeks which did not appear to have been caused by her haste.

"It sounds very unkind, but I was not thinking of you, dear," she said. "It is late, I suppose. Where have you been?"

Lucy came up to the window, tossing her straw hat and light jacket on the sofa as she passed.

"Leslie, you said something about adventures when I was starting—"

"Did I?" said Leslie. "And have you had any? Let me look at you? You look flushed and excited. What is it, Lucy?"

"Yes, I have had an adventure," she said, her soft, guileless eyes drooping for a moment, then lifting themselves candidly to Leslie's again. "But let me begin at the beginning, as children say. Leslie, you must go and see the village. It is the dearest little place in all the world, and just like one of the pictures one sees at the Academy. You will want to sketch it the moment you see it, I know. Well, I went to the shop—oh, the funniest shop you ever saw! You go down two steps into it, and even then it is only just high enough for you to stand up in. And they sell everything—tapes, treacle, soap, snuff, laces, biscuits—everything! And the woman that keeps it is the mother of one of our girls, and she made ever so much of me, and sent her best respects to you—'the beautiful teacher,' as she said the girls all called you!"

"Is it all fiction, or only the last sentence, Lucy?" said Leslie.

"My dear Leslie, I have heard them call you so myself!" said Lucy. "I went to the butcher's—the butcher is one of nature's noblemen, and took my order for four mutton chops as if I were a princess ordering a whole sheep—and then I went out into the country beyond, and if I were to tell you what I think of it you would say I was exaggerating—"

"Which you never do, of course," put in Leslie, gravely.

"It is simply heavenly!" continued Lucy, ignoring the insinuation. "Such lovely meadows and tree-covered hills, and there is a delicious river full of trout—so a man who was working close by said. Can you throw a fly, Leslie? I can, and I will teach you. It is the jolliest fun in the world, fishing. And when I got to the opening out of the valley, I saw a tremendous house—a great white place on the brow of a hill. It took me quite by surprise, for I had no idea that there were any great people living near us—well, not exactly near, for this must be four or five miles off. I asked a man who lived there and he said that it belonged to a lady—Lady—there! I have forgotten the name after all, and I wanted to remember it to tell you."

"Never mind," said Leslie.

"She is an awfully great lady, and tremendously rich, my informant said. I wish I could remember her name! It was rather a pretty one. Well, then"—she paused a moment, and her color came and went—"I thought I would rest for a little while, and I sat down on a big stone, up a little grassy lane, and while I was sitting there quiet as a mouse, I heard the sound of a horse's hoofs on the short turf and, so suddenly it made me jump, a huge horse came galloping up. He saw me and shied—goodness, how he shied! I thought the man on his back must be thrown, but he sat there like—like a rock! But he swore—I don't think he saw me at first, Leslie; in fact, I am sure he didn't, for when he did he raised his hat as if to apologize for the bad words, and then rode on."

"Is that all?" said Leslie, with a smile. "I thought you were going to say, at the very least, that he stooped down and caught you up and you would have been carried off into captivity but for a gallant young man who ran up and seized the horse, etc., etc., etc."

"Leslie!" remonstrated Lucy, laughing and blushing. "He didn't stop a moment or speak, of course, but rode on straight away. But, Leslie, you never saw such a handsome man or such a sad-looking one—"

"The Knight of the Woful Countenance," said Leslie.

Lucy laughed, but rather gravely.

"Well, if you had seen him I don't think you would have laughed, Leslie; he looked so wretched and weary, and—I don't know exactly how to describe it —so reckless! He seemed as if he didn't care where he was riding or whether the horse kept straight on or fell."

"So that he kept straight on and didn't fall on or run over you, it is all right," said Leslie. "But, Lucy dear, I don't think you must be out so late and alone again, especially if there are reckless young men riding about the roads and lanes."

"Yes," said Lucy; "but I haven't come to the end of my adventures yet, Leslie."

"Not yet?"

"No," said Lucy, almost shyly. "Of course, I was rather startled by that horse thundering by—it was so very big and it passed so near, almost on to me, you know—and I suppose I must have called out." She blushed. "It was very foolish, I know, and I know you wouldn't have done so."

"Don't be too sure! Did the knight come back, Lucy?"

"No, no," and the blush grew more furious, "of course he did not. I don't suppose he heard me; but some one else did, for there came up the moment afterward a gentleman—"

"Not another on horseback, Lucy? Don't be too prodigal of your mounted heroes."

Lucy laughed.

"No, this one was not on horseback; he was walking, and was quite a different-looking man to the other, though he was nearly, yes, nearly as good looking."

"Two handsome young men in one evening; isn't that rather an unfair allowance?" said Leslie.

Lucy smiled.

"I knew you would make fun of it all, Leslie," she said, "and I don't mind in the least. I like to hear you, and, after all, there was nothing serious in it."

"I should hope not, Lucy."

"Leslie, you really don't deserve that I should tell you any more—you don't, indeed."

"Pray, don't punish me so severely," responded Leslie; "my levity only conceals an overpowering curiosity. What did the second stranger say or do?"

"Well, he said—and he couldn't say much less, could he?—'are you hurt?'"

"How you must have screamed! I suppose if I had been listening I should have heard you here."

"And of course I said no," continued Lucy, severely ignoring this remark, "and that I had only been a little startled by the horse. He asked me if I knew who it was, and when I said 'no', he looked as if he were going to tell me, but instead he asked if I knew the way to the railway station."

"Now don't say that you told him and that he raised his hat and went off," said Leslie, with mock earnestness.

Lucy laughed, but said, shyly: "Well, I told him, but he didn't go—just at once. He asked me one or two other questions—which was the nearest village, and so on—and, of course, I had to answer that I was a stranger, and then we both laughed, or rather he smiled, for he seemed very grave and preoccupied. I think he was a lawyer or something of that sort. He looked like a business man; and presently he said, as if accounting for his being there, that he had walked from White Place—that was the house on the hill-side—and that he was going back to London, and—and—well, that's all!"

"Are you quite sure that was all?" asked Leslie, with burlesque severity.

Lucy's fair face flushed.

"Y-yes. Oh!—I'd got a fern-root in my hand; I meant to put in the garden below the window—and he noticed it, and said that he wished they had them in London, and—well, I offered it to him—"

"Lucy!"

Lucy jumped up.

"Really—really and honestly, Leslie, I did it without thinking! and he took it at once without any fuss or nonsense. You see, he was a gentleman," she added, with delicious simplicity.

Leslie shook her head with a smile.

"It is all too evident that you are not to be trusted out alone, my dear," she said. "Why, Lucy!"—for something like tears had began to glitter in Lucy's gentle eyes—"why, you silly girl, I am only in fun! Why should you not direct a stranger to the railway station, and why shouldn't you give him the fern he coveted, poor, smoke-dried Londoner. There was nothing wrong in it."

"You are quite sure, Leslie? Afterward—afterward, as I was walking home, it seemed to me that I had perhaps, been—unladylike." The awful word left her lips in a horrified whisper.

"My dear, you couldn't be if you tried," said Leslie, with quiet decision. "Now run and put your things away and we will talk it all over again while we are having supper. 'Unladylike!'" She took the gentle, 'good'-looking face in her hands and kissed it. "You are very clever, Lucy, but that is the one thing you could never attain to."

They sat for a long time over their simple meal, talking of their school, discussing the various capacities of the pupils, arranging classes, and so on; and once or twice Leslie referred to Lucy's 'adventures,' and declared that she did not believe a word of them, and that Lucy had invented the whole to amuse her, little suspecting that the big house Lucy had seen was the famous White Place belonging to Lady Eleanor Dallas, that the horseman was Lord Yorke Auchester, and that the stranger who "looked like a lawyer" and who had walked off with Lucy's fern was Ralph Duncombe.

CHAPTER XXXIV.

WAS YORKE HAPPY?

Lady Eleanor was happy, and, unlike a great many persons, was not ashamed to admit that she was.

"Why should I be ashamed or try to hide my joy?" she said to Lady Denby, who remarked her niece's high spirits, and her evident satisfaction with her own condition and the world in general. "I am happy! happy! happy! and every one may know it."

"They do know it, my dear," said Lady Denby, dryly.

"And they are welcome to!" retorted Lady Eleanor, laughingly. "I count myself the luckiest girl in the world! I am young, not hideously plain, rich—very rich, Mr. Duncombe says—by the way, aunt, you will be very careful not to mention his name in Yorke's hearing—and I am going to marry the man I have been in love with ever since I was so high. I wake in the middle of the night—and I am glad to wake—and I tell myself all this over and over again. It seems too good to be true, sometimes; but I know it is all true when the morning comes. Oh, yes, I am happy at last!"

"And Yorke is very happy, too?" said Lady Denby. And the moment after the question had left her lips she was sorry she had asked it, and she hastened to add: "But of course he is. Men generally look poorly when they are particularly happy, I've noticed, just as they invariably blow their noses when they want to cry!"

"Why shouldn't he be happy?" said Lady Eleanor, after a pause; but her face had grown almost grave and almost troubled. "As you say, men don't go about as if they were dancing to music, as we women do, and they don't sing as we do. And—and if Yorke is not boisterous—Why did you say that?" she demanded, suddenly changing her tone and turning upon Lady Denby anxiously and nearly angrily. "Do you think he looks dissatisfied—as if—as if he were sorry?"

"My dear child, your love for that young fellow is softening your brain," responded Lady Denby, quietly. "Of course, I have noticed nothing. He is quiet; but I suppose most men who are on the brink of matrimony are quiet. They hear the clanking of their chains as they are being forged, and are thinking of the time when they will be riveted upon them. No man really likes being married."

“There shall be no chains for Yorke!” said Lady Eleanor, softly; “or, if there must be, then I will cover them with velvet. You shall see—you shall see!”

Certainly, Yorke did not go about as if to invisible music, or sing as he went; and he was, as Lady Denby put it, quiet—very quiet. But if he was not boisterous, he was everything else that a woman could desire in a betrothed. He spent a portion of each day at Kensington Palace Gardens. He was always ready to accompany Lady Eleanor to the park, the theater, concerts, balls, and even shopping. Indeed, the patience with which he would stroll up and down Bond Street or Oxford Street, smoking cigarette after cigarette, while Lady Eleanor was shopping, was worthy of the highest commendation, and immensely calculated to astonish his wild bachelor friends. What he thought about as he paced slowly up and down the hot pavements of those fashionable thoroughfares heaven only knows! At any rate, it is well that Lady Eleanor didn’t.

Every morning he rode with her in the park—there was no need to sell his horse now or to sack Fleming—and the loungers on the rails as they raised their hats to his beautiful companion growled enviously: “Lucky beggar! going to marry the prettiest and richest girl of the season! Some men get all the plums in this world’s pudding!” Altogether he spent a great deal of his time in the society of his betrothed; but there were still some hours of the day in which he was free to amuse himself after his own devices, and he might have passed a very pleasant time, for there was still a large contingent of his friends in town, and there were outings at the Riverside Club, drives to Richmond, and so on. But Yorke was seen in none of the places where the youth of his sex most do congregate; and he spent the hours of his freedom in long walks into the country around London, or in the smoking-room of the quietest of the clubs. And he was always alone—alone, with that strange, absent look in his eyes—that far-away look which lets out the secret, and tells all who see it that a man’s mind is wandering either backward or forward; generally backward.

All the world knew of his engagement, and every man who met him congratulated him—all the world except the Duke of Rothbury, from whom no word of congratulation had come.

“Have you written to Godolphin?” Lady Eleanor had asked, shyly, and Yorke, with a little start, had said “no;” that there was no occasion. He would see it in the papers. “But he may not. They only get Galignani in Switzerland; at least, I never could get anything else,” said Lady Eleanor. But Yorke had put off writing. He would not have admitted it to himself, but he shrunk from writing to Dolph and telling him that he, the duke, was right, and that Leslie was forgotten. Forgotten! Of what was he thinking as he strode through the country lanes, as he sat in a corner of the smoking-room, silent and moody, but of Leslie? Always Leslie!

The time comes when everybody—excepting a few millions—leaves London.

"Shall you go to Scotland, Yorke?" Lady Eleanor asked. She knew he had half a dozen invitations this year. He was never without them any autumn, but this year they were more numerous than usual. Yorke Auchester running loose and up to his ears in debt, and Yorke Auchester engaged to Lady Eleanor Dallas were two very different persons and by a singular coincidence everybody who had a house and a moor in the Highlands invited him. But he said he would not go to Scotland.

"I'm tired of it!" he said. "The place is eaten up by tourists at this time of the year. I'd rather stay in London!"

"Well, then, I will not go. I was going to the Casaubon's, but I will send an excuse—"

"Oh, no, don't do that!" he said, with the most unselfish alacrity. "Don't you stay up in town for my sake; it's beastly dull now, I know."

Lady Eleanor thought a moment.

"I will tell you what I will do," she said. "Aunt and I will go to White Place. It is just a nice distance from town, and—and if you should ever think of running down, why—aunt will be glad to see you, sir."

The ladies went to White Place, and Yorke stayed in town. But, of course, he ran down to the big house very frequently, and when he went he was made much of, as was only right and natural. Would not the place be his own some day, or at any rate would he not be the lord and master of the mistress of it? Indeed, the servants received him as if he were already master, and understood that their quickest and shortest way of pleasing their mistress was by winning the favor of this handsome lover of hers. Everything was done that man—ah! and woman; and how much quicker is woman—could do to amuse and please him. A stud of horses filled the stables—his own being the most honorably housed—the keepers received carte blanche as to the game; a suite of rooms in the best position, and so luxuriously furnished that poor Yorke laughed grimly when he first entered them—was set apart for him. Lady Eleanor would have filled the house with guests, but it seemed that Yorke was not in the humor for company. "Which is so nice and sweet of him!" murmured Lady Eleanor. His favorite wine had been brought down from London, and the cook had a list of the dishes to which his lordship was most partial. Happy! If he was not happy he was the most ungrateful man among the sons of them.

"You are spoiling him, my dear," Lady Denby ventured to remonstrate gently. It was the morning that Lady Eleanor had given orders for a special wire from the station to the house, so that his highness might let them know when he was coming. "You are spoiling him all you know how, and that's always a bad thing for a man, especially before marriage; because, you see, when he is married he will expect to be spoiled a great deal more—and you haven't left yourself any room."

"I dare say," Lady Eleanor retorted. "I don't care. Besides, it isn't true. You can't spoil Yorke."

"Do you mean that nature has done it for you already?" said Lady Denby, sweetly.

"Nature!" flashed Lady Eleanor, her face flushing proudly; "nature spoiled him! Oh, where is there a handsomer man, a stronger, a finer than my Yorke?"

"My dear, you are a raving lunatic," remarked Lady Denby, in despair.

Certainly if he were being spoiled Yorke did not grow less careful in his devoirs. He was as ready, as on the day of his engagement, to attend his betrothed; and when they walked and drove together he was always close at her side, and never wanting in those attentions which the woman finds so precious when they are paid by the man she loves. And with it all she watched him so closely, was so careful not to bore him. In the matter of business, for instance, most women having so much money would have wanted to talk over with her future husband this investment and the other; but Lady Eleanor knew Yorke better than to attempt anything of the kind. Ralph Duncombe still remained her guide, philosopher, and friend in business matters, and it was understood between Ralph Duncombe and her—without a word having passed—that his name was never to be mentioned in Lord Auchester's hearing, and that they were never to meet.

One day, however—the day Yorke had galloped past Lucy in the lane, they had very nearly met face to face, for Ralph Duncombe had left the house only a few moments before Yorke had entered. Yorke had come down from London for a few hours, and had ridden with Lady Eleanor, and she had thought that he was going to remain for dinner; but quite suddenly he had announced that he must get back to town; once or twice lately he had had similar fits of restlessness, and had come and gone unexpectedly. Lady Eleanor did not press him to stay; his chains, even now, should be covered with velvet; and he had ridden off, having arranged to leave his horse at the station, to be fetched by a groom.

He trotted down the drive quietly enough, looking back once or twice to smile and wave his hand at Lady Eleanor, who stood on the steps watching him; but once out of sight he stuck the spurs into the horse, and the high-spirited animal bounded off like a shot from a gun.

And as he tore across the lawns and down the road, the devil that sat behind Yorke Auchester taunted and upbraided him after the manner of devils.

"You ungrateful hound! why can't you be happy? Why can't you rest and be content? You are going to marry one of the loveliest women in England; you are going to be rich—rich! you, who hadn't a penny—haven't a penny of your own; you are envied by every man who knows you, and thousands who don't, but have only read of you in the papers! What do you want, man—what do you want?"

And all Yorke could answer with a groan was, "One more moonlit night at Portmaris with Leslie by my side. Leslie, Leslie!"

The horse was in a lather when they reached the station; but his master was not tired—that was one of his troubles, the difficulty of getting tired enough to be sleepy—and directly he got to town he set off walking, and the devil of unrest trudged behind him, as he had sat behind him on the horse.

He, Yorke, and the demon with him, turned into the club at last, and Yorke ordered some dinner. The footman brought him the carte de jour, but Yorke flicked it from him.

"Bring me what you like," he said indifferently, and he was eating it as indifferently when Lord Vinson sauntered up.

"Halloo, Auchester!" he said. Yorke nodded absently, not to say, surlily. "All alone? I'll join you."

He sat down, and after studying the carte with devout attention, ordered his dinner, and then, having disposed of his soup, wanted to talk.

"Just seen Finetta," he said. Yorke looked up swiftly, but said nothing; and Vinson went on, as he picked the bones from his red mullet. "'Pon my soul, I think all women are mad—I do, indeed!"

"Why?" said Yorke. He was bound to say something.

"Why, take Fin, for instance. There she is at the top of the tree, earning thousands a year, a regular popular favorite; and, hang me, if she doesn't shirk her work at the theater three days out of six, and actually talk about cutting the shop altogether! Seems to have lost her senses lately. And she used to be so cute at one time, eh?"

Yorke said nothing, but bowed at his plate.

"By the way, you and she have had a row, haven't you?" said Vinson, after a moment or two.

"A row? No. Why?"

"Oh, well, I didn't know. But when I mentioned your name the other day, she just flared up in a way to make a man see stars. Awful! I don't know what she isn't going to do to you!"

"She's welcome to do all she likes, when she likes, and how she likes," said Yorke, fiercely. "For God's sake talk of something else!"

Now, when a man is told to "talk of something else," he usually obeys by talking of nothing; and Vinson made haste with his dinner, and left the table, muttering something about wanting to see the evening papers.

"Seems to me that Auchester is going out of his mind," he said to a friend; and he nodded behind the paper toward Yorke. "Snapped me up just now as if he meant to knock my head off. Too much luck, that's what's the matter! Who's the favorite for the sweepstakes, eh?"

He unfolded the paper as he spoke, and glanced down the columns, and as he did so he uttered an exclamation.

"What's the matter with you?" demanded his friend.

"Hush!" whispered Vinson; and he clutched the man's arm and led him to a part of the room out of reach of Yorke's glowering eyes. "By great goodness! talk of luck! Look here! Oh, Moses! did you ever?"

"Let me see!" said his friend impatiently. "You clutch that paper as if—What is it? Eh? Oh!"

They both stared at the paragraph to which Vinson pointed in silence for a moment or two. Then Vinson said in a whisper:

"Do you think he has seen it?"

"Not he! Do you think he would sit like that?" retorted the other man.

"Then—then we ought to break it to him, eh?" said Vinson. "By George! I don't half like the job. Here, you come with me!"

They both approached the table, and Yorke nodded to the other man, but did not extend a warmer greeting.

"Not in Scotland, old man?" said Vinson, quaking a little.

"What do you mean?" demanded Yorke, glaring at him. "I'm here, as you see."

"Not even yachting? Er—er—when did you see Lord Eustace last—your uncle, you know?"

Yorke looked from one to the other as if he thought they had lost their senses.

"What?" he said, impatiently. "When did I see—Why do you ask?"

"Oh, show it to him!" said Vinson, desperately. "I told you I should mull it!"

The other man held the paper to Yorke and pointed to a paragraph, and Yorke taking it—and not too courteously—out of his hand, read this:

"We regret to announce the death of Lord Eustace Auchester and his two sons. His lordship was yachting in the Mediterranean, and the vessel, being overtaken by a sudden squall, capsized. Their lordships and the crew, four in number, were all lost. Lord Eustace Auchester was the heir to the Dukedom of Rothbury, which will now descend to his nephew, Lord Yorke Auchester."

Yorke gazed at the printed words for a time as if he failed to grasp their significance. Then his face paled—paled slowly till it was white as death.

"Hold up, old man!" said Vinson. "Dash it all, I wish I'd broken it better! Here, take some wine!"

But Yorke, pushing the wine from him, rose, the paper still in his hand, and, as if he had forgotten the presence of the two men, stared wildly before him. Then, to their horror, he broke into a hoarse laugh.

"Why, she should have waited!" he exclaimed, bitterly, and as if he were speaking to himself. "Yes, if she had waited she would have been a duchess, after all!"

CHAPTER XXXV.

THE HEIR APPARENT.

Yorke walked straight out of the club, leaving the two men staring at each other in amazement.

"Good Lord! poor Auchester is clean off his balance. Do you think it is the shock—that it was because we did not break it gently enough?"

The other man shook his head.

"N-o, I don't think so. He's been very queer in his manner lately, and—But who the devil did he mean when he said, 'She might have been a duchess?'"

Yorke strode along Pall Mall bewildered and stunned. At first he was too confused to feel anything; then regret and grief came uppermost. He was genuinely sorry. You may dislike your uncle and cousins, and yet be far from wishing them dead; and Yorke's eyes were moist, and there was a lump in his throat as he thought of his three kinsmen lying at the bottom of the Mediterranean.

Then he began to realize what their unexpected and tragic death meant to him. There was only Dolph between him and the dukedom, and poor Dolph could not make old bones, and as it bore down upon him with its full significance, the terrible bitterness which had overwhelmed him at the club recurred. The turn of the wheel of fortune had come too late. If it had happened a month—five weeks earlier, he would not have been driven into a corner, the only way out of which was by a marriage with Eleanor Dallas.

"Too late!" he muttered. "Yes! if it had come sooner I might have kept Leslie;" but his heart revolted against his thought, and he swore under his breath, "No, no! It was the title she wanted, not me. It is better that she has gone!"

He went home and saw by Fleming's face that he had heard the sad news. Poor Fleming tried to look cut up, but it was hard work, seeing that he had been saying to himself since the moment he had read the paragraph, "My master will be a duke!"

"Dreadful news, my lord," he said, in the tone proper to the occasion.

"Yes, yes, Fleming," said Yorke, gravely.

"Your lordship will go over, I suppose?"

Yorke started slightly. He had not as yet thought of this, his obvious duty.

"Yes," he said. "Get some things ready and look out the time-table."

"Yes, my lord. Your lordship will go down to White Place first?" suggested Fleming, respectfully.

Yorke hesitated, but he assented.

"I'm to go abroad with you, my lord?" said Fleming tentatively, and Yorke nodded.

"You can if you like—just as you like," he said.

"Thank you, my Lord, I will go," said Fleming. "Your lordship may want things done, and I may be useful."

"You are always that," Yorke said; and it was just such simple expressions of appreciation as this that won the regard and devotion of Fleming and his kind.

Yorke went off to White Place that night. He was tired, but he could not sleep in the train, though he tried. His mind was too overburdened with thought. Late as it was, the ladies were up, and they had heard the news from a servant who had brought an evening paper from town.

Its effect upon Lady Eleanor was strange, and puzzled Lady Denby at first, for Lady Eleanor let the paper drop from her hand, and stood staring before her with an expression in her eyes which was rather that of some vague dread than sorrow.

Lady Denby went to her and drew her to a couch.

"It is terribly sudden, and I am not surprised at your being upset, dear," she said. "But—What is it, Eleanor? You are not going to faint?" for Lady Eleanor had swayed and fallen back with the look of dread still in her eyes.

She recovered after a moment, and the tears came.

"Oh, poor things, poor things! Oh, it is dreadful; but God forgive me, it was not of them I was thinking but of—of Yorke and myself!"

"Of Yorke?" said Lady Denby, puzzled still.

"Yes," said Lady Eleanor, in a low and half-shamed voice. "Don't you see the —the wedding must be put off now!"

Lady Denby stroked her hand soothingly.

"Yes, of course, dear; but there is nothing in that to frighten you; for you look frightened, Eleanor."

"Seems like—like a judgment on me; as if heaven were angry and meant to throw obstacles in the way——."

"Oh, my dear Eleanor!"

"Yes! You don't know—you don't understand what I feel! And I felt so happy, so safe! and now—How long do you think it will be necessary to put it off?"

Lady Denby was very nearly shocked.

"The suddenness of this terrible news has upset you, Eleanor," she said, gravely; "but for heaven's sake don't talk so—so callously."

"You do not know!" repeated Lady Eleanor, with a deep sigh. "It is not that I do not feel for them. Ah, yes, I do, keenly; as keenly as you can; but—but it is as if it were fated that something should occur to prevent our marriage." She was silent for a moment; and then she said, as if to herself: "He will be the duke. I am sorry."

"Sorry!" Lady Denby stared at her.

"Yes," said Lady Eleanor, in the same low, reflective voice. "Yes; I would rather he was what he is, and—and poor. I would rather that he owed everything to me. Now—now it will be I who will owe much to him."

"That is as fine a sample of pride as I have ever met with," said Lady Denby.

"Is it?" said Lady Eleanor. "You do not know or understand. Do you think"—she looked up with a look of pain in her beautiful eyes—"do you think that if he were free he would wish me now to be his wife?"

"Eleanor, I have often said, in jest, that your affection for Yorke was undermining your reason; but in solemn truth I begin to think that there is some truth in my assertion. Dry your eyes and compose yourself. He will be here presently; he is sure to come the moment he hears the news. He will have to go over and see about the funeral."

"No, no; why should he?" said Lady Eleanor, then she flushed as if with shame. "Yes, yes, of course! and you think he will come?"

"There he is!" said Lady Denby, as they heard Yorke's step in the hall. "For heaven's sake don't breathe to him the charming sentiments you have favored me with."

Lady Eleanor shook her head and bit her lips to bring the color into them.

"Do not fear," she said. "It is only when I am alone or with you that I show my doubts and fears."

Yorke came in and took her in his arms and kissed her.

"You have heard the news, Eleanor, I see," he said gravely.

"Yes, it is dreadful, dreadful! To think that all three should be gone—those two poor boys! You are going over, Yorke?" for he had got on his traveling ulster.

"Yes; I am going to meet Fleming at Charing Cross to-morrow morning. I shall have to go back at once."

"At once! It was good of you to come so far just to say good-by; but you are always good to me, Yorke," and she laid her head on his shoulder. "This—this will make a difference to you, dearest?"

He did not affect not to understand her.

"Yes," he said, simply. "Two days ago there seemed little chance of my being the Duke of Rothbury. Now—but I hope and trust dear old Dolph will live to be a hundred."

"And I, and I!" she responded fervently. "I would rather have you as you are, Yorke; far, far rather."

"I'm afraid that this sad affair will delay our marriage, Eleanor," he said, and he said it as regretfully as he could.

"Yes," she whispered, her face still hidden on his shoulder—"Yes, it must, I suppose; but"—he could almost feel her blush—"but not for long?" she asked, nearly inaudibly.

"I don't know," he stammered. "I—we shall see. I must find Dolph. He was in Switzerland, but I think it is very likely that he has moved down south with the cooler weather. He will be cut up. He liked poor Eustace better than any of us did. I must go now, dear," he said, presently.

"So soon?"

"Yes, I am afraid so. Is there anything you want me to do—anything I can tell Dolph?"

She shook her head.

"There is only one thing I want," she said, in a low voice, "and that is—you! Come back as soon—the first moment you can, Yorke, and—and don't forget me!"

He would have been a far worse man than he was if he had not been touched by the depth of her love, and he kissed her with greater warmth than he had ever before shown her.

When he had gone Lady Eleanor threw herself down on the sofa and hid her face in her hands, and Lady Denby, when she came in an hour later, found her thus.

Do it as luxuriously as you may, the journey from England to the south of Italy is a tiresome and aggravating one, and Yorke reached Policastro—the place at which the bodies were lying—worn out mentally and physically. It was fortunate that the devoted Fleming had accompanied him, and never did his devotion display itself more plainly or to better advantage. There were a number of persons, busybodies, there, who would have surrounded Lord Auchester at once—the whole coast was in a state of excitement over the catastrophe—but Fleming kept them at bay, and insisted upon his master taking some rest before he commenced the painful duties necessitated by the circumstances.

"His lordship isn't going to see any one to-night," he assured the landlord of the hotel. "Not if it was the King of Italy himself. If anybody wants to know anything, let them come to me."

The landlord only half understood, but he was considerably awed by Fleming's tone, and departed shrugging his shoulders and spreading out his hands after the manner of his nation.

In the morning Yorke went and identified the bodies and arranged for the funeral, and was returning to the hotel when he met Grey, the duke's valet.

"His grace has just arrived, my lord. I came to meet you," he said. "I hope your lordship is well?" he added, respectfully, and with rather a serious glance at Yorke's face.

Yorke nodded.

"All right, thank you, Grey," he said. "And the duke?"

Grey hesitated.

"About as well as usual, I hope, my lord," he said, quietly. "This sad affair has upset him, of course, and—and he hasn't been very strong lately—not since we left England, indeed, my lord. Your lordship will find him looking thinner," he added, as if to warn Yorke.

Yorke quickened his pace, and Grey led him to the duke's room.

The room was darkened by the drawn blinds, and Yorke, coming out of the sunlight saw but indistinctly for a moment; then, as the duke raised himself on the couch, he started and found speech difficult. The duke was but a shadow of even his former self, and the hand which he extended was so thin that Yorke was afraid to press it.

"Why, Dolph," he said, with forced cheerfulness, "this is a surprise! How did you come here?"

"We have been traveling night and day, as you have no doubt," said the duke, and his voice sounded much thinner and more feeble than when Yorke had last heard it. "Pull up an inch or two of one of the blinds and let me look at you."

Yorke did so, and came back to the couch, and the duke, after scanning his face, fell back with a faint sigh.

"And so you are going to be the next duke, after all. How you and I have fretted—No, I don't know that you ever cared much, but I did—and it has all come right at last! The Providence that 'shapes our ends, rough-hew them as we will,' has decreed that poor Eustace and his boys should go down there in the bay and that you should reign in his place!"

"I wish they were all alive still," said Yorke, with sincerity.

"I know you do," responded the duke. "But I can't help thinking, as I have always thought, that you will make a good duke, Yorke. You have the presence and the moral strength, and a better temper than poor Eustace. He was too fond of his money. But of the dead let us speak nothing but good. And now about yourself. Why did you not write and tell me of your engagement? Never mind; I understand. And if I did not write and tell you I was glad, you knew it without any epistolatory assurance from me. You have done wisely, Yorke, very wisely. Eleanor has everything that a man wants in a wife—youth, beauty, wealth and station. She will make a splendid duchess, Yorke."

"Yes," said Yorke, staring at the carpet moodily.

"I suppose I must hang on until you are married," said the duke, as cheerfully and coolly as if he were talking of somebody else. "Once or twice lately I have been inclined to throw up the sponge, but somehow I've got a hankering to see you settled; and then I suppose I shall want to live long enough to take the next heir on my knee. Men are never satisfied. But I don't suppose I shall be able to hold out till then."

"For heaven's sake, don't talk such arrant nonsense!" Yorke said, emphatically. "You are no worse than you were."

The duke smiled at him calmly but significantly.

"My dear fellow, I am hanging on to life by my eyelashes," he said, in a matter-of-fact tone.

"You must get back to England as quickly as possible," said Yorke, trying to speak in an assured and perfectly confident voice. "There is nothing like

England in the winter, after all. Come back and let Eleanor nurse you."

"That's an inducement, certainly," said the duke. "Eleanor and I were always good friends."

There was silence for a few moments; then the duke, after glancing once or twice at Yorke's grave face, said, in a low voice that faltered:

"There—there is no news of—of—"

He stopped.

"Of whom?" said Yorke, with a frown, though he knew well enough.

"Of Leslie," said the duke, and a faint flush passed over his emaciated face.

Yorke shook his head.

"No," he replied, clearing his throat. "No, I have seen nothing and heard nothing of her since I left Portmaris."

"She must have gone out of England," said the duke, knitting his brows. "Her father being an artist—as he thinks himself, poor fellow—would be ready enough to come abroad here on the Continent. It is strange that I have not run across them."

Yorke said nothing, but the frown on his forehead deepened and darkened.

"When I shuffle off this mortal coil you will find in my will that I have mentioned—Leslie." He paused before the name. "You won't mind, Yorke? She wouldn't take any money from me alive, but she may not mind when I'm gone. After all, it was a cruel trick we—no, I—played her, Yorke," he said, in a remorseful tone.

"It was!" said Yorke, curtly. "But it was a test, and she failed in it."

The duke sighed. Silence again for a moment or two; then, as if he were giving speech to a thought that had occurred to him before, and often before, this he said, hesitatingly:

"Do you think—mind, I only ask you the question for the sake of asking it; I have no reason for doing so—but do you think that there was the slightest chance of our having made a mistake?"

"What do you mean?" demanded Yorke.

"I mean—well, it is difficult to say exactly what I mean. But you know—or perhaps you don't know—how sick men brood and brood over a thing. You see, we have so much time on our hands lying on our backs and counting the flies on the ceiling, that we think over things a great deal more closely than men in sound health. And—and at times a doubt has crossed my mind." He stopped. "There is no ground for it. I am sure I could not have been mistaken; she spoke only too plainly the morning we parted. Besides, there is the fact of her breaking her appointment with you; of leaving you without a word beyond the message she sent by me."

"And the message she sent by Arnheim. I met him the other day and he gave it to me; I went off too quickly on the other occasion for him to do so. It was like that she sent by you; she wished to see me no more," said Yorke, grimly.

"Yes, yes! There could be no mistake, and yet—well, I have lain and thought of her as she was when we first met her, do you remember?"

Yorke smiled grimly. Did he remember?

"So girlish and innocent; so quick to be pleased, and so grateful," he sighed.

"Yes; sometimes it has seemed impossible to me that she should have been so base and mercenary. But there could be no mistake, as you say. And, mind, I should not have said this if you had still been unsettled and hankering after her; but now——."

"Don't say it now, either!" broke out Yorke, springing to his feet and pacing up and down. "For God's sake, don't talk of—of that time or of her. I—I can't bear it! I beg your pardon, Dolph; but don't you see—don't you understand that though a man may cover up his wound and cease to complain, the heart may sting and ache still? I want to forget—to forget! and—and if there is any doubt—but there can't be—I've got to shut my eyes and ears to it—to put it away from me. If I did not—if I entertained it for a moment—well—" He stopped and laughed bitterly. "That way madness lies! You and I had better agree to taboo the subject. The sound of her name—How soon can we leave this place?" he broke off.

The duke sighed.

"You must get back as quickly as possible," he said. "Eleanor will miss you. The wedding need not be put off very long. You are already practically the duke. I shall pass over all the business of the estate to you at once, and it is right and fitting that you should be married. The world will see that. Three months, too, will be long enough to wait; the wedding can be a perfectly quiet one."

"Very well," said Yorke, dully. "Settle it as you like."

"Yes! it can't be too soon," said the duke, thoughtfully. "You've got to consider me, you know," and he laughed. "Look here, my lord, you may as well begin to take the burden on your shoulders. Give me that dispatch-box; there are some letters Grey has been bothering me about. It is something about the trees in the Home park at Rothbury. Cut ‘em down or let ‘em stand, just as you think proper. They will be yours, you know, very shortly, thank God!”

CHAPTER XXXVI.

THE NEW LOVE.

A fortnight later Lucy was returning from a rather lengthy ramble. She had a companion, one of the school-girls, this being the universal holiday, Saturday afternoon, and they both carried a basket full of roots and leaves; for whenever Lucy went out she managed to bring home something for planting in the little garden of which she and Leslie were so fond and proud.

"I hope you're not getting tired, Jenny," she said to the girl who tripped on proudly beside her.

"Oh, no, Miss Lucy."

"Well, I'm glad you are not," remarked Lucy; "for we are a long way from home yet."

"And it is going to rain," added Jenny, with that placid indifference to the weather which distinguishes country children.

"What; and I have brought no umbrella, and you have only that thin cloak, Jenny. But perhaps you are wrong. I always notice that when people say it is going to rain, it invariably turns out fine, perhaps for weeks."

"It's going to rain now, Miss Lucy," repeated Jenny, still more confidently; and a moment or two afterward she added, "There!"

Lucy felt a spot on her face and seized the girl's basket.

"You must let me carry this, Jenny, because we shall have to hurry all we know. It will never do to go in wet through. What would Miss Leslie say?"

This formula, which she found of great service when admonishing the children, lent speed to Jenny's small feet, and Lucy and she hurried along the road. But quickly as they went the rain caught them up, and presently it came down in a torrent.

Jenny laughed, and Lucy, being rather careful of her clothes, and inclined to take matters seriously, was constrained to laugh too.

"We must get under a tree," she said. "There, squeeze up against the trunk, and I will stand in front of you and shelter you as well as I can. Oh, what would I give for an umbrella!"

Jenny leaned against the tree and amused herself by twisting a spray of brown ivy leaves into a wreath, and looking up at the weather now and again; and Lucy was rapidly sinking into that semi-indifferent, semi-despairing condition which such circumstances produce, when she heard the rattle of a cart coming along the road.

"Jenny, there is a cart, and I believe it is going to Newfold," she said, with a sudden hopefulness. "Perhaps it is someone we know—one of the tradespeople. If so, we will ask them to give us a lift."

"They won't wait to be asked, Miss Lucy," said Jenny, shrewdly, and indeed truthfully, for the two school-teachers were already favorites in Newfold.

"Here it is now," said Lucy; then she sighed disappointedly. "It is a dog cart—a gentleman's dog-cart," she said. "Bother!"

It came abreast of them and was spinning past, when suddenly the gentleman who was driving seemed to see them, and after a moment's hesitation he pulled up the horse.

"You mustn't stand under that tree," he called out.

Lucy colored and started for two reasons; one, because she had been brought up in habits of obedience, and generally did what she was told, no matter who told her, and especially if the order was issued in a commanding voice, and this was a commanding voice. The other reason was that she recognized the voice itself. It was the gentleman she had met in the lane, and to whom she had given the fern root.

"Come away," he said, gravely; then he appeared to recognise her, for he jumped down and, still holding the reins, came forward and raised his hat, Jenny laughing to see the rain pour off the brim.

"I beg your pardon," he said. "I did not see who it was for a moment, the rain is pelting so. But all the same you really must not stand there. There is thunder in the air, and it is dangerous standing under a tree—lightning you know!"

Lucy uttered a little cry, then laughed and blushed.

"Of course. How foolish of me not to think of it! But when you called out I was afraid I was doing some injury to the tree by trespassing."

He laughed—a grave, short kind of laugh, which, however, seemed to Lucy to suit him somehow.

"How wet you are!" he said. "Have you been standing here long?"

"Ever since it began," replied Lucy with a little shrug of her shoulders—a trick she had unconsciously caught from Leslie. "And we are waiting till it stops."

"I am afraid you will have to wait a long time," he remarked. "It has set for a wet evening. May I ask where you are going?"

"To Newfold," said Lucy.

"Newfold? Ah, yes! Will you let me offer you a lift? I am going there, or, at any rate, very near there—as far as the London road goes."

"Oh, no, thank you," said Lucy, flushing. He looked disappointed; then he glanced at Jenny.

"The little girl is getting very wet. She will take a chill," he said, gravely.

"Oh, do you think so?" exclaimed Lucy, with instant alarm. "Oh, dear! And I am afraid she is not very strong. It doesn't in the least matter so far as I am concerned, for I never take cold. I am used to the country and rough weather; but Jenny——."

Jenny grinned at the idea of her being in any danger from an autumn storm, but she was too wise to make any remark, for she was dying for a ride in the handsome dog-cart.

"I think you had better let me take her—and you," he said; and seeing that she still hesitated, he cut the Gordian knot by lifting Jenny into the cart and holding out his hand for Lucy.

Then when she was seated he got out a big carriage umbrella and put it up for them, and quickly slipping off his waterproof, arranged it on the seat behind so that it completely covered them.

"Oh, but you will get wet!" remonstrated Lucy, much distressed; but he laughed and made light of the business.

"We Londoners like getting wet sometimes," he said. "It is a change, you see. In London we take as much care of ourselves as if a spot of rain would kill us."

"Oh, I know," said Lucy, with shy pride. "I have lived in London for some time."

"I thought you said you were used to the country?" he remarked.

"So I am—I was born in the country," Lucy explained, in her frank, simple manner—a manner, by the way, which possesses a greater charm for some, indeed most, men, than all the cultivated artificialities.

"I have lived all my life," she said—"all my life"—as if she were at least ninety—"in the country until I went up to London to cram for my exam."

"Your exam.?" he said, invitingly, and yet not obtrusively, and there was nothing in the interest displayed in his face which indicated presumptuous or idle curiosity.

"Yes," said Lucy, blushing faintly; "I am a teacher."

"A governess?" he said.

"No, a teacher," corrected Lucy, with fine emphasis. "I am one of the teachers at the village school. There are only two—I mean teachers. I am the second."

"And do you like being a teacher?" he asked. His voice was as grave as ever, but the expression of interest seemed increasing; the pleasant face looked so pretty and innocent and girlish under the shadow of the big umbrella; the clear, low voice rang so true and sweet. It seemed to the weary city man as if he had stopped to pick up one of the wild flowers from the hedge-row.

"Oh, yes," said Lucy, promptly.

"I thought so by the way you spoke," he said, with a smile; and Lucy laughed and blushed again.

"I like it very much," she said. "But, then, ours is such a nice school, and the girls are all such good girls, aren't they, Jenny?"

"Yes, Miss Lucy," assented Jenny, from under the wrap into which she had nestled.

"Self-praise, eh?" he said.

"Oh, but she is really a very good girl," said Lucy, in a confidential whisper, which seemed to make them more intimate. "They are all good, and so we are both as happy as we can be."

"We both?" he said.

"I mean my fellow-teacher; my principal," said Lucy, "Miss—" She was about to tell him the name, but stopped, remembering that he was a stranger and that Leslie might not like to be so confidential, about herself, at any rate.

"I am very glad you are so happy," he said. "Do you know, I had been on the point of visiting your school."

"You?" said Lucy, opening her eyes with surprise; and, as he noticed, with something else—a faint but unmistakable pleasure.

"Yes," he said. "It belongs to a lady who is a friend of mine. She is kind enough to let me see to some of her business matters."

"The kindness seems to be on the other side," said Lucy, laughing.

Ralph Duncombe colored and found himself laughing too.

"Well," he said, "let us say we are both kind. I was going to explain that she had asked me to do something in connection with the school. I forget what it was now."

"Perhaps it was the roof," said Lucy, eagerly. "It is rather bad in one or two places, and the other morning two or three spots of water came through. Oh, I hope it was the roof!"

"It must have been," he said, with due gravity; "and I will see that it is put right at once. Is there anything else that wants doing, Miss—Miss Lucy, I think you said your name was?"

"Yes, Lucy Somes," she said, thinking hard, and trying to remember if there was anything else wrong at her beloved school. "N-o, I don't think there is anything else the matter, excepting the roof."

"Perhaps I had better come and see for myself, he said, in a matter-of-fact way.

"Are you—an architect?" Lucy inquired, rather timidly.

Ralph Duncombe smiled.

"No; I am nothing nearly so clever. I am only an ordinary business man, very hard worked and very glad to run away from the city and into the fresh air."

"Ah, yes; how you must enjoy it!" said Lucy, with a sympathetic little sigh, "to get away from the crowd and the heat and the smoke."

So they talked, and as Ralph Duncombe listened to the sweet young voice it seemed to him as if there was a power in it to soothe his weary, restless spirit; and when Lucy suddenly exclaimed, as if she were quite surprised that they should have reached the spot so soon, "Why, here is the corner!" he pulled the horse up with evident reluctance.

"I'll drive you around to the school," he said; but Lucy declined, and so earnestly that he could not persist.

He lifted them down, and cut short Lucy's blushing thanks.

"It is I who ought to be, and am very much, obliged to you, Miss Somes," he said, "for you have made one part of my lonely drive very pleasant. I hope you won't be any the worse for your wetting."

"Oh, but I am as dry as a bone—and so is Jenny," said Lucy, blushing still more. "Good-by—and you will not forget the roof?"

"No, no," he said; "but I must come and see it myself."

He sat bolt upright in the cart, watching them as they ran along the road shining with the rain, and a strange feeling took possession of him. How lonely he had been before he saw them! How lonely all his life was! He was rich, fearfully rich, and yet there was not a streak of sunshine in his life. His love for Leslie Lisle had clouded it over as with a pall. Oh! why had the fates dealt with him so unkindly? Why had he not given his heart to some girl like the one who had just left him—one who would have returned his love, and borne for him the sweet name of—wife?

For the first time in his life Ralph Duncombe found himself thinking tenderly and wistfully of some other woman than Leslie Lisle.

He thought of her several times the next day. Her sweet girlish face came between him and a most important letter he was writing; and once during the morning his chief clerk came in and found him—the great city man—sitting with his head leaning on his hands and his eyes fixed vacantly on the window.

When Saturday came around again he remembered that he must go round to White Place to see Lady Eleanor. He had the horse harnessed, and drove along the road, light now with the autumn sunshine, and every inch of the way he thought of Lucy. When, in the afternoon, he reached the corner where he had set her and Jenny down, he pulled up, stared straight in front of him for a moment, then suddenly turned the corner and drove to the school, and his heart beat as it had not beaten since he said good-by to Leslie as he saw Lucy's girlish figure in the garden. She wore a plain cotton frock; a big sun hat, much battered and sunburned, was on her head, and the prettiest and most useless of rakes in her hand. She almost dropped this apology for a tool when she saw him, and the color ran up her cheeks as she came to the gate.

"You have come to see the roof!" she said. "That is kind of you."

"Yes, I have come to see the roof!" he said.

He had forgotten all about it; but he could scarcely say he had come to see her.

"I am so sorry," said Lucy; "but my friend—the principal, you know—is out. She does not often leave the house and garden, even for an hour, excepting to go to church; but I persuaded her to go down to the village this afternoon. I am so very sorry!"

"So am I," responded Ralph, with mendacious politeness. "May I come in?"

"Oh, yes, please!" said Lucy. "But the horse?"

"He will stand till this day week," said Ralph. "But I'll hitch the reins over the palings all the same."

"This way," said Lucy, eagerly; and she led him to the school-room. He stared up at the very small hole in the roof with the deepest gravity apparently; but in reality he was thinking how sweetly pretty the face beside him looked as she upturned to gaze aloft.

"All right," he said, with a laugh. "I'll see that it is put straight. You are sure there is nothing else?"

"N-o," said Lucy, "nothing. Oh, yes! the gate to the meadow is so very old that that the donkey in the next field pushes it open, and—"

"Let us go in and see it," said Ralph, promptly. "We may as well do everything that wants doing at once."

They went to the meadow, and he examined the gate and admired the view across the fields, and on Lucy telling him it was much better from the edge of the wood, he wandered off in that direction, and, somehow or other, they found themselves sitting on the stile that led into the plantation and talking, as Lucy put it afterward, "like old friends"—so much so, indeed, that it was with quite a start that Lucy heard the clock strike five.

"Oh, I have not offered you any tea!" she exclaimed, remorsefully. "Please come into the school-house. My friend will be back by this time, and she will be quite angry at my want of hospitality."

Ralph, picturing to himself a middle-aged school-mistress as the 'principal,' glanced at his watch hesitatingly; but seeing a look of disappointment beginning to cloud Lucy's face, rose promptly.

Why should he not go in to tea with her? It was the last time he would see her, having an opportunity of listening to the sweet young voice; and at the thought a sudden pang shot through his heart. He had spent his life following a will-o'-the-wisp. Leslie Lisle, even if he found her, could never be his. Why should he not ask this pretty, innocent-eyed girl—

"Lucy," he said, suddenly, and yet gently.

She started at the sound of the Christian name, and turned her eyes upon him questioningly.

"Don't be frightened," he said, still more gently, but with an earnest gravity that thrilled her. "And yet I am afraid I shall frighten you. Do you know what it is I am going to ask you? No, you cannot guess. Lucy, since last Saturday I have been thinking of you every day!"

"Of me?" The words left her lips in a whisper, and the color deepened in her cheeks.

"Of you!" he said, fervently. "I love you, Lucy. Will you be my wife?"

She stepped back, her eyes opening wide, her parted lips tremulous. But when he took her hand she did not shrink back further, and she did not attempt to take the hand away.

They wandered hand in hand about the lanes for an hour, while the horse contentedly nibbled at the grass at the bottom of the garden hedge, and during that hour Ralph told her who and what he was—told her everything, indeed, excepting his love for Leslie Lisle—and Lucy was still in 'love's amaze' as they made their way back to the house.

"You must come in, if only for a moment," she said as he was unfastening the reins. "I want to tell her—my fellow-teacher—to—to—to show you to her." Her eyes sunk and her voice trembled. "I know she will be so glad! Besides, I —I couldn't tell her about it all by myself. It is so sudden—so dreadfully sudden—that I should die of shame!" and her face grew crimson as she laughed.

"All right," he said; "I will come in; but it must be only for a moment, Lucy."

She opened the gate, and as she did so something glittering on the path caught her eye.

She stooped and picked it up.

"Why, it's a ring!" she exclaimed—"a gentleman's ring! You must have dropped it as you came in—Ralph."

"Not I!" he said, shaking his head.

He had not worn a ring since—since he had given his to Leslie.

"But you must have done," she said, with charming persistence. "No gentleman has passed this gate excepting you, sir."

He laughed.

"Let me see," he said.

He took the ring, looked at it, and the smile fled from his face, which suddenly went pale. It was the ring he had given Leslie! He stood, dumb with amazement.

"Well?" she said, linking her arm in his, and so intent on the ring that she did not notice his pallor and constraint.

"Yes," he said, and his voice rang out with a strange doubt and trouble—"yes, it is my ring!"

CHAPTER XXXVII.

"POOR GIRL!"

Ralph Duncombe stood looking at the ring as a man looks upon some trinket he has happened on that belonged to some dearly loved friend long since dead. The ring he had given to Leslie! Back in a flash came the memory of that morning he had given it to her. The sea, the beach, the lovely face floated before his eyes and made him giddy. He had just asked this sweet, innocent girl to be his wife; he had no right, no wish to think of Leslie as a lover, and yet—ah, well, in the heart, as in heaven, there are many manoeuvres, and for the moment the old love filled the biggest place in Ralph Duncombe's heart.

"What is the matter?" asked Lucy, with faint wonder at his silence and stillness. "Is it so very precious a ring? Let me look at it. Would you have been very sorry if you had lost it?"

"Very," he said, scarcely knowing what he said.

"How glad I am that I found it! You must have dropped it as you came in. How careless of you!"

"No," he said, bravely; he could no more prevaricate before that sweet innocence than lie outright. "No, Lucy, I did not drop it just now. I parted with it a long while ago, and I have not seen it since until now."

Lucy gazed up at him open-eyed.

"Then how did it come here?" she asked, in an awestruck whisper. "To whom did you give it? A gentleman, of course?"

"No," he said, after a moment's hesitation. "It was to——."

Before he could add 'a woman,' a voice low and clear, a voice which thrilled him and awoke the echo—thank God, for Lucy's sake—only the echo—of his old passion, was heard in the doorway.

"Lucy, are you there?"

It was Leslie's voice! Ralph Duncombe started, and in the shock of surprise seized Lucy's arm.

"Who is that?" he breathed, in a hushed whisper, his eyes fixed on the doorway.

"Why, how nervous you are!" she said, laughing softly, but a little timidly, for she had seen him start, and felt the pressure of his hand. "Who should it be but my friend, Miss Lisle?"

"Miss—Lisle!" he repeated.

Something in his voice startled Lucy, and she shrank from him the slightest bit in the world. But he noticed it, and he put his arm round her.

"Your—your fellow teacher is called Leslie Lisle?" he said.

"I didn't say 'Leslie,'" said Lucy, half-frightened; "but it is Leslie."

As she spoke, a tall, slim figure in a white dress appeared against the dim background of the open doorway, then came towards them, then stopped.

"Is that you, Lucy? You are not alone——." As she stopped her eyes glanced quickly from one to the other, dilating as she looked; then her face grew crimson, and she spoke his name: "Ralph!"

"Leslie!" he answered, and made a movement towards her; then, as if suddenly remembering the wondering, frightened girl on his arm, stopped.

"You—you know one another!" said Lucy, at last, in a kind of gasp. "Oh, what does it mean?"

Ralph Duncombe, the ever ready, self-possessed city man, the man whose clerks regarded him as of iron rather than flesh and blood, stood biting his lip, and staring at the white figure motionless and dumb.

But the gods made women quick, and that glance from one to the other had told Leslie all their story. Trembling a little, but outwardly calm, she glided towards them.

"Yes," she said, slowly, distinctly, "Mr. Duncombe and I know each other. We are old, very old friends——."

"Friends?" fell from Lucy's quivering lips, and spoke doubtfully in her wide-open eyes.

"Yes, dear," said Leslie, softly, "great friends—nothing more." The last two words were breathed rather than spoken, and Lucy's lips opened with a deep sigh of relief, and the hand that had been gradually slipping, slipping from Ralph's arm, tightened again.

"This—this is a surprise, Les—Miss Lisle," he said at last, and his voice sounded almost harsh from his emotion. "Where have you been? What has happened?" he glanced at the black scarf, at the black ribbons on her sleeves, and his voice faltered.

Leslie's head drooped for a moment, then she raised it bravely.

"Yes!" she said, answering his unspoken question. "Months ago. I will tell you about it—presently. Will you both go in? You have something to tell me, I see," and she smiled. "I will come directly. I have lost something——."

Lucy took Ralph's hand and held it up.

"It is found," she said, and pointed to the ring solemnly. "It was to you he gave it, was it not, Leslie?" and a dark, a terrible fear, a pang almost of jealousy shook her heart.

Leslie motioned to Ralph to be silent, and taking Lucy's hand drew her towards her.

"Yes, Lucy," she said, in a low voice, every word thrilling intensely. "The ring was given to me by Mr. Duncombe. It was given to me as a pledge of friendship. It was a farewell gift. Given without requital; a pledge and a token that if ever I needed the donor's help I had but to send it as a message to find that help. Since the day he gave it to me I have not seen Mr. Duncombe, but I have not forgotten him nor ceased to cherish my ring. And yet," a sad little smile curved her lip. "I have lost it twice——."

Somehow, these last few words went farther to reassure Lucy than anything else could go. Lovers do not lose their love tokens! If Leslie had cared for Ralph, she would have taken better care of her ring.

"I—I don't understand—ah, yes, I do! I see it all!" she said, with a little sob, and looking from one to the other. "I understand it all! It is very natural," her voice choked a little. "Who could see you, know you, without loving you ——."

"Hush, hush!" whispered Leslie in her ear. "That was so long ago that he has forgotten it. There is only one woman in the world he loves, and she is here!" and she drew Lucy's face against her bosom with a loving pressure.

Ralph Duncombe stood, as a man in such a situation must stand, silent and awkward. It seemed as if both had clean forgotten him, but suddenly Leslie held out her hand to him.

"We have not shaken hands yet," she said, with a little laugh, "and we are keeping you outside in the most inhospitable fashion. Pray come in!" and she went in, still holding Lucy to her.

"Now let me turn up the lamp; how the evenings draw in, do they not? Supper is ready, and——." Then she broke down, and sinking into a chair, leant her head in her hands.

Lucy knelt beside her and soothed her.

"It is her father she is thinking of," she whispered to Ralph with womanly instinct; she knew that Leslie would have died rather than weep over a lost lover before that lover and the woman who had won him. "It is of her father; the sight of you has brought it all back to her! Oh, how wonderful it all is! To think that you——."

"I'd better go!" said Ralph, with a man's aptitude at doing the wrong thing.

"No, no! wait till she has got over it. She will be all right in a moment; you don't know how brave she is."

Indeed, almost in a moment Leslie had dried her tears.

"Forgive me!" she murmured penitently. "How selfish you must think me! and I am so full of happiness at her happiness too! And it was to this gentleman—this old friend of mine—you gave the fern root, and it was he who drove you and Jenny home in the rain!"

"Yes! isn't it like a fairy story, Leslie? And you are really glad?" she asked wistfully.

Leslie took the upturned face in her hand.

"Gladder than I have ever been in my life—than I have been for, ah! so long!" she corrected herself. "If I could have chosen your future for you I would have chosen just this that fate has planned. You will make each other very, very happy, I know! Now sit down, Mr. Duncombe. I will promise not to—not to cry again. Lucy, cut some bread. I will be back in a moment."

As she left the room, Lucy stole half timidly up to Ralph.

"Oh, how could you think of me after—after loving her!" she whispered.

He bent his head and kissed her.

"Say no more, Lucy," he said gravely. "Let the past bury its dead. Yes I—I loved her; but she—I was no more to her, never could have been more to her, than just a friend. I know it now; are you satisfied, dearest?"

She looked into his eyes for a moment, a look which seemed to sink into his soul; then she let her head fall on his breast with a sigh of peace. When Leslie came down there were no tears in her eyes, and presently, of her own accord, she spoke of her father's death, and told Ralph Duncombe how she had met with Lucy, and how they had passed their exams and obtained the school. But not one word did she say of Yorke. Ralph noticed this.

"And why did you not send to me?" he said reproachfully.

Leslie shook her head.

"You were too proud!" he said.

"Yes, that was it," she admitted quietly. "I was too proud."

"And it would have given me much pleasure to have helped you!" he said. "Is there nothing I can do now? Can you think of nothing?"

Leslie shook her head with a faint smile.

"We have everything we want, have we not, Lucy?" she said.

Lucy blushed. She certainly had.

"No, there is nothing," continued Leslie, then she stopped and he looked up quickly.

"There is something you have thought of?" he said.

Leslie's head drooped thoughtfully.

"Yes, there is something," she said. Lucy got up as if to leave the room; but Leslie put out a hand and stayed her. "No, dear, it is no secret; besides, if it were, you must not keep secrets from each other. Wait a moment."

Lucy and Ralph exchanged glances.

"Do you know anything?" he asked.

Lucy shook her head.

"No," she replied in an awed whisper, "she has told me nothing of her past—nothing. We love each other like sisters, and I think there is no one in the world half so good or sweet as Leslie, but I should not dare—yes, that is the word—to ask for her confidence."

Leslie came back into the room. She had a small packet in her hand, and she laid it on the table before Ralph Duncombe.

"I am going to ask you to do something for me," she said with a smile that flickered sadly, as if it were very near tears. "I wish you to give this to the person to whom it is addressed."

Ralph Duncombe took up the packet.

"The Duke of Rothbury!" he said aloud.

Lucy opened her eyes.

"You may open it," said Leslie in a low voice. "It is of value—great value, I believe. If it had not been I would have sent it by post. Yes, open it."

Ralph Duncombe opened the packet and stared amazed.

"It is of great value," he said gravely; "and—and I am to give it to the Duke of Rothbury?"

"Yes," said Leslie, her lips quivering. The sight of the sorrow which she was trying to hide stirred him past repression.

"He gave you this?" he said.

"Yes, but—but do not ask me any questions, please," she faltered.

Her color came and went.

"It is not necessary," he said. "You have suffered, and at his hands——."

"No—no——."

"But it is yes, yes!" he said, with restrained passion, and with a strange perplexity. Great heaven, what a mistake Lady Eleanor had made! It was not Lord Auchester then, but the Duke of Rothbury Leslie had been going to marry.

"I will give it him," he said sternly.

Leslie looked up with a sudden glance of apprehension.

"Give it to him; but that is all!" she said meaningly. "There is nothing to be said—or done."

"You mean that if—if he has injured you, you have forgiven him?" he said.

"Long, long ago!" she breathed. "You may say that, if—if there should be occasion, but no more."

He bowed his head.

"It shall be as you wish," he said; "your word is a law to me."

"I knew you would do it for me," she said in a low voice; "would understand."

Then, as if she wished the subject to be closed, she began to talk of his and Lucy's strange meeting, and their future.

"It is the greatest pity in the world that you should have happened to be passing the day Lucy was frightened by the wild horseman, for the Government will lose one of its best teachers."

"And I shall gain one of the best of wives!" he murmured. They talked for half an hour, and Leslie seemed as light-hearted as they, but presently she stole out of the room, looking over her shoulder in the doorway with a "good-night."

"Do you understand it?" whispered Lucy, as he took her in his arms to say farewell. "Does it mean that Leslie might have been a duchess?"

"Yes, I think so," he said. "I don't quite understand it; I feel as if I were groping in the dark with just a glimmer of light. But, anyhow, I know, I am sure that the fault, if there was any, was his, and I wish that she had left me free to tell him so and exact reparation."

"Ah, but that is just what you must not do!" said Lucy sternly. "It is just what Leslie does not want. You are to give him back the diamonds and say nothing excepting that she forgives him!"

He nodded with a sigh.

"Poor Leslie! How she must have suffered!"

"Yes, you can see that by her face, even now; and it is ever so much happier and brighter than when I saw it first. Ah, Ralph, I wish she were as happy as we are!"

Ralph Duncombe, as he drove along the road to White Place with the diamond pendant in his pocket, felt like a man struggling with a tremendous enigma. Lady Eleanor had evidently made a terrible and unaccountable blunder in stating and believing that it was Yorke Auchester whom Leslie was going to marry. How could she have made such a mistake? And what had happened to break off the marriage? Had the duke jilted Leslie? At the thought—though he was in love with Lucy now—his face grew red with anger and he felt that, duke or no duke, he would have called him to account but for Leslie's injunction.

When he reached White Place he found Lady Eleanor pacing up and down the room with an open letter in her hand, and she turned to greet him with a smile on her flushed face.

"You have good news?" he said.

"Yes." She nodded twice with a joyous light in her eyes. "I have heard from Lord Auchester. He is coming back the day after to-morrow. He and the Duke of Rothbury——."

Ralph started, and his face darkened.

"The Duke of Rothbury?" he said. "I am glad of that, Lady Eleanor, for I wish to see him. And, Lady Eleanor, I have something to tell you—something you will be glad to hear. There has been a strange and awkward mistake. It was not Lord Auchester who was going to marry Miss—Miss Lisle, but the Duke of Rothbury."

Lady Eleanor's face paled, and she caught her breath.

"Not—Yorke! The duke! Ah, no, no! That cannot be!"

"Pardon me, but I am right," he said, rather sternly.

She shook her head.

"No, no; I saw—" She stopped, and the color flew to her face. "I saw him buying the—the wedding ring."

Ralph stared at her, then he smiled grimly.

"He may have bought a ring, but not for himself," he said. "It may have been for the duke, for it was the duke she was going to marry, Lady Eleanor."

"How—how do you know?"

"Miss Lisle herself told me."

She started.

"She! Where—where is she?"

"She is the teacher at the school at Newfold."

Lady Eleanor sank into a chair, and looked up at him with frightened eyes.

"Here—so near? Oh, let me think!" and she clasped her hands over her eyes.

"That is what I have been doing; thinking," he said grimly. "It has been a terrible blunder. I do not know all the circumstances—scarcely any, indeed—of the case; I only know that it was the duke to whom she was engaged."

"Was? Then it is broken off?"

"Yes," he said gravely. "By Miss Lisle—for good and sufficient reasons, I am certain."

She looked at him keenly.

"You know her—you have known her all along." She saw him color, and added in a breath—"Ah, I understand!"

"Yes," he said, "I have known Miss Lisle a long time. I had hoped once to induce her to become my wife, but——."

"And now?"

"I am engaged to another lady," he said, rather stiffly. "Miss Lisle refused me. That is all that need be said on that point, Lady Eleanor."

She inclined her head.

"It has been a terrible blunder," she said thoughtfully. "But—ah, what a load your news has removed from my heart! Not Lord Auchester, but the duke!"

She closed her eyes and drew a long breath. Yorke was all her own now!

"Can you tell me the duke's address. Lady Eleanor?" he asked after a pause.

"His London house is in Grosvenor Square. He will go there, and not to Rothbury, on his return to England. Do you want to see him?" she added. "Why?"

"I have a small matter of business with his grace," he replied.

Lady Eleanor looked at his grave face apprehensively.

"You will not——."

"Tell him anything that has occurred? Scarcely, Lady Eleanor," he said. "That which you and I did in regard to these bills and Lord Auchester's money affairs must forever remain secret. Erase it from your memory."

"Ah, if I could!" she murmured. "When I think of the possibility of his knowing——."

"It is not likely that he will ever know," he said. "The secret is yours and mine alone. You say that Lord Auchester is returning the day after to-morrow?"

"Yes."

"In that case, Lady Eleanor, my visits to White Place must cease. You will not need any help of mine in the future—I need not say that I should be as ready and willing to be of assistance to you as I have ever been—but it will be better that all communication between us should cease. You will not misunderstand me?"

"No, no! I understand," she said. "I am very grateful for all you have done. But for you I should not be as happy as I am."

"I am glad to have helped you to that happiness, however slightly," he said. "And I trust that you may be happier still in the future. Good-by, Lady Eleanor."

He held her hand for a moment or two, then left her. He had no desire to see her again. If he could have done so, he would have wiped from his memory the plot in which he had been concerned with her to drive Lord Auchester into her arms; indeed, as he drove through the silent night he felt heartily ashamed of it. He thought of Leslie and Lucy throughout the journey with a strange sense of confusion. He loved the gentle girl who had given him her heart, but he would remain Leslie's friend and champion. That the Duke of Rothbury had in some way behaved badly to her he felt assured, and but for his promise to Leslie he would have called him to account. As it was, he had bound himself to the simple return of the diamond pendant.

He carried it in his breast pocket for the two following days, and on the third went to Grosvenor Square.

"Yes, sir; his grace is at home, but I do not know whether he can see you. I will ask his gentleman."

Grey came into the hall, and shook his head as Ralph Duncombe preferred a request for an interview.

"His grace only returned yesterday, and is very tired, sir," he said. "I am afraid he cannot see you."

Ralph Duncombe wrote on the back of his card, "From Miss Lisle," and enclosed it in an envelope.

"Give that to his grace," he said.

Grey came back after a few minutes.

"His grace will see you, sir. Follow me, if you please," and he led the way to the study at the back of the hall.

The duke was lying on the adjustable couch, and the sight of his wasted form and deathlike face startled Ralph Duncombe and drove all the anger from his heart.

The duke signed to Grey to withdraw, then raised himself on his elbow and looked at Ralph Duncombe keenly.

"You wish to see me?" he said.

"Yes," said Ralph, and unconsciously he lowered his voice.

"And you come from—Miss Lisle?" A faint, very faint color tinged the transparent face.

"I do, your grace. I am charged with a simple mission. Miss Lisle bids me return this to your grace," and he held out the packet.

The duke took it and opened it, and gazed at the pendant as it flashed in the palm of his hand.

"She told you to return it to me? I did not give——." He stopped.

"I was to return it to the Duke of Rothbury," said Ralph, rather sternly.

"To—the—Duke of Rothbury; yes, yes," said the duke in a low voice, and the color deepened in his face. "You have come from Miss Lisle? You know where she is; may I ask her address?"

"I cannot give it to your grace," said Ralph.

The duke flashed his eyes—they glittered in their dark rings—then he let them fall, and sighed.

"I understand. At least you will tell me whether she is well and—and happy?"

Ralph Duncombe's wrath smouldered.

"She is well now, and I trust happy," he said.

"Now? Has she been ill?"

"Ill and in great trouble. Her father is dead——."

The duke raised himself to an upright position, then sank back.

"Poor girl, poor girl!" he murmured.

Ralph Duncombe flushed.

"Miss Lisle neither asks nor would accept your pity, your grace," he said, sternly. "I am ignorant of the events connected with that gift or its return. I do not wish to know anything about it, but of this I am assured—that Miss Lisle desires to hold no further communication with you."

The duke was silent for a moment.

"Very good," he said at last. "I understand. But I think if she knew how much I desire her forgiveness for the deceit I practised upon her, and how near I am to that land which forgiveness cannot reach, she would not refuse to forgive me."

"I have discharged my mission," said Ralph coldly. He could not bring himself to convey Leslie's forgiveness.

The duke touched an electric bell.

"I wish you good day, sir," he said, and sank back with a sigh. But, after Ralph Duncombe had gone, he opened his hand and looked at the diamond pendant, which still lay in his palm.

"Yorke had given her this," he said musingly. "But why did she send it to me? Why? What shall I do with it? Give it to him? Dare I do so just now? Will it be safe to call up sleeping memories? Had I not better wait until—until after the wedding?"

He decided that he would do so, and carefully placing the pendant in the drawer of a cabinet that stood near his elbow, he sank back again and closed his eyes. But his lips moved long afterwards, and "Poor girl, poor girl!" came from them, as if he were still thinking of her.

CHAPTER XXXVIII.

"VENGEANCE IS MINE."

The weeks rolled on, and the wedding morn of Yorke and Eleanor Dallas stood but three days off. It was to be a quiet wedding, in consequence of the death of Lord Eustace and his two sons; but the heir to the great dukedom of Rothbury could not be married without some slight fuss, and the society papers contained interesting little paragraphs concerning the event. The happy young people were to be married at a little church in Newfold, a picturesque village near Lady Eleanor Dallas's seat, White Place. There were to be only two bridesmaids, cousins of the bride, and the great Duke of Rothbury himself was to be the bridegroom's best man, provided that the duke should be well enough, the paragraphist went on to say, adding that, as was well known, the duke had been in bad health of late. After the ceremony the young couple were to start for the South of France, and on their return it had been arranged that they should go to Rothbury Castle, the seat of the duke, who intended handing over the management of the vast estate to his heir.

Lady Eleanor read these and similar paragraphs until she had got them by heart. To her the days seemed to drag along with forty-eight hours to each, and they had appeared all the longer in consequence of Yorke's absence, for on the plea of having to make his preparations, and business for the duke, he had not paid many visits to White Place since his return from Italy. But though Eleanor felt his absence acutely she was too wise to complain.

"I shall have him altogether presently," was the thought that consoled her. "All my own, my own with no fear of anything or anybody coming between us."

But she was terribly restless, and wandered about the grounds, and from room to room, 'where bridal array was littered all around,' as if she were possessed of some uneasy spirit.

"If one could only send you into a mesmeric sleep and wake you just before the ceremony, my dear Nell, it would be a delightful arrangement for all concerned," said Lady Denby. "It is the man who is generally supposed to be the nervous party in the business, but I'll be bound Yorke is as cool as a cucumber."

If not exactly as cool as that much abused vegetable, Yorke certainly showed very little excitement, and as he walked into the duke's study on the evening of the third day before that appointed for the wedding, the duke, glancing at him keenly, remarked on his placidity.

"You take things easily, Yorke," he said.

"As how?" said Yorke, dropping into a chair, and poking the fire.

"Well, you don't look as flurried as a nearly married man is supposed to look."

"I am not flurried," he said. "Why should I be?" and he looked round with the poker in his hand. "Fleming has seen about the clothes, the banns have been put up, and the tickets taken. There is nothing more to be done on my side, I imagine. No, I am not at all flurried."

"But you look tired," said the duke. "Is everything all right at Rothbury?" Yorke had just come from there.

"Yes," he replied listlessly. "I saw Lang about those leases and arranged about the timber, and I told them to have everything ready for you. I am glad you are going to winter there, Dolph. You will be as comfortable, now that the whole place is warmed by that hot water arrangement, as if you were at Nice, and will have the satisfaction, in addition, of knowing that you are benefitting the people around. They complained sadly of the place being shut up so much."

"Well, you can alter that," said the duke. "You like the place and can live there five or six months out of the year. I believe it is supposed to be one of the nicest places in the kingdom."

Yorke nodded and leant back, his eyes fixed on the fire.

"You dine here to-night?" asked the duke after a pause.

Yorke nodded again.

"Thanks, yes. I'll take my dinner in here with you, if you don't mind."

"No, I don't mind," said the duke with a smile of gratitude and affection lighting up his wan face. "I wish you were going to dine in here with me for the rest of my life; but that's rather selfish, isn't it? Don't be longer away than you can help, Yorke. It may happen that Eleanor will get tired of the Continent; if she should, come home at once."

"Very well," said Yorke. "I am in her hands, of course."

"Of course, and you couldn't be in better or sweeter."

"No," assented Yorke absently. "Did you send back that draft of the leases I posted to you?"

"Eh?" The duke thought a moment. "No, I didn't. I forgot all about them."

Yorke smiled.

"You see that it is time I handed in my checks and allowed a better man to take the berth," said the duke cheerfully. "I'm very sorry, especially as you have taken so much trouble about the business. Let me see, where did I put them? I'm ashamed to say I've forgotten. Look in that bureau drawer, will you?"

Yorke got up and sauntered across the room. He looked very tall and thin in his dark mourning suit of black serge, and the duke noticed that he was paler than when he had seen him last, paler and more tired looking.

"Never mind," he said. "Let the lawyers make out fresh ones."

"Oh, I'll find 'em," said Yorke. "You have stuffed them in somewhere," and he opened drawer after drawer, in the free and easy manner in which a favorite son opens the drawers and cupboards of a father. "I'll back you for carefully mislaying things, especially papers, against any man in England—excepting myself."

"Grey always sees to them. He has spoilt me," remarked the duke apologetically.

"That's what I tell my man Fleming," said Yorke. "I should mislay my head if he didn't put it on straight every morning when he brushed my hair."

The duke laughed.

"They are a pattern pair," he said. "Don't trouble. Ring for Grey."

But Yorke in an absent mechanical fashion still sauntered round the room searching for the missing drafts, and presently he opened the drawer of the small cabinet which generally stood beside the duke's couch, but which this evening was immediately behind him.

Yorke opened the drawer and turned over the things, and was closing it again when his eyes caught the glitter of diamonds.

"You keep a choice collection of things in these drawers of yours, Dolph," he said.

"What is it?" asked the duke.

Yorke pulled out the pendant.

"Only diamonds," he said, "and very handsome ones, too. Where on earth did you get them, and who are they for? Perhaps I'd better not go poking about any longer, or I shall come upon some secret——." He stopped suddenly. He had been speaking in a tone of lazy badinage, scarcely heeding what he was saying, until suddenly he recognized the pendant.

"Oh, I've no secrets," said the duke. "What is it you have found! Ah!" He had swung himself round by the lever and saw Yorke gazing at the pendant lying in his hand.

"Where did you get this?" demanded Yorke. The duke looked at his face as he asked the question. It was grave, with curiosity and surprise; but the duke was glad to see that it showed no keener emotion, and told himself that Yorke was forgetting Leslie.

"Do you recognize it?" he asked.

"Yes," said Yorke slowly. "It is a thing I gave——." He stopped. "How did it come here? Where did you get it?"

"It was brought to me," said the duke in a low voice.

"Brought to you? Why to you?" Yorke demanded, looking up from the pendant. What memories it awakened!

"I cannot tell you."

"Who brought it?"

"A man by the name of—I forget. His card is in the drawer."

Yorke looked.

"No, it is not here."

"Then it is lost. His name—his name—yes, I remember. It was Duncombe. Ralph Duncombe."

"Ralph Duncombe?" Yorke spoke the name two or three times. He seemed to think that he had heard it before, but he could not recall it. He put the pendant in his pocket, and went and stood before the fire with his back to the duke.

"Did he give no message—no explanation?" he asked.

"No," said the duke. "He acted as if he thought I had sent the thing to her."

Yorke did not look round. Why had Finetta sent back the pendant, and why had she sent it to the duke instead of to him, Yorke?

"You don't want to talk about it?" said the duke after a pause.

"No, I don't," assented Yorke grimly. "There are some things one would prefer to forget."

"Ah, if one could, if one could!" muttered the duke.

The dinner came in soon afterwards; and the two men talked of the approaching marriage, of the plans for the winter, of the game at Rothbury, of everything but the diamond pendant. Then suddenly Yorke, who had been answering in an absent-minded kind of way, uttered an exclamation.

"What is the matter?" demanded the duke.

"Nothing," said Yorke sharply. Then he looked at his watch. "Do you mind my leaving you before the coffee?"

"Not a bit. Where are you going?"

Yorke made no reply, perhaps he did not hear. He got up, and rang for Grey to bring his hat.

"I shall not be back till late, Dolph," he said. "Don't sit up."

He had remembered suddenly where he had seen this Ralph Duncombe's name. It was the man who had hunted him down to the ruin from which Eleanor had saved him; and it was by this man Finetta had sent back the diamond pendant. There was only one conclusion to be drawn from the coincidence; it was Finetta, then, who had sought to revenge herself for his desertion of her, by planning his ruin and disgrace. It was she who had brought about this marriage of his, this marriage which would enslave him for life.

Yorke was not a bad-tempered man, nor a malignant, but at that moment he was possessed of a burning desire to confront Finetta, and charge her with her perfidy.

He went down the Strand and entered the Diadem. The stall-keeper looked at him with lively surprise and interest.

"Glad to see you back, my lord," he said, with profound respect.

Yorke took the programme and glanced at it.

"Miss Finetta appears to-night?" he asked.

"Oh, yes, my lord! She will be on in a few minutes."

Yorke sat bolt upright in his stall, glaring at the stage. There were several persons in the front of the house who knew him, but he looked neither to the left nor the right. His heart was on fire. The false-hearted woman! She had pretended to bid him farewell in peace and friendship, and had betrayed him! Yes, he would wait until the performance was over, and would go round and confront her. There should be no scene, but he would tell her that her baseness was known, and, if possible, shame her.

It was a foolish resolve, but, alas! Yorke was never celebrated for wisdom.

The orchestra played the opening to the second act, the usual chorus sang, and the usual comic man cracked the time-honored wheezes, and then the band played a few bars of an evidently well known melody, for the gallery greeted the music with an anticipatory cheer, and a moment afterwards Finetta bounded on the stage. There was a roar of delighted welcome, and amidst it she came sailing and smiling gracefully down to the footlights, her dark eyes flashing round with a half-languorous, half-defiant gleam in them of which the public was so fond.

Then suddenly she saw the well known face there in the stalls. For a second she paused in her slow, waltzing step, and looked at him with a look that he might well take for fear. The conductor of the band glanced up, surprised; it was the first time Finetta had ever missed a step. But before he could pull the band together and catch up the lost bar she had gone on dancing, and danced with her accustomed grace and precision.

Yorke watched her with a grim fury. This smiling, dancing jade had plotted to ruin him, had tried to drive him into a debtors' court—worse, had forced him to marry Eleanor Dallas! He could have sprung up there and then and accused her of her vileness; and the desire to do so was so great that he was on the point of rising to leave the theater and await her at the stage door, when suddenly he saw her falter and stumble, and the next instant—the same instant —she had disappeared, and in the spot where she had just stood was a gaping hole.

The house rose with a gasp, a sigh of horror that rose to a yell of indignation and accusation.

It was the old story: 'Someone had blundered' and left the trap door unbolted, and London's favorite dancer had danced upon it and gone down to the depths beneath.

The audience rose, yelling, shouting, pushing this way and that; the curtain was lowered, the lights turned up, and the manager, in the inevitable evening dress, appeared, with his hand upon his heart. He assured the audience that Miss Finetta was not hurt—not seriously hurt—and that though it would not be wise for her to dance again that evening, he trusted that she would appear again to-morrow night, etc., etc.

Yorke waited till the plausible excuse was concluded, then he quietly—in a dream, as it were—went out and round to the stage door.

And one line of the Book he had, alas! read too seldom, rang in his ears as he went: "Vengeance is Mine!"

The stage door keeper knew him in a moment, but in answer to Yorke's inquiry if he could see Miss Finetta, shook his head.

“I don’t know, sir! There’s a rumor that she’s kil——.”

Yorke pushed by him and made his way to the dressing rooms. There was a crowd of chorus girls and supers surging to and fro in the corridor and clustered together in little knots; all talking in hurried whispers.

They made way for Yorke and he knocked at the door of Finetta’s dressing room. The manager opened it.

“Is it the doctor—oh, it’s you, my lord!” he said in a whisper. “It’s an awful thing! In the middle of the season, too!”

“Is she——,” began Yorke in a low voice, hoarse with agitation. But low as it was it was heard by someone within the room, for Finetta’s voice, weak and hollow with pain, said:

“Is that you, Yorke? Let him come in!”

CHAPTER XXXIX.

FINETTA'S CONFESSION.

Yorke went in. Finetta was lying on the sofa, lying with that awful inert look which tells its own story. Her shapely arm hung down limply, helplessly; across her face, white as death, a thin line of blood trickled, coming again as fast as the trembling dresser wiped it away. One or two women stood near her, silent and apprehensive.

She lifted her eyes heavily and tried to smile.

"I—I thought you would come," she said painfully. "I saw you in the stalls."

Yorke bent over her, all the anger sped from his heart.

"Are you hurt, Fin?" he said in a low voice.

"Yes," she said. "Badly, I think. Some—some fool left the trap unbolted; or —" a gleam of fire shot into her eyes for a moment—"or was it done on purpose, eh? There's one or two here who wouldn't be sorry to have me out of the bills. Well, they'll have their wish for a short time."

"Have you sent for a doctor?" Yorke asked the manager.

He nodded.

"Doctor! I don't want any doctor here," said Finetta sharply. "I want to go home. Take me home, Yorke. Never mind what they say. Take me home, if you have to do it on a stretcher."

"Very well," he said.

The manager drew him outside.

"You can't do it, I'm afraid, my lord. She's too hurt to be moved."

"Don't listen to him, Yorke!" Finetta's voice came to them. "Take me home."

A long slight table stood in the passage. Yorke wrenched the legs off and called to a couple of carpenters. Then, with the help of the manager and dresser, he laid Finetta on this impromptu stretcher and carried her to the brougham which was waiting outside.

"Drive slowly," he said to the man.

"No, let him go fast," panted Finetta. "I can bear it," and she clenched her teeth. Yorke sat beside her and supported her, and she lay with her head on his shoulder, her teeth set hard, her hands grasping each other, and no cry or groan passed her lips.

At the sound of the brougham wheels Polly came to the door, and uttered a cry of alarm at the sight of her sister lying limp and helpless in Yorke's arms.

"Oh, Lord Yorke!" she gasped.

"Don't be frightened, Polly," he said. "Finetta has met with an accident."

They carried her upstairs.

"Get her undressed and into bed," he said. "I'm going for a doctor."

"You—you will come back, Yorke?" Finetta managed to say.

"Of course," he said. "Keep up your heart, Fin. You'll be all right."

He got the doctor, and while he was upstairs making his examination Yorke paced up and down the sumptuous dining-room in which he had spent so many pleasant, merry hours.

It seemed an age before the doctor came down.

"Well?" asked Yorke anxiously.

The doctor looked down with the professional gravity.

"She is very badly hurt," he said. "Oh, no," he added, seeing Yorke start and wince. "I don't say that it will kill her, but—you see she struck the edge of the trap with her back. I think I should like to have Sir Andrew."

"Yes, yes!" said Yorke. "I will send for him at once——."

"Oh, to-morrow will do, my lord," said the doctor. "He could do no more for her than I can accomplish, and she is—unfortunately—in very little pain. But there seems to be something on her mind, something in which your lordship is concerned, and she is very anxious to see you."

"I will go to her," said Yorke at once.

They went upstairs, and Finetta turned her great eyes upon them.

"What has he been telling you, Yorke?" she asked feebly. "Am I going to die? Don't be afraid, I'm not a milksop, and I shan't go into hysterics and make a scene. I suppose I've got to die, as well as other people."

"No, no, there is no talk of dying, Fin," he said.

"Then what is it? Why do you both look so glum?" she said, impatiently. "There's nothing much in falling down a trap: I've seen heaps of people do it. What is it? Am I going to be laid up long? Ask him how soon I shall be able to dance again?"

"Better be quiet," said the doctor, with his hand on her pulse.

"You answer my question," she retorted as furiously as her weakness would allow.

"I'll answer any questions you like to-morrow," he said soothingly. "I want you to rest now."

"They're all like that—a pack of old women," she said, "and they think we're all old women too! Rest! ah, if he could give me something that would make me rest——. Don't go, Yorke; not yet. I—I want to say something to you. It's a long time since you were here, Yorke," and she sighed.

He sat down beside the bed and held her hand, and she turned her eyes upon him gratefully, then averted them and groaned faintly.

"Did I hurt you, Fin?" he asked.

"No, no!" she replied. "It wasn't that. It—it was something I was thinking of."

"You mustn't talk," said the doctor.

She opened her lips and grinned at him contemptuously.

"Why mustn't I? Do you think I am going off my head? Well, there—but don't leave me, or if you do, come again to-morrow, Yorke," and she turned her head away and closed her eyes.

Yorke sat beside her through the night, holding her hand. At times she seemed to fall into an uneasy slumber, from which she would wake and look from him to Polly with a vacant gaze which grew troubled when it rested on his face, and then she would sigh and close her eyes again. Toward morning she fell into a deep sleep, and Yorke went home, but only remained long enough to change his clothes, and returned to St. John's Wood. He found Sir Andrew there, and the great man greeted him with a significant gravity; but before he could speak Finetta turned her eyes to Yorke.

"Ask him to tell me the truth of the case, Yorke!" she said, in a voice much weaker than that of last night. "I'm not afraid. He says I'm not going to die; but ask him how soon I shall get back to the Diadem!"

Sir Andrew smiled, but it was the smile which masks the face of the physician while he pronounces sentence.

"Not yet awhile, my dear young lady," he said.

"Not yet—ah!" She tried to sit up, but sank back and fixed her dark bold eyes on him. "You mean! What is it you mean? Not—not——," her voice quivered and broke. "Oh, God, you mean that I shall never dance again!"

The doctor looked down. She read his answer in his face, and silenced Sir Andrew's conventional protest.

"You—you needn't lie. I—I can see it in your faces. Oh!" and a low but heart-breaking cry rose from her white lips. "Oh, never, never again! Never to dance again! Oh, Yorke, Yorke, tell them to kill me! I'd rather die—rather, ten thousand times rather! Never to dance again. It isn't true," she burst out, her tone changed to weak fury and resentment. "You don't know. You can't tell. Doctors are fools, all of 'em. Send them away, Yorke. I hate the sight of them standing there like a couple of undertakers. What, not to dance again! It's a lie! It's a——." Then she covered her face with her hands, and her whole body shook and trembled.

The paroxysms passed, and she drew a long breath and put out her hand to Yorke.

"It's true," she said, in a faint voice, "I feel it. Don't—don't mind what I said, gentlemen. It—it's knocked me rather hard. You see, I've got nothing to—to live for but my dancing. I'm—I'm nothing without that. Oh, God, what an end! To lie here——," she turned her head away and groaned.

Yorke held her hand in silence.

What could he say? The doctors went; the morning passed; he sat and held Finetta's hand as she dozed heavily.

Every now and then she stirred and opened her eyes, saw and recognized him, and with a sigh closed them again, as if his presence soothed and comforted her.

He left her in the middle of the day, promising to return in a few hours. He was to be married in two days time, and there were things to be done and settled. He found a letter from Lady Eleanor awaiting him—a loving, passionate letter, reminding him of some trifle in connection with their wedding trip. He put it in his pocket, scarcely read, and in the afternoon returned to Finetta. Her eyes turned to the door with painful, feverish eagerness as he entered, and she smiled gratefully and yet, as it seemed to him, with a curious mixture of fear and sadness.

"You—you are very good to me, Yorke," she said. "Better—better than I deserve."

"All right, Fin," he said, pressing her hand. "You'd do the same for me; old friends, you know."

"Yes," she said, "old friends." She was silent a moment or two, then with an effort she said, "Yorke, I've got something to tell you. And—and I think I'd rather die than say it."

"Don't say it then," he said promptly. "What's it matter? You've got to keep quiet, the doctor said——."

"But I've got to say it," she broke in with a moan. "I can't sleep or rest while it's on my mind. You can't guess what it is, Yorke?"

"No. Never mind. Let it slide till you get better, Fin."

She shook her head as well as she could.

"That would be a long time to keep it," she said. "Yorke, what brought you to the theater last night?"

He started slightly. It might almost be said that he had forgotten the diamond pendant, which was still in his waistcoat pocket.

"Why, I came to see you, of course," hereplied.

"Yes," she said, her large eyes fixed on his. "Yes, but why? I saw your face, Yorke, and there was mischief in it. I saw that you had found out something, if not all."

"Found out what?" he asked carelessly. "Oh, you mean about the pendant? What made you send it back, Fin?"

She looked at him with a puzzled frown.

"What pendant? What are you talking about?"

"The diamond ornament you sent back," he said. "But there, don't worry ——."

"Diamonds I sent back? Is that likely? But what diamonds? You never gave me any."

He tried to smile banteringly; he thought her mind was wandering.

"Never mind. There!" He took the pendant from his pocket and laid it in her hand. "Take it back again, and keep it this time."

She looked at it, and from it to him.

"I never sent this to you—I never saw it before," she said.

"All right, it doesn't matter——."

"Never! You say you gave it to me. When? When?"

"I sent it to you the night—the day after we parted," he said.

Her eyes dilated, and she put her hand to her head.

"You—sent this—this to me? You must be out of your mind, or I am. And you say I sent it back!"

"Look here, Fin," he said soothingly, "I know what it is you want to say to me, and I want to save you the trouble and worry of saying it, so I will tell you that I know all, and that I forgive you, if that's what you want."

Her face twitched, and her eyes fell from his.

"You know all!" she faltered.

He nodded gravely.

"Yes. And I'll own up that I was mad. I came to the theater last night to have a row with you. But that's all past, clean past. And after all you didn't do me any damage, Fin—not the damage you meant to," he corrected himself as the thought of his coming marriage flashed across him. "It would have been all up a tree with me if a—a friend hadn't found the money at the last moment; but as it turned out we got the best of you and your friend, Mr. Ralph Duncombe."

She gazed at him with knitted brows.

"Mr. Ralph who? I never heard the name before. What are you talking about?" she demanded.

"Never mind."

"Answer! Tell me!" she broke out. "Explain what you are driving at, or I shall go clean mad."

He bit his lip.

"Why don't you let it rest?" he said wearily. "I tell you I'm ready to forget it, that I've forgiven you. After all it was tit for tat, and only natural. And it was clever, too, in a way. Did you think of it yourself, Fin, or did this strange gentleman, this new friend of yours, hit upon the idea of buying up my debts and hunting me into a corner——."

He stopped, for with a tremendous effort she had raised herself.

"Stop!" she panted. "This—this is all new to me. I know nothing of it. It's not that I wanted to tell you about. Not that. I never bought your debts. I never heard this man's name before in my life. Ah"—for his face had gone white —"you believe me! It wasn't me who planned that."

"Not you? Then who?"

She fell back.

"Ah," she breathed, "I—I can guess. Oh, Yorke, this you have told me makes it all the harder for me. But I must tell you. It weighs on my heart like—like lead. Ever since I fell, all the while I've been lying here her face has haunted me. I see it waking and sleeping, all white and drawn, with the tears running down it as it was when I told her."

"Whose—whose face? Whose?" he said, a vague presentiment mingling with his amazement and confusion.

"The young lady's—Leslie Lisle's," she gasped.

He sprang to his feet, then sank into the chair again, and sat breathing hard for a moment.

She waited till she had regained strength, then hurried on.

"It was me who—who separated you. Yorke, wait, don't—don't speak. It—it was a chance that helped me. I'd followed you to that place, Portmaris, and I was caught by the tide, and she tried to save me, and we climbed the cliff, and when I fainted she found the locket with your portrait in my bosom. See," and she drew the locket out and held it to him.

He took it mechanically and uttered a cry—a terrible cry.

"I gave you this! It's false! You stole it! Oh, Fin, forgive me—forgive me, but I feel as if I were going mad!" and he covered his face with his hands.

She let her hand rest on his arm timidly.

"Hold on!" she panted. "Let me tell you all as it happened. The tangle's coming straight. There's—there's been some devil's work besides mine! She saw the portrait and—and recognized it. I told her that you'd given it to me—as you had——."

"No, no! I sent it to her the same day as I sent this thing to you."

She gazed at him perplexedly for a moment; then she laughed a mirthless laugh.

"My God!" she said, "I see! You put them in the wrong papers! and I thought you—you cared for me still; and—and I told her so. And she believed it!"

"You told her—she believed it!"

"Yes," she panted hoarsely. "She believed it, and gave you up! She couldn't do otherwise after finding that locket and—and the lies I told her. I said you were going to marry me——."

She stopped and looked at his face, white and set.

"You—you could kill me even as I lie here, Yorke," she said, in a dull, despairing voice. "I can see it in your eyes."

He turned his eyes away.

"Go—go on!" he said, almost inarticulately.

She put her hand to her brow.

"I left her there, looking more dead than alive, and came back to town, and I thought you'd come back to me. I—I waited, and one day I saw you in Hancock's buying the—the ring; and I knew she'd taken you back, and all in the moment I—I told her, and then I got frightened at what I'd done. And when I saw that she had managed to do what I had failed over, and had separated you from Leslie Lisle and got you for herself——."

He rose and stretched out his hands to her as if he would stop her.

"Her? Who?"

"Who?" she opened her eyes upon him. "Why, Lady Eleanor Dallas! It's she you are going to marry, isn't it?"

He went to the mantel shelf and dropped his head upon his arms; then he came back and sank into the chair again with his hands thrust into his pockets, his head upon his breast.

"It's—it's a bad business, Yorke," she panted wearily. "But—but don't be too hard on me, or on her. For she loves you, Yorke! Ah! that's been the trouble all round; we've all loved you too well!" and she turned her face away and closed her eyes.

He sat and stared before him like a man dazed. For one moment he had felt convinced that Finetta's disclosure was the outcome of delirium; but as she had gone on with her confession, he knew that she was speaking of realities.

They had misjudged Leslie after all; she had not left him because she had discovered that he was not a duke! The reflection was the only one relieving streak of light in the gloom. What should he do? What could he do? Where was Leslie? And even if he found her, how could he desert Lady Eleanor? How could he throw her over on the very eve of their wedding day? She had not sinned against him, as Finetta had done; her only sin, as Finetta had so truly said, consisted in loving him too well. No, even if he knew where Leslie Lisle was, he could not desert Eleanor. He must marry her and try—as he had been trying all this time—to tear Leslie's image from his heart. But, ah, how much harder this feat had become since Finetta's disclosure.

She looked round at last.

"You are still here, Yorke," she said. "You haven't gone? I thought—I thought you'd have left me directly, and that I shouldn't have seen you again."

He laughed, scarcely knowing what he did.

"Not much use in that, Fin," he said drearily, hopelessly. "You acted like—well, like a woman, I suppose——."

"Oh!" she moaned. "I acted like a demon. I hadn't any pity, any mercy! I watched her getting whiter and whiter—I heard her cry out as if I'd stabbed her——."

He put up his hand to silence her. "That—

that will do, Fin!" he said hoarsely.

"But I should have given in to her and kept back the lies if you hadn't sent me this."

She put her hand to her bosom and drew out the locket. "That gave me the pluck and the obstinacy. I thought after all you cared for me——." She stopped. "It was a mistake all round, and—and—so I don't care to keep it any longer. Take it, Yorke."

He shook his head; but she put the locket in his hand.

"Do you think I'd keep it now I know you didn't mean it for me, but for her? Not me! Take it and—well, give me the other."

He suffered her to close his hand over the locket; and she took the pendant and laid it on the pillow.

"I know now why she put her hand to her bosom once or twice; this was lying there. Poor girl! Yes, I can be sorry for her, for I knew what she felt. But it's too late now, Yorke, I suppose. You've got to marry Lady Eleanor, eh? Well," as he remained silent, "let's hope that poor young thing has forgotten you!"

Yorke got up and strode up and down, biting his lip and shutting and opening his hands.

"Better go now, Yorke," she said with a sigh. "I know you hate the sight of me; that's only natural——."

"No, no, Fin!" he said with a frown. "I'm not so bad as that; but I feel confused and half mad. God forgive us all, we all seem to have conspired to work her harm! Even Dolph—and I who loved her! Yes, I'd better go, Fin; but I will come back——."

"No, you won't," she said quietly, "at least, not till after your marriage. But, Yorke——."

"Well?" he asked.

"If—if you should ever find her—Miss Lisle," she said, in a low, hesitating voice, "I wish—I wish you'd tell her I'd made a clean breast of it; and—and ask her to come and see me. She'd come; she's one of that sort of women that are always ready to forgive; and she'll forgive me right enough when she sees me lying here helpless as a log, and remembers how hard I fought beside her up that beastly cliff that day! Go now, Yorke, and—well, I don't know that God would bless you any the sooner for my asking Him. But you have been very easy with me, Yorke, after all I've done to make you wretched."

Her voice died away inaudibly at the last words, and she took the hand he gave her and laid it on her lips.

Yorke went out with the locket in his hand, and a burning fire in his heart and brain.

This butterfly o' the wind, this dancing girl, had wrecked Leslie's and his lives! Wrecked and ruined them irreparably. She had spoken of his finding Leslie; but where could he look for her, and, indeed, would it not be better that they should never meet again? He had got to marry Eleanor—and the day after to-morrow; Finetta's confession—like most confessions by the way—had come too late!

In a frame of mind which beggars description he went to Bury Street and resumed his packing; then, in the midst of it, he remembered that he had promised to go to White Place that evening.

This butterfly o' the wind, this dancing girl, had wrecked his life! As he thought of this, he found the locket in his pocket, and transferred it to that of the waistcoat he was putting on.

CHAPTER XL.

"MY SWEET GIRL LOVE."

When he got down to White Place—he had walked from the station—he found Lady Denby alone.

"Eleanor has gone out," she said, "but only for a stroll. As you did not come by the usual train she gave you up. Why didn't you wire?"

"I forgot it," he replied absently.

Lady Denby laughed ironically.

"What is the use of having a special wire if you don't use it?" she said. "Have you had your dinner?"

"Oh, yes," he replied, though he had eaten nothing since the morning.

Lady Denby looked at him curiously.

"You are not looking very well, Yorke," she said. "You seem tired and fagged, and a change is what you want."

"Well, I shall get it directly," he said, with unconscious grimness. "Which way has Eleanor gone? I'll see if I can find her."

"She said something about going to the village," Lady Denby replied; "but I don't expect she will get beyond the grounds. Have some coffee or something."

He mixed a brandy and soda, more to please her than himself, and then went out.

Remembering what Lady Denby had said, he should have kept to the park, but he was not thinking of Lady Eleanor or the way she had taken, and he went straight out of the gate and along the road to the village.

He was thinking, alas! not of the woman he was going to marry in two days' time, but of Leslie Lisle; thinking that, perhaps, some day he should meet her. What would he say to her then? Would it be just simply "How do you do, Miss Lisle?" and go on his way again? Ah, no! Let him meet her when he might, sooner or later he would have to tell her how they had been separated, and why, when the knowledge of Finetta's perfidy had come to him, it was too late to go back to her! He would have to tell her that, would have to clear himself in her eyes!

He walked on, wrapt in bitter thoughts, haunted by the spectre which takes the shape of 'It might have been,' and found himself far on the London Road. He had, all unconsciously, passed the village, and he would have still kept striding along, but that a heavy shower, which had been threatening for some time, came pelting down. So he turned back at a slower pace, and, as most men do when they are getting wet, thought of a pipe.

He found his pipe and a tobacco pouch, but his match box was absent. He hunted in the corners and crevices of his pockets for a match, but unsuccessfully, and he was about to give up the idea of a smoke, when he came upon the school and school-house. He stopped and looked at it absently; he had been so absorbed in gloomy reverie as he passed it on his way from White Place that he had not noticed it.

He stood by the little white gate in the close-cut hedge for a moment or two to see if any one was about of whom he could ask a light; then, as no one appeared, he pushed open the gate, walked up the narrow, weedless path, and knocked at the door.

A neat, a remarkably neat, little handmaid answered the knock, and in severe accents said:

"Round to the back-door, my man."

Yorke had his coat collar turned up, and his short pipe in his mouth, and the little maid had taken him for a tramp or a pedlar.

He smiled, and entering into the humor of the thing, obediently, not to say humbly, went round the house and presented himself at the back-door.

"Well, what is it?" asked the girl.

"Oh, I only want a light for my pipe," said Yorke. "Will you be good enough to give me one?"

She saw her mistake in a moment, and grew crimson.

"Oh, I beg your pardon, sir, but we have so many tra—er—so many strange kind of people come knocking."

"Then you do well to be careful," he said.

She ran and brought him a box of matches, and he lit his pipe and thanked her, raising his hat, and was turning to go out of the garden, when she said:

"Wouldn't you like to wait till the heaviest of the rain is over, sir?"

Yorke would have declined, but that he was afraid she might think he was wounded by her mistaking him for a tramp, so he said:

"Thank you, I'll stand up under the hedge for a minute or two," and he stood under a couple of the limes that bordered the side of the garden, and puffed at his pipe. It did occur to him to wonder whether Lady Eleanor had got back to White Place before the storm broke, and whether she, in her turn, would wonder where he was; but he was just in that frame of mind in which a man is glad to stand still and smoke and think, and keep as far away as possible from friends and acquaintances. Besides, after the next two days he might find it difficult, if not impossible, to smoke a pipe in solitude. So he leant against the trunk of the lime and went over in his mind all the details of Finetta's confession. He saw it all as plainly as if he had been present at the scene between her and Leslie. He understood how quick Leslie would be to surrender him to the woman who had, as she thought, a prior right; how greatly Leslie's maiden pride and jealousy would aid Finetta in her task. And as he thought, his soul rose in bitter protest against the fate which had wrecked both their lives.

He finished his pipe, and was refilling it, and had his hand upon the tobacco pouch, when suddenly he heard a voice singing.

He paid no attention for a moment, then his hands grew motionless, and he clutched the pouch tightly, and he looked up with a sudden flush, a sudden light flashing in his eyes. For the voice was singing this song:

My sweet girl love, with frank blue eyes,
  Though years have passed, I see you still,
  There where you stand beside the mill,
Beneath the bright autumnal skies.

Then he laughed, laughed with a bitter, self-mockery.

"I'm going out of my mind," he said, with intense self-scorn. "Here's some girl singing a silly ballad, which no doubt sells by the thousand, and I'm actually trying to persuade myself that the voice is like Leslie's, just because I once heard her singing it! Yes, I'm going mad, there's no doubt of that," and half-angrily he pressed his cap on his forehead, savagely struck a light and lit his pipe, and prepared to march out, though it was still raining in torrents. But as he passed the front window, framed in the red autumnal leaves of the Virginian creeper, he heard the voice more distinctly, and he stopped and began to tremble, looking hard toward the window.

"I am a fool!" he told himself. "I have been thinking of her so constantly. I am so much upset that I should think any young girl I happened to meet like her, any voice I heard like hers. This one, for instance, is—is——."

The perspiration broke out upon his forehead, and the hand that held the pipe shook, for at that moment the last words of the song died away with a peculiar little trill, a soft little sigh, which he remembered in Leslie's voice, and hers alone, most distinctly.

"It is easily proved," he muttered, and he stole across the small square of grass up to the window, and looked in.

For a moment or two the room seemed dark, the objects within it indistinct; then he saw a girl seated at the piano, a slim, graceful figure in some black, softly draping stuff, that of itself seemed to speak of Leslie. She was seated with her back toward the window, but as he leant on the window-sill she moved her head, and a cry burst from him. It was Leslie!

He drew back from the window-sill and leant against the wall, under the dripping Virginian creeper, his heart knocking against his ribs, his lips parched and dry.

What should he do? Go into the house and speak to her? Ah, not now! Not now, just before his marriage! And yet—oh, God!—how hard it was! Leslie in there—Leslie in there, still deeming him false, and a few words would undeceive her. He took a couple of steps to the door, then pulled up, and in another moment or two he would have rushed down the path and out of the gate, but there rose, even as he turned, the sweet, sad voice again, and his resolution melted like wax in a furnace. He opened the door, went along the passage, paused a moment to collect some fragment of self-possession and self-restraint, then entered the parlor.

He stood gazing at her with hungry, longing eyes, and an ache in his heart, which grew almost unendurable, then he said as softly as he could:

"Leslie!"

She stopped singing, but did not turn her head. She had, in fancy, heard him breathe her name so often.

"Leslie!" he repeated, drawing nearer.

Her hands grew motionless on the keys, and she looked round. Then she rose slowly, like a ghost, her face growing whiter and whiter, her eyes dilating, and "Yorke" breathed from her parted lips.

"Leslie!" he said again. "Oh, Leslie!" and he held out his arms to her.

She seemed to struggle against the potent influence he exerted, then she came nearer, swaying a little, like one walking in her sleep.

"Oh, my darling, my darling, is it you? Really you?" he said in a subdued voice, as if he feared to startle, frighten her.

She was almost in his arms, her bosom heaving, her lips quivering, when she seemed to remember; and with a cry, the saddest he had ever heard, she swayed away from him, extending one hand as if to keep him off.

He caught the hand, and held it in a grasp like that of a vice.

"You shrink from me, Leslie? Oh, my dearest—to shrink from me!"

She seemed to struggle for voice, and found it at last.

"Why—why have you come?" she breathed.

"Why have you hidden from me?" he responded, and there was almost a touch of indignation in the earnest, pleading voice. "Why did you do it, Leslie? Oh, God, if you knew what I have suffered——."

"You—have—suffered?" she repeated. "Ah, no, not you! It is I——." She stopped and sighed deeply.

He almost forced her, by her hand, into a chair and knelt beside her.

"Leslie, Leslie!" he cried, striving hard to speak calmly and coolly. "Listen to me. I'll try and explain. I'll try and tell you how this cruel thing has been brought about. It will be hard work, for the words sound like a jumble in my ears, and it is all I can do to keep myself from taking you in my arms—ah, don't shrink, don't be frightened! I will leave you to be the judge when—when you have heard all. Leslie, that woman Finetta——."

She started and turned her face from him.

"Leslie! Leslie! She lied. She told you she was to be my wife. It was not true, then or ever! As Heaven is my witness, there was not even love between us, on my side. I had parted from her two days before——."

"Oh, hush!" she broke out with a kind of jerk. "I remember every word—every word. It is burnt into my heart."

"It was false!" he said vehemently. "I can understand, imagine, all she would say! She is an actress—would have deceived a woman of the world, much more easily one all innocence and purity like yourself, dearest."

She looked at him as if a glimmer of hope was dawning, then her face clouded again, and she tried to take her hand from his, but unsuccessfully.

"You—you forget," she murmured. "The portrait. You sent it to her the day you sent my gift to me! Your portrait!"

He could have groaned.

"No," he thundered, gripping her hand. "I sent that to you!"

"To—me?" fell from her lips.

"Yes, to you! The diamond thing I sent to her—listen and believe me, Leslie. Look in my eyes! Ah, dearest, do you think—how could you ever have thought—that I would be false to you? Why, I should never have believed you false to me, though an angel had whispered it. I sent the pendant to her because we had been good friends, and—and—ah, I must speak openly—because I knew that she wished we might be something more. It was a parting gift—a parting gift—from friend to friend, that was all! But fate chose that I, like a fool, should misdirect the packages! Leslie, the portrait was for you, the diamonds for her! Ah, think, consider, dearest! Should I send such a thing to you? To you, whose taste is so pure and refined!"

She began to tremble, and he drew still nearer to her.

"Why—why—did you not come—and—tell me this sooner?" she almost wailed.

He hung his head for a moment, then he looked up and met her eyes steadily.

"Leslie, I will tell you all. I—I have wronged you cruelly. I have been a fool. Yes, so great, so insensate a fool as to believe that, having learned the imposition we had practised on you, having discovered that I was not the Duke of Rothbury, you repented of our engagement——."

"You were not the Duke of Rothbury," she said, her brows knit; "are you not?"

"Oh, if Dolph were only here!" he groaned. "No, dearest, I am not; and at that time there was little chance of my ever being the duke. It is Dolph—Mr. Temple—as we called him, who is the duke. It was a whim—a freak of his. Oh, you see!"

Yes, she saw, and the color came to her face, and a proud, wounded look into her lovely eyes.

"And—and you thought that it was because I believed you to be a duke—and only because of that—that I——."

"Leslie, here on my knees I plead guilty. You cannot despise me more than I despise myself! But, dearest, think! The last words you spoke to Dolph the morning you parted with him! Think, was there not some slight excuse?"

She hung her head.

"It—it is all past now," she said at last with a deep sigh. "We cannot re-live it all! Ah, no!"

And she turned her face away as a tear rolled down her cheek. Before that tear he lost his self-command. He forgot Lady Eleanor, forgot that his wedding-day, as fixed, was within a few hours, and he caught her in his arms. She uttered a low cry, and bent away from him, her hands against his breast; but before the fire, the anguish of appeal, in his eyes her own fell; she trembled and quivered like an imprisoned bird, then felt herself crushed against his breast.

"Oh, my darling, my darling!" he murmured brokenly. "As if you and I could part again! No, no, never again while life lasts! Never again, dearest. Oh, don't cry!" He kissed the tears away, and laid her face against his lovingly, protectingly. "Don't cry, Leslie, or I shall think you can never forgive me! And——." He looked at the black dress. "Where is your father?"

"Oh, Yorke, Yorke!" she sobbed.

"Hush, hush! dearest! And you bore it all alone!" he groaned. "And I should have been by your side to help and comfort you! What shall I say, what shall I do, to prove my remorse? It was all my fault!"

"No, no," she responded, woman-like. "Not all, Yorke! I—I ought not to have believed that—that woman. I felt that she was not—not a good woman, and I ought not to have trusted her. But the portrait, Yorke! It all seemed so clear, so conclusive."

"I know," he said gravely; "I have heard it from her own lips."

"From her own lips?"

"Yes," he said gently. "She has confessed it all. If she sinned, she has been punished. Finetta, the dancing girl, will never dance again; she is helpless and crippled for life."

Leslie uttered a low cry of horror and shuddered.

"Oh, God forgive me! and I was just wishing she might be punished. Oh, Yorke, where is she? I—I cannot forget her temptation, and I—I will try and forgive her!"

"She wants to see you, dearest!" he said; "I left her this morning with a prayer for your forgiveness on her lips. I will take you to see her, and she will explain all that may be still dark. See, she sent you this," and he put the locket in her hand. "But, dearest, I want to hear all about yourself. Why are you here—and are you here alone?"

"I am the teacher here," she said. "Let me go now, Yorke, dear!"

"No, no!" he said, "I cannot!" and he held her still closer. "Tell it to me with your head lying on my shoulder, your heart to mine——." He stopped suddenly, and Leslie following his eyes, would have broken from him, for two persons had entered, Lucy and Ralph Duncombe, but Yorke still held her.

Lucy uttered a low cry of amazement, and the color flew to her face.

"Oh, come away," she whispered to Ralph.

But he strode in and confronted Yorke with indignant menace.

"No!" he said, sternly; "I am Miss Lisle's friend, and it is my duty to protect her!"

"To protect her!" repeated Yorke mechanically, and staring at him.

"Yes!" said Ralph. "Leslie—Miss Lisle—do you know who this gentleman is?"

Leslie, white and red by turns, raised her eyes.

"Yes!" she said, almost inaudibly.

Ralph Duncombe started.

"You know who he is? And—and that he is engaged—to be married to Lady Eleanor Dallas the day after to-morrow!"

CHAPTER XLI.

"IT IS THE TRUTH."

Leslie looked at Ralph Duncombe vacantly for a moment, as if she had failed to understand him; then the color began to ebb from her face and left it white, and she strove feebly to release herself from Yorke's enfolding arms.

He did not speak, but he glared at Ralph Duncombe in a kind of half-dazed fury.

Lucy was the first to break the awful silence which followed Ralph's announcement.

"Oh, no, no, it is not—it cannot be true! There must be some mistake, Ralph," she exclaimed, almost inaudibly.

Ralph Duncombe bit his lip. He had spoken in the first heat of his amazement and indignation, and was, perhaps, sorry that he had done so, or, at any rate, that he had spoken so precipitately.

"It is true," he said doggedly. "Ask him! It is for him to explain."

All eyes were fixed on Yorke. The two women's with an anxious, expectant look in them, as if they were only waiting for his contradiction and denial.

But his face grew as white as Leslie's, and after looking round wildly he hung his head and groaned.

Leslie drew herself away from him slowly, her gaze still fixed on him, her bosom heaving, and dropped the locket from her hand. It went with a dull thud to the floor. She had been in Paradise a moment or two ago, had been filled with a joy which in its intensity almost atoned for the past months of sorrow and anguish; and now she was plunged back into the depths again.

It was Lucy who spoke again. Losing her timidity in her anxiety for the friend she loved so dearly; she glided to Yorke, and put her hand on his arm.

"Oh, speak, sir!" she implored him. "Say that it is not true! Don't you see that she is waiting?" And she looked over her shoulder at Leslie.

Yorke followed her eyes, then looked down at her pretty, anxious face despairingly.

"I cannot!" fell from his lips.

Lucy shrank back from him, and stole her arm round Leslie to support her.

"You cannot! Oh!"

Ralph Duncombe came further into the room.

"He cannot deny it," he said. "I know—am a friend of Lady Eleanor Dallas. I know this gentleman, though he does not know me. He is Lord Auchester, the heir, now, to the Duke of Rothbury, and he is engaged to marry Lady Eleanor. The wedding is to take place the day after to-morrow. I am sorry—yes, I am sorry—that I blurted out the truth! but the sight of him—well, I am an old friend of Miss Lisle's, and I claim the right to protect her. If his lordship considers that I have exceeded a friend's privilege he is at liberty to demand any satisfaction I can give him."

Yorke raised his head. His face was set and white, his eyes heavy with despair. He felt as the ancient gladiator felt at the moment the fatal net caught him in its meshes, and the dagger was descending to strike him to the heart; as the miserable wretch in the dock feels when the sentence of death is being pronounced. For a moment it seemed as if he could not speak, and he wiped the cold sweat from his face mechanically; then he said in a low, broken voice:

"It is the truth!" He looked at Leslie, scarcely imploringly so much as hopelessly, despairingly. "I had forgotten it! Yes," he went on almost fiercely, "I had forgotten it! I was so happy that I lost all memory of it! You, sir, who came as an accuser, who no doubt, think me an utter blackguard and lost to all sense of honour, shall be my judge as well as my accuser."

Ralph Duncombe shook his head.

"I do not wish——," he began; but Yorke silenced him with a gesture that was full of the dignity of despair.

"Hear me, please! Miss Lisle and I were engaged to be married—that is, months ago. We met at a place called Portmaris, and—" he glanced at Lucy —"sir, I loved her as truly and devotedly as you can love this young lady. We were to have been married——."

"You!" exclaimed Ralph Duncombe. "No, it was the Duke of Rothbury to whom she was engaged."

Yorke sighed.

"No, it was to me," he said. "I exchanged titles with my cousin, the duke; why, need not be explained. Leslie—Miss Lisle understands. It was a foolish trick, and, like most follies, has brought trouble and sorrow in its wake. But for that stupid freak—. We were to have been married, but on the eve of our marriage we were separated, torn apart by a wicked lie, which, aided by a wrongly addressed envelope, served to ruin our happiness. Miss Lisle thought I had deceived her, and, acting on the promptings of a heart that is all truth and purity, she cast me off. I lost her in all senses of the word, and I felt that I deserved to lose her. Now, sir, call your imagination to your aid. Look on this young lady whom you love, and try and put yourself in my place. Picture to yourself my state and condition, having lost all that made life worth living! Ah, you can!" for Ralph Duncombe looked down and bit his lip.

Yorke passed his hand across his brow and sighed heavily, and for a moment seemed as if he had finished his explanation; then he looked up, as if awaking suddenly.

"I was in that state in which a man might win pity from his worst enemy; but I had an enemy—of whose existence I was and am still ignorant—and he chose that moment to hunt me into still greater straits. I have been a fool in more senses of the word than one. I was heavily in debt. It was because of that millstone of debt that I had induced Miss Lisle to consent to a secret marriage. My enemy, whoever he was, discovered this; he bought up all my debts and liabilities, and constituting himself my sole creditor, he came down upon me with all the weight of those debts, meaning to crush me. I should have gone under, never to rise again. I should have been ruined and disgraced, should have brought disgrace upon the name I bear and all connected with me. But ——." He paused, and his face worked. "There was one who—who had some little regard for me, and—and she stepped in and saved me; lifted me out of the mire and set me on my feet again; saved me from the consequences of my folly, and saved the old name from shame. Gratitude is a poor word to describe what I felt toward her! I—I made the debt I owed her still heavier by asking her to take that which she had saved. And—and in the goodness of her heart she consented! From that time until now—until now!—I have been true to her in deed and intent. I have striven to forget the woman to whom I had given my heart, there at Portmaris, the woman who was all the world to me"—his voice broke—"the woman whom I lost on our wedding eve! To-day, to-day only, have I heard from the woman who separated us a full confession of the deception by which she effected her purpose. But I knew it was too late to regain my lost happiness. Too late! I never expected to see Miss Lisle again, scarcely hoped to do so, excepting that it might be once before I died, that I might say to her, 'With all my faults and follies, I was true to you, Leslie!'"

Leslie, standing rigid and motionless, moaned faintly.

He cast an agonized look at her.

"Then—then I came by the merest chance to this cottage. I heard her voice. I stole in, and in the joy of meeting her, and reconciliation with her, in that great joy the past was blotted out from my mind, and I forgot—I say I forgot that I was betrothed to another, that I was within a few hours of being wedded to another."

His voice died away, and he stood with downcast head and vacant eyes. Then he looked up.

"There is my story, sir! You say that you are a friend of—of Miss Lisle's. It is for you to demand—exact satisfaction for the wrong that I have done her. But, mind, that wrong dates only from to-day! I have loved her——." He broke down for a moment; then went on almost sternly, "What I have to do, what I can do to atone, I will do! I—I can never hope for Miss Lisle's forgiveness ——."

Leslie's hands writhed together, and Lucy's arm held her still more firmly.

"I can never hope to see her again. But I will say this in her hearing, that I would lay down my life to wipe out the past, to render her happy in the future."

Leslie's hands stole up to her face.

"For the rest," he went on, "I will tell Lady Eleanor all that I have told you. It is her due. She shall be the judge; she shall dispose of my future. I owe her much more than can be told."

He stopped, then looked up, and there was a light in his eyes which made Lucy shrink.

"One thing more. I have spoken of the way in which I was hunted down. That part of the business is a mystery still. But I am going to solve it! I am going to find Mr. Ralph Duncombe."

Lucy broke from Leslie, and with a cry of terror flung herself on Ralph's arm, and looked over her shoulder at Yorke's stern face.

Yorke stopped and started, his face grew red and then white, and he strode forward.

"What!" he cried, under his breath. "Are you——."

Ralph Duncombe put Lucy from him gently, and came a step forward to meet him.

"Yes," he said gravely, "my name is Ralph Duncombe."

"You!" said Yorke, as if his amazement over-mastered his anger. "Do you mean that it is you who bought up my debts and hunted me down?"

"It was I!" said Ralph stolidly.

"But—but——." Yorke groaned. "Why? Why, what harm did I ever do you? Why, man, I never saw you before to-day. I never saw your name until I read it in the writs! Why? Why?" and he stood with clenched hands, the veins standing out on his forehead.

Ralph bit his lip, but he looked full into Yorke's blazing eyes.

"Why did you do it?" demanded Yorke in a low voice, which was all the more ominous for its quietude. "What was I to you that you should concern yourself in my affairs? That you should try and ruin me? It was you who drove me——," he was going to say "into a marriage with Lady Eleanor," but he stopped himself in time. "Why did you do it?"

Ralph Duncombe remained silent for a moment, then he said:

"My lord, I desired to break off the engagement between you and Miss Lisle."

"You? Why? Ah——."

The light flashed upon him; then he glanced at Lucy, who stood, trembling, with one hand upon Ralph's arm.

"Yes," said Ralph. "But Miss Lisle had rejected me, she would never have been my wife, and, in saying this, I will say no more! I have another reason."

"That reason?" demanded Yorke, with barely restrained fury.

"I decline to answer," said Ralph.

Yorke made a movement as if to seize him or strike him. Lucy screamed, Leslie seemed as if to spring between them, then flung herself on her knees beside a chair, and this recalled Yorke to himself.

"Forgive me," he murmured, casting a glance at her; then in a loud tone he said to Ralph significantly:

"This is not the place for a scene, Mr. Duncombe. I shall demand an explanation from you elsewhere. I—I will go now." He put his hand to his brow, and his face lost its fury as he turned it to Leslie, kneeling, with her face in her hands. "Yes, I will go now. Good-by, Les—Miss Lisle. Forgive me all the trouble and sorrow I have caused you! God knows, as I said, I would lay down my life to win a day's happiness for you! I—I think in your heart of hearts you know that. I—I have been a wretchedly unfortunate man! It is all my own fault, I dare say, and yet——. Well! All the talking in the world will not talk out the past, will not help me through the future! Good-by! God bless you, Leslie."

His voice broke into a kind of sob, and he strode toward the door.

As he did so, as, half-blind with misery, he fumbled at the handle, the door opened from the outside, and a tall figure stood on the threshold.

It was Lady Eleanor Dallas! She was wrapped in a very dark cloak, dripping wet, above which her beautiful face gleamed white as that of a Grecian statue.

She held the door, and leaned against it to support herself, and the hand she raised, as if to stop him, shook and quivered as if with ague.

"Stop, Yorke!" she moaned, rather than said.

CHAPTER XLII.

LOVE AND PRIDE.

"Eleanor!" he said hoarsely.

She looked at him as if she found it impossible to speak for a moment; then she drew herself upright, and pushed the wet hair from her forehead.

"Yes, it is I," she said, in a low voice, in which agony and pride struggled for the mastery.

"Where—where did you come from? How long——."

"Yes," she said, answering his unfinished question, "I have been listening. They told me at home that you had gone out to look for me, and I followed you. I heard your voice as I was passing, and I came into the garden. I have been standing by the window and——. Every word!" fell from her white lips.

"You—you should not have listened," he said "Come away," and he put out his hand as if to draw her outside; but she did not move.

"I am going presently," she said, speaking as if with an effort. "I—I want to say something. Yorke——." She seemed as if she were about to break down, but mastered her emotion and came a step or two farther into the room. "Yorke, you have not heard all yet, not the whole truth. He," she glanced at Ralph Duncombe, "could not tell you, but I will."

A presentiment of what was coming fell on Yorke and he tried to stop her.

"No!" he said. "Say no more, Eleanor, but come home with me."

"I cannot," she said. "I must speak. Miss Lisle——." She drew nearer to Leslie, who had risen and stood against the window, her hands clasped, her head turned away. "Miss Lisle, you have been cruelly wronged. And by me!"

Leslie started and looked up quickly. Lady Eleanor gazed at her, seeing her face distinctly for the first time, and so the two stood and looked at each other —these two beautiful women who were fated to love the same man!

"It was I who—who separated you from Lord Auchester."

Yorke held up his hand to stop her.

"Eleanor!"

But she did not remove her eyes from Leslie's face.

"Yes, I. It was I who employed Mr. Duncombe to buy the debts and summon Lord Auchester."

Ralph Duncombe looked up.

"Is—is this necessary, Lady Eleanor?" he said gravely. "I am ready to take all the responsibility."

"No," she said. "It was I! The woman Finetta told me that the marriage was to take place, and I did all I could to prevent it. You wonder that I should admit it?" she smiled, with a mixture of pride and despair. "I have told you that I have been standing by the window there, and have heard all. Do you think that I would hold Lord Auchester to his promise, that I would consent to his marrying me now that I know he is in love with another woman?"

Her eyes flashed and her lips curved haughtily, though her voice was as low as before.

"I tell you this now," she went on, "that Lord Auchester may not hold Mr. Duncombe to blame. The sin, if sin there was, was mine, and I atone for it!" As she spoke the last words she glided across the room and stood in front of Leslie.

"Miss Lisle, if I were to say that I am sorry, you would not believe me. You are a woman like myself, and—you will understand! I knew Lord Auchester before you did, and"—she looked round haughtily—"I loved him. If there is any shame in that, I accept it. He knew that I loved him."

"For God's sake, be silent—come away!" exclaimed Yorke almost inaudibly.

She glanced at him as if she scarcely saw him.

"It was the happiest, proudest day of my life when he asked me to be his wife, and—and in the conviction that I could, and should, make him happy, I did not regret the means by which I had won him. I forgot, you see," she smiled bitterly, "that the day of reckoning might come. It has come and I face it! All the world may know the story——."

"No, no! Oh, no!" panted Lucy, whose gentle heart was melted by the agony which she knew this proud woman was suffering.

Lady Eleanor did not even look at her.

"I do not care who knows!" she said. "I have made my confession, and I have done with it." She made an eloquent gesture with her hands.

There was silence for a moment; then she said, addressing Leslie, in a low, distinct voice:

"I do not ask for your forgiveness, Miss Lisle. If I stood in your place I should find it as impossible to forgive as you do. I will not even utter the conventional wish that you may be happy. I tried to ruin your happiness in securing my own, and I have failed. Let that console you, as it will torture me! If you need further consolation, take it in the assurance that he has loved you all the time he has been promised to me. Yes!" she said with a deep sigh, "I have felt that all through. His heart was always yours, never mine. If this evening's work had never been, if we had married, he would have gone on loving you, and my punishment would have been greater than it is."

She was silent a moment; then, still looking at Leslie, she said, inaudibly to the rest:

"That woman, Finetta, lied when she spoke of you. Yes! I can understand how he came to choose you before me!"

She turned and drew her cloak round her and moved to the door. Yorke started as if roused from a kind of stupor, and went forward as if to accompany her, but she drew away from him.

"Your place is here," she said icily, "not with me!"

He stopped, irresolute, half dazed by conflicting emotions, and she looked over her shoulder at Ralph Duncombe.

"I ordered my carriage to follow me," she said in a dull, mechanical voice. "Will you see if it is on the road, Mr. Duncombe?"

He started forward and offered his arm; but Yorke motioned him aside and took her hand.

"No!" he said hoarsely. "My place is by your side. You are my promised wife, Eleanor!"

He spoke the words in the tone a man might use who is about to lead a forlorn hope which must end in death, as a man who is resigning all chance of happiness. She understood and smiled bitterly as she drew her hand from his.

"Pardon me, Lord Auchester," she said pointing bitterly to Leslie, "there stands your promised wife," and with one long look into his face she turned and left them.

Yorke was a gentleman. He could not let the woman whom he was pledged to marry in a few hours go out into the night like an outcast. He followed her and Ralph Duncombe.

"Eleanor," he said in deep agitation, "you will let me come with you?"

The sound of wheels was heard on the muddy road, and she stood and listened to them rather than to him.

"Eleanor, think what you do!" he said. "I stand by my promise, my engagement, notwithstanding——."

"Notwithstanding that I obtained it by a fraud!" she said, turning her eyes upon him. "Yes, I knew you would say that; and I am grateful. But you forget, Yorke, I heard every word you said. You would give me—what? not yourself, not your heart? You cannot, it belongs to her. Go to her! Forget me!" Then her voice broke, her pride melted, and she held out her arms to him, her white face drawn and haggard. "Oh, Yorke, I loved you so! No, do not come near me! I am not so degraded as to accept such a sacrifice! You love her, and I do not wonder! No, I do not wonder! She is more beautiful than I am, and better, a thousand times better! You will make her happy, and—oh, how much more is this! she will make you happy. Good-by! Go back to her! Plead to her, kneel to her, to forgive you. You will find it hard, these good women are always harder than we are! She would not have done as much to win you as I have, and will therefore, be all the slower to forgive! But go! And—and ——." The carriage was drawing near. She threw back the hood of the cloak and flashed all her proud white loveliness upon him. "When you think of me, think of me as I am at this moment, at the moment I relinquished you!"

He stood motionless, and she drew near and laid a white hand upon each of his shoulders, looked into his eyes, a lingering farewell look; then as Ralph Duncombe opened the carriage door, she let her hands drop slowly and got into the carriage. Ralph was following her, but she stayed him with a gesture.

"No, no! Alone! Alone!" came from her parted lips.

The word "Alone! Alone!" fell like a funeral knell upon Yorke's ear; it was the last word he was to hear from Lady Eleanor's lips for many a year.

The two men stood and gazed after the carriage; then Yorke turned upon Ralph Duncombe.

"At any rate, I have a man to deal with now!" he said savagely.

"And one who will not shrink from the encounter, my lord," responded Ralph promptly.

"You have to account to me for your conduct Mr Duncombe," said Yorke. "You have interfered in my affairs most unwarrantably. What have you to say?"

Ralph Duncombe flushed angrily and a passionate retort rose to his lips, but he crushed it down.

"You have every right to demand an explanation, Lord Auchester," he said with an unnatural calmness, "and I give it you. I interfered because I once loved Miss Lisle, and because I did not consider you a fit husband for her. I judged you by the estimate I had formed on hearsay. I thought that I was doing Miss Lisle a service in helping to prevent the marriage."

Yorke swore.

"Even your anger shall not stop me in confessing that I erred," Ralph went on. "I was wrong, I admit it. But I did what I did for the best."

"The best!" groaned Yorke.

"Yes! You cannot but know the character the world gives you. A spendthrift—one who carried on an intrigue with a dancing woman——."

Yorke held up his hand.

"No more, sir!" he said sternly.

But Ralph went on doggedly:

"I thought I was acting wisely and righteously in preventing your marriage to such a woman as Leslie Lisle. I admit I was wrong; and I am ready to yield you any satisfaction you may desire."

Yorke looked into the honest face, into the steadfast eyes, for a moment; then he sighed.

"You are right. I was never worthy of her! What man of us all is?"

"None!" said Ralph. "But, notwithstanding, I say, go and ask her to be your wife, Lord Auchester."

Yorke seemed staggered by this knockdown advice, and hung his head. Then he looked up, breathing hard.

"I will," he said, and he strode into the house, Ralph Duncombe remaining outside.

Leslie had sunk into a chair, and Lucy was kneeling beside her, holding her hands and murmuring those inarticulate words of sympathy and consolation which only women can utter—for at such times a man is always an imbecile and a fool.

Yorke strode in and bent over the chair.

"Leslie," he said, in a hoarse, broken voice. "Leslie, I have come back to you. I don't know what to say to you, except that I love you, that I have never ceased to love you since the first day we met there at Portmaris. Will you forgive me? Will you be my wife, Leslie?"

A profound silence followed his impassioned words. Lucy, kneeling, held

Leslie's hands.

"Speak to him, dear," she whispered, the tears rolling down her face. "Speak to him, Leslie."

But Leslie could not speak. She was a woman, just a woman, and she found it hard to forgive his betrothal to Lady Eleanor. All else counted for nothing. But that——! She sat motionless and dumb.

"I understand," he said, almost inaudibly. "You are right. Well—good-by, Leslie, good-by!"

"Leslie!" whispered Lucy in an agony.

But still Leslie did not move, but sat, her face hidden, her hands tightly clasped.

"It's no use," said Yorke. "It is more than I could hope for! Good-by, Leslie!"

"Leslie, dear, dear Leslie, he is going!" whispered Lucy. But Leslie remained motionless and silent, and Yorke, with a groan, left them.

"Well?" said Ralph, as Yorke came out into the darkness and the rain.

Yorke shook his head.

"I have failed," he said grimly.

"What? Stop!" exclaimed Ralph moved to pity by the despair and hopelessness of the voice. "Why, man, she loves you!"

Yorke shook his head again.

"Not now," he said, in a dull, heavy way. "She did, but now I have lost her. The best, the sweetest——." His voice broke.

Ralph Duncombe seized his arm.

"Wait!" he said. "You are wrong! If ever a woman loved a man, Leslie Lisle loves you!"

Yorke disengaged his arm from Ralph's grasp.

"There is no hope for me," he said, despairingly. "I have lost her," and he passed through the gate, and was swallowed up by the darkness.

Lady Eleanor reached White Place, and went straight to her own room, and presently Lady Denby came to her.

"Good heavens, Eleanor, what have you been doing to yourself?" she exclaimed, as she stared at the dripping cloak. "Why, you are wet to the skin! You will catch your death of cold. Where is Yorke?"

"Yorke?" said Lady Eleanor, with a spasmodic laugh. "Yorke will not trouble you again, aunt. He has gone!"

"Gone!"

"Yes, for good! There will be no wedding the day after to-morrow."

"My dear Eleanor, are you mad?"

"No, I am sane at last," said Lady Eleanor. "The engagement is broken off. Do you remember my telling you, when I heard of Eustace's death, and his boys', that I was afraid things would go wrong? Well, they have gone wrong. For Heaven's sake, don't stare at me like that! Tell my maid to pack my clothes; I shall leave here to-morrow."

"But—but, what has happened?" demanded Lady Denby.

Lady Eleanor laughed harshly.

"He has found the girl he has been in love with all this time. It is not me he wanted to marry, but her. That's all! Tell them to pack up!"

"But—but, my dear Eleanor!"

Lady Eleanor flung her wet hair from her face.

"There is no 'but,'" she said wearily. "He has gone. Let us go away out of England, no matter where. And—and the day after to-morrow was to be my wedding day! No wedding day will ever dawn for me!"

She sank upon a sofa and hid her face and lay motionless for an hour, Lady Denby standing near. Then suddenly Lady Eleanor started and raised her head.

"What was that?"

"I heard nothing," said Lady Denby.

"I heard a horse; some one has ridden out of the courtyard. It is Yorke. That is the last of him!"

It was Yorke. He had walked swiftly through the lane to White Place, and going straight to the stable had saddled his horse.

"It's a dark night, my lord," said the groom, who held the lantern, and he looked curiously and apprehensively at the stern face. "An' the ground's soft and slippery, my lord," he added.

Yorke did not, however, seem to hear him, but tossing him a sovereign leapt into the saddle and went out of the courtyard at a canter. The horse was fresh and somewhat startled at being taken out so late and into the darkness, and under ordinary circumstances Yorke would have let him go easy until he quieted down, but to-night he had no thought for the horse or himself, or anything else; and when they had got outside the park and on the London road he let the animal have its head, and even touched it with his heel. This was quite enough, and they went spinning along the slippery road at a breakneck pace. It was very dark, the rain was still coming down in good old English fashion, and the horse was getting more and more nervous as he felt, by some instinct, that his master was riding carelessly and recklessly. Yorke scarcely knew whether he was riding or walking until suddenly he saw something white flash along the ground in front. It was only a white cat, but if it had been a ghost the horse could not have been more frightened. He stopped almost instantly and shied, and, on Yorke's striking him, reared. Yorke was a good rider and kept his seat, but when he struck the horse again and tried to force him over, the animal, half mad with fright, reared still higher, until he stood as upright as a circus horse; then, losing his balance, slipped on the greasy road and came down backward on the top of Yorke.

It was done in a moment, with scarcely any sound save the clatter and splash of the horse's hoofs as he rose and shook himself, trembling and panting, and in the silence of the night Yorke lay motionless, his whole length stretched out upon the ground, the rain beating down upon his upturned face.

Ralph Duncombe had gone to the inn and the two girls, left alone, were still in the parlor. Leslie had scarcely changed her attitude, and seemed sunk in lethargic indifference, which was really the result of exhaustion, and though she listened to Lucy's arguments and prayers, made no response to them.

Lucy pleaded hard for Yorke. With a woman's quick insight she had pierced the haze by which his actions and motives seemed obscured, and had jumped at, rather than worked out, the whole truth.

"Are you going to let him go, Leslie," she asked for the twentieth time, "after all he has suffered?"

"I have suffered also," said Leslie at last.

"But through no fault of his! Or, at any rate, not entirely through his fault. Is it because he changed titles with the duke that you are so angry, and will not forgive him?"

Leslie shook her head.

"I do not care about that," she said simply.

"Is it because he was so great a friend with that dancing woman?"

Leslie's face flushed, but she shook her head.

"No," said Lucy quickly. "He had not seen you then, remember. He said good-by to her after he had met you. You needn't want any more than that. What is it then? Ah, it is because of his engagement to Lady Eleanor!"

Leslie turned her face away her brows drawn together.

"But think, dear!" pleaded Lucy. "What could he do? Lady Eleanor had saved him from ruin—he did not know that it was she and Ralph who had driven him into a corner; remember, she had saved him, and he knew that she loved him, and he thought that you had thrown him over. Oh, Leslie, he only did what any man would have done. Forgive him, dear! He loves you with all his heart and soul, any one—a woman especially—can see that. There, you are trembling! Leslie, let your heart speak for you. Let me send for him!" and she rose, as if she meant to sally out that moment and bring Yorke back, but Leslie caught her arm.

"No," she said with a set face. "I must think. I cannot forget that he was going to be married to—to Lady Eleanor the day after to-morrow. It is better that he should keep to his engagement to that lady."

She could forgive him everything but his betrothal to Lady Eleanor.

As she spoke she kissed Lucy and went to her own room. In crossing the parlor she saw the locket with Yorke's portrait lying on the floor. She paused a moment, a moment only, then went on, and left it lying there.

But half an hour afterward, when all was still, the door opened, and she entered the room and picked up the locket, gazed at the portrait, and was about to press it to her lips, when she stopped and shuddered, remembering in whose keeping the locket had been. Indeed, she was about to drop it on the floor again, when a singular sound broke the stillness. It was as if some one were moving in the garden. She thrust the locket into the bosom of her dress and went to the window. The rain had ceased, and there was a glimmer of moonlight between the clouds. By this uncertain light she saw something standing on the small lawn. She was rather frightened for a moment, till she saw it was a horse. She was not in a condition of mind to care very much about the garden, but she thought of Lucy's pride in it, and fondness for it, and she opened the door and stole out, intending to drive the horse, which she suspected had strayed from one of the adjoining meadows, through the gate.

But when she got near it she saw that it was saddled. She did not immediately realize the significance of this fact. Then it flashed upon her, and she ran into the house and into Lucy's room. Lucy was still dressed, and seemed to expect her.

"I heard you moving about, dear," she said lovingly, "and I knew you would come to tell me that you had forgiven him and taken him back."

"No, no!" exclaimed Leslie. "Come—come at once!"

They ran down hand in hand, and Lucy uttered a cry of alarm as she saw the horse.

"Oh, my dahlias, Leslie! Oh, oh!"

"Hush!" said Leslie in a whisper. "Don't you see? It is saddled! There has been an accident. Get the lantern, Lucy! Quick! I will catch the horse!"

"No, no, you cannot!"

But Leslie went up to the great creature guardedly, and after a moment's fidgeting he allowed her to get hold of the bridle.

Lucy was back with the lantern in a moment or two, and stood trembling; it was Leslie who was calm and cool now.

"Look, Lucy, there is blood on his shoulder and back! He has fallen, and—and I am afraid for his rider. Wait!"

She snatched the lantern from Lucy's hand, and running to the road, examined it.

"Thank God for the rain!" she said fervently. "See, every hoof mark!"

She slung the bridle over the gate, and holding the lantern close to the ground, followed the tracks. It was Lucy who first saw the motionless figure lying in the road, and she uttered a faint scream.

In another moment she was kneeling beside it, and then she stretched out her arm as if to hide the white, blood-stained face from Leslie.

"Keep back! Don't come near!" she gasped in a paroxysm of terror. "Oh, Leslie, Leslie, it is he!"

Leslie sank on to her knees, and put Lucy's arm aside, and looked at the face.

"He is dead!" she screamed. "Dead! I have killed him!" And uttering heartbroken wails like some wild, distraught creature, she took his head upon her bosom and held it there, calling upon his name in an agony of despair and remorse.

CHAPTER XLIII.

"LESLIE, YOUR WIFE!"

Lucy stood and wrung her hands, looking round helplessly, almost terrified out of her senses by Leslie's terrible outburst of passionate grief. But her helplessness lasted only for a moment or two. She bent down and shook, literally shook, Leslie's shoulder.

"He is not dead!" she said, "but he will be if we let him lie here!"

She had hit upon the surest way of rousing Leslie. She stopped the awful wailing, held Yorke's face from her and looked at it—oh, with what a scrutiny!—then sprang to her feet.

"Help me!" she said through her clenched teeth, and she put her arms around Yorke's broad shoulders, and raised him from the ground. She felt strong enough to carry him by herself! Between them they carried him into the house and into Lucy's room.

"Now I will go for the doctor," said Leslie, with a calmness which terrified Lucy almost as much as her grief had done, but Lucy snatched up her shawl.

"No, I will go! You must stay with him! You—you will not break down, Leslie?"

A smile crossed Leslie's white face; and, sufficiently answered, Lucy sped away.

When she came back with the doctor they found that Leslie had—heaven only knows how—got off Yorke's saturated coat and waistcoat, and washed the blood from his face; and she stood outside the door holding Lucy's hand, calm and composed, while the doctor made his examination. Then he called them in.

"No bones broken, thank God!" he said; "the horse must have fallen on him, and I was afraid——. But he has struck his head, and there is mischief in a blow like this. He will want careful nursing." He looked from one to the other, and Leslie moved forward a little. The doctor nodded. "Very good," he said, as if accepting her; and he began at once to give her the necessary instructions. "When he comes to he must be kept quiet."

Ralph, who had been fetched by the doctor's man, entered the room, and the doctor sent him into the village for some things he required; on the way Ralph roused the postmaster and sent a telegram to the Duke of Rothbury.

The two girls and the doctor watched beside Yorke throughout the morning, but he still lay motionless and apparently lifeless.

The doctor's face grew graver as the hours passed, and he drew Ralph aside.

"Better send for his friends," he said; "I had hoped to bring him round before this; there is Lady Eleanor Dallas——."

Ralph started. He and the rest of them had forgotten her.

He got on Yorke's horse, and rode full pelt for White Place.

"Their ladyships left by the first train this morning for the Continent, sir," said the butler; "Paris, I think, but I'm not sure; I was to wait till they sent their address."

Ralph rode back and whispered the result of his message to Lucy; she looked relieved.

"I—I am not sorry!" she said. "If she had come Leslie would have gone, perhaps! No, I am not sorry! Oh, Ralph, if he should die!"

In the afternoon a fly drove up to the door and Grey helped the duke out. He was as white as the face that lay on the pillow upstairs, and for a moment or two he could not speak, but sat with lightly folded hands listening as Ralph told the whole strange story.

"Take me to him," he said at last.

They took him upstairs, and he started at sight of Leslie beside the bed; then he held out his hand, and Leslie put hers into it without a word; indeed, almost indifferently and without removing her eyes from Yorke's face. For her all the world lay there, hovering between life and death!

He stood watching Yorke for some time, then he went downstairs again.

"Will he live?" he asked the doctor.

The doctor gave the usual shake of the head and shrug.

"It is a difficult case, your grace," he said vaguely.

The duke put his hand before his eyes for a moment or two. "If he should die it will kill her!" He had been watching Leslie's face as well as Yorke's.

Two days passed. A stillness like that of death itself reigned over the little house. Toward evening Lucy implored Leslie to go to her room and take some rest.

"And leave him?" was the only response, and she held the limp hand still more tightly. The night fell and Leslie had sunk on her knees with her face on the dear hand, praying silently, when she felt the hand against her cheek move. She raised her head and motioned to Lucy and the doctor and they drew back.

The hand moved again, and presently the thrill that was almost an agony in its intensity, ran warm through Leslie's heart, for she saw the eyes she had watched hour by hour open slowly.

There was no life or intelligence in them for a minute or so, but Leslie bent over him and whispered his name. They lighted up, and a smile flickered on his face and his lips moved.

She bent still lower and heard him—surely no other could have caught those faint accents!—whisper her name.

"Yes, it is—Leslie!" she said.

He smiled again, and his fingers closed over hers weakly and yet clingingly.

"That's—that's right, my darling!" he said. "I knew you'd come! I've driven Stevens at the club half wild about that telegram; but I'll—I'll give him a five-pound note. Leslie——."

"Yes," she murmured.

"I've got the certificate, license, whatever you call it, and we'll be married to-day——."

Her face flushed and the tears blinded her.

"I'm too busy now to tell you how I love you for trusting me, dearest, but I'll tell you after its all over. The snuggest little church! I've got everything read —Where's a cab—Where——."

He stopped and a shudder ran through him, and the expression of his face changed swiftly.

"Leslie!" he cried, in a voice of grief and dread. "Where are you? I have lost you! Lost you; Leslie, come back to me! Oh, God, she has gone, gone forever! Come back to me, dearest, dearest!"

The doctor stepped forward hurriedly with a grave anxiety in his manner; but Leslie motioned him back.

She put her arm round Yorke and laid her face against his—her own scarlet and white by turns—and in a voice inaudible to the rest, whispered:

"I am here, dear Yorke! Don't you know—have you forgotten? It is I, Leslie —your wife!"

He looked puzzled for a moment, then a smile broke over his face and he laughed as he turned his face to her.

"I—I must have been dreaming, Leslie!" he said joyfully. "Yes, that's it! What an idiot I am! I forgot we were married yesterday! Think of it! Where are we? On the steamer—in Italy—where? My—my head feels queer, and the things work about me. Just—just tell me again, dearest."

"It is Leslie—your wife," she murmured, her love telling her what he wanted.

"Yes, yes!" he murmured, with a laugh of infinite content. "Married yesterday, of course; stupid things, dreams. Leslie! My wife! Married yesterday!"

Then with a sigh of blissful assurance and perfect peace he closed his eyes and fell asleep on her bosom.

Lucy stood crying, the tears were rolling down the duke's wan cheeks, and even the doctor found it necessary to turn his head away.

Then Lucy found herself outside the room sobbing on Ralph Duncombe's shoulder.

"Oh, I am so happy, so happy!" she sobbed. "It is all right now!"

"All right?" he said with masculine density.

"Yes, don't you see? Didn't you hear!" opening her eyes. "She is bound to marry him now! Why, it's almost as if they were married already."

CHAPTER XLIV.

HUSBAND AND—BROTHER.

The great duke who built Rothbury Castle was no fool.

He chose the best of the hills, placed his house on the brow amidst a belt of oaks and elms and surrounded by park-like lawns. He made the body and the two wings in a long facade facing due south, and all along the front he ran a terrace of white stone with flights of broad steps leading down to the lawns and Italian gardens, which were then in vogue.

From this terrace a view was obtained which was almost, if not quite, as grand as that which enraptures the gaze from Richmond Hill; while looked at from below, the castle presented an appearance which might well be described as magnificent. Each succeeding duke had done what he could to improve, or at any rate maintain, the ancestral home, and all England was proud of Rothbury Castle.

On an evening in June the duke was seated in his bath-chair in a corner of the terrace looking wistfully and expectantly towards the most distant part of the drive, which wound round and about the tall elms like a yellow snake. Beside him stood Grey, also looking expectant, and every now and then covertly glancing at his watch behind his master's back.

Just below the terrace was an arch composed of laurels, studded with roses; the great flag and the Rothbury arms floated from one of the towers and other flags flapped in the soft breeze from Venetian masts, and lines stretched from point to point of the castle and grounds. Servants in their dark claret livery hurried to and fro or stood in groups looking toward the same spot on which the duke's eye was fixed. The hall door was open wide, and at the foot of the stairs stood the general servants of the household—all of them, from the stately housekeeper in satin to the scullery-maid in her black stuff dress and white apron. In fact, the whole place was in a state of pleasant excitement, and no one excepting the duke in his chair seemed able to keep still in one place for more than a minute at a time.

"That train's late, Grey," said the duke with a painfully poor attempt at indifference. "It always is late. See that I write to the Traffic Director about it, will you? It is something shameful the way this line is mismanaged. It must be twenty minutes late, I know!"

"Not quite, your grace; about a quarter, I should say," said Grey, pulling out his watch.

"Oh, put that watch away!" said the duke. "You have lugged it out twenty times during the last half hour. Do you think I haven't seen you? I wish to heaven you'd go away if you must fidget."

"Beg pardon, your grace," said Grey from behind, and hiding a smile. "Shall I wheel your grace in, the air is rather——."

"Nonsense! It's as hot as—as a furnace. Are they coming yet? They seem to forget that I'm a director of this beastly line! By George, I'll go down to their next board meeting and make it hot for them! More accidents occur from the unpunctuality of trains than anything else. Ah, what's that?"

"They're coming, your grace!" exclaimed Grey.

The duke made a movement as if he were about to rise, then he sank back with a sigh.

"Go and tell them; they can't see as well as we can. See that everything is ready."

"Yes, your grace; but there's no need, they've seen the carriage," he added, as the servants began to move about like a hive of bees, and then, as if by mutual consent, swarmed upon the principal flight of steps from the terrace.

The carriage, with its four white horses, swept along the avenue, the postilions cracking their whips and keeping their steeds at a smart gallop; and presently Yorke, who had been leaning forward, said:

"The first view of the castle, Leslie!"

Leslie bent forward eagerly and a faint cry of amazement and delight escaped her.

"Oh, Yorke, how lovely, how lovely!" she murmured. "I had no idea it was so large or so beautiful. It is an Aladdin's palace! And look, Yorke, there is an arch of flowers! How kind of them! Oh——," she drew a long breath and sank back. "I think I am a little frightened by it all!"

He leant his arm on the side of the carriage and looked at her with a smile on his lips, and the light of a passionate love in his eyes.

The view before them was beautiful enough in all conscience, but the loveliness beside him transcended it! Six months of such happiness as falls to few mortals had done wonders for Leslie. It had brought back the color to her face, the light to her eyes, the music of youth's joy and love's ecstasy to her voice. It was the Leslie of Portmaris with something added, a something too delicately intangible for words, but the charm of which all felt who met and talked with her.

If it was possible Yorke had grown to love her with a deeper and more passionate love since their marriage, and his pride in her beauty had verged on the ridiculous; and sometimes Leslie, made to blush under his gaze, would put her hands over her eyes. The intensity of his love almost frightened her; and she was as one who fears for the safety of a precious vase which fate may overturn or some malignant wand cast from its pedestal and shatter.

The six months of happiness had wrought wonders for Yorke also. The wan and haggard, the hopeless, listless expression had vanished from his face, and in its place was a look of contentment and youthful energy which gave him back all the brightness that had helped to win Leslie's heart.

It was, indeed, the old Yorke with his ready laugh and jest who sat beside his sweetheart-wife, as they bowled toward their future home.

"There you are!" he said presently. "You can see the terrace now. By George, what a mob! It's a regular reception! There'll be a speech for certain! Do you think you are equal to returning thanks, my lady? Just think over a few 'graceful phrases,' as the newspapers put it—something neat and short."

"Oh, don't Yorke!" she pleaded. "If you knew how my heart was beating ——."

"Let me feel it," he said promptly, seizing upon the excuse.

"No, no, sir! You mustn't! Fleming may look round any moment," and she cast a glance of mock warning at that important individual seated on the box. "But you may hold my hand, if you like. Isn't it trembling?" and she turned her eyes upon him piteously, though a soft smile played upon her parted lips. "Oh, Yorke, I feel so—so small before all this. I ought to have been six feet high, and very, very stately! And instead I feel so tiny and insignificant! There is one good thing. I shall be able to get behind you and hide myself. Do you know that you have grown dreadfully big, Yorke?"

He laughed.

"Have I? I dare say. Happiness, like laughter, makes one grow fat. I shouldn't be surprised if I developed into a kind of Daniel Lambert. There was one fat Rothbury. I'll show you his portrait, and if you like it I'll try and live up to it. Oh, what lots I have to show you! But, I forgot, I must leave that to Dolph! The dear old chap will love to trot you around the place, for he's proud of it, though he is always growling and calling it a barracks, and an overgrown show. Dear old Dolph! Now—oh, you are not going to cry!"

"No, no!" Leslie responded, wiping her eyes stealthily. "It—it was only the sun in my eyes. Oh, Yorke, how good Heaven has been to us in every way! Think how sad it would have been to have come home and found him gone from us!"

Yorke nodded with momentary gravity.

"Yes, Heaven has been very good to us, dearest," he said in a low, fervent voice. "In that as in all things."

The horses tore along as if they knew they were being eagerly waited for, and presently the sound of cheering rose and swelled into a volume as the carriage passed under the arch. As it passed Leslie looked up and uttered an exclamation of delight.

"Oh, look, Yorke!" she cried. "Yorke, look!"

Half a dozen of the prettiest of the village school-girls stood on a bower on top of the arch, and the moment the carriage was underneath they began to sing and throw roses into it.

"Stop, stop for one moment!" pleaded Leslie. "I—I want to speak to them. Oh, I can't, I can't!" she cried. "You speak, Yorke! Thank them, oh, thank them!"

They could not stop, and in despair Leslie snatched up one of the roses and kissed it at the children, and waved her hand.

"That's better than a speech," said Yorke delightedly. "Look at them clapping their hands, and hear them shouting. Commend me to Lady Auchester for doing the right thing in an emergency. Here we are!" he exclaimed, as the carriage drew up at the steps, and four grooms ran forward to the horses' heads, and he got out and held his hand to her.

As they passed up the steps, lined on either side by the servants, the cheers were redoubled, mingled with shouts:

"Welcome home, my lord! Welcome home, my lady!"

At the top of the steps stood the gray-haired butler. Yorke nearly spoiled his short speech by shaking hands with him, but the old fellow stammered it out, and Yorke, with his wife on his arm, looked round with his bright smile, and opened his lips.

But, as he said afterward, a lump came into his throat, and for a moment or two he could not utter a word, and even then he found himself stammering as the butler had done, as he said:

"Thank you, thank you! I should like to tell you how deeply I feel your kindness, but I can't, somehow! But I do feel it very much, and so does my wife, my dear wife——," he stopped suddenly, and in the unexpected silence, a voice—it was that of the little scullery-maid, who had edged forward—was heard distinctly—"Oh, isn't she lovely!"

A proud light flashed into Yorke's eyes, and he held his head high.

"Yes," he said, "she is lovely! But she is something better than that; she is good—good!"

One touch of nature like this makes the whole world kin, and a shout went up which echoed and re-echoed round the old walls.

Leslie stood 'covered with blushes,' but her hand closed on her husband's, and with a loving, grateful pressure, as she looked up at him with a pride which equaled his own.

Then Yorke went quickly across the terrace—the servants drawing back with true delicacy—to where the bath-chair stood, and in another instant the duke's hand was grasped in his. But after an affectionate glance at his happy face the duke motioned him aside, and held out both hands towards Leslie.

"My welcome comes last, but it's not the least, my dear," he said.

Leslie stood for a second hesitating, her color coming and going, then she bent down and kissed him on the forehead.

His thin face flushed, and he held her a moment, patting her arm in the way a man does when he is having a hard fight with his emotion.

"You're both looking very well, young people," he said, but without removing his eyes from Leslie's face. "Very well—and absurdly happy."

Leslie laughed, and her eyes dwelt on him with an expression of satisfaction and rejoicing, which he did not understand until she said:

"And you—oh, how well you look, how different."

He shook his head with one of his quaintly grim smiles.

"Yes. I'm very sorry, and I hope you'll both forgive me for being so inconsiderate, but I was never half so well in my life. I'm afraid I'm going to be a nuisance, and keep poor Yorke waiting for the title for a year or two."

"All right, Dolph," said Yorke in his old breezy voice. "We'll tell you when we're tired of waiting."

"Do, do!" he said. "Mind, that's a promise! Now you are tired, and you want to rest before dinner. Yorke, you'll have to do the honors of the house; Leslie won't care to wait while I limp along."

Leslie drew his arm through hers and looked down at him with the smile which a sister bestows upon a beloved and afflicted brother, and with an added tenderness too subtle for analysis.

"I will not go without you," she said. "Lean upon me, or rather I will lean upon you, for I am a little tired, and you are quite strong."

The duke's face flushed with pleasure and satisfaction as he got up.

"Very well," he said.

They entered the vast hall, and he pointed out the great staircase upon which Royalist and Roundhead had fought till the stairs ran with blood—the stains were there still, under the carpet; the old oak carving; the tattered banners which the Rothburys of old had borne in many a fight for king and country; the tapestry hangings, which not even Windsor could match; the oriel window of stained glass, brought piece by piece from Flanders; the long line of family portraits. Then he took her through the state apartments, with their gilded carvings and priceless furniture, grand lofty rooms, as splendid as anything she had seen, even in palatial Venice; to the library, which a studious, book-loving duke had constructed with infinite care and pains, and filled with rare and choice editions; to the smaller rooms in which he and she and Yorke would live, and which with their modern decorations and furniture were the epitome of elegance and comfort. Then they went up the great staircase and along the broad corridors, lined with pictures and statuary.

"These are your rooms," he said, opening a door, and smiling as Leslie uttered a cry of amazement and delight. "You like them?" he said quietly, but evidently delighted at her delight. "I'm glad of that. It has been an amusement for me while you have been away getting them ready. I hope you'll find all you want, but you must remember that I'm only a miserable bachelor, and make allowances if you miss anything."

"What shall I say to him, Yorke?" she said, appealing to Yorke helplessly.

The duke drew her on as if to escape her thanks.

"You shan't be bothered with more rooms now," he said. "To-morrow you shall see it all. You must get acquainted with your own house, you know, as soon as possible."

As he spoke Yorke, who had walked beside them too moved for speech, stopped before the half opened door and pushed it open.

It was a plainly furnished room—very plainly, no silks or satins or inlaid furniture here, but an ordinary iron bedstead, and dressing table and washstand of plain deal.

"My room," said the duke simply.

Leslie stopped and peeped in, then she stood still, surprised and touched at its simplicity.

"Why have you given us all the beautiful things, and left none for yourself, duke?" she said reproachfully.

He laughed.

"Oh, I'm simple in my tastes," he said. "But I half thought of furnishing this room as a boudoir for you, there is such a pretty view. Come in!"

She went in and to the window, but she did not look at the view, for her eye was caught by a picture hanging on the wall at the foot of the bed.

It was the picture her father had painted, and "Mr. Temple" had bought.

She looked at it in silence and the tears filled her eyes; then she turned her lovely face to the duke and tried to speak.

"All right, my dear," he said in a low voice. "I like to have it there. It reminds me of old times. Reminds me of the Portmaris days, when, blinded by my own conceit, I thought all women were false and worthless. You have opened my eyes, my dear, and I see more clearly now! There! There!" for her tears fell fast. "That is all past now."

He paused for a moment, then lifted his eyes to her face with a tender regard, and murmured:

> Love took up the harp of life, and smote on all its chords with
> might,
> Smote the chord of Self, that, trembling, passed in music out
> of sight—

"I suppose he has told you how it was with me, my dear?"

Leslie's eyes dropped for an instant, then she raised them and looked into his, and her hand closed tightly on his thin one.

"Well," he said with a smile, "you must cut your heart in two, and give one-half to your husband, and the other to—your brother!"

CHAPTER XLV.

THE CUP OF HAPPINESS.

Six weeks later, when the world of fashion was ringing with the praises of Lady Auchester's beauty and amiability, and the society papers were prophesying that the future Duchess of Rothbury would become the most popular of the leaders of ton, Leslie and Yorke drove in a hansom to St. John's Wood.

They were very silent during the journey, and when they stopped at the house in which the famous Finetta of the Diadem had held so many merry parties, Leslie got out of the cab alone.

She was inside the house nearly an hour, and when she came out with her veil down and re-entered the cab she did not speak for some time, but held her husband's hand in eloquent silence.

"Well, dearest?" he said at last.

"Yes, I am glad I came," she said, in a low voice. "Very glad. Oh, Yorke, how changed she is! I scarcely knew her. You remember how strong and self-reliant she was? Now——," she stopped with a little sob. "And yet she is so happy and cheerful. She spends all her time thinking and working for others; the poor girls at the theater where she was, come and see her, and she helps them in all sorts of ways. While I was there the clergyman came in, and he spoke a few words to me outside her room. He said that if there ever was a really good woman she was one."

"Poor Fin!" said Yorke, under his breath.

"No, no," said Leslie; "not pity, Yorke. She does not need that, for she is happier now lying there, than ever she was in the old days of her strength and triumph. I told her all about you, and Lucy and Ralph, and she wants me to take Lucy to see her. She and Lucy will just suit each other. And Yorke——," she paused and held out her tiny fist to him. "She has given me something; for a wedding present, she said. Guess what it is."

"I give it up," he said quietly.

She opened her hand and showed him the diamond pendant.

"'I thought you would come some day,' she said, Yorke, and if you could have seen her face when she said it! 'And so I kept it for you.'"

One day Lord Auchester and his wife, and Mr. and Mrs. Ralph Duncombe were staying at a country house in the North. It was an extremely pleasant party, of which those two ladies were, by general consent, admitted to be the belles, and the hostess, not unnaturally proud of having the famous Lady Auchester under her roof, decided to give a big dance which should include all the neighboring county families and their guests.

Half an hour before the opening of the ball, while Leslie was dressing, the hostess, Lady Springmore, came in to her in a great flush of excitement and distress.

"Oh, my dear Lady Auchester, I am so sorry!" she exclaimed, when Leslie had sent her maid away. "I am heartbroken about it, and I don't know what to do."

"What is it, Lady Springmore?" asked Leslie, more amused than frightened at her hostess' fluster. "Has the floor fallen in, or the ices gone wrong?"

"No, no, my dear! It's—it's something concerning you and Lord Auchester," and she clasped her hands and sank into a chair.

"Then I'd better call my husband," said Leslie, looking toward the next dressing-room, where Yorke was brushing his hair and whistling "like a ploughboy," as Leslie often declared.

"No, no. And yet—oh, I'd better tell you at once. My dear Lady Auchester, the Marlows have got Lady Eleanor Dallas staying with them—and she's coming here to-night!"

Leslie blushed, but she said quietly, "Well?"

"Well!" echoed the hostess in a kind of despair. "Don't you see, dear? She doesn't know you are here, and—and—oh, what shall I do?"

"Do nothing," replied Leslie, as quietly as before.

"But—but will it not be awkward and unpleasant for you, dear Lady Auchester?"

"Yes," said Leslie, in her old, downright way. "Yes; it will be both awkward and unpleasant, but if we ran away from all the awkwardness and unpleasantness in life we should spend our time in perpetual flight. I see you know our story, Lady Springmore."

"Oh, every one does, my dear," murmured that lady apologetically.

"Just so," said Leslie calmly. "Well, if you are kind enough to ask my advice, it is: Do nothing. The world is so small that Lady Dallas and we are sure to meet sometimes, and—well," she smiled, "do you think that we shall make a scene in your pretty ballroom? Wait!"

She opened the door of the dressing-room an inch or two and called to Yorke.

"Hallo!" he called back. "What is it? Want me to come and admire you in your warpaint, I suppose? Shan't! Tired of admiring you!"

"Oh, hush, hush!" said Leslie, blushing like a rose. "Lady Springmore is here, Yorke. She has come to tell us that—that Lady Eleanor Dallas is coming to-night."

"The devil!"

"No, dear, Lady Eleanor," said Leslie, sweetly and naively.

He came to the door and poked his head round; then he saw by her face what he was expected to say, and said it like a good and docile husband.

"Delighted to see any guest of yours, Lady Springmore!" he said, bobbing his head at her, and promptly disappeared.

An hour or two later, when the ball was in full swing, Leslie heard the footman announce Lady Eleanor Dallas.

She had been waiting for it, and was prepared. Lady Eleanor entered. She was thinner, and looked pale, and rather listless, and the air of pride and hauteur were more pronounced than of old.

Superbly dressed, she moved through the crowd with a faint smile of greeting for her acquaintances; then suddenly she saw Leslie. She stopped for just one instant, and the blood rushed to her face; then she came toward her, and, Leslie coming forward too, they met each other half way, so to speak.

The few conventional words were spoken, and by that time Lady Eleanor had recovered her presence of mind, and was once more the stately, haughty patrician who suffers and is silent.

"Your husband is here, Lady Auchester?" she said, quite calmly.

"I will bring him to you," said Leslie, promptly.

She found Yorke, and put her arm through his, pressing it to give him courage, for in all cases like this the bravest man is as like as not to prove an arrant coward.

"She is here, Yorke! Now, mind!"

"Oh, Lord!" he groaned. Then he pulled himself together quite suddenly. "If she can go through it, I can!" he said, grimly.

In another moment they were facing each other—Yorke with an unconsciously stern face, Lady Eleanor with a faint smile which masked more than pen can tell.

"How do you do, Lord Auchester?" she said, giving him her hand.

Yorke took it, and for a moment he found that it trembled; but he said afterwards that he thought it was only fancy.

Then, without another word, she turned and moved away.

They met—they were bound to meet—often in the after years, but it was never more than "How do you do, Lord Auchester?" "I hope you are well, Lady Eleanor?" until Leslie's first girl was born.

There had been a good deal of fuss—as the duke said, who made more fuss than any one else—over the birth of the son and heir; but this child, the first girl, was hailed as if she were the most wonderful production the world had ever seen, and Lucy was regarded with boundless envy because she was chosen as godmother.

But the day before the christening Leslie received a magnificent set of pearls, inclosed in a box of white ivory, inside which was a slip of paper, bearing, in Lady Eleanor's handwriting, this inscription:

"To my godchild, Leslie Eleanor Auchester."

Yorke was amazed and bewildered, but Leslie understood in an instant.

"What does it mean?" he demanded, staring at her, and almost letting the casket drop.

"It means that she is going to transfer her love to our—no, your—little one, Yorke," she said. "Oh, don't you see? And we thought she hated us!"

She caught up her baby and kissed it, and laughed and cried over it, in her joy and thankfulness, for every time she had met Lady Eleanor her tender heart had ached. But now this little mite had removed the only thorn in Leslie's bed of roses.

"Yes, she shall have her," she said.

"Eh?" exclaimed Yorke, staring. "What! Altogether? I say!"

"Oh, not altogether!" said Leslie, with a little gasp, and clutching her baby tighter. "No, not altogether, but—but nearly! Oh, Yorke, Yorke, my cup of happiness is full now. Quite, quite full!"

[THE END.]